THE PENGUIN CLASSICS

FOUNDER EDITOR (1944–64) E. V. RIEU

HONORÉ DE BALZAC was born in Tours in 1799, the son of a civil servant. He spent nearly six years as a boarder in a Vendôme school, then went to live in Paris, working as a lawyer's clerk then as a hack-writer. Between 1820 and 1824 he wrote a number of novels under various pseudonyms, many of them in collaboration, after which he unsuccessfully tried his luck at publishing, printing and type-founding. At the age of thirty, heavily in debt, he returned to literature with a dedicated fury and wrote the first novel to appear under his own name, *The Chouans*. During the next twenty years he wrote about ninety novels and shorter stories, among them many masterpieces, to which he gave the comprehensive title the *Human Comedy*. He died in 1850, a few months after his marriage to Eveline Hanska, the Polish countess with whom he had maintained amorous relations for eighteen years.

HERBERT J. HUNT was educated at Lichfield Cathedral Choir School, the Lichfield Grammar School and Magdalen College, Oxford. He was a Tutor and Fellow at St Edmund Hall from 1927 to 1944, then until 1966 he was Professor of French Literature and Language at London University and from 1966 to 1970 was Senior Fellow of Warwick University. He published books on literature and thought in nineteenth-century France; he was also the author of a biography of Balzac, and a comprehensive study of Balzac's writings: *Balzac's 'Comédie Humaine'* (1959, paperback 1964). His translation of Balzac's *Cousin Pons* appeared in the Penguin Classics in 1968. He died in 1973.

HONORÉ DE BALZAC

History of the Thirteen

TRANSLATED AND
INTRODUCED BY
HERBERT J. HUNT

PENGUIN BOOKS

Penguin Books Ltd, Harmondsworth, Middlesex, England
Penguin Books, 625 Madison Avenue, New York, New York 10022, U.S.A.
Penguin Books Australia Ltd, Ringwood, Victoria, Australia
Penguin Books Canada Ltd, 2801 John Street, Markham, Ontario, Canada L3R 1B4
Penguin Books (N.Z.) Ltd, 182–190 Wairau Road, Auckland 10, New Zealand

—

Histoire des Treize first published 1833–5
This translation first published 1974
Reprinted 1978, 1980

—

—

Made and printed in Great Britain by
Hazell Watson & Viney Ltd, Aylesbury, Bucks
Set in Monotype Garamond

Contents

Introduction

AT the age of thirty Honoré de Balzac,[1] after ten years of varying activities, began work on that cycle of novels, short stories and reflective studies which, by 1840, he had decided to call *The Human Comedy*. By 1848, Balzac being worn out and almost moribund, his productivity having ceased, the work comprised over ninety items. It was in 1834 that the idea came to him of dividing both present and future works into 'Studies': Studies of Manners, Philosophical Studies and Analytical Studies (very few of these latter materialized). His Studies of Manners, subdivided into types of 'Scenes', began in 1829 with *Scenes of Private Life*. Around 1832–3 he started to develop a new category, *Scenes of Provincial Life*, and, almost simultaneously – he wrote fast and furiously, and was generally occupied with several stories at a time – a third category: *Scenes of Parisian Life*. The evolution of the three other types of scene: Political, Military and Country Life, does not concern us here.

History of the Thirteen (*Ferragus*[2] and *The Duchesse de Langeais* were first published in 1833–4, *The Girl with the Golden Eyes* in 1835) laid the foundation of the Paris 'Scenes', for even though Chapters 1 and 4 of *The Duchesse de Langeais* have their action in Majorca, the core of the action is in Paris. Moreover Balzac almost goes out of his way to characterize aspects of the Parisian way of life in this trilogy of fictions. *Ferragus* gives a description (minute as always with Balzac) of certain unsavoury areas of that city, with an intimate glance at the interrelation between criminal and harlot types

1. For a general account of Balzac's life and work see Select Bibliography, p. 19.
2. *Ferragus* had appeared beforehand in the periodical *La Revue de Paris*; the beginnings also of *La Duchesse*, in *L'Echo de la Jeune France*.

and, at the end, a gruesome but masterly satire on bureaucratic red tape as it concerns the attempt to obtain official sanction for the cremation of Clémence Desmarets. *The Duchesse de Langeais* includes a searching criticism, practically a denunciation, of the French aristocracy almost hermetically sealed in the Faubourg Saint-Germain. We are shown a class clinging to its titles and privileges, failing to follow the example of the English aristocracy by recruiting its ranks from lower but more vigorous elements in the community, and failing thereby to take up its natural mission as a guiding force in the new political, social and economic structure created by Revolution and Empire. Balzac's personal motives for this criticism will be considered later. More than a quarter of *The Girl with the Golden Eyes* is devoted to a vivacious evocation of five classes, 'spheres', or 'circles' in Paris – proletariat, lower bourgeoisie, upper or professional bourgeoisie, the world of artists and the aristocracy – with their multifarious occupations and preoccupations; all of them wasting their lives in the avid quest for gold and the pleasures they hope it will buy: *propter vitam vivendi perdere causas*. All are inhabitants of a Dantesque inferno, of which Balzac was already constituting himself the historian (see p. 318 and note 6). *Ferragus* in particular, with its subordinate theme of the fanatically devoted father (p. 123) points directly to that 'histoire parisienne' – eminently Parisian – *Old Goriot*, which, by the end of 1834, was already coming into print.

*

Another conspicuous feature of this trilogy is that it purports to be the history of a secret society. *The Thirteen* brings out an amusing though perhaps regrettable trait in Balzac's psychology. He had from youth onwards a taste for the mysterious and the terrible, the cloak-and-dagger element so characteristic of the 'Gothic' novel or the 'novel of terror'. In his years as an apprentice writer (1819–24) he himself had dabbled in this genre. He had invented a criminal gangster, Argow the Pirate, who appears in *Le Vicaire des Ardennes* (1822) and *Annette et le criminel* (1824). Even after the pseudonymous 'Horace de Saint-Aubin' had blossomed out into Honoré de Balzac, melodramatic elements were liable to crop up in his novels: the 'Parisian captain' in *The Woman of Thirty* and, above all, the criminal leader Vautrin in *Old Goriot* and *A Harlot High and Low* (the sequel to *Lost Illusions*). He himself was to found a 'secret society' in 1838 – the *Chevaux Rouges* – one which, however, never succeeded in being anything more than a spasmodically functioning dining-club. Hence, thanks to the boyish gusto which Balzac retained throughout life, his creation of the Thirteen in 1833–5.[3] Only five of the prominent members are ever named, and four of them appear in this trilogy: Ferragus, Armand de Montriveau, the Marquis de Ronquerolles and Henri de Marsay. The Preface gives a description of the association. Ferragus uses their services fairly extensively in the novel that bears his name. Armand de Montriveau calls upon them, first of all when he is preparing his threatened vengeance on Antoinette de Langeais, and again, in the final chapter, for the abduction of 'Sister Thérèse' from the remote convent from which she only emerges as a corpse. Henri de Marsay has the aid of Ferragus and Ronquerolles when he is preparing to punish Paquita Valdes because she has made him 'pose for another person'.[4] The members of this association are rich, all-powerful, sinister and unscrupulous. They even seem to possess preternatural powers. On p. 75 Ferragus seizes Auguste de Maulincour by the hair and shakes his head several times, thereby inducing a disease which brings him lingeringly to death. It has been maintained that this is plausible as a method of administering arsenic,[5] but it is easy to remain sceptical on this score. Armand de Montriveau, when Antoinette tries to repel his advances

3. It is only just to add that in early nineteenth-century France, following the turbulent times of the Revolution and Empire, many criminal adventurers were thrown up, with the result that truth was often at least as strange as, if not stranger than, fiction.

4. See below, p. 376.

5. By rubbing a solution of arsenic into the hair. See the Classiques Garnier edition, Introduction, p. 31: a suggestion made by the Académie des Sciences in 1955.

with allusions to her marriage bonds, boasts of possessing power over fate, though in fact he may merely be referring to the diabolical resourcefulness of the Thirteen (p. 222). But no such Anne Radcliffe rationalization is possible in the case of Henri de Marsay: he is positively credited with an occult power which enables him to condemn to death anyone he chooses; a power due, it seems, to a pact he has made with the demon (p. 363): here we are definitely back in the ambience of the 'Gothic' novels as developed by Monk Lewis and Maturin, indeed by Balzac himself in his novel of 1822, *Le Centenaire*. We can now leave this aspect of the trilogy while observing that, when all is said and done, the Thirteen do not unduly obtrude and that the essential interest of the three fictions is a psychological one.

But readers will notice that one of these figures – Ferragus – bears the title *Chef des Dévorants* (Chief of the Companions of Duty). Balzac explains (pp. 23–5) what the 'companionships' were, though not with complete accuracy. A brief definition of them here will help to show why Balzac attached Ferragus to them. The *Compagnonnages* were associations of guilds of skilled craftsmen which had survived from the Middle Ages and which, it appears, still subsist, picturesquely and anachronistically, in the twentieth century. They claimed to date back, like the freemasons, to the time when Solomon was building the Temple at Jerusalem. They were divided into three 'rites' or *devoirs* (duties): Children of Solomon, or Companions of the Duty of Liberty; Children of Master Jacques; and Children of Papa Soubise. They had their secrets, their ritual initiations, their passwords and customs: for instance, each postulant, before passing out as a fully fledged *Compagnon*, had to make a tour of France practising his craft (joiner, weaver, stone-mason, ironworker, etc.), receiving hospitality at each stage of his tour in a lodging-house kept by a 'mother'. Contrary to what Balzac says on p. 25, all members of these three societies were *Dévorants*, that is to say, members of a *devoir*; but the title *Dévorants* was more specially applied to the Children of Master Jacques. In the early nineteenth century they were famous for their rivalries and quarrels, which often led to bloodshed and murder. They were arousing much interest at the time when Balzac was writing. One Agricol Perdiguier (whose nickname – see Balzac's remarks on nicknames on p. 24 – was Avignonnais-la-Vertu) was to publish in 1839 his *Livre du Compagnonnage*, which inspired the novelist George Sand, always tenderly sympathetic towards the working classes, with her fiction of 1840, *Les Compagnons du Tour de France*. The reasons which determined Balzac to make Ferragus a leader of *Compagnons* are not far to seek: Ferragus, alias Gratien Bourignard, is an escaped convict. He is the most sinister member of the Thirteen, even though he ends up as a pathetic, even comic figure; and the violence for which the *Compagnons* were notorious, but above all their tradition of loyalty to the members of their *devoir* (see p. 24), afforded him a means of heightening the melodramatic element in his novel.

*

These quasi-extraneous elements having been dealt with, we are now free to consider the three novels in their essential themes. Stripped of its melodramatic excrescences, and allowing for the interest contained in Balzac's evocation of the *grisette*, Ida Gruget, and her relations with Gratien Bourignard, *Ferragus* is a middle-class tragedy. Jules Desmarets is a middle-class Othello, with a young military fop – Auguste de Maulincour – to take the role of Iago. It is a genuinely tragic love story, a striking contribution to the many studies extant of connubial bliss being destroyed by suspicion and misunderstanding, one which culminates in conjugal anguish and premature death; one which may perhaps be put on a level with Madame de La Fayette's great novel of 1674, *La Princesse de Clèves*, even though it falls short of it in respect of perfect taste, classical sobriety and restraint. Does the turn of events command the reader's total adherence? He may feel a little restive as he advances from p. 77 onwards: why at this stage could not husband and wife discuss their difficulties frankly, with Clémence revealing the truth that her father is a criminal fleeing from justice? The answer is that people rarely behave reasonably in moments of emotional stress. Jules and Clémence miss the opportunity to come to terms. Her rapid collapse and death, recounted in such lavish detail, accord with a romantic convention of the time: emotional disruption may well involve physical disintegration. Balzac was of his era in subscribing to this. There is much here over which few late-twentieth-century readers will shed tears with Balzac. They will be less likely to withhold their admiration from the dry irony of the Père-Lachaise descriptions, which Balzac was scarcely to surpass even in *Cousin Pons* (1847).

The Duchesse de Langeais brings us closer to Balzac's personal history, as also to his political commitments between 1831 and 1833. It is not too much to say that the Revolution of July 1830, which elevated Louis-Philippe of Orléans to the throne as 'roi des Français', left Balzac cold. His scepticism about the 'bourgeois monarchy' brought him into contact with a leader of the legitimate royalist party, the Duc de Fitz-James. His already conservative opinions became more and more pronounced and, early in 1832, he began to contribute to a legitimist periodical, *Le Rénovateur*. This was essentially a temporary adherence, although Balzac was to remain a reactionary throughout his life. He had his ideas (expressed in the second chapter of *The Duchesse de Langeais* and elsewhere) on what the legitimists ought to do in order to take effectual action: this was too much for them, and it was not long before they dropped him, and he dropped them. But towards the end of 1831 he had become emotionally involved. Fitz-James's niece, the Marquise de Castries, started a pen-friendship, at first anonymous, with him. He discovered who she was. They met. He fell in love both with her and with the prospect of having a marquise for a mistress. Their friendship reached the tender stage. In the early autumn of 1832 they went off on a holiday together – to Aix-les-Bains in Dauphiné and then on to Geneva. All this time Balzac had been wooing her assiduously, but she refused to accord him her ultimate favours. They parted, he furious, dejected, humiliated; and he brooded over the humiliation for some time to come. Regarding himself as the victim of a heartless coquette (though she did have valid reasons for refusing herself) he naturally took to the pen to avenge, or at any rate to compensate, himself; initially in the first, unpublished version of his *Country Doctor* (1833), and then in *The Duchesse de Langeais*.

This novel is therefore the study of a society coquette and of the wiles she adopts in order to enslave an impressionable, but heroic and austere ex-soldier. She goes too far and 'toys with the axe' (the original title of the novel was *Touch not the Axe!* – see p. 251). Montriveau plans an exemplary punishment for her: branding with a hot iron. At this juncture the coquette in her disappears and the true woman asserts herself. Henceforth she is wholly his and even makes shameless advances to him (the reactions of her kinsfolk to this conduct enable Balzac to display his gift for satire, so much more effective than his predilection for sentimental effusion). Montriveau is too obdurate. She flees the world and becomes a nun, and he does not succeed in recapturing her alive.

One must not of course exaggerate the personal element in this story, but it is certainly there. It is a case of wish-fulfilment. The all-conquering Balzac, transformed into a heroic aristocrat, brings a proud society queen to his feet. But if that were the sole interest of the novel, it would scarcely be sufficient. Balzac, as always in his fictions in which personal reminiscences are blended, rises above them. He has sense enough to let Antoinette de Langeais put potent arguments to Montriveau in favour of resistance to the selfish impulses of a would-be seducer (p. 234 and elsewhere). Throughout the novel he emphasizes one theme: the difference between passion and true love (see p. 266 ff.), clinched in the ironical conclusion of p. 305: 'From now on be content with passion. Love is an investment we ought to think out cautiously.'

And so, discounting the personal element in the story, we should ask ourselves also, with regard to the psychological element, what credibility we can accord to the picture of Antoinette's surrender and self-humiliation when she comes under the threat of the branding-iron. 'Duchesses are tough,' says de Ronquerolles, 'and women of her kind are more amenable to cruelty than to kindness.' Who could doubt that this is sometimes true in certain cases? What perhaps is nowadays less acceptable to us is Antoinette's reaction after apparent rejection: retirement to a convent, espousal with God, romanticism at its worst! Similarly, in *The Girl with the Golden Eyes*, Henri de Marsay's half-sister, after stabbing Paquita to death, exclaims: 'I've only God left to love!' and announces her intention of taking the veil.

So we come finally to the third novel – a very short one. It represents an incursion into what was then virtually still a forbidden zone. Homosexuality had been frequently treated by the less respectable of eighteenth-century novelists, and it was at least hinted at by a few of Balzac's own contemporaries. He himself had already treated it discreetly in a short story of 1830, *Sarrasine*. Vautrin, his master-criminal, making his first appearance in *Old Goriot* (1834–5), is a homosexual, though Balzac does not over-emphasize the fact. There were a few cases of lesbianism in real life known to him. Hence perhaps the fact that in *The Girl with the Golden Eyes* Balzac by no means draws a veil over realities. No more than de Marsay does he express horror or distaste at the idea of the lesbian relationship between Paquita and Margarita (p. 377); he seems rather to be more concerned with the question of verisimilitude. How indeed, we ourselves may ask, is it conceivable that Paquita should become infatuated with such an unspeakable cad[6] as Henri de Marsay? The explanation is that he is almost a replica of his half-sister Mariquita. It is the 'call of the blood'. Balzac then seems to treat the theme with less moral misgivings than Baudelaire was to show in *Les femmes damnées* (*Les Fleurs du Mal*).

His treatment of the physical side of sexual relations is interesting. Balzac is only too often fulsomely sentimental about love, even that side of it which he frequently refers to as 'the poetry of the senses'. In *Ferragus* he is mainly concerned with the chaste voluptuousness of conjugal love; in *The Duchesse de Langeais* with the preliminary approaches

6. My judgement, though evidently not Balzac's!

to extra-marital union. Sentimentality is therefore predominant here, whereas in *The Girl with the Golden Eyes* he is frankly dealing with sensual, sexual experience. He goes as far as it was feasible to go in that age (while remaining more or less respectable), and no doubt this must appear cautious and unenterprising in our permissive times. There is some evidence that Balzac regarded himself as being, in spite of the Castries humiliation, well-nigh sexually irresistible. Hence (though this may be further wish-fulfilment) the prowess he awards to de Marsay, a new Don Juan. Hence the fatuous remark 'to women's credit' which we read on p. 345. And hence, in part at least, his complacent recording of poor Paquita's submissiveness.

*

An explanation of Balzac's dedications would not be out of place. He prided himself on his descriptions of music, which were at first rather naïve. It was not until he wrote *Gambara* (1837) and *Massimila Doni* (1839) that, having received some competent coaching from a German musician named Struntz (the prototype for Schmucke in *Cousin Pons*), he became less amateurish in such descriptions. *Ferragus* is dedicated to Hector Berlioz because of the *Dies Irae* bravura passage (pp. 137–9), which Balzac felt had its parallel in Berlioz's *Symphonie Fantastique* of 1830. *The Duchesse de Langeais* is dedicated to Franz Liszt because of the descriptions of Sister Thérèse's organ-playing in Chapter 1. In *The Girl with the Golden Eyes* we turn to the sister art of painting. It is dedicated to Eugène Delacroix because here, inspired as he was by Delacroix's striking experiments in colour tonality, Balzac was attempting a pictorial composition whose motif should be the mystic significance of certain dominant colours: white for innocence, red for passion, black for death. Paquita's boudoir (p. 365 ff.), supposed to be similar to, if not identical with, Balzac's own salon in his Chaillot set of rooms, is decorated according to a similar scheme of dominant colours – 'The human soul is strongly attracted to white, love has a delectation for red, and gold gives encouragement to the passions because it has the power to realize their dreams' (p. 366). There is no doubt that he was trying to achieve in words something like the effects Delacroix achieved on canvas.

One further point: readers of Balzac will be familiar with his system of 'reappearing characters', which he began to put into practice round about 1834–5, whereby he planned to knit his fictitious society into something like coherence by showing such and such a person now in the forefront, now in the background of his 'Scenes'. Of the characters in *The Thirteen*, de Marsay is the most important from this point of view: he is almost ubiquitous in *The Human Comedy*, becoming Prime Minister in 1832 but dying relatively young in 1834. Ronquerolles, Montriveau, Navarreins, the Vidame de Pamiers, Lord Dudley and others put in desultory appearances. Ida Gruget is mentioned elsewhere. Madame de Sérisy's main role is in *A Harlot High and Low*. Paul de Manerville's main appearance is in *The Marriage Contract* (1835), at the end of which story, after the collapse of his marriage, Balzac sends him off to India. Antoinette de Langeais appears in the background of *Old Goriot*; there she is on the point of departure for Majorca. Naturally enough, Ferragus does not appear elsewhere.

*

To conclude, the three novels of *The Thirteen* are not perhaps to be counted among Balzac's best, even though they must be allotted an important place in the evolution of *The Human Comedy*. Yet, although they have their defects, they also have many attractive features – even perhaps the cloak and dagger element. That adventurous lady the Duchesse de Berry, mother to the legitimate heir to the French throne, was at this time rampaging about France in a vain endeavour to raise support for the restoration of the Bourbon monarchy. She was enthralled by *Ferragus* and waited impatiently for its sequel to appear! In actual fact, people attached to Balzac are able to take pleasure in both the qualities and the defects of these novels – and even in the absurdities. They may excite irritation, but they may also provide amusement and inspire affection for this strange man. So it was at any rate with such masters of the novel as Marcel Proust and Henry James.

In translating this work, I have used the Classiques Garnier edition, and am much indebted to its editor, Professor Pierre-Georges Castex, for the help and enlightenment his text has given me.

Select Bibliography

Biography: ANDRÉ MAUROIS, *Prometheus: the Life of Balzac,*
Bodley Head, 1965. H. J. HUNT, *Honoré de Balzac. A Biography,*
1957. Reprinted 1969, Greenwood Press, New York, with indispensable corrigendum sheet bringing it up to date.
General Studies: PHILIPPE BERTAULT, *Balzac and The Human
Comedy,* New York University Press, 1963. H. J. HUNT, *Balzac's
Comédie Humaine* Athlone Press, 1964: an analysis of Balzac's work
in the course of its evolution. F. W. J. HEMMINGS, *Balzac, An
Interpretation of La Comédie Humaine,* Random House, New York,
1967. FÉLICIEN MARCEAU, *Balzac and His World,* W. H. Allen,
1967: a study of the characters in *The Human Comedy* which unfortunately takes no account of the stages by which these characters
came into being in Balzac's imagination.

Preface

IN Paris under the Empire thirteen men came together. They were all struck with the same idea and all endowed with sufficient energy to remain faithful to a single purpose. They were all honest enough to be loyal to one another even when their interests were opposed, and sufficiently versed in guile to conceal the inviolable bonds which united them. They were strong enough to put themselves above all law, bold enough to flinch at no undertaking; lucky enough to have almost always succeeded in their designs, having run the greatest hazards, but remaining silent about their defeats; impervious to fear; and never having trembled before public authority, the public hangman or even innocence itself. They had all accepted one another, such as they were, without regard to social prejudice: they were undoubtedly criminals, but undeniably remarkable for certain qualities which go to the making of great men, and they recruited their members only from among men of outstanding quality. Lastly – we must leave out no element of the sombre and mysterious poetry of this story – the names of these thirteen men were never divulged, although they were the very incarnations of ideas suggested to the imagination by the fantastic powers attributed in fiction to the Manfreds, Fausts and Melmoths of literature. Today this association is broken up, or at least dispersed. Its members have peaceably submitted to the yoke of civil law, just as Morgan, that Achilles among pirates, gave up buccaneering, became a colonist and, basking in the warmth of his domestic fireside, made profitable use, without any qualms of conscience, of the millions he had amassed in bloody conflict under the ruddy glare of burning ships and townships.

Since the death of Napoleon, a chance event about which

the author must still keep silent has dissolved the bond between these men, whose secret activities were as strange as any to be found in the most 'Gothic' of Anne Radcliffe's novels. The somewhat unaccountable permission to narrate in his own fashion a few of the adventures which happened to them – whilst respecting certain stipulations – was given to him only recently by a member of this anonymous band of heroes whose underground activities permeated the whole of society: a man in whom he believes he discerned a vague desire for celebrity. He was still youthful in looks, with fair hair, blue eyes and a soft, clear voice which seemed to suggest a feminine type of character: pale of face, mysterious of manner. He was agreeable in conversation, claimed to be no older than forty, and might well have belonged to a very high social class. He seems to have taken an assumed name. He was not known in society. Who was he? No one knows.

Perhaps this unknown man, by taking the author into his confidence about these extraordinary events, wished to see them as it were re-enacted in order to enjoy the emotions they might arouse in the minds of the public – a sentiment analogous to that which Macpherson experienced when the name of the poet he created – Ossian – became a household word in all languages. For the Hebridean schoolmaster, this was no doubt one of the most thrilling, or at any rate one of the rarest, sensations a man may procure for himself: genius incognito. To write, as Chateaubriand did, *L'Itinéraire de Paris à Jérusalem*, is to stake one's claim on the human glory of a century: but to endow one's century with a Homer ... is not this to encroach on God's creative function?

The author of this work is too familiar with the laws of narration not to know what commitments he is undertaking in writing this short preface. But he also knows the *History of the Thirteen* well enough to be certain that his narrative will never fall short of the interest such a programme should inspire. Dramas dripping with gore, scenes bristling with terror, novels teeming with clandestine decapitations have been confided to his ears. If there were any reader not yet sated with the horrors which in recent times have been coldly served up to the public, we might regale him with nonchalant atrocities and amazing family tragedies: let him but say the word. But the author has preferred to select some less violent adventures, those in which the storms of passion are in the end appeased and woman emerges radiant in virtue and beauty. Let this be said to the credit of the Thirteen: such episodes do occur in their history, which one day perhaps will have the honour to be offered to the public as a supplement to that of the pirate gangs, those special communities which were so amazingly enterprising, so captivating in spite of the crimes they committed.

An author must disdain to convert his story, when it is a true one, into a sort of toy with a secret spring and, as some novelists do, drag his reader through four volumes from one subterranean chamber to another, merely in order to show him a dried-up skeleton and tell him by way of conclusion that his bogey effects have been obtained by means of a door hidden behind a tapestry or a corpse inadvertently left under floor-boards. Although the author has an aversion for prefaces, he felt impelled to proffer these remarks as an introduction to the following fragment. *Ferragus* is an initial episode invisibly linked to the *History of the Thirteen*, and the power wielded by this organization, although acquired by natural means, alone can explain the apparently supernatural agencies at work. Narrators of fiction may be permitted a measure of literary waywardness, but once they become historians they must forgo the benefits afforded by the use of apparently eccentric titles – some slight successes have already been achieved nowadays on this basis. It therefore behoves the author of this work briefly to explain the reasons which have forced him to accept a title which may seem far-fetched.

'Ferragus' is a name which, in accordance with an ancient custom, any chief of *Dévorants* may adopt. The day he is elected, the chief makes his choice from among the dynastic names of these *devoirs* and takes the one which pleases him most, just as a newly elected Pope chooses the pontifical dynasty to which he desires to belong. Thus, among the *Dévorants*, you have Trempe-la-Soupe IX, Ferragus XXII, Tutanus XIII, Masche-Fer IV,[1] in the same way as the Church has its Clement XIV, Gregory IX, Julius II, Alexander XVI, etc.

But what are the *Dévorants*? *Dévorants* is the name given to one of the tribes of *Compagnons*, whose origins must be sought in the great mystic association formed among the craftsmen of Christendom for the rebuilding of the Temple of Jerusalem. These *Compagnonnages* still exist in France at an artisan level. Their traditional loyalties, since they have a strong hold on unenlightened minds which are too uneducated to go back on the oath they have sworn, might well be applied to formidable enterprises if some rough-hewn genius thought of taking control of the diverse associations. They could in fact provide a storehouse of unquestioning tools. From time immemorial, from town to town, the *Compagnons* have had their *obade*, a kind of halting-place in the tour they make around France: a hostelry kept by a 'mother', an old woman, more or less a gypsy, having nothing to lose, knowing all that is going on in the locality and devoted through fear or habit to the tribe she lodges and feeds as its members come and go. To sum up, this community, always changing but obedient to unchanging customs, can keep an eye open in every direction and carry out a command without questioning its validity: for the oldest among these *Compagnons* belong to the age when people still clung to certain beliefs. Moreover, the entire organization professes doctrines which are convincing enough, esoteric enough, to sweep all its adherents off their feet once they are carried to their logical consequences. Furthermore, the *Compagnons*' attachment to their rules is so passionate that the different sections fight bloody conflicts between themselves in defence of certain matters of principle. Fortunately for public order at the present moment, when a *Dévorant* has ambitions he starts

---

1. The meanings of these strange nicknames are far from clear; *Trempe-la-Soupe:* 'one who soaks his bread in his broth'; *Masche-Fer:* 'iron-chewer'?

up in business, makes his fortune and withdraws from the
Compagnonnage. Many interesting things might be told about
the Companions of Duty, the rivals of the *Dévorants*,[2] and all
the different sects of workmen, their usages and brotherhoods;
also about the relations between them and the freemasons.
But here such details would be out of place. The author will
merely add that under the pre-revolutionary monarchy it was
not exceptional to find a Trempe-la-Soupe serving a life
sentence in the galleys, but still exerting remote control
over his confraternity and piously consulted by it; and then,
if he managed to get free, he would be certain of finding aid,
succour and deference wherever he went. For a loyal *Compagnon*, to see his leader in a convict-prison is just one of those
misfortunes for which providence alone must be blamed.
This does not dispense the *Dévorants* from paying obedience
to the authority they have created and put above them. Their
king is in temporary exile, but he is still their king. Thus
then we may completely account for the romantic prestige
attached to the name of Ferragus and the *Dévorants*.

Returning to the Thirteen, the author feels that the details
of this history, so nearly verging on romance, give him
justification enough for abdicating yet one more of the
finest privileges a novelist may still enjoy; one which, if it
were put up to auction in the literary market, might reach a
very high bid: that of foisting on the public as many volumes
as *La Contemporaine* has to run to.[3] The Thirteen were all
hard-bitten men like Trelawney, Lord Byron's friend and,
so it is said, the prototype of the Corsair; they were all of
them fatalists, men of courage with romantic minds; they
were bored with the humdrum life they led and were drawn
towards violent enjoyments by long-repressed urges which
by now had become irresistible. One day, one of them, after
re-reading *Venice Preserved*, after admiring the wonderful
spiritual affinity existing between Pierre and Jaffeir, began to

2. Balzac's ideas in this matter lack clarity. See Introduction, p. 10.
3. A series of scandalous 'Memoirs' which had appeared round
about 1830. This rather obscure sentence seems to be satirically directed
against long-winded authors of the time.

ponder over the virtues peculiar to social outcasts, the integrity which reigns in the galleys, the honour which prevails among thieves, and the privileged, inordinate power that such men can acquire by concentrating all their purposes into one single will. He decided that man was greater than men. He saw the possibility of society falling totally under the sway of outstanding people who would join to their natural intelligence, their acquired knowledge and their financial resources a fanaticism white-hot enough to fuse these different forces into one propulsive urge. From then on, immense in its activity and intensity, their hidden might, against which the social order would have no defence, would overturn obstacles, paralyse their opponents' wills and confer their collective power on each individual member. This association, living in society but apart from it and hostile to it, accepting none of its principles, recognizing no laws or only submitting to them out of sheer necessity, devoted to one single cause, acting entirely and solely for any one of its members when he called for their collective assistance; this life led by freebooters in yellow gloves and sporting a carriage; this intimate collaboration between exceptional men, cold and mocking, smiling and cursing as they made their way through a false and petty society; the certainty of being able to bend everything to a whim, to plan a skilful stroke of vengeance, to be sure of unanimity in thirteen hearts; also the unbroken happiness of nourishing a private hatred against men, of being able to withdraw into oneself with the assurance of being one move ahead of the foremost public figures; this religion of pleasure and egoism made fanatics of thirteen men who founded a sort of Society of Jesus in favour of the devil. It was at once horrible and sublime. The pact was struck. And so in Paris there were thirteen brethren who were entirely at one another's disposal but did not recognize one another in public, although they met together in the evenings like conspirators, concealing no thoughts from one another, each in turn drawing on riches similar to those of the Old Man of the Mountain, having a foot in every salon, their hands in every coffer, elbowing their way through every street, a head on every pillow, unscrupulous in their furtherance of every whim. They had no leader, for not one of them could claim supremacy; quite simply, priority was given to the liveliest passion or the most urgent need. They were thirteen kings – anonymous, but really kings; more than kings: judges and executioners too, they had equipped themselves with wings in order to soar over society in its heights and depths, and disdained to occupy any place in it because they had unlimited power over it. The author may perhaps discover the reasons for their eventual abdication; if so, he will disclose them.

He may now begin his narration of the three episodes of this history which he himself found especially attractive because of the Parisian flavour of the details and the strange contrasts they reveal.

Paris, 1831

FERRAGUS:
CHIEF OF THE COMPANIONS OF DUTY

To Hector Berlioz

I

Madame Jules

IN Paris there are certain streets which are in as much disrepute as any man branded with infamy can be. There are also noble streets; then there are streets which are just simply decent, and, so to speak, adolescent streets about whose morality the public has not yet formed an opinion. There are murderous streets; streets which are more aged than aged dowagers; respectable streets; streets which are always clean; streets which are always dirty; working-class, industrious, mercantile streets. In short, the streets of Paris have human qualities and such a physiognomy as leaves us with impressions against which we can put up no resistance. There are streets of doubtful gentility in which you would not like to live, and other streets in which you would willingly reside. Some of them, like the Rue Montmartre, are like mermaids – lovely heads, but fish-tails at the other extremity. The Rue de la Paix is a wide street, a main street, but it inspires none of those spontaneously lofty meditations like those which come upon an impressionable soul in the middle of the Rue Royale; it certainly lacks the majesty reigning in the Place Vendôme. If you wander along the streets of the Île Saint-Louis, look for no other cause of the uneasy sadness that takes possession of you than the solitariness, the dejected appearance of its houses and forsaken mansions. This island, the cemetery so to speak of the Old Regime tax-farming magnates, is as it were the Venice of Paris. Stock Exchange Square is all rattle, bustle and harlotry. It is beautiful only in the moonlight, at two in the morning; in the day-time an epitome of Paris, at night-time a dream-vision from Greece. Is not the Rue Traversière-Saint-Honoré a street of ill fame, with its shabby, double-windowed houses in which, as you mount from storey to storey, you climb upwards to vice, crime and poverty?[1] The narrow streets facing north which only enjoy a touch of sunlight three or four times a year are sinister streets where murder is done with impunity: justice today fights shy of them, though in the old days perhaps the *Parlement* would have summoned the lieutenant of police and roundly called him to account, or at least would have delivered formal judgement against the street as it once did against the canons of Beauvais Cathedral for wearing wigs at mass. In the meantime Benoiston de Châteauneuf's research has proved that twice as many murders were committed in these streets as in any others. We can sum all this up in one example: does not the Rue Fromenteau hold the record for murder and prostitution?

These observations, which outside Paris would have no application, will no doubt be comprehensible to those men of thought and study, those poetic voluptuaries who, as they saunter through Paris, are adept at gathering a whole harvest of enjoyable experiences, one which undulates like a field of ripe corn within the city walls – and also to those for whom Paris is the most delightful of monsters: here a pretty woman, farther off a poverty-stricken old hag; here as freshly minted as the coin of a new reign, and in another corner of the town as elegant as a lady of fashion. A monster, certainly, from head to foot: its head is in the garrets, inhabited by men of science and genius; the first floors house the well-filled stomachs; on the ground floor are the shops, the legs and feet, since the busy trot of trade goes in and out of them. And what an ever-bustling life this monster leads. Scarcely has the last distant rattle of carriages from the ballrooms died down in the centre before its arms are already stirring on the outer reaches and slowly awaking from torpor. Every door yawns open and turns on its hinges like the articulations of a huge lobster, invisibly operated by thirty thousand men or women, every one of whom occupies a space of six square feet per person, with a kitchen, a workshop, a bed, children

1. In early nineteenth-century Paris, it is a fact that different classes and degrees of affluence might well be housed in the same building; the higher the storey the greater the indigence.

and a garden; he or she can see but dimly in it and yet has to see everything. Imperceptibly these joints begin to crack, movement is passed on from one to another, the streets become noisy with talk. By midday all is alive, the chimneys are smoking, the monster eats; then it roars and stirs its thousand legs. A wonderful sight! But, O Paris! He who has not admired your sombre landscapes, shot here and there with streams of light, and your deep, mute, blind alleys; he who has not listened to your murmurings between midnight and two in the morning, still knows nothing of the real poetry within you, or of the strange, broad contrasts you offer. Only a few devotees, people who never walk along in heedless inattention, sip and savour their Paris and are so familiar with its physiognomy that they know its every wart, every spot or blotch on its face. For all others, Paris is still the same monstrous miracle, an astounding assemblage of movements, machines and ideas, the city of a thousand different romances, the world's thinking-box. But, for the devotees, Paris is sad or gay, ugly or beautiful, living or dead; for them Paris is a sentient being; every individual, every bit of a house is a lobe in the cellular tissue of that great harlot whose head, heart and unpredictable behaviour are perfectly familiar to them. They then are the true lovers of Paris: they raise their eyes at this or that street corner and know they will see a clock-face; they tell a friend whose snuffbox is empty to go through such and such a passage, and that there they will find a tobacco shop on the left, next door to a pastry-cook's, a man with a pretty wife. For these men, these poets, travelling through Paris is a time-consuming luxury. Could you really grudge spending a few minutes watching the dramas, disasters, tableaux, picturesque incidents which arrest your attention in the heart of this restless queen of cities, plastered with posters and yet not having one single clean corner, so much does she pander to the vices of the French nation? Who among us has not had the experience of leaving home in the morning for the other side of Paris and still lingering in the centre of it at dinner-time? Such among us will find an excuse for this preamble – a rambling one, but yet one which can be summed up in one single observation, one which is useful and novel, in so far as any observation can be novel in Paris where nothing is novel, not even the statue erected yesterday on which a street urchin has already carved his name. Here it is: there are streets or street ends, there are certain houses unknown to most people in polite society which a woman belonging to it cannot enter without the most cruelly hurtful things being thought about her. She may be rich, she may pass through some of these Parisian byways in a carriage, on foot or in disguise, but she will be compromising her reputation as a respectable woman. But if by chance she comes there at nine in the evening, the conjectures which an observer will allow himself to make may lead him to fearful conclusions. Lastly, if this woman is young and pretty, if she enters some house or other in one of these streets; if the approach to this house is a long, dark and stinking alley; if at the end of this alley the pale glimmer of a lamp is flickering and this glimmer outlines the hideous face of an old woman with bony fingers – I say this truly in the interest of young and pretty women – this woman is lost. She is at the mercy of the first male acquaintance who comes upon her in these Parisian marshes. Furthermore there is a kind of street in Paris where such an encounter may be the prelude to an appallingly tragic drama, a drama of blood and passion, a drama of our modern school. Unfortunately few people will be convinced of or understand this dramatic possibility any more than they will understand Romantic drama itself. One is loath to tell a story to a public for whom local colour is a closed book. But who can ever pride himself on being understood? We go to the grave misunderstood: so the women say; and so say the writers.

At half-past eight one evening, in the Rue Pagevin, during a period when this street had not a single wall on which some obscene graffiti were not inscribed, looking towards the Rue Soly, which was the narrowest and least passable of all Paris streets not excluding the most crowded corner of the least frequented alley; in the beginning of February, about thirteen years ago, a young man, thanks to one of those

chances which do not occur twice in a lifetime, was making
his way on foot round the corner of the Rue Pagevin into
the Rue des Vieux-Augustins, on the right-hand side, just
where the Rue Soly begins. At this point the young man,
whose actual residence was in the Rue Bourbon, discerned
in the woman behind whom he was unconcernedly walking
some vague resemblance to the prettiest woman in Paris,
a person of impeccable and delightful character with whom he
was secretly and passionately in love – hopelessly too, for
she was happily married. His heart immediately gave a bound,
an intolerable flush of heat ran from his diaphragm into every
one of his veins, a cold shiver ran down his back and his head
swam. He was in love, young, well acquainted with Paris
and perspicacious enough to realize what ill repute could be
incurred by any elegant, rich, young and pretty woman
walking alone in that locality with furtive, perhaps guilty
steps. Could it really be she, in so disreputable a spot, at
such a time in the evening?

The young man's love for this woman may appear very
romantic, the more so because he was an officer in the Royal
Guard. Had he been an infantryman it might still have seemed
plausible; but as a high-ranking cavalry officer he belonged
to that branch of the French service which expects to make
the most rapid conquests and draws as much vanity from its
love-making technique as it does from its uniform. However,
this officer's passion was genuine: it was what might well seem
a *grande passion* to many young people. He loved this woman
because she was virtuous. He was indeed in love with her
virtue, her decorous gracefulness, the impression she gave of
saintly innocence: these were the dearest treasures his unavowed passion most adored. She was truly worthy of
inspiring the kind of platonic love which occasionally
sprang up like a flower amid the blood-drenched wastes of
medieval times. She was worthy to be the secret guiding
principle of all a young man's actions. A love like this is as
lofty and pure as the blue vault of heaven: a love without
hope, to which one clings because it never brings disillusion;
a love which is prodigal of ecstatic joys, particularly at an

age when the heart is aflame, the imagination razor-sharp and the vision clear.

Paris by night can produce singular, strange, unimaginable effects. Only those who have spent time observing them are aware what a thing of fantasy a woman may become after dusk. At one moment the creature you are following, by chance or by design, looks willowy; at another her stockings, if they are immaculately white, convince you she has dainty and shapely legs; then her figure, although wrapped in a shawl or a pelisse, appears to be youthful and voluptuous in the semi-darkness; finally the wavering flare from a shop or a street-lamp throws on this unknown woman a fitful but almost always deceptive gleam which awakens and fires the imagination and sends it hurtling into the realm of unreality. At that point the senses are aroused. All is colour and animation. The woman is totally transfigured; her body is embellished; at moments she is no longer a woman but a wild spirit, a will-o'-the-wisp who with high-power magnetism draws you along … to a respectable home, where the poor woman, a middle-class housewife, alarmed by your menacing footsteps or the clink of your boots, slams her door in your face without even taking a look at you!

The flicker of light from a cobbler's shop window cast a sudden illumination on the well-turned figure of the woman walking ahead of the young man. No other than *she*, the young man thought, could have such a waist! She alone had the secret of those chaste movements which so innocently bring out the beauty of the most shapely proportions. There was no mistaking the shawl and velvet hat she wore in the daytime. Her grey silk stockings were spotless and her shoes free from any speck of mud. Her shawl fitted closely round her waist and shoulders and vaguely outlined their attractive contours; the young man had seen these white shoulders in the ballroom and knew what beauty the shawl concealed. By the way a woman of Paris winds her shawl around her and trips along the street, a man of discernment can guess the secret of her mysterious errand. There is a certain tremulousness, a certain lightness both in her person and her manner of walking; she seems to weigh less; she moves, or rather glides along, like a shooting star; she flies away, wafted by a thought which the folds and movements of her dress reveal. The young man quickened his pace, overtook the woman and turned round to look at her. But she had already disappeared down an alley through a gate which clattered and whose bell began ringing as it closed behind her. The young man turned back and saw her reach the end of the alley, acknowledge an old porteress's obsequious salute and climb a twisty staircase whose lower steps were brightly lit: the lady was climbing nimbly and briskly, as an impatient woman might be expected to do.

'But what can she be impatient about?' the young man wondered as he stood back and flattened himself against the wall on the opposite side of the street. And, for his future misfortune, he scrutinized every storey of the building as attentively as a police agent on the track of a conspirator.

It was the kind of house that exists in its thousands in Paris: mean, vulgar, narrow, of jaundiced tone, with four storeys and three sets of windows. The shop on the ground-floor and the mezzanine belonged to the cobbler we have mentioned. On the first floor the shutters were closed. Where was the lady going? The young man thought he heard the tinkle of a door-bell at the second-floor flat. In fact, in a room with two brightly lit windows a lamp moved and suddenly lit up the third window, hitherto in darkness: that of the first room in the flat, no doubt the salon or the dining-room. Immediately the silhouette of a woman's hat was vaguely outlined, the door was shut, the first room became dark again, then the two other windows recovered their red glow. At that point the young man heard a cry: 'Look out!' and received a slap on the shoulder.

'Can't you keep your eyes open?' a rough voice asked – that of a workman carrying a long plank over his shoulder. He passed on: his voice was the voice of Providence, which was saying to this inquisitive man: 'What are you meddling with? Mind your own business and leave Parisians to their own concerns.'

The young man folded his arms. Then, since no one could see him, he let tears of rage fall down his cheeks without bothering to wipe them away. He felt ill, in fact, at the sight of the shadowy figures playing on the two lit-up windows. His glance happened to light on the higher end of the Rue des Vieux-Augustins and he noticed a cab standing alongside a portion of wall where there was neither house-door nor lighted shop.

'Can it be she or not?' A vital question for a lover. And this particular lover went on waiting, for twenty minutes, a century in fact. After which the woman came out, and then he really recognized the person with whom he was secretly in love. But he would not be convinced. The unknown woman walked up to the cab and got into it.

'The house won't run away. I can examine it any time,' the young man told himself. He ran after the carriage in order to dissipate his lingering doubts: before long he had none left.

The cab halted in the Rue de Richelieu at a flower shop near the Rue de Ménars. The lady got down, entered the shop, sent a shop assistant out with the cabman's fare, and came out after choosing some marabou feathers. Marabou feathers for jet-black hair! Being a brunette, she had wanted to see what effect this plumage could have against her head. The young cavalry officer could almost hear what words passed between the lady and the flower-girls.

'Madame, nothing goes better with dark complexions. Dark persons are usually too well-defined in outline and marabou gives their toilette the requisite soft-focus effect. As Madame la Duchesse de Langeais has said, it gives a woman a touch of shadowiness, a touch of the Ossianesque, and it's very up to date!'

'Very well. Please send them immediately.'

Then the lady briskly turned into the Rue de Ménars and went back home. When the main door of the house in which she lived closed to, the amorous young man, having jettisoned all his hopes and, worse still, his most cherished beliefs, staggered through Paris like a drunken man and before long found himself in his own flat without knowing how he had reached it. He flung himself into an armchair, held his head between his hands, spread his feet over the hearth, drying and even scorching his sodden boots. It was a critical moment for him, one of those moments in human life when character changes and the conduct of the best of men depends on the luck or ill-luck of the first thing he does. Providence? Fate? Make your choice.

This young man belonged to a good family though not one of very ancient nobility; but there are so few really old families left today that all young people claim long lineage. His grandfather had purchased his post as Councillor in the *Parlement* of Paris and had risen to the post of President.[2] This man's sons, well provided with this world's goods, entered the services and contracted marriages which gained them admission to Court. The Revolution had swept this family away, except for a headstrong old dowager who had refused to emigrate. Flung into prison, threatened with death but saved by the Ninth Thermidor,[3] she recovered her property. At the appropriate moment, round about 1804, she recalled her grandson to France: Auguste de Maulincour, sole remaining scion of the Charbonnon de Maulincour family. The kindly dowager brought him up with triple devotion: that of a mother, a noblewoman and a headstrong dowager. At the Restoration the young man, then eighteen, joined the Red Guards, went with the royal family to Ghent when Napoleon returned from Elba, became an officer in the Household Guards, left them to join the cavalry of the line, and was recalled to the King's Guard. Now, at twenty-three, he was major in a cavalry regiment: a proud position due to his grandmother who, despite her age, was good at pulling strings.

This double biography summarizes the history, general

2. The pre-revolutionary *Parlements* (thirteen in all)were not 'parliaments' in the English sense. They were High Courts of Justice, divided into various 'chambers', each of which had a 'president' or chairman.
3. July 1794: the day of a revolt in the National Convention that overthrew Robespierre and his allies and brought the Reign of Terror to an end.

and particular (allowing for variants) of all the families of *émigrés*: they had debts, estates, dowagers – and a measure of wordly wisdom. Madame la Baronne de Maulincour was on very friendly terms with the aged Vidame de Pamiers, a former Commander of the Knights of Malta. This was one of those eternal friendships of sixty years' standing, indestructible because they are underlaid with secrets of the human heart which, if time allowed, would well repay the attempt to divine them. But an explanation in twenty lines would have no flavour. They could run to forty volumes, no less interesting than the Abbé Prévost's *Dean of Kilrean*, a work much talked of by young people who have made up their minds about it without having read it. And so Auguste de Maulincour belonged to the Faubourg Saint-Germain by virtue of his grandmother and the vidame; the fact of dating back for two centuries justified his adopting the airs and opinions of aristocrats who claimed to go back to the reign of Clovis. This tall, slim, pale young man, of delicate appearance, but a man of honour and true courage, ready to fight a duel on the slightest pretext, had not yet proved his mettle on any battlefield, although he sported the Cross of the Legion of Honour.

Here we come visibly to one of the most conspicuous, though perhaps the most pardonable of the mistakes made by the Restoration government. The young people of those times belonged to no precise period: they were divided between memories of the Empire and memories of the Emigration,[4] between the ancient traditions of the royal Court and the studied calculations of the bourgeoisie, between religious observance and fancy-dress balls, between Louis XVIII, who had his eyes glued on the present, and Charles X, who looked too far into the future; they were moreover obliged to respect the royal will even though the monarchy was taking the wrong course. This young generation, completely bewildered, blind but yet clear-sighted, counted for nothing in the eyes of the dotards who thought only of

4. The exit of the aristocracy from France which began late in 1789 and only completely ended in 1814.

keeping the reins of government in their doddering hands. If they had retired and 'Young France', still mocked at by the elderly Doctrinaires, whom one might well call the *émigrés* of Restoration times, had been able to come forward, the legitimate monarchy might have been saved.

Auguste de Maulincour had fallen victim to the ideas common among these young aristocrats, and this is how it came about. The Vidame de Pamiers, though seventy-seven years old, was still a man of alert intelligence; he had seen a lot, lived a lot, and could tell a good story. He was a man of honour and a ladies' man, though his views on women were thoroughly odious. He loved and despised them. Their supposed honesty and depth of feeling he dismissed as hypocritical stuff and nonsense. In their company this one-time lady-killer pretended to believe in them, never contradicted them, tried to bring them out. But when this question cropped up among his cronies, the vidame maintained the principle that the seduction of women and the synchronization of several love affairs should be a young man's sole preoccupation rather than going out of his way and meddling with public concerns. It is tiresome to have to sketch so superannuated a portrait. But has it not been in circulation everywhere? Let us face the facts: could even the picture of an Imperial grenadier be more stereotyped? Nevertheless the vidame exerted on the destiny of Monsieur de Maulincour an influence which we cannot but emphasize: he had his own way of giving him advice and was trying to convert him to the eighteenth-century doctrine of *galanterie*. The dowager baroness, a sentimental and pious woman who took up a half-way position between God and the vidame and was a very model of grace and gentleness, though blessed with such a persistency of purpose as triumphs over everything in the long run, had wanted her grandson to preserve the splendid illusions of life and brought him up in the soundest principles. She transmitted all her own delicacy of feeling to him and made a timid man of him and apparently a very stupid one. His sensibility was preserved intact, was not blunted by contact with the world and remained so chaste, so vulnerable that he was acutely offended by actions and maxims to which mundane society attached no importance. Ashamed of being so sensitive, he concealed it under a mask of self-assurance and suffered in silence while joining others in mocking at things which, left to himself, he would have admired. He suffered a further disappointment: through one of those whims of chance which are fairly frequent, he, a man of gentle melancholy and an idealist as regards love, met in the object of his first passion a woman who had conceived a horror for the Teutonic brand of sentimentality. He lost confidence in himself, took to day-dreaming, immersed himself in self-pity and complained of not being understood. And yet, since we yearn the most ardently for the things we find it hardest to get, he continued to worship women and pay them those ingeniously tender, those delicately feline attentions at which women themselves are so adept and of which they perhaps desire to preserve the monopoly. In truth, although women complain of being inadequately loved by men, they have little use for men who are half feminine of soul. All their superiority consists in persuading men that they are inferior to them when it comes to loving. That is why they are quick to drop an admirer when he is so inexperienced as to cheat them of the fears they like to parade, the delicious tortures of ill-founded jealousy, the emotional flutterings that spring from deluded hopes, the vain expectations, in short the whole retinue of pleasurable woes attendant upon women: they hold the Charles Grandisons in horror. What could be more uncongenial to their nature than a peaceful and perfect love? What they want is emotion: unclouded happiness is no happiness for them. There are of course angelic exceptions: women with enough strength of soul to carry love to infinity; they are among women what a fine genius is among men. A great passion is as rare as a masterpiece of art. Love other than this is merely a matter of accommodations and vexations – fleeting, paltry like everything that is petty.

In the midst of these undisclosed sentimental disasters, while he was looking for a woman capable of understanding him – a quest which, incidentally, is the most extravagant folly of our age in so far as love is concerned – Auguste met, in a social milieu completely alien to his own, in a moneyed circle second only to that of the big banking community, a perfect creature, one of those women who are so pure, so set apart and who inspire so much respect that love needs all the support long and familiar acquaintance can give it before it dares to express itself. And so Auguste abandoned himself entirely to the delights of that deepest and most touching kind of passion, a love based purely on admiration. It was a matter of innumerable repressed desires, nuances of passion so vague and yet so profound, so fugitive and yet so forceful that one scarcely knows how to qualify them; they are comparable to perfumes, cloud effects, the play of sunlight and shadow, everything in nature which throws out intermittent gleams, flares up and dies down, leaving lingering emotions in the heart. At the time of life when a man is spiritually youthful enough to take to melancholy, cherish distant hopes and find something more than a woman in a woman, what greater bliss can befall him than to be so much in love that the touch of a white glove, the feel of a strand of hair, a word or a glance exchanged can bring more joy than the most passionate possession can give to an accepted lover? Thus, only those who have been rebuffed, plain women, unhappy men, lovers who worship in silence, shy people of both sexes, know what treasures can reside in the voice of a beloved person. Since its resonances have their *fons et origo* in the soul itself, they have such power to thrill that they bring two hearts so violently together and convey the speaker's meaning so lucidly, and so truthfully, that a single inflexion can precipitate the conclusion of a sentimental drama. How bewitching for a poet is the melodic accent of a sweet voice! What thoughts it awakens! How refreshing the balm it spreads! Love can be heard in the voice before the looks avow it.

Auguste, a poet as all lovers are – there are poets who merely feel and poets who express feeling, and the former are the happiest – had savoured all these initial joys, so full and so manifold. The lady he loved had as caressing a voice as the most scheming of women could ever have wished for as an easy means of seduction: that kind of silvery voice which, though it falls gently on the ear, has a particularly vibrant quality for the heart it perturbs and disturbs, soothes and confuses. But yet this woman was paying evening visits to the Rue Soly, leading off from the Rue Pagevin; her furtive appearance in a squalid house had just shattered a most exalted passion! Auguste was converted to the Vidame de Pamiers' way of reasoning. 'If she is betraying her husband, he and I will take our revenge,' he said.

There was a remnant of love in this *if*. Descartes's philosophic doubt is a tribute of courtesy which must always be paid to virtue. At this moment the Baron de Maulincour remembered that his lady was due at a ball in a house where he was on calling terms. He put on a dress suit without delay, left his flat, arrived and slyly looked round for his beloved in all the rooms. Madame de Nucingen, seeing him bustling about, told him: 'You won't find Madame Jules. She isn't here yet.'

'Good evening, my dear,' said a voice.

Auguste and Madame de Nucingen turned round. Madame Jules was just arriving, dressed in a white, simple and becoming dress, her head adorned with those very marabous which the young baron had seen her choose at the florist's. The sound of this beloved voice was like a stab in the heart. Had he managed to acquire any right whatsoever to feel jealous about this woman, he might have petrified her with the words: *Rue Soly*! But if a comparative stranger like himself had repeatedly uttered it in Madame Jules's ear, she would have been astounded and asked him what he meant. He could only give her a stupid stare.

For malevolent and cynical people it is perhaps highly amusing to know a woman's secret, to be aware that her chaste demeanour is a pretence, that there is deep duplicity behind her serenity of countenance, that an appalling drama is being enacted under the cover of an unruffled brow. But some souls find sadness in such a spectacle, and many even of the scoffers, once they are back at home and alone with their consciences, anathematize society and despise such a woman. That is how Auguste de Maulincour felt in Madame Jules's presence. A paradoxical situation! They had no closer relationship than that existing in society between people who exchange a word or two no more than seven or eight times during the winter season. And here he was calling her to account for a liaison of which she was innocent, and passing judgement on her without her even knowing of what she was accused.

Many young men have found themselves in a similar position, have hurried home in despair at having broken for ever with a woman they had secretly worshipped and now secretly condemn and despise. Hence arise monologues which no second person hears, uttered within the four walls of a solitary retreat; hence storms of emotion which surge up and die down again without ever emerging from the depths of the heart; hence admirable scenes of imaginary expostulation which would call for the painter's brush.

Madame Jules went to look for a seat, leaving her husband to move round the salon. Having found a chair, she appeared to be embarrassed, and while chatting with a neighbour was throwing glances at her husband, Monsieur Jules Desmarets, the Baron de Nucingen's stockbroker. Here is the story of their life together.

For five years before marrying, Monsieur Desmarets had worked in a stockbroker's office and had no other resources than a clerk's meagre salary. But he was one of those men whom penury rapidly instructs and who make a bee-line for their objective; a dogged young man, one of those who take no account of obstacles and are capable of outwearing the patience of Job. So, as a young man, he had all the republican virtues attributed to the poorer peoples of this globe: he led a sober life, never frittered away his time and fought shy of distractions. He was waiting. Moreover, nature had provided him with the very great advantage of good looks. His calm, untroubled brow, the placid but expressive cut of his countenance, his simplicity of manner, everything about him betokened a life of hard work and resignation, a lofty, imposing personal dignity and an unostentatious nobility of heart capable of rising to any situation. His modesty inspired a measure of respect in all who knew him. Moreover, living alone as he did in the heart of Paris, he only mixed with society now and then, during the brief moments he spent in his employer's salon on public holidays. In this young man, as in most people who live this kind of life, resided passions of astounding depth: passions too vast ever to be compromised in trivial matters. His modest means obliged him to live austerely, and bouts of hard work enabled him to conquer any temptation to irrational conduct. After pondering over figures until his cheeks grew pale, he found relaxation in the obstinate effort to acquire the sum of knowledge which today is so indispensable to anyone who wishes to make his mark in society, in commerce, at the bar, in politics or literature. There is one reef on which men of sterling character come to grief; their very integrity. They meet a penniless girl, fall headlong in love, get married and spend the rest of their lives in a contest between poverty and love. The attempt to balance the family budget quenches the most ardent ambition.

Jules Desmarets came up square against this reef. One evening, in his employer's house, he met a young woman of rare beauty. Only unhappy people starved of affection and wasting their bloom of youth in continuous labour know what swift havoc a passion can wreak in a solitary and unappreciated heart. They are so convinced that they are in love, their whole being is so immediately and powerfully concentrated on the woman of whom they are enamoured that they draw from her very presence an emotional delight which often they do not succeed in communicating to her. This kind of egoism is the most flattering of all for a woman who is able to divine the passion that may be hidden behind apparent immobility, one which may strike so deep that some time is needed before it can come to the surface. People in this sorry case, living like anchorites in the heart of Paris, have all the enjoyments of an anchorite's existence; sometimes they are unable to resist temptation; but more often they are deceived, betrayed and misunderstood, and very rarely are they permitted to gather the sweet fruits of love; love which for them is always like a flower fallen from heaven. One smile from the woman in question, a single inflexion of her voice were enough to kindle infinite passion in Jules Desmarets. Fortunately this passion, while yet unavowed, was so ardent, so concentrated that it naïvely revealed itself to her who inspired it. From then on a bond of religious love united them. To put the matter simply, they joined hands together in full view of the world, like two children, brother and sister, threading their way through a crowd every member of which gives way to them admiringly.

The girl was in one of those painful predicaments in which human egoism places some children. She had no civil status; only her name, Clémence, and her age, were recorded in the civil register. She had very little to live on. It delighted Jules Desmarets to learn these unhappy facts. If Clémence had belonged to some opulent family he could scarcely have hoped to win her; but she was a poor love-child, the fruit of some extra-marital passion: so they got married. This event heralded a series of lucky events for Jules Desmarets. Everyone envied him his luck, and jealous people thereafter accused him of having nothing but luck, taking account neither of his virtues nor of his courage. A few days after her daughter's marriage Clémence's mother, accepted as her godmother in social circles, advised Jules to buy a stockbroker's practice and promised to find the necessary capital. At that time these practices were still reasonably priced. That very evening, in his own employer's salon, a rich capitalist, on this lady's recommendation, offered Jules the most advantageous bargain possible, gave him the wherewithal to exploit his broker's licence, and by the next day the fortunate clerk had purchased his employer's post. In four years' time Jules Desmarets had become one of the richest members of his company; clients of importance had come forward and increased the number of those his predecessor had bequeathed to him. The confidence he inspired was unlimited, and it was impossible for him not to detect, in the manner business came his way, some mysterious influence due to his mother-in-law or some secret protection which he himself attributed to providence. At the end of three years, Clémence lost her 'godmother'. By now Monsieur Jules, known by this designation in order to distinguish him from his elder brother whom he had set up as a notary in Paris, had an income of about two hundred thousand francs a year. There was not, in the length and breadth of Paris, a second example of the happiness enjoyed by this couple. For five years the exceptional love they bore each other had been troubled only by a slander for which Monsieur Jules exacted the most sensational retribution. One of his former comrades alleged that Madame Jules was accountable for her husband's fortune and explained it as being due to the dearly-bought protection of an important person. Jules challenged the scandalmonger to a duel and killed him. The devotedness of the young couple, in no wise impaired by married life together, was very much admired in society, even though it aroused envy in certain women. It was respected as an ideal ménage and everyone paid tribute to it. Monsieur and Madame Jules were sincerely liked, perhaps because nothing is more pleasant to contemplate than the sight of a happy couple. But they never stayed long at soirées, impatient as they were to steal away to their love-nest like a pair of turtle-doves who have lost their way. In actual fact, this love-nest was a big, handsome mansion in the Rue de Ménars in which a feeling for art moderated the luxury which moneyed people traditionally display. The Desmarets couple gave lavish hospitality, even though they found social obligations uncongenial. Jules tolerated society, knowing that by and large a family needs it; but both he and his wife felt out of place in it, like hothouse plants put out in stormy weather. With natural tact, Jules had carefully concealed from his wife both the slander and the death of the slanderer who had come near to disturbing their conjugal bliss. Madame Jules was sensitive and artistic in temperament and had a taste for luxury. A few imprudent women, despite the terrible lesson the duel should have taught them, whispered to one another that Madame Jules must often find herself short of money, reckoning that the twenty thousand francs her husband allowed her for clothes and pocket-money were scarcely sufficient. As a matter of fact they often found that she was better dressed at home than when she went out in the evening. It was her pleasure to dress up only for her husband, wishing to show him in this way that he meant more to her than society. A true love this, a pure love, above all a happy love, in so far as love can be happy when the public regards it as something furtive. And so Monsieur Jules, still a lover, and ever more and more in love as one day succeeded another, happy to satisfy all his wife's wishes, even her whims, felt a little anxious because she had so few – as if this were the symptom of some malady or other.

Auguste de Maulincour had the misfortune to come up against this conjugal passion and fall madly in love with Clémence. However, in spite of this idealistic infatuation, he managed not to make himself ridiculous in society. He conformed to all the requirements of military etiquette; and yet, even when he drank a glass of champagne, he maintained an air of reverie and silent disdain for existence; his face had the nebulous expression which for various reasons is characteristic of blasé people, people who find life too devastatingly hollow, those who believe they are dying of consumption or heart disease. To nourish a hopeless passion, to be disgusted with life: these are poses frequently adopted in society today. But a man might more hopefully try to capture the heart of a sovereign lady than aspire to the conquest of a happily married woman. Therefore Auguste de Maulincour had good reason for feeling grave and solemn. A queen has certainly the vanity which goes with power, her lofty state protects her against herself; but a pious bourgeoise is as well protected as a hedgehog or an oyster: both have rude armour.

At that evening's gathering the young officer was standing near the object of his unavowed passion, who was certainly not conscious of having committed a double infidelity. There Madame Jules stood in all her naïvety, the last woman in the world to assume a pose: gentle, majestically serene. How unfathomable is human nature! Before starting to speak, the baron looked alternately at husband and wife. What were his reflections? In a flash he went through all Young's *Night Thoughts*. During this time music was echoing throughout the rooms. A thousand candles were shedding their light. It was a ball given by bankers, one of those blatantly festive occasions by means of which the worshippers of dull gold – the gold of commerce – insolently emulated the gay, gilded sociability of the Faubourg Saint-Germain, without foreseeing the day when the Bank would invade the Luxembourg Palace and place its own representative on the throne. At that time political conspiracies were dancing their way along and taking as little account of future governmental collapses as of future bank failures. The receptions which Monsieur le Baron de Nucingen⁵ gave in his gilded salons had the peculiar animation which Parisian society – joyous enough at least in appearance – imparts to Parisian festivities, for there men of talent lend their wit to dolts, and in requital the dolts lend them their typically self-satisfied air. This exchange enlivens the proceedings. But a Paris soirée is always like a firework display: wit, coquetry and pleasure blaze up and die away like sky-rockets. The morning after, wit, coquetry and pleasure alike are forgotten.

'So then,' Auguste said to himself by way of conclusion. 'The vidame is right about women? Admittedly all the women who are dancing here are less irreproachable than Madame Jules appears to be. But Madame Jules goes to the Rue Soly!' The Rue Soly preyed on his mind and made him sick at heart.

'And so you never dance, Madame?' he asked her.

'You have asked me that three times this winter,' she replied with a smile.

'That is perhaps because you have never answered the question.'

'That is true.'

5. The powerful, unscrupulous banker and financier who plays an important part in *The Human Comedy*.

'I well knew that no truth could be got from you – or from any other woman.'

Madame Jules went on laughing.

'After all, Monsieur, if I really told you why, you would think it silly. I don't believe it is deceitful to withhold secrets which most people would mock at.'

'The disclosure of any secret, Madame, depends upon a friendship of which no doubt I am unworthy. Yet you could have nothing but the noblest of secrets: do you think I could make a jesting matter of things which should command respect?'

'Indeed,' she said. 'You, like all other people, make fun of our purest sentiments and slander them. In any case, I have no secrets. It is my right to love my husband openly. This I proclaim, and am proud of it. And if you make fun of me when I tell you that I dance with no one but him, I shall have a very poor opinion of your qualities of heart.'

'Have you never danced with anyone but your husband since you married him?'

'I have not, Monsieur. I have never leaned on any other arm than his, and I have never felt the touch of any other man.'

'Has your doctor not even felt your pulse?'

'Ah! There you go making fun of me.'

'No, Madame, I admire you because I understand you. But you let us hear your voice, look at you, and after all you even permit our eyes to admire you . . .'

'Oh, that is what vexes me,' she said, interrupting him. 'Yes, I could have wished it were possible for a married woman to live with her husband as a mistress does with her lover, for then . . .'

'Then how did it come about that, two ho:.rs ago, you were walking along the Rue Soly in disguise?'

'Where on earth is the Rue Soly?' Her clear voice betrayed no emotion, her features gave no twitch, she gave no blush and was in no wise put out.

'What? Did you not climb to the second floor of a house in the Rue des Vieux-Augustins, at the corner of the Rue

Soly? Did you not have a cab waiting for you a few yards away, and did you not return through the Rue de Richelieu and call at the florist's there, where you chose the marabous you are now wearing?'

'I did not leave my house this evening.'

While uttering this lie, she kept a smiling countenance as she fanned herself. But anyone who had had the right to slip his hand to the back of her girdle would perhaps have found that it was moist. At this moment Auguste remembered the lessons the vidame had taught him.

'Then it was someone remarkably like you,' he added, pretending to believe her.

'Monsieur,' she replied, 'if you are capable of following a woman and spying on her, allow me to tell you that it is a very reprehensible thing to do. I do you the honour of disbelieving you.'

The baron left her, took his stand in front of the fireplace and appeared to be lost in thought. His head was lowered, but he was keeping a furtive eye on Madame Jules. She, not bearing in mind the play of the mirrors, cast two or three glances at him in which there was a hint of terror. Then she made a sign to her husband, rose to her feet and took his arm in order to walk round the salons.

When she passed by Monsieur de Maulincour, he was chatting with a friend, and said out loud, as if he were answering a question: 'She's a woman who certainly will not sleep easy tonight.' Madame Jules halted, threw him a dignified and very contemptuous look, and then went on without realizing that a further look, had her husband but noticed it, might well have put her happiness at risk as well as the lives of two men. Shortly after Auguste, a prey to the fury which he was bottling up in the depths of his being, left the house vowing that he would get to the bottom of this intrigue. Before leaving, he went round again looking for Madame Jules, but she had gone. What a turmoil was raging in the young man's head, stuffed with romantic notions like all those who have never known a love so transcendent as the one they imagine! His adoration for Madame Jules now took a new shape: he loved her in a jealous rage, with the delirious anguish of one who is not without hope. As a faithless wife, she was no longer on a pedestal. Auguste could now abandon himself in thought to all the felicities of successful courtship: the whole gamut of sensual pleasures was now open to his imagination. In short, if had lost the angel in her, he was discovering a most entrancing demon. He went to bed, building innumerable castles in the air, finding romantic motives for justifying Madame Jules but not really believing in them himself. Then he resolved to devote all his efforts, from tomorrow onwards, to finding out the cause of and the interests involved in this mysterious affair. It was a novel he might read: better still, a drama to unfold, one in which he would have a part to play.

2

Ferragus

SPYING is a very agreeable occupation when conducted on one's own behalf or in furtherance of a passion: it furnishes the pleasures a thief enjoys while one remains respectable. But one must be prepared to boil with rage, roar with impatience, get one's feet frozen by standing about in the mud, endure extremes of temperature and live on frustrated hopes. On the strength of a single clue one must set off for an unknown goal, fall short of it, take to cursing, improvise elegies or dithyrambs addressed to oneself, utter imbecilic exclamations in the hearing of a gaping passer-by, upset barrow-women and their apple-carts, rush about, relax, loiter in front of a window, lose oneself in conjecture ... But the hunt is on! Hunting in Paris! Hunting with all its hazards except the hounds, the guns and the tally-ho! Only scenes in a gambler's life are comparable to these. Furthermore, you need a heart swollen with love or vengefulness in order to lie in ambush in Paris like a tiger waiting to pounce on its prey, and consequently to enjoy all the incidents which may occur in this or that quarter of Paris, adding a further interest to those they already have in abundance. For this, must one not possess some multiplicity of soul? Must one not live through a multiplicity of passions and sentiments – simultaneously?

Auguste de Maulincour flung himself zealously into this fevered existence because he was sensible of all the woes and pleasures it brought. He went about Paris in disguise, kept watch at every corner of the Rue Pagevin and the Rue des Vieux-Augustins. He hurried like an errand-boy from the Rue de Ménars to the Rue Soly and back again, having no idea what Nemesis might await him, what reward or punishment might accrue from such assiduity, such activity, so

many stratagems. However he had not yet reached the stage
of impatience that brings exasperation or perturbation. There
was hope in his loiterings, since he reckoned that for a day or
two Madame Jules would not risk returning to a locality
where her presence had been noticed. And so he had devoted
these early days to getting familiar with that particular street.
Being a novice at spying, he dared question neither the porter
nor the cobbler in the house which Madame Jules was
visiting; but he hoped to provide himself with an observation post in the house exactly opposite the mysterious set
of rooms. He was studying the lie of the land and trying to
temper impatience with caution and prevent his passion
from giving him away.

One day early in March, while he was still cogitating
plans for a decisive stroke, as he left his observation post
after one of the stretches of sentry-go which so far had given
him no information, he was returning home at about four
o'clock in order to deal with a matter relating to his duties as
an officer when, in the Rue Coquillière, he was caught in one
of those cloudbursts which suddenly choke the gutters and
whose every drop resounds like a bell as it plops into the
puddles of the public thoroughfare. When this happens a
pedestrian in Paris has to stop short, take refuge in a shop or a
café – if he has enough money to pay for the hospitality he
is obliged to seek – or, if urgency demands, under a *porte-
cochère*, where poor or shabbily dressed people take shelter.

Why is it that none of our painters has yet tried to make a
lifelike sketch of a swarm of Parisians grouped, during a
downpour, under the dripping porch of some mansion or
other? Where else could so rich a picture be found? First
of all there is the reflective or philosophical pedestrian who
loves to watch the patterns etched by the rain on the lead-grey
atmosphere, a sort of chasing similar to the fitful spurts of
glass in fusion; or else the eddies of foaming waters that the
wind rolls over the roofs like gusts of luminous spray; or else
the wayward spewings from the bubbling, frothing spouts;
or else other innumerable, admirable trifles which idlers
take a delight in studying, however ill-humouredly the owner

of the premises tries to drive them along with his broomstick. Then there is the voluble pedestrian who complains and converses with the portress as she stands poised on her broomstick like a grenadier on his rifle; the penniless pedestrian who flattens himself two-dimensionally against the wall with no concern for his rags and tatters, inured as they are to the wear and tear of the streets; the scholarly pedestrian who scans, spells out or reads the posters without ever finishing his reading; the jovial pedestrian who makes mock of people when they meet with mishap in the streets, laughs when women get bespattered with mud and makes faces at men or women looking out through their windows; the silent pedestrian who gazes up at the windows in every storey; the business pedestrian armed with a satchel or carrying a parcel, computing the gains or losses the downpour will cause; the friendly pedestrian who bursts in like a bomb with a 'What weather, gentlemen!' and pays his respects to everybody; and finally there is the genuine bourgeois of Paris, the man with the umbrella, who knows all about downpours, predicted this one, left home against his wife's advice and has taken possession of the concierge's chair. Every member of this chance assembly, conforming to his own particular bent, scans the heavens, hops this way and that, either in order to avoid the mud, or because he is in a hurry, or because he sees other citizens rushing along helter-skelter, or because the courtyard behind the *porte-cochère* is sodden and terribly likely to give him a mortal cold if he ventures into it, so that he feels it would be like stepping from the frying-pan into the fire. There is only one other kind of pedestrian – the prudent one who, before he steps out again, looks for breaks in the clouds, and patches of blue sky.

And so Monsieur de Maulincour took refuge, in company with a motley crowd of pedestrians, under the porch of an ancient mansion with a courtyard which looked like a great chimney-flue. All along its green gypsum-stained walls, efflorescent with damp, there were so many leads and conduits, and so many storeys in its four main blocks, that it was reminiscent of the cascades round the Château de Saint-Cloud. Water streamed down in all directions, bubbling, leaping, babbling. It was black, white, blue, green; it swirled and furled under the portress's broom. She was a toothless old hag. She was broken in to such downpours and seemed to welcome them as providing an opportunity for sweeping out into the streets a medley of flotsam which, had an inventory been made, would have furnished an interesting revelation of the life and habits of each tenant in the building: scraps of printed calico; tea-leaves; petals of faded, mutilated artificial flowers; vegetable peel; waste paper; fragments of metal. With every sweep of her broom the old woman was exposing to view the contents of the gutter – that dark crevice sectioned into draught-board squares into which all concierges frantically sweep their refuse. Our forlorn lover was taking this picture in – one of the thousand pictures that kaleidoscopic Paris offers every day. But his inspection was only mechanical, that of a man absorbed in thought. Then all at once, raising his eyes, he found himself face to face with a man who had just joined the throng.

He was, or seemed to be, a beggar, but not the typical Paris beggar – a creation to whom no human language can give a name. No, this man came from a new mint, had been coined without any reference to the ideas evoked by the word 'beggar'. This unknown person did not stand out as one of those odd Parisian characters we frequently find so striking among the down-and-outs whom Charlet has sometimes hit off with a rare accuracy of observation: coarse, grimy faces, raucous voices, red, bulbous noses, toothless but menacing mouths. They are cringing yet terrible, because the profound intelligence which gleams in their eyes seems out of keeping. Some of these brazen-faced vagabonds have a mottled, chapped, veiny complexion, deeply corrugated foreheads, sparse and dingy hair – like that of a wig which has been consigned to the rubbish bin. All of them are cheerful in degradation and degraded in enjoyment; marked with the seal of debauchery; and their silence is a kind of reproach flung at the world. Terrifying thoughts are revealed in the posture they maintain. They are as ready to steal as to whine for alms. They are past the stage of repentance and they shuffle cautiously round the gibbet without ever getting caught in the noose; innocent, they wallow in vice; vicious, they are steeped in their own brand of innocence. You may smile at them, but they always give you food for thought. One of them is the epitome of a stunted civilization and includes every element in it: honour among thieves, patriotism, virtue; also the maliciousness behind a vulgar misdemeanour and the subtlety behind a neatly-engineered felony. Another puts on a mask of resignation: he is a clever mimic, but a stupid man. All of them are drawn towards an orderly and industrious way of life, but they are thrust back into the mire by society, which cannot be bothered to find out how many poets, great men, intrepid heroes and splendid organizing abilities there may be among these beggars and bohemians of Paris: a sovereignly good and a sovereignly wicked community, like all the masses of men who have known suffering; inured to unheard-of ills and kept constantly at mud-level by some fatal power. All of them cherish a dream, a hope, a vision of happiness: a lucky gamble, a win in the national lottery, a litre or two of wine.

There was nothing of this strange manner of life in the person who was very unconcernedly leaning against the wall opposite Monsieur de Maulincour, who looked like a figure of fantasy which a clever artist might have sketched on the reverse side of some canvas in his studio. This long, gaunt man, concealing profound and frigid thought behind his leaden visage, congealed all pity in the heart of interested people by the impression his ironical attitude and black looks made on them, both of which announced his claim to treat with them on equal terms. His face was off-white and his wrinkled cranium, bald on top, vaguely resembled a block of shaped granite. Some sparse locks of flat, grey hair, plastered down on each side of his head, reached down to the collar of his coat, grimy and buttoned up to the neck. He reminded one simultaneously of Voltaire and Don Quixote: he was a mocker and yet a melancholy man;

full of scorn and philosophy but half-demented. It looked as if he had no shirt. His beard was long. His shabby black cravat, threadbare and torn, showed a bulging, heavily furrowed neck with gross veins standing out like cords. His eyes were ringed with black and blue circles. He could not have been less than sixty. His hands were clean and white. He wore leaky, down-at-heel boots. His blue trousers, patched here and there, were blanched with a kind of nap which made them revolting to look at. Perhaps because his wet clothes were giving forth a fetid odour, perhaps because the normal smell of poverty emanating from Parisian hovels clung to him, just as civil service offices, sacristies and hospitals have their particular fetid and rancid stench, the people standing next to this man moved away and left him to himself. He cast a calm and expressionless regard at them and then transferred it to the officer. It was like the celebrated glance of the Prince de Talleyrand: lustreless and lacking warmth; the kind of impenetrable veil behind which a steely soul conceals deep emotions and diabolically accurate calculations about men, situations and events. His face was inscrutable, his mouth and forehead impassive. But his eyes drooped with a noble and almost tragic deliberateness. In fact drama was implicit in the very flicker of his faded eyebrows.

The sight of this stoical figure induced in Monsieur de Maulincour one of those wayward reveries which start with a commonplace query and in the end provoke a multitude of speculations. The storm had passed over. Monsieur de Maulincour saw no more of this man than the skirt of his frock-coat brushing against the boundary-stone. But as he moved away he found at his feet a letter which had fallen to the ground. He guessed that it belonged to the unknown man whom he had seen thrust back into his pocket a scarf he had just been wearing. The officer took up the letter in order to give it to the man, but he could not help reading the address:

> *To Mister Ferragusse*
> *rue des Grans-Augustains korner of the rue Soly,*
> PARIS

This letter was not stamped, and the address on it prompted Monsieur de Maulincour to withhold it, for he was in the grip of a passion, and in the long run most passions weaken scruples. The baron had the feeling that this find would prove to be opportune, and he decided to hold on to the letter in order to obtain right of entry into the house of mystery by restoring it to the man who had dropped it and who, he felt sure, lived in this dubious-looking dwelling. Already certain suspicions, vague ones like the first glimmers of daybreak, were leading him to assume some relationship between the man and Madame Jules. Jealous lovers indulge in all sorts of suppositions; it is by so doing, and by choosing out the most plausible of their conjectures that judges, spies, lovers and observant people pierce through to the truth they are after.

'Is the letter for him? Is it from Madame Jules?'

His restless imagination assailed him with a thousand questions; but he smiled on reading the opening words of the letter. Here it is, verbatim, in its splendid naïvety, with its uncouth spelling. It had to be given in its entirety or not at all. True, punctuation had to be supplied, for the screed itself contained no commas, no indications of pauses, no exclamation marks even: a fact which might well tend to invalidate the system of punctuation which our modern authors have devised in order to show what great ravage all great passions can cause.

HENRY!

I made a lot of sacrifises for you and one of them was not to give you noos of me, but somethink inside me forses me to tell you wot rong youve done me. Oh, I kno write enuff that your to far gone in wikkedness to pitty me. Youve an eart of stone. Its deff to Natures calls. But never mind. I must tell you wot rong youve dun me and wot an orrible posishun youve put me in. Henry, you new wot I suffered when I was in trubble the first time; but you put me in it agen and left me in the depths. I tell you strate, I felt I could put up with it becos I thort you loved me and respekted me. Now Ive nothing to ope for. Its threw you Ive lost all that mattered, all that maid life worth living: relashuns, frends, honner and reputation. I gave all this up for you and all I ave left

is disgrase, shame and, I tell you strate, poverty. I only needed
one think more: to know I meant nuthing to you and that you ated
me. Now I kno that, I'll stick to wot I desided. My minds maid up.
I wont disgrase my family, I'm going to end my suffering. You
neednt try to put me off it, Henry. Its horrible, I no, but wot else
can i do in my posishun? No help, no support, no frend to comfort
me. I cant go on, its settled. So then, in two days, Henry, in two
days Ida wont be worthy of your esteme. But I take my oath on
this: Ive an eesy conshience becos Ive never seased to deserve
your frendship. Oh Henry my dear – for Ill never change towards
you – promise youll forgive me for the career Im starting on.
Its luv thats given me currage and will keep me strate. Ill always
be thinking of you and that will keep me from falling. But dont
you ever forget its you that drove me to this: the blame is yours.
I hope God wont punnish you for your missdeeds. On my nees
I beg Him to forgive you, for if I new you were unhappy that
would be the last straw for me. Im down to my last penny, but Ill
take no help from you. If youd loved me I might have axcepted
it as coming from a frend. But Ill take nuthing out of pitty, I
coudnt stand that and Id feel more of a coward for that than for
wot Im planning to do. I only ask you won thing: I dont no how
long Ill be in Madame Meynardies establishment, but mind you
keep away from it while Im there. Your last too visits gave me a
start I shant get over for ages. I wont go on about the way you
behaved. You hate me, you sed. That's written in my eart and
frose it stiff with fright. God help me! Just when I need evry bit
of currage Ive got, I dont know wether Im on my head or my eels.
Henry luv, before Ive put a five-bar gate between us, give me one
last proof you don't despize me even if you don't luv me enny
more. Altho Im still fit to look you in the eye, Im not asking to
have a word with you. I feel so weak and I still luv you so, anything cud happen. But for pitty's sake write me a word back. Itll
give me currage to bear my trubbles.

Its thru you I went rong. But your the only man I ever fell for
and Ill never forget you.

IDA

The life-story of this young woman, this tale (so laconically
related) of love betrayed, of baleful joys, of grief, poverty
and appalling resignation; this poem by an anonymous but
essentially Parisian author, recorded in this grimy letter, set
Monsieur de Maulincour pondering for some moments. In

the end he wondered whether this Ida might be a relative of Madame Jules, and whether the evening rendezvous he had chanced on had not been necessitated by some charitable purpose. Could the old pauper have been Ida's seducer? A scarcely credible supposition! As he threaded his way through the labyrinth of his reflections, which ran this way and that and cancelled each other out, the baron came to the Rue Pagevin and saw a cab stationed at that end of the Rue des Vieux-Augustins which stands next to the Rue Montmartre. Any standing cab had some meaning for him. 'Could it be hers?' he wondered. His heart beat fast and furious. He pushed through the little gate with its tinkling bell, but with drooping head and a certain shamefacedness, for an inner voice was asking him: 'Why are you poking your nose into this mystery?'

He walked up a few steps and came face to face with the old portress. 'Monsieur Ferragus?' he asked.

'Don't know him.'

'What? Does Monsieur Ferragus not live here?'

'No such person in this house.'

'But, my good woman . . .'

'I'm not a good woman, Monsieur. I'm a concierge.'

'But, Madame,' the baron went on. 'I have a letter to hand over to Monsieur Ferragus.'

'Ah, Monsieur! If you have a letter,' she said with a change of tone, 'that makes a difference. Will you show it me?' Auguste showed her the folded letter. The old woman gave a doubtful nod, hesitated, seemed minded to leave her lodge in order to go and inform Monsieur Ferragus about this unforeseen event, and then said: 'Very well, go up, Monsieur. You must know where it is . . . ' Giving no reply to this remark, by which the cunning old woman might have intended to set a trap for him, the officer ran briskly upstairs and gave a sharp tug at the bell of the second-floor flat. His lover's intuition told him: 'She's there.'

The unknown man he had met at the porch, Ferragus himself, the man through whom Ida had 'gone rong', opened the door. He was wearing a dressing-gown of flowered material,

thick flannel trousers and dainty carpet-slippers. His head was
neatly groomed.

Madame Jules, who was looking through the door of the
inner room, turned pale and fell back on to a chair.

The officer dashed towards her. 'Can I do anything for you,
Madame?' he cried.

But Ferragus thrust his arm forward and repulsed the
officer so brusquely that Auguste felt as if an iron bar had hit
him in the chest.

'Stand back, Monsieur!' the man said. 'What do you want
with us? You have been prowling round this quarter for
five or six days. Do you belong to the police?'

'Are you Monsieur Ferragus?' asked the baron.

'No, sir.'

'Nevertheless,' Auguste continued. 'I must return this
paper to you. You lost it in the porch of the house where
both of us were sheltering from the rain.'

As he spoke and proffered the letter to this man, the baron
could not help throwing a glance round the room into which
Ferragus was admitting him: it was excellently but simply
decorated. A fire was burning in the hearth. Near to it was
a laid table more sumptuously served than seemed appropriate to this man's apparent status and his very mediocre
lodging. Farther away, on a settee in the second room, which
was within his range of vision, he perceived a heap of gold
coins and heard a sound which could not be anything but
that of a woman weeping.

'Yes, this paper belongs to me, and I thank you,' said the
unknown man, turning round in such a way as to intimate to
the baron that he desired his immediate departure.

Auguste's curiosity was too great for him to pay attention
to the intense scrutiny of which he was the object. He did not
notice the almost mesmeric glances which the unknown man
was darting at him; had his eye met this basilisk glare he
would have realized the danger in which he stood. His
passion being too great for him to think of himself, he bowed,
went downstairs and returned home, trying all the time to
find some meaning behind the conjunction between these

three persons: Ida, Ferragus and Madame Jules. Figuratively speaking, this was like trying to fit in the odd-shaped sections of wood in a Chinese puzzle without having any clue. But Madame Jules had seen him, Madame Jules visited this house, Madame Jules had lied to him. Maulincour proposed to pay her a visit the following day. She could not refuse to see him since he had made himself her accomplice and was involved knee-deep in this obscure affair. He was already assuming despotic airs and thought of imperiously demanding that Madame Jules should make a clean breast to him about everything.

During that period Paris had a building mania. Paris may be a monster, but it is the most monomaniacal of monsters. It falls for a thousand fantasies. At one moment it takes to brick-laying like a lord enamoured of the trowel. Then it tires of the trowel and takes to military exercises, dresses from head to foot in the uniform of a national guard and spends its time drilling and smoking. Then suddenly it gives up military parades and throws its cigar away. Then it falls into the slough of despond, goes bankrupt, sells up and files its petition. But a few days later it puts its affairs in order, sallies forth in holiday and dancing mood. One day it will get sticky hands and mouth through eating barley sugar. Yesterday it was buying Weynen paper.[1] Today the monster has toothache and treats it by applying anti-toxic plasters to all its walls. Tomorrow it will lay in a stock of cough mixture. It has its day-to-day manias, but also its manias for the month, the season, the year. Accordingly, at that moment, the whole population was demolishing or rebuilding something or other, somehow or other. Few were the streets free from scaffolding, with its long poles, its stock of planks hitched on to crosspieces and hoisted on putlogs from storey to storey: frail constructions trembling under the feet of the masons but strengthened with rope-work, white all over with plaster and seldom guaranteed against the assault of passing carriages by the regulation wood fencing which had to surround all building areas whether building was actually in process or

1. A brand of writing-paper which then was all the rage.

not. There was something nautical in these masts, ladders, riggings and the shouts of the masons.

It so happened that, a dozen or so yards from the Maulincour mansion, one of those ephemeral erections had been set up in front of a house which was being built in freestone. The next day, just as the Baron de Maulincour was driving past this scaffolding in his cabriolet on his way to Madame Jules's house, a stone measuring two cubic feet, which had been hoisted to the top of the poles, slipped through its rope cradle, whirled round and crashed down on to the flunkey sitting in the rear of the cabriolet. A shout of terror made the scaffolding vibrate and the masons tremble; one of them was painfully clinging to the long poles in danger of death – it looked as if the stone had grazed him as it fell. A crowd quickly gathered. All the masons climbed down, maintaining with oaths that Monsieur de Maulincour's cabriolet had put their crane out of true: two inches more, and the stone would have crashed down on the officer's head. The manservant was killed and the carriage smashed.

This accident made quite a stir in the quarter and the newspapers reported it. Monsieur de Maulincour, quite sure that he had not collided with anything, lodged a complaint. The local magistrate was called in, and his inquiry established the fact that a small boy with a lath was standing guard and warning passers-by to keep clear. The matter went no further. Monsieur was the worse off for the loss of his manservant and the fright he had sustained. He stayed in bed for several days, for the shattering of the back part of the cabriolet had given him some bruises, and the nervous shock ensuing from the accident threw him into a fever. He did not go to call on Madame Jules.

Ten days after this occurrence, on leaving his house for the first time, he was making for the Bois de Boulogne in his repaired cabriolet when, on the way down the Rue de Boulogne at the place where the sewer lies, opposite the Chambre des Députés, the axle broke clean through the middle. The carriage was moving swiftly and the two wheels were brought so violently together that his skull might well have been smashed; but the hood offered some resistance and preserved him from this danger. None the less he was severely injured in the side. For the second time in ten days he was taken home in a state of collapse to the weeping dowager.

This second accident gave him some misgivings and vague suspicions about Ferragus and Madame Jules. In order to clear them up, he kept the broken axle in his room and sent for his carriage-builder. The latter came, inspected the axle and the break in it, and proved two things to Monsieur de Maulincour: firstly, that the axle was none of his making – he supplied none without his initials being roughly carved on it, and he had no idea by what means this axle had been substituted for the original one. Secondly, the fracture in this faulty axle had been brought about by means of a cavity, a sort of interior hollow, by blow-holes and flaws very cleverly contrived.

'Sure enough, Monsieur le Baron,' the coach-builder said, 'you've got to be pretty clever to fix up an axle like that, to make it look so natural.'

Monsieur de Maulincour asked his coach-builder to say nothing about this mishap, and concluded that he had been duly warned. These two attempts on his life had been so skilfully arranged as to show that he was up against resourceful enemies.

'It's war to the death,' he told himself as he tossed about in bed. 'A Red Indian kind of war: unforeseen attacks, ambushes, betrayals. A war declared in Madame Jules's name. Who then is the man she belongs to? What power then does Ferragus have at his command?'

Monsieur de Maulincour was a brave man and a soldier, but he could not repress a shudder. Among all the thoughts that came flooding in upon him, there was one against which he was defenceless and without courage: might his secret enemies not soon resort to poison? Immediately, under the dominion of fears which were much aggravated by his temporary debility, the diet to which he was subjected and his feverishness, he sent for an old woman who had long been attached to his grandmother and loved him almost as a mother:

simple people are capable of sublime devotion. Without taking her completely into his confidence, he commissioned her to buy secretly and day by day, in different localities, whatever food he needed, urging her to keep it locked up and to bring it straight to him without letting any other person come near it whenever she served it up to him. In short he took minute precautions to safeguard himself from that kind of death. He lived alone, was ill and confined to bed, and therefore had plenty of time to think of self-protection, and that is the only preoccupation which leaves human egoism clear-sighted enough to think of everything. But the unhappy invalid had allowed his life to be poisoned through fear, and despite all efforts suspicion had cast its dark shadow on every hour he lived. And yet the two attempts at assassination taught him one of the qualities most indispensable to politicians: it helped him to understand what profound dissimulation must be exercised when the great interests in life are at stake. To keep one's own counsel is nothing; but to keep it for long in advance, to be able, if necessary, to forget a fact for thirty years, as Ali Pasha did, in order to bring off an act of vengeance which one has been planning for thirty years, is a phenomenon worthy of study in a country in which very few men are capable of dissimulating even for a month. Monsieur de Maulincour's life was henceforward wrapped up in Madame Jules. His mind was perpetually given to serious ponderings on the means he could employ in this blindfold conflict with unknown adversaries. Every obstacle he encountered augmented his undeclared passion for this woman. Madame Jules continued to occupy a central position in his thoughts and feelings, and she acquired more attractiveness from her presumed vices than from the undoubted virtues which had originally made her the object of his idolatry.

The sick man, wishing to reconnoitre the enemy positions, decided that there would be no danger in letting the old vidame into the secret of the situation. The commander loved Auguste as if he were his own child. He was shrewd, adroit and of a diplomatic turn of mind. And so he came for a talk with the baron, gave comprehending nods as he listened, and they took counsel together. The good vidame was unable to share his young friend's assurance when Auguste affirmed that nowadays the police and civil authorities were competent to unravel all mysteries, and that if it became absolutely necessary to call upon their services he would obtain powerful support from them.

The old man gave a grave reply. 'The police, dear boy, are superlatively incompetent, and the civil authorities are incredibly feeble when it comes to dealing with individual matters. Neither police nor public officials are able to read people's minds. One might reasonably expect them to look into the causes which have led to a given fact, but they are singularly ill-equipped for the task, because *ipso facto* they lack the personal interest which makes all things clear to a man who needs complete knowledge. No human power can prevent an assassin or a poisoner from reaching the heart of a prince or the stomach of an honest citizen. Police work should above all be concerned with human passions.'

The commander strongly advised the baron to go away to Italy, from there to Greece, from Greece to Syria, from Syria into Asia, and not to return until he had convinced his secret enemies of the regret he felt, thus tacitly making his peace with them. Alternatively he should stay at home, and even keep to his bedroom, since there he could be safe from any further attack which Ferragus might make and only emerge from it when he was sure of destroying him. 'You must never approach an enemy,' he gravely told him, 'until you are ready to knock him on the head.'

Nevertheless the old man promised his young friend to use all the astuteness with which Heaven had favoured him in order that he might, without compromising anyone, reconnoitre the enemy territory, map it out completely and thus pave the way for victory.

The commander had an old manservant of the Figaro type, as cunning a rascal as had ever assumed human shape. He had proved to be diabolically nimble-witted, as physically tough as a convict, as agile as a pickpocket, as subtle as a woman. But, for lack of practice, since the reconstitution of Parisian

society which has driven conventional comedy-valets into
retirement, his particular talent had fallen into disuse. This
superannuated gentleman's gentleman was devoted to his
master as to a superior being; but year by year the wily vidame
added a considerable sum to the wages of his erstwhile steward
of gallantry. This gratuity materially reinforced the bond
of natural friendship between them and provided the old
man with attentions which the most loving of mistresses
would never have invented for an ailing lover. In this jewel
among stage lackeys, this relic of the eighteenth century,
this minister who was incorruptible because he had no
passions to satisfy, the commander and Monsieur de Maulincour placed their entire confidence.

'Monsieur le Baron might well ruin everything,' said the
great man in his livery on being called to counsel. 'Let him
eat, drink and sleep in peace. I take the whole matter upon
myself.'

In fact, a week after this conference, just as Monsieur de
Maulincour, completely recovered from his illness, was
lunching with his grandmother and the vidame, Justin came
in to give his report. Then, with the false modesty affected
by talented people, he said, as soon as the dowager had returned to her rooms: 'The man who is out for Monsieur le
Baron's blood is not called Ferragus. The real name of this
diabolical man is Gratien, Henri, Victor, Jean-Joseph Bourignard. This Gratien Bourignard is a former building contrac-
tor, once a very rich man and into the bargain one of the most
handsome bachelors in Paris, a Lovelace who might well have
led a Grandison astray.

'My information goes no further than this. Bourignard
was a simple journeyman, and the Companions of the Order of
Dévorants elected him as their leader under the name of
Ferragus XXIII. The police should know all that if the police
were capable of knowing anything whatsoever. This man
has moved house. He no longer lives in the Rue des Vieux-
Augustins: he hangs out now in the Rue Joquelet. Madame
Jules Desmarets often goes to see him. Quite often her husband, on his way to the Stock Exchange, takes his wife to

the Rue Vivienne; or else she takes her husband to the Stock Exchange. Monsieur le vidame is too versed in such matters to require me to tell him if the wife has the husband in leading-strings or vice versa. Madame Jules is so pretty that I would put my money on her.

'All that is positive fact. This man Bourignard often goes to No. 129, a gaming house. Saving your respect, sir, he's a rake who's fond of women and gives himself the airs of a man of quality. More still: he often wins at the gaming-tables, he's a consummate actor, can get up in any part and leads a most eccentric life. I don't doubt he has many domiciles, for most of the time he evades what Monsieur le Commandeur calls "parliamentary inquiries". Nevertheless, if you wish it, sir, he can be disposed of in an honourable way by taking his habits into account. It's always easy to get rid of a man who goes for the women. All the same, this capitalist is talking of moving house yet again. Now then: have Monsieur le Vidame and Monsieur le Baron any orders to give me?'

'Justin, you have done well. Don't go any further until I tell you. But keep an eye on everything here, so that Monsieur le Baron need have nothing to fear.

'My dear boy,' he continued, addressing Auguste. 'Return to normal and forget Madame Jules.'

'No, no,' said Auguste. 'I'll not give way to Gratien Bourignard. I want to get him in my power – and Madame Jules too.'

That evening, Baron Auguste de Maulincour, who had recently been promoted to senior rank in a company of the Household Guards, went to a ball given at the Elysée-Bourbon Palace by Madame la Duchesse de Berry.[2] Certainly no danger was to be feared for him there. And yet the Baron de Maulincour left the ballroom with an affair of honour on his hands, one for which no reconciliation was possible. His adversary, the Marquis de Ronquerolles, had strong motives for his grievance against Auguste, which arose from his former liaison with Monsieur de Ronquerolles' own sister,

2. Wife of the Duc de Berry, who was heir to the throne and was assassinated in 1820.

the Comtesse de Sérisy. This was the lady who disliked Teutonic sentimentality, but this made her all the more demanding as regards the slightest details in her make-up as a prude. By an inexplicably unlucky chance, Auguste made a harmless joke which Madame de Sérisy took amiss and at which her brother took offence. They discussed the matter in a corner, in whispers. Like well-bred people, they kept the matter quiet. It was not until the following day that chatter arose in aristocratic and court circles. Madame de Sérisy was warmly defended and Maulincour regarded as being completely in the wrong. August personages intervened. Seconds of the highest distinction were imposed on Maulincour and Ronquerolles and every precaution was taken to ensure that neither of the duellists should be killed. When Auguste found himself face to face with his adversary, admittedly a bit of a rake, but one who was acknowledged to be a man of honour, he could scarcely regard him as an instrument of Ferragus, the leader of the *Dévorants*. Yet he felt inwardly impelled to give voice to inexplicable forebodings and to question the marquis.

'Gentlemen,' he said to the seconds, 'I certainly do not refuse to exchange pistol-shots with the Marquis de Ronquerolles. But first of all I declare I was in the wrong. I will make whatever apologies he may desire – publicly if he wishes – because when a lady is concerned I believe that a gentleman cannot incur disgrace by apologizing. I therefore appeal to his good sense and generosity: isn't it rather silly to fight when the man in the wrong might win? . . .'

Monsieur de Ronquerolles was unable to accept this way of settling the affair. Thereupon the baron, now more suspicious, walked up to his adversary.

'Very well, Marquis,' he said. 'Give me your word as a gentleman, in the presence of these gentlemen, that you are inspired by no other motive for seeking satisfaction than the one with which we are openly concerned.'

'Sir, you have no right to put such a question to me.' And the marquis went and took up his position. It had been agreed in advance that they should exchange one single pistol-shot.

Monsieur de Ronquerolles, in spite of the settled distance which seemed to make Monsieur de Maulincour's death very problematic if not impossible, brought the baron down. The bullet went through his ribs, only just below the heart, but happily without damaging any organs.

'You took too good aim, Monsieur,' said the Guards officer, 'for your motive to have been merely to avenge extinct resentments.' Monsieur de Ronquerolles thought he had killed Auguste and could not repress a sardonic smile on hearing these words.

'Caesar's sister, sir, must be above suspicion.'

'Madame Jules, as always,' Auguste retorted.

Then he fainted, without being able to complete a mordant jest which died on his lips. He lost a lot of blood, but his wound was not dangerous. After a fortnight during which the dowager and the vidame lavished on him the care which old people can give – such expert care as it takes a lifetime of experience to acquire – his grandmother one morning gave him a rough talking-to, and made it plain to him to what mortal anxiety she was being subjected in her extreme old age. She had received a letter signed 'F' in which the history of the espionage to which her grandson had stooped was related in close detail. This letter reproached Monsieur de Maulincour with acts unworthy of a gentleman. It alleged that he had posted an old woman at the cab-stand in the Rue de Ménars: an old spy ostensibly occupied in selling coachmen the water from her casks, but in reality commissioned to keep watch on the comings and goings of Madame Jules Desmarets. He had spied upon a most inoffensive man in order to worm out all his secrets, upon which the life or death of three persons depended. He alone had opted for the pitiless conflict in which, having already received three injuries, he would inevitably succumb, because his adversaries had sworn his death and would use every means to encompass it. By now Monsieur de Maulincour could not even avoid his fate by promising to respect the mystery in the life of these three persons, since it was impossible to accept the words of a nobleman capable of falling as low as any police agent – and with no other motive than the irrational purpose of disturbing the lives of an innocent woman and a respectable old man.

This letter had little effect on Auguste in comparison with the tender reproaches he received from the Baronne de Maulincour: he had shown a lack of respect for and trust in a woman, and spied on her without having any right to do so! And should a man spy even on the woman who loves him? His grandmother poured out a spate of the sort of excellent arguments which never prove anything; they flung the young baron, for the first time in his life, into one of those towering rages in which germinate and from which emerge the most fateful acts in a man's life. He came to the following conclusion: 'Since this is a duel to the death, I must use every means at my disposal to kill my enemy!'

The commander immediately, on Auguste's behalf, sought out the chief of civil police in Paris and, without introducing either the name or person of Madame Jules into the account of this adventure (although she was in fact at the bottom of it), he told him of the fears roused in the Maulincour family by an anonymous person bold enough to threaten death to a Guards officer in defiance of the law and the police. The police official expressed surprise by lifting his green spectacles, blew his nose several times and offered snuff to the vidame, who stood on his dignity and averred that he did not take it, although his nostrils were brown with it. Then the assistant-superintendent took notes and promised that, with the help of Vidocq[3] and his sleuth-hounds, he would bring this enemy of the Maulincour family to book in a very few days, there being no secrets hid from the Paris police force. A day or two later the superintendent came to see the vidame at the Maulincour house and found the baron entirely recovered from his recent wound. Then he expressed in official jargon his thanks for the clues they had so kindly furnished, and informed Auguste that Bourignard had been condemned to twenty years' penal servitude but that he had miraculously escaped from the chain-gang on its way from Bicêtre to

3. Head of the French Criminal Investigation Department in Imperial and Restoration times.

Toulon. The police had been trying to catch him for thirteen years, knowing that he had had the impertinence to return to Paris, where he had eluded all attempts to capture him, even though he had been involved in a number of shady affairs. In short, this man, who had had a most eventful life, would certainly be pounced upon in one of his domiciles and delivered over to justice. The police official terminated his unofficial report by telling Monsieur de Maulincour that if he attached enough importance to the affair to witness Bourignard's arrest, he might come the following day at eight in the morning to a house in the Rue Sainte-Foi whose number he gave. Monsieur de Maulincour spared himself the bother of seeking this corroboration, trusting, with the respect and reverence which the Paris police inspires, in the diligence of the civil organization. Three days later, having read nothing in the newspaper about the arrest, which should surely have provided material for an interesting article, Monsieur de Maulincour conceived some anxiety, but this was dispelled by the following letter:

Monsier le Baron,
I have the honour to inform you that you need entertain no further fear regarding the matter in question. The so-called Gratien Bourignard, alias Ferragus, died yesterday in his domicile, No. 7, Rue Joquelet. Any suspicion we might have had about his identity has been destroyed by the facts discovered. We called in two doctors – that of the Mayor and the prefecture of Police – and the Superintendent of Police carried out sufficient investigation to make matters certain. Moreover, the reliability of the witnesses who signed the death certificate, and the testimony of those who tended the aforesaid Bourignard during his last moments (including that of the worthy curate of the Bonne-Nouvelle church, to whom he made his last confession, for he died a Christian death) rule out the slightest possible doubt.

Your obedient servant ...

Monsieur de Maulincour, the dowager lady and the vidame felt immeasurably relieved. The good old lady kissed her grandson with a tear in her eye and went off to render thanks to God. The dear old soul had made a novena for Auguste's

welfare and believed that her prayer had been answered.
'All is well,' said the commander. 'Now you can go to the
ball you told me about. I see no reason why you shouldn't.'

Monsieur de Maulincour was the more eager to go to this
ball because Madame Jules was sure to be there. It was a
party given by the Prefect of the Seine *arrondissement*, at
whose house the two social sets of Paris used to meet as if
on neutral territory. Auguste scoured the various salons
without meeting the woman who was exerting so much
influence on his life. He made his way into an empty boudoir
in which gaming-tables were still awaiting players, and sat
down on a divan, with a turmoil of contradictory ideas about
Madame Jules passing through his head. Then a man took
hold of the young officer's arm, and the baron was stupefied
to recognize the pauper of the Rue Coquillière, Ida's Ferragus,
the man who had lived in the Rue Soly, Justin's Bourignard,
the convict pursued by the police, reported dead the day
before.

'Monsieur, not a cry, not a word,' Bourignard said. Auguste
recognized his voice, but certainly no one else would have
recognized the man. He was elegantly dressed, and on his
dress-coat were the ribbons of the Order of the Golden
Fleece and the star of another order. 'Monsieur,' he continued
with the hissing voice of a hyena, 'you are justifying all the
steps I am taking by calling in the police. You will come to
grief, Monsieur, without fail. Do you love Madame Jules?
Does she love you in return? By what right do you disturb
her peace and blacken her reputation?'

Another person approached. Ferragus arose in order to
leave.

'Do you know who this man is?' Auguste de Maulincour
asked as he gripped Ferragus by the collar. But Ferragus
nimbly slipped free, seized Monsieur de Maulincour by the
hair and mockingly shook him several times by the head.
'Will nothing but lead drive some sense into it?' he asked.

It was Monsieur de Marsay who had witnessed this scene.
'I do not know him personally,' he replied, 'but I know that
this gentleman is Monsieur de Funcal, a very rich Portuguese.'

Monsieur de Funcal had disappeared. The baron followed him without being able to overtake him. When he arrived beneath the peristyle he saw Ferragus in a glittering carriage looking at him mockingly as it clattered away.

'Monsieur, I beg you,' Auguste said as he returned to the salon and accosted de Marsay, with whom he was on speaking terms. 'Where does Monsieur de Funcal live?'

'I don't know. But no doubt someone here can tell you.'

The baron questioned the Prefect and learned that the Comte de Funcal was staying at the Portuguese Embassy. At that moment, imagining that he could still feel Ferragus's icy fingers in his hair, he perceived Madame Jules in all the splendour of her beauty: fresh-looking, graceful, unpretentious, radiant with the immaculate femininity which had captured him in the first place. For Auguste she was now nothing more than a hateful, infernal creature. His eyes were bloodshot with hatred as he looked at her. He waited for an opportunity to speak to her alone and said: 'Madame, your hired assassins have missed me for the third time.'

'What do you mean, Monsieur?' she asked, turning red. 'I have heard that you had met with several regrettable accidents, and they gave me much concern. But how can I be accounted responsible?'

'But you must know that the man of the Rue Soly has put desperadoes on my trail?'

'Monsieur!'

'Madame! From now on not I alone, but others also, will call you to account, not only for my well-being, but also for my life.'

At this juncture Jules Desmarets came up.

'So you have something to say to my wife, sir?'

'If you wish to know what it is, sir, come to my house.'

Whereupon Maulincour departed, leaving Madame Jules pale and almost fainting.

3

A wife under suspicion

THERE are very few women who, once in their lives, with regard to an undeniable fact, have not found themselves faced with a sharp, searching, trenchant interrogation, a questioning pitilessly carried out by their husbands. The mere apprehension of it imparts a slight chill; the first word of it enters the heart like the point of a dagger. Hence the axiom: *all women lie*. A white lie, a venial lie, a noble lie, a horrible lie: but lie they must. It follows, admitting this 'must', that they have to be adept at lying – and women in France are admirable liars. Our way of life is such a good school for imposture! In short, woman is so naïvely impertinent, so dainty, so graceful, so convincing when she lies; she so fully recognizes the utility of falsehood for avoiding in social life the violent shocks destructive of happiness, that she finds it as indispensable as the cotton-wool in which she keeps her jewellery. It follows that falsehood forms the basis of language for women and that truth becomes merely exceptional; when virtuous, they tell the truth as a matter of whim or speculation. Moreover, according to their character, some women lie with a laugh on their lips; others with a tear in their eye, others solemnly, others angrily. After having started in life by pretending to be insensitive to the homage they find most flattering, they often end up by lying to themselves. Which of us has not admired their apparent self-possession at the very moment when they are trembling lest the secret treasure of their love should be discovered? Which of us has not studied their ease and facility of manner, their freedom of wit in meeting the most embarrassing situations? On such occasions they show no signs of strain; deceit flows softly down as snow drops from the skies. And then, with what art they detect the truth in others! With

what subtlety they employ the strictest logic regarding the
impassioned questioning in which they always detect some
secret in the heart of a man ingenuous enough to adopt an
interrogatory attitude towards them! Is not questioning a
woman as good as delivering oneself over to her? Will she
not tumble to everything you wish to conceal from her and
talk volubly without telling you a thing? Yet some men claim
that they can contend on equal terms with the woman of
Paris! With a woman who can parry your lunges with a
phrase: 'How inquisitive you are! How does that concern
you? Why do you want to know? Ah! You're jealous!
And suppose I don't choose to answer?' In short, with a
woman who knows a hundred and thirty-seven thousand
ways of saying *no* and can ring endless changes on the
theme *yes*. Could not a thesis on *yes* and *no* provide one of
the finest diplomatic, philosophical, logographical and moral
research subjects still to be investigated? But to carry out so
diabolical an inquiry an androgynous genius would be
needed, and so it will never be attempted. And yet, of all
the topics which do not find their way into print, is that
not the one about which women know most and are best
able to put into practice? Have you ever studied the flair,
the pose, the *disinvoltura* of a falsehood? Take a look.

Madame Desmarets was sitting in the right-hand corner
of her carriage and her husband in the left-hand corner.
Having succeeded in mastering her feelings as she left the
ball, Madame Jules was affecting a calm demeanour. Her
husband had said nothing to her and was not yet saying
anything. Jules was looking through the window at the
black walls of the silent houses which he was passing; but
suddenly, as if some thought had brought him to a decision,
as they were going round a street corner, he scrutinized his
wife, who seemed to be feeling cold in spite of the fur-lined
pelisse in which she was wrapped. He thought she looked
pensive, and perhaps she really was pensive.

Of all communicable things, thought and gravity of mood
are the most contagious. 'What can Monsieur de Maulincour have said to you to upset you so much?' asked Jules.

'And what does he want me to go to his home to learn?'

'Well, he can't tell you anything at his house that I can't tell you now,' she replied.

Then, with the feminine subtlety which always takes a little of its lustre from virtue, Madame Jules waited for him to probe further. He turned his glance aside to the houses and continued his study of the carriage entrances. Would not any further interrogation have been equivalent to a suspicion, a challenge? To suspect a woman one loves is a crime. Jules had already killed one man without having suspected his wife. Clémence had no idea how much true passion and profound reflection were contained in her husband's silence; Jules was just as ignorant of the extraordinary conflict which was going on in Clémence's heart. And the carriage rumbled on through the silent streets of Paris, bearing away a married couple who loved each other to the point of idolatry, who were gently and closely leaning against each other on their silk cushions, but none the less were separated by an abyss. In the elegant broughams coming home from the ball between midnight and two in the morning, how many strange scenes take place, even if one thinks only of those broughams whose lamps light up both street and carriage, those whose glass is clear, in fact the broughams of legitimate love in which couples can squabble without fearing that they may be seen by passers-by, because the registry office has conferred on them the right to sulk, fight, exchange kisses in a carriage, elsewhere and everywhere! In consequence, how many secrets are revealed to nocturnal pedestrians, to the young people who had driven to the ball in a carriage but had been obliged for one reason or another to go home on foot! It was the first time that Jules and Clémence had sat thus, each in his own corner. Normally they sat very close together.

'It's very cold,' said Madame Jules.

But her husband did not hear, for he was studying all the dark signs over the shops.

'Clémence,' he said at last, 'forgive me for the question I am going to ask you.' He drew close to her, put his arm round her waist and pressed her close to him.

'God help me, here it comes!' the poor woman thought.

'So then,' she said, anticipating his question, 'you want to know what Monsieur de Maulincour had to say to me. I'll tell you, Jules, but not without misgivings. Dear God, can we have secrets from each other? For some moments now I have seen you struggling between your consciousness of the love that is between us and indeterminate fears. But have we not a clear consciousness of our love, and do not your suspicions make everything dark? Why not keep to the daylight you enjoy? When I have told you everything you will want to know more still; and yet I do not myself know what is behind this man's strange words. Well then, perhaps some fatal quarrel will arise between you two. It would be far better that we should both of us forget this unhappy moment. But in any case, swear that you will wait for this singular adventure to explain itself naturally. Monsieur de Maulincour has declared to me that the three accidents which happened to him – the stone which fell on his footman, the collapse of his carriage and the duel he fought over Madame de Sérisy – were the result of a plot I had laid against him. Then he threatened to explain to you the motive I had for wanting to assassinate him. Can you make any sense out of all that? What worried me was the impression I felt when I saw the demented look on his face, his wild eyes and his violent and disconnected words. I thought he had gone mad. Just that. Now I should not be a woman if I had not noticed that during the last year I have become what they call the "object" of Monsieur de Maulincour's passion. He has seen me nowhere else than in ballrooms; nor has he made anything but the insignificant remarks that one makes in ballrooms. Perhaps he wants to disunite us so that one day he may get me alone and defenceless. Can't you see? You're frowning already. Oh! how I hate society. We're so happy without it! Why then go looking for it? Jules, I beg you, promise me to forget all this nonsense. Tomorrow we shall doubtless learn that Monsieur de Maulincour has gone out of his mind.'

'It's all very strange,' Jules said to himself as he stepped down from his carriage at the bottom of his own staircase. He offered his arm to his wife and together they climbed to their apartments.

In order to unfold this story truly and in all its detail and to follow it through all its twists and turns, we ought here to divulge some of the hidden facts of love and steal behind the panelling of a bedroom: but in the manner of Nodier's Trilby, without startling Dougal, or Jeannie or anybody. We must be as chaste as our noble French tongue strives to be and as bold as Gérard's brush had been in his picture of Daphnis and Chloe. Madame Jules's bedchamber was a holy of holies. Only she, her husband and her chambermaid had right of entrance. Opulence has fine privileges, the most enviable of them being those which give the greatest scope to the expression of our feelings, bring them to fruition through the accomplishment of the innumerable whims they inspire, surround them with a radiancy which magnifies them, with the studied attentions which purify them and the delicate touches of courtesy which add yet more to their attractiveness. If you hate al fresco luncheons and badly served meals, if it gives you some pleasure to see a glisteningly white damask tablecloth, a silver-gilt cutlery service, exquisitely delicate china, a gilt-bordered, richly sculptured table, lit with diaphanous candles and then, under emblazoned silver globes, the miracles of the choicest cuisine; if you want to be consistent, you must then spurn attics and house-tops, streets and street-walkers; you must say good-bye to garrets and grisettes, to umbrellas and galoshes, you must abandon them to people who pay for their dinner with vouchers. Also you must understand the basic principle of love: it can only be achieved in all its grace on carpets from the Savonnerie, under the opal glimmer of a marmoreal lamp, between discreet, silk-lined walls in front of a gilded fireplace, in a room muffled from all noises by Venetian blinds, shutters and billowy curtains, whether these noises come from the streets or from neighbouring flats. You must have mirrors which make play with human shapes and reflect to infinity the woman you would wish to be multiple and whom love does indeed render multiple. You must have very low divans and a bed which, with a sort of secretiveness, allows its presence merely to be divined; and, in this dainty chamber, fur rugs for bare feet, candles with glass shades amid draped muslins, so that one may read at any time of night; also flowers whose scent is not too heavy, and linens whose fineness of texture would have contented even Anne of Austria.

Madame Jules had carried out this delicious programme, but that was only a beginning. Any woman of taste could do as much, even though the planning of these things requires a stamp of personality which gives originality and character to this or that ornament, to this or that detail. Today more than ever before, there reigns a fanatical craving for self-expression. The more our laws aim at an impossible equality, the more we shall swerve from it by our way of living. In consequence rich people in France are becoming more exclusive in their tastes and their attachment to their personal belongings than they were thirty years ago. Madame Jules knew what this programme entailed and put everything in her home into harmony with the luxury which went so well with their conjugal love. 'Sixty pounds a year and my Sophie' or 'Love in a cottage': only starvelings talk like this. Black bread is all right to start with, but having become gourmets if they really love each other, they come round to regretting the gastronomic pleasures they cannot afford. Love loathes poverty and toil. It prefers to die rather than pinch and scrape.

Most women, returning from a ball and in a hurry to get to bed, cast off their dresses, their faded flowers and the bouquets which by now have lost all fragrance. They toss their dainty shoes under a chair, patter about in shapeless slippers, take the combs from their hair and let it fall down loose. It matters little to them that their husbands see the hooks and safety-pins and artificial contrivances which had sustained the elegant structure of their hairstyle and head-dress. The mystery is gone, the veil is down; the husband sees all the make-up. Her corset, at most times discreetly concealed, lies about if the drowsy chambermaid has forgotten to stow it away. In fact the counterfeit woman is there in her entirety, in her bits and pieces: whalebone hoops, arm-holes stiffened with gummed taffeta, deceptive frippery, hair which came from the *coiffeur*. *Disjecta membra poetae*: the sham poetry, so much admired by those for whom it had been devised and elaborated, the pretty woman in fact, encumbers every corner. The loving husband, yawning his head off, is then confronted with the real woman, also yawning. There is no elegance in her disorder; she has a crumpled night-cap on her head, the one she wore last night and will wear again tomorrow night. 'After all, husband, if you want a pretty night-cap to ruffle afresh every night, increase my dress allowance.' And that is how life is. A wife is always old and disagreeable to her husband, but always smart, spruce and bedecked for the other man, for every husband's inveterate rival, namely for society which slanders or tears all wives to shreds.

But Madame Jules, inspired by true love – for love, like everything else in existence, obeys the instinct of self-preservation – behaved very differently. She drew, from the constant benefits her happy married life conferred upon her, the strength needed to perform the trifling duties which should never be neglected because they keep love alive. For that matter, do not these little cares and attentions proceed from a sense of personal dignity which is ravishingly becoming? Are they not a sort of flattery? Are they not a way of respecting the beloved person in one's own person? And so Madame Jules had forbidden her husband to enter the dressing-room in which she divested herself of her ball-room dress, and from which she emerged in her night attire mysteriously adorned for the mysterious rites in which she delighted. When she entered the bedroom, always elegant and graceful, Jules saw her as a woman coquettishly wrapped in an elegant dressing-gown, her hair gathered quite simply into rich tresses, for, dishevelled or not, she did not refuse to her husband's love either the joy of gazing at it or fondling it. As a wife, she was then always more simply herself, more beautiful than she had made herself for society. She had taken a bath to revive her beauty, and all the artifice she employed consisted in her being whiter than the muslin she wore, fresher then the freshest perfume, more seductive than the most practised courtesan, and lastly always tender and therefore always adored. This admirable understanding of a woman's craft had been Josephine's great secret for keeping Napoleon captive, just as it had been Caesonia's technique with Caius Caligula and that of Diane de Poitiers with our Henri II. But if it was so amply rewarding for women in their late forties, what a weapon it was in the hands of younger women! In such a situation a husband ecstatically enjoys the reward he reaps for his fidelity!

That evening, returning home after a conversation which had chilled her with fright and was still causing her the liveliest anxiety, Madame Jules took special care with her *toilette de nuit*. She wanted to be ravishing and she *was* ravishing. She had drawn close about her the cambric of her wrap, left her bosom half open and let her black tresses fall down over her rounded shoulders. Her perfumed bath gave her an intoxicating fragrance. Her bare feet were encased in velvet slippers. Armed with these advantages, she approached him with dainty steps and put her hands over his eyes. He was in his dressing-gown, with one elbow leaning on the mantelpiece and one foot resting on the bar, and she saw that he was pensive. Then she whispered in his ear, which she nibbled as she warmed him with her breath. 'A penny for your thoughts, my friend!' Then she clasped him closely in her arms in an attempt to wean him from his black thoughts. A woman who loves knows the full extent of her power. The greater her virtue, the more effectively she can exercise the art of wheedling.

They went to bed. As she fell asleep Madame Jules said to herself: 'Decidedly, Monsieur de Maulincour will bring some misfortune to us. Jules is worried and distraught and is keeping his thoughts to himself.' It was about three o'clock in the morning when Madame Jules was awakened by a presentiment which had startled her from sleep. She had at once a physical and a moral perception of her husband's absence. She could no longer feel Jules's arm round her neck, the arm within whose fold she had slept happy and peaceful for five

years without ever tiring it. Then a voice within her had said:
'Jules is suffering. Jules is weeping.' She raised her head,
sat up, found that her husband's place was cold, and discovered him sleeping in front of the fire with his feet on the
fender and his head leaning against the back of a large armchair. His cheeks were wet with tears. The unhappy wife
jumped from her bed and leapt to her husband's lap.

'Jules, what's the matter? Are you suffering? Speak, tell
me what's wrong. If you love me, tell me.' Impulsively, she
showered on him a spate of most tenderly loving words.

Jules knelt at his wife's feet, kissed her knees and hands and,
with fresh tears streaming from his eyes, said: 'Dearest
Clémence, I am very unhappy! To suspect one's mistress –
you are my mistress – is to love her no longer. But while I
suspect you, I still adore you ... The words that man said
this evening went straight to my heart. I can't forget them,
and they have destroyed my peace of mind. There's some
mystery behind all this. I'm ashamed to say it, but your
explanations haven't satisfied me. My reason throws out
glimmers of suspicion which my love for you makes me
reject. I'm terribly divided in mind. Could I have remained
where I was, with your head on my breast, while suspecting
that you might be harbouring thoughts unknown to me? –
Oh, I believe you, I believe you!' he cried out passionately as
he saw her sadly smiling and opening her mouth to reply.
'Say nothing. Give me no reproach. The slightest word from
you would kill me. In any case, could you say a single thing
to me that I have not been saying to myself for the last
three hours? Yes, there have I been for the last three hours,
watching you as you slept, so beautiful, admiring your pure
and peaceful forehead. Yes indeed, you have always shared
your thoughts with me, have you not? I alone have a place
in your soul. When I gaze at you, when I look into your eyes,
I see right into you. Your life is still as pure as your glance
is clear. No, no secrets are hidden behind that limpid eye.'

He rose and kissed her eyes. 'Let me confess to you, beloved
creature, that for five years what has every day increased my
happiness has been the knowledge that you had none of the

natural affections which always take a certain toll of love.
You had neither sister, father, mother nor companion, and
I occupied neither first nor second place in your heart: I was
sole possessor. Clémence, tell me once again all the sweet
things you have so often told me. Don't scold me, console
me, I'm unhappy. I undoubtedly have to reproach myself
for a vile suspicion, whereas no spark of remorse burns
in your heart. That being so, my beloved, could I have stayed
so close to you? How could two hearts so completely united
repose on the same pillow when the one suffers and the other
is at peace? ... What are you thinking about?' he cried
out abruptly as he saw that Clémence was wrapped in thought,
dismayed and unable to restrain her tears.

'I am thinking of my mother,' she replied in a grave tone.
'You could not know, Jules, what grief your Clémence feels
when she has to remember her mother's dying farewell, to
hear her voice once more, the sweetest kind of music; when
she has to think of the solemn pressure of a dying woman's
icy hands, while she still feels the pressure of yours at the
moment when you are giving me overwhelming proof of
the love which delights my soul.' She pulled her husband
to his feet, locked him in her arms with a nervous strength
which was greater than ever a man could muster, kissed his
hair and bathed him with her tears. 'Oh! I would be ready to
be cut in pieces for you! Tell me truly that you are happy
with me, that for you I am the most beautiful of women,
that for you I am a thousand women in one. My darling,
you are loved more than any man will ever be. I don't know
what people mean by talking of "virtue" and "duty", Jules:
I love you for yourself; it makes me happy to love you, and
I shall go on loving you more and more till I die. I take
pride in my love and I believe I shall never have any other
feeling in my life. What I am about to tell you is perhaps
shocking: I am content not to have a child and don't really
want one. I feel more of the wife in me than the mother.
And yet you have misgivings about me. Listen, darling,
promise me to forget, not the time we have just spent in
tenderness mingled with doubt, but the words that madman

uttered. That, Jules, is what I demand of you. Promise that you will not see him or go to his house. I am convinced that if you take one further step into this labyrinth we shall fall into an abyss in which I shall perish – though even then your name will be on my lips and your heart in my heart. Tell me why you rank me so high in your soul but so low in reality. You, who advance so much credit on your clients' material fortune, cannot do me the charity of writing off a suspicion! On the first occasion in your life when you can prove that you have unlimited faith in me, you would dethrone me from your heart! Between a madman and myself, you choose the madman! Oh, Jules!'

She paused, pushed back her hair which was falling forward over her brow and backward over her neck, and added in heart-rending tones: 'I have said too much. One word should have been enough. If any shadow of doubt, however slight, remains on your brow and in your mind, just realize that I shall die of it!'

She was unable to repress a shudder. She turned pale.

'Oh! I will kill that man!' Jules said to himself, taking his wife in his arms and carrying her to her bed.

'Let us sleep in peace, my angel,' he added. 'I swear to you that all is forgotten.'

At this consoling word, repeated more caressingly still, Clémence fell asleep. Then Jules, as he watched her sleeping, said to himself: 'She is right. When love is so pure, it is tarnished by suspicion. To so limpid a soul, to so tender a flower, any slur must bring death.'

When, between two mutually affectionate beings who share each other's life at every moment, a cloud looms up, quickly dissipated though it may be, it leaves some traces of its passage in their souls. Either their tenderness becomes more keen, just as the earth is more beautiful after rain, or the shock reverberates like the distant rumbles of thunder when the sky is serene again; but there is no going back to life as it was before, and love must either increase or diminish. At breakfast next day Monsieur and Madame Jules paid each other the sort of attentions which are not free from affectation.

The looks they exchanged were full of an almost forced gaiety, like those which appear to be the effort of people anxious to deceive themselves. Jules was a prey to involuntary doubts, his wife to positive fears. And yet they had slept as if sure of each other. Was the embarrassment they felt due to mutual distrust, to the memory of their nocturnal scene? That they did not know themselves; but their love for each other had been and was still too pure for the at once cruel and soothing impression of the previous night not to leave its mark on their souls. Both of them were intent on effacing it and each of them was eager to take the initiative in mending the rift between them. They could not help brooding over the primary cause of the first misunderstanding they had ever had. For two people in love it is not a question of positive grievances: pain is still far off, but there is a sort of sorrow which it is difficult to depict. If there is some sort of relationship between colour and spiritual perturbation; if, as Locke's blind man says, scarlet has the same effect on the eye as a fanfare has on the ear, the reaction of melancholy they felt may well be credited with a grey tonality. But love brought to sadness, that love which is still vividly sensible of a bliss which has been momentarily disturbed, affords pleasures which, being a blend of pain and joy, are entirely novel. Jules was studying the intonations of his wife's voice and gazing into her eyes with the youthful ardour which had animated him when he had first fallen in love with her. Then the memory of five completely happy years, Clémence's beauty and the ingenuousness of her love swiftly obliterated the last vestiges of a pain which had been intolerable. This next day was a Sunday, on which there was neither Stock Exchange nor any other business. And so husband and wife spent their day together, getting closer in heart to each other than they had ever been, like two frightened children who instinctively squeeze and cling tightly to each other. To a married couple there sometimes comes a day of complete happiness, due to chance, having no link either with yesterday or tomorrow: short-lived blossoms! Jules and Clémence drew delicious enjoyment from this one, as if they felt that this was the last day of their life as lovers. What name can be given to that unknown power which forces travellers to press onwards before there have been any omens of a storm, or which brings forth resplendent life and beauty in a doomed man a few days before his death and inspires him with most optimistic projects; that which prompts a scientist to turn up his nocturnal lamp at the moment when it is giving him perfect light; that which puts a mother in fear of the excessively penetrating glance thrown on her child by a perspicacious man? We all of us come under this kind of influence in the great catastrophes of our life, and we have not yet either named it or studied it; it is something more than presentiment but still something less than prevision.

All went well until next day. On Monday Jules Desmarets, forced to put in an appearance at the Stock Exchange at the appointed time, did not leave the house without asking his wife, as usual, if she wished to take advantage of his cab.

'No,' she said. 'The weather's too bad for going out.'

In fact it was pouring with rain. It was about half past two when Monsieur Desmarets went to the Ring and the Treasury. At four o'clock, as he left the Stock Exchange, he found himself face to face with Monsieur de Maulincour, who was waiting for him with the feverish pertinacity which is born of hatred and vengefulness.

'Monsieur,' said the officer, taking the stockbroker by the arm. 'I have important information to give you. Listen to me. I am too straightforward a man to have recourse to anonymous letters likely to disturb your peace of mind, so I preferred to talk to you. Please believe that if my life were not at stake, I should certainly not in any way meddle with someone else's private affairs, even if I thought it was my right to do so.'

'If what you have to say concerns Madame Desmarets,' Jules replied, 'I shall beg of you, sir, to say nothing.'

'If I said nothing, sir, you might before long see Madame Jules in the dock of an assize court alongside a convict. Do you still wish me to say nothing?'

Jules turned pale, but his handsome face quickly assumed

a calm demeanour. Then, dragging the officer beneath one of the porches of the temporary Stock Exchange where they then were, he said, in a voice which concealed deep inner emotion: 'Monsieur, I will listen to you. But it will be a duel to the death between us if . . .'

'Oh, I agree to that,' Monsieur de Maulincour exclaimed. 'I hold you in the greatest esteem. You talk of death, Monsieur. You are no doubt unaware that your wife may have had me poisoned last Saturday evening. Yes, sir, since the day before yesterday, something extraordinary is going on inside me; fever and a mortal languor are seeping through my hair into my skull, and I know perfectly well what man touched my hair during the ball.'

Monsieur de Maulincour related, without leaving out one single fact, both the story of his platonic love for Madame Jules and the details of the adventure with which this scene began. Anyone at all would have listened as attentively as the stockbroker; but Madame Jules's husband had a right to be more astonished at it than anybody in the world. In this his true character came out: he was surprised rather than downcast. Having become a judge – the judge of the woman he adored – he found within his soul the rectitude of a judge, and also a judge's inflexibility. Being still a lover, he thought less about his shattered life than about that of his wife: he paid heed, not to his own grief, but to a far-off voice saying within him: 'Clémence is not likely to be lying! Why should she betray you?'

'Monsieur,' said the Guards officer as he finished, 'being certain that on Saturday evening I recognized in Monsieur de Funcal the Ferragus whom the police believe dead, I immediately put an intelligent man on his tracks. When I reached home, by a lucky chance I remembered the name of Madame Meynardie, quoted in the letter of that Ida, the presumed mistress of my persecutor. Armed with this single item of information, my emissary will swiftly enlighten me about this terrifying adventure, for he is more skilful in discovering truth than the police themselves are.'

'Monsieur,' the stockbroker replied, 'I am unable to thank

you for this piece of confidence. You tell me there will be proof and witnesses; I shall await them. I shall courageously seek out the truth in this strange affair, but you will permit me to remain sceptical until the facts are clearly proved to me. In any case, you shall have satisfaction from me, for you must appreciate that this affair calls for it.'

Monsieur Jules returned home.

'Jules, what's the matter?' his wife asked. 'You are terribly pale.'

'It's cold outside,' he said, striding slowly across this room which was so redolent of happiness and love, this tranquil room in which a devastating storm was gathering.

'You haven't been out today?' he asked in apparently nonchalant tones.

No doubt he was impelled to ask this question by the latest of a host of thoughts which had rushed through his mind under the stimulus of jealousy, but which were part of a lucid sequence of meditation.

'No,' she replied with an assumed accent of sincerity.

At that moment Jules noticed a few spots of water on the velvet hat in his wife's dressing-room, the one she usually wore in the mornings. Monsieur Jules was a man of violent disposition, but also of great delicacy, and it went against the grain with him to challenge his wife's veracity. When such a situation arises between certain beings, all is over between them for life. Yet these drops of rain were like a flash searing through his brain. He left his room, went down to the concierge's lodge and said to him: 'Fouquereau, I guarantee you three hundred francs per annum if you tell me the truth. I shall throw you out if you deceive me; and you will get nothing at all if, having told me the truth, you tell anyone else about my question and the answer you have given me.'

He paused in order to look his concierge straight in the eyes and drew him into the light coming from the window.

'Did Madame go out this morning?'

'Madame went out at a quarter to three and I think I saw her come in half an hour ago.'

'That is true, on your honour?'

'Yes, sir.'

'You shall have the income I promised you; but if you say anything, remember what I said ... you would lose it all.'

Jules returned to his wife.

'Clémence,' he said, 'I need to get my household accounts in order, so don't take offence at what I am going to ask you. Have I not given you forty thousand francs since the beginning of the year?'

'More,' she said: 'forty-seven.'

'Would you be able to remember what you did with them?'

'Of course,' she said. 'In the first place I had several of last year's bills to pay.'

'This will get me nowhere,' Jules said to himself. 'I'm setting about it the wrong way.'

At this moment Jules's manservant came in and handed him a letter which he opened composedly. But once he had glanced at the signature he read it avidly.

Monsieur,

For the sake of our tranquillity and your own, I have decided to write to you without having the advantage of being known to you; but my position, my age and the fear of some disaster force me to beg you to show some indulgence in the trying predicament in which our family finds itself, to its distress. Monsieur Auguste de Maulincour has for some days been showing signs of mental derangement, and we are afraid lest he disturb your happiness with vain fancies about which he had talked to the Commandeur de Pamiers and myself in the course of a first onset of fever. We therefore apprise you of this sickness, which no doubt is still curable. It has such grave and important effects for the honour of our family and my grandson's future that I count on your entire discretion. If the Commandeur or I, Monsieur, had been able to come to your house we would have saved ourselves the trouble of writing to you; but I have no doubt you will accede to the request a mother makes you to burn this letter.

Sincerely yours,
BARONNE DE MAULINCOUR,
née DE RIEUX

'All this is torture!' Jules exclaimed.

'Tell me, what is going on in your head?' his wife asked him, giving signs of acute anxiety.

'I have come,' Jules replied, 'to the point of wondering if it is you who have had this warning sent to me in order to dispel my suspicions. So imagine what I am suffering,' he added, throwing the letter across to her.

'Wretched man!' said Madame Jules, letting the paper fall. 'I pity him, although he is doing me much harm.'

'You know he has spoken to me?'

'Ah!' she said, terror-struck. 'You went to see him in spite of giving your word not to!'

'Clémence, our love is under sentence of death. We have stepped beyond the ordinary conventions of life. And so let us jettison trivial considerations in the midst of such great perils. My dear, tell me why you went out this morning. Wives sometimes think they are entitled to tell us little fibs. Don't they often take pleasure in making a secret of the treats they are preparing for us? Just now, no doubt, you gave me a careless answer, a no for a yes?'

He went to her dressing-room and brought back her hat. 'Look and see. I don't want to play the jealous guardian, but your hat gives you away. It has rain-drops on it. So: you went off in a cab and caught these rain-drops either when you went to find a conveyance or as you came out of it. But a wife can leave her house in all innocence, even after telling her husband that she was not going out. There are plenty of reasons for changing one's mind. Is it not one of your rights to have your whims? Women are not obliged to be always of the same mind. You may have forgotten something, a service to render, a visit to pay or a good turn to do someone. But there's nothing to prevent a wife from telling her husband about it. If they're friends, why should she blush to admit such things? Well, Clémence, my darling, it's not a jealous husband who's talking to you: it's your friend, your lover, your brother.' He threw himself at her feet, passionately. 'Say something. Not to justify yourself, but to calm my horrible sufferings. I well know you went out. Well, what did you do and where did you go?'

'Yes, I did go out, Jules,' she replied with a quavering voice, although her face was still calm. 'But ask me no more. Trust me and wait. Otherwise you will store up endless remorse for yourself. Jules, darling Jules, what is love without trust? I confess that at this moment I am too upset to give you an answer. But I am not a deceitful woman. I love you. You know well I do.'

'Ringed round with everything which can shatter a man's faith and rouse his jealousy – for clearly I don't hold the first place in your heart, clearly you and I are not one person ... Well, Clémence, I still prefer to believe you, to put my trust in what your eyes tell me! If you were deceiving me, you would deserve ... '

'A thousand deaths, for sure,' she broke in.

'I myself hide no thought of mine from you. But you, you ... '

'Say no more. Our happiness depends on silence on either side.'

'But I want to know what all this is about!' he exclaimed in a violent fit of rage.

Just then a woman's cries were heard and the yelps of a shrill little voice came to the married couple from the ante-room. 'I tell you I *will* come in!' it shrieked. 'Yes, I *will* come in. I want to see her. I *will* see her!'

Jules and Clémence ran into the drawing-room and soon they saw the doors flung open violently. Suddenly a young woman showed herself, followed by two servants who told their master: 'Sir, this woman has forced her way in. We told her that Madame was not at home. Her answer was that she knew Madame had gone out but that she had seen her come in again. She insists that she'll stay at the door until she has talked to Madame.'

'Leave us,' Monsieur Desmarets said to his servants.

'What do you want, Mademoiselle?' he added, turning to the stranger.

This *demoiselle* was a type of woman one only meets with in Paris. She is made in Paris, like the mud of Paris, the pavements of Paris, just as the water of the Seine is manufactured

in Paris, in great reservoirs through which Industry filters it
ten times before delivering it to the many-faceted carafes in
which, muddy though it was before, it now sparkles clear
and pure. She is therefore a truly original creature. She has
many times been hit off by the draughtsman's crayon, the
caricaturist's brush, the black-and-white artist's graphite, but
she eludes all analysis because she is as uncapturable in all
her moods as is Nature herself, as mercurial as Paris itself is.
In fact, only one radius of the social circle attaches her to
vice; she escapes from it by the thousand other points of the
social circumference. What is more, she only allows one
trait of her character to be divined, the only one for which
she incurs reproach: her best qualities are hidden, and she
glories in her naïve licentiousness. Incompletely rendered in
the plays and books which have set her in the limelight in
all her glamour, she will never be truly represented except
in the garret she lives in, because in all other surroundings
she will be either calumniated or flattered. Once she is rich,
she becomes corrupted; while she remains poor she is misunderstood. How indeed could it be otherwise? She has too
many vices and too many good qualities. She is too likely to
die nobly in a gas oven or to take refuge in withering cyni-
cism. She is too beautiful and too hideous. She is too much
a personification of Paris, which she eventually supplies with
toothless portresses, laundry-women, crossing-sweepers
and beggar-women; but she sometimes also furnishes them
with insolent countesses, adulated actresses, opera-singers
sure of applause. In former times she even supplied the
monarchy with two virtual queens. Who would be able to
seize hold of such a protean person? A woman in every sense
of the word, but less than a woman and more than a woman.
A painter of manners can only cope with certain details in
so vast a portrait: a complete one would reach out to infinity.

She was a Paris *grisette*,[1] but a *grisette* in all her glory.
A *grisette* who goes about in a cab, happy, young, beautiful,

1. The author's definition and description are so complete that no
further elucidation is needed, except perhaps an explanation of the
term *grisette*: in its eighteenth-century meaning a working-class girl who

but still a *grisette*, complete with claws and scissors, as provocative as a Spanish girl, as cross-grained as a prudish
Englishwoman standing out for her conjugal rights, as
coquettish as a great lady, though more outspoken and unin-
hibited; a genuine lioness making her sortie from the little
flat which she has dreamed of for so long with its red calico
curtains, its furniture garnished with Utrecht velvet, its
tea-table, its coffee-set of hand-painted china, its settee, its
little moquette carpet, its alabaster clock and glass-shaded
candles, its cream-painted bedroom, its soft eiderdown; in
short, everything which rejoices the heart of a *grisette*: having
a charwoman, once a *grisette* herself, one who has won her
stripes and now sports a moustache: invited to theatre parties;
wearing a galaxy of curls; possessed of silk dresses and hats
galore; to sum up, every felicity that can be bought at a milli-
ner's counter except the carriage and pair which only figures
in a shop-girl's imagination as the field-marshal's baton figures
in a soldier's dreams.

Yes, this particular *grisette* possessed all that as a reward
for – or in spite of – a genuine affection, just as a few others
often acquire it for a chore of one hour a day, a kind of impost
exacted by an old man and nonchalantly paid. The young
woman who stood before Monsieur and Madame Jules was
so barely shod that one could scarcely see a thin black line
between the carpet and her white stocking. This type of shoe,
so well recaptured by Parisian caricaturists, constitutes a
grace which is peculiar to the Parisian *grisette* but becomes
clearer to an observer's eye thanks to the care with which she
makes her clothing cling to and neatly delineate her proportions. This unknown person was then – to make use of a
picturesque expression created by the French soldier – a
neat little package, in a green frock with a shoulder-piece
which allowed one to guess the shapeliness of her bust:
actually it was plainly visible, for her drooping cashmere shawl
was only maintained in position by its two ends which she

---

wears cheap grey dresses; by Balzac's time it had come to mean a young
woman of low class and easy virtue trying to establish some claim to
respectability.

held half twisted round her wrists. She had delicate features, pink cheeks against a white complexion, sparkling grey eyes, a prominently bulging forehead and carefully smoothed hair which leaked out in large curls from her tiny hat on to her neck.

'My name is Ida, Monsieur. And if the lady I'm privileged to speak to is Madame Jules, I've come to make a clean breast of everything I've got against her. It's bloody mean, when you're well off and nicely settled as you are, to try and rob a girl of a man I'm as good as married to, one who's talking of putting things right and making an honest woman of me. There's lots of nice young men round about – isn't that true enough, sir? – to have a bit of fun with, without robbing me of a man who's getting on in years and just suits me fine. Blow me, I've no posh house, me. Love's all I have. I hate fancy men and I hate money. I've got a heart, I have, and . . . '

Madame Jules turned to her husband: 'Monsieur, you will spare me from hearing any more of this,' she said; and she returned to her bedroom.

'If this is your lady,' said Ida, 'it looks as if I've made a bloomer. But so much the worser. Why does she come to see Monsieur Ferragus every day?'

'You're making a mistake, Mademoiselle,' said Jules, stupefied. 'My wife is incapable . . . '

'Oh! So you're spliced, you two!' said the *grisette*, manifesting some surprise. 'Why then, Monsieur, it's worse still, isn't it, for a woman who's lucky enough to be married good and proper, to be messing about with a man like Henri . . . '

'Who do you mean by Henri?' Monsieur Jules asked Ida, dragging her into an adjoining room in order that this wife should hear nothing more.

'I mean Monsieur Ferragus.'

'But he's dead,' said Jules.

'All my eye! I went to Franconi's Circus with him last night and he brought me home as was right and proper. Anyway, your missus can tell you what's what about that. Didn't she go to see him at three o'clock today? I know she did.

I waited outside in the street for him, seeing how a nice man, a Monsieur Justin – perhaps you know him, a little old man with trinkets hanging from his watch-chain who wears stays – had told me Madame Jules was cutting me out. A name like that, Monsieur, is well known among pretend ones. Excuse me, since it is your name, but even if Madame Jules were a duchess at court, Henri's so rich he can treat himself to anything he fancies. My business is to stick to what I've got, and that's what I've a right to because I love Henri! He's the first man I fell for; my love and my future are wrapped up in him. I'm afraid of nothing, sir. I'm a good girl, I've never told lies or stolen a thing from anybody. Even if I had a crowned queen up against me, I'd go straight up to her, if she tried to rob me of the man who's going to marry me, and I'd be quite capable of killing her, crowned queen or not: all beautiful women are equal, Monsieur ... '

'That's enough, quite enough,' said Jules. 'Where do you live?'

'No. 14, Rue de la Corderie-du-Temple, Monsieur. Ida Gruget, corset-maker, at your service, for we make quite a lot of them for gentlemen.'

'But where does the man you call Ferragus live?'

'Well, sir,' she said, pressing her lips tightly, 'to begin with, he's not just a man. He's a gentleman, richer maybe than you are. But why ask me his address when your wife knows it? He told me not to tell anybody. Do I have to answer your questions? I'm not at confession nor at the police station, thank God. I'm not at anybody's bidding.'

'Suppose I offered you twenty, thirty, forty thousand francs if you told me where Monsieur Ferragus lives?'

'Nothing doing, nothing brewing!' she said, adding a vulgar gesture to this singular reply. 'I wouldn't tell you for all the money there is. Here's where I take myself off. How do I get out?'

Appalled, Jules let Ida go without further ado. The whole world seemed to be collapsing under him, and the sky above him was clattering down.

'Dinner is served,' his valet told him.

Both valet and butler waited in the dining-room for about a quarter of an hour without their master and mistress coming in.

The chambermaid came in to say: 'Madame will not be dining.'

'What's wrong then, Joséphine?' the valet asked.

'I don't know. Madame's in tears and is going to bed. No doubt Monsieur has some little affair on in town, and it's been found out at a very bad moment, see? I wouldn't answer for her life. Men are all so blundering! They're always making scenes without thinking what they're up to.'

'Not at all,' the valet replied in a low voice. 'It's the other way round. It's Madame who ... well, you know what I mean. What time would Monsieur have to go gallivanting? He hasn't slept out once in five years. He comes down to his office at ten o'clock, and only goes out at twelve o'clock to lunch. In fact, he lives an open and steady life, whereas Madame slips off every day at three, goodness knows where.'

'So does Monsieur,' the chambermaid said, taking her mistress's part.

'But Monsieur goes to the Stock Exchange ... Anyway, I've told him three times that dinner's ready – might as well talk to a dummy.'

Monsieur Jules came in. 'Where is Madame?' he asked.

'She has a migraine and is going to bed,' the chambermaid replied with an important air.

Monsieur Jules then said to the servants: 'You may clear away. I shall keep Madame company.' And he went to his wife's room.

He found her weeping and stifling her sobs in her handkerchief.

'Why are you crying?' he asked. 'You need expect neither violence nor reproach from me. Why should I avenge myself? If you have not been faithful to my love, it just means you were not worthy of it ... '

'Not worthy! ... ' These repeated words were audible despite her sobs, and the accent with which she pronounced them would have melted any other man but Jules.

'In order to kill you I should perhaps need to love more passionately than I do. But I should not have the courage. I would rather kill myself and leave you to your – could we call it happiness? – and with whom? ... ' He broke off.

'Kill yourself?' cried Clémence, throwing herself at Jules's feet and clasping them.

But he tried to break free of this embrace, shook his wife off and dragged himself over to his bed. 'Leave me,' he said.

'No, no, Jules!' she cried. 'If you no longer love me I shall die. Do you want to know the whole truth?'

'Yes!' He took hold of her, gripped her violently, sat on the edge of the bed and kept her wedged between his legs. Then, gazing dry-eyed on her lovely face, now flame-coloured, but furrowed with tears, he repeated: 'Come, tell me.'

Clémence renewed her sobbing.

'No. It's a dead secret. If I revealed it, I ... No, I cannot. Have pity, Jules.'

'You're still deceiving me.'

'Ah! You say "you", not "thou",' she exclaimed. 'Well, Jules, you may think I am deceiving you, but before long you'll know the whole truth.'

'But this Ferragus, this convict you visit, this man who has grown rich in crime: if he's not yours, if you don't belong to him ... '

'Jules!'

'Well, is he your unknown benefactor? The man to whom we seem to owe our fortune, as people have already said.'

'Who has said that?'

'A man I killed in a duel.'

'Oh God! Already one person dead!'

'If he is not your protector, if he does not furnish you with money, if it is you who give him money, why then, perhaps he's your brother?'

'Well,' she said. 'Suppose that were true?'

Monsieur Desmarets folded his arms. 'Why should you have hidden it from me?' he continued. 'Have you and your mother been taking me in? For that matter, does one go to visit one's brother every day, or almost every day? Does one?'

His wife had fainted at his feet.

'She's dead,' he said. 'But suppose I were wrong?'

He leapt to the bell-pull, summoned Joséphine and carried Clémence to her bed.

'This will kill me,' said Madame Jules as she came to.

'Joséphine,' Monsieur Desmarets shouted. 'Go and fetch Monsieur Desplein. Then go and find my brother and beg him to come here as soon as he can.'

'Why your brother?' asked Clémence. But Jules had already gone out.

For the first time in five years, Madame Jules went to bed alone and was obliged to admit a doctor into her inviolate bedroom. These two things gave her keen pain. Desplein found that Madame Jules was in a very bad state: never had a violent emotional disturbance occurred at a worse moment. He was reluctant to rush matters and postponed his diagnosis until the next day, after giving some prescriptions which were not acted upon because emotional preoccupations made Clémence forgetful of physical remedies. Dawn came before Clémence fell asleep. She had been kept awake by the dull murmur of a conversation of several hours' duration between the two brothers. But the thickness of the walls prevented any word which might have revealed the subject of this long conference from reaching her ear. Eventually Monsieur Desmarets the notary departed. The quietness of the night, also the singular sharpness of senses which passion confers, allowed Clémence to discern the scratching of a quill and the involuntary movements of a man engrossed in writing.

Those who habitually stay up at night and have observed the different effects of acoustics through deep silence are aware that often a slight reverberation is easy to perceive even in the places where equal and continuous murmurs have had no distinctive resonance. At four o'clock this noise ceased. Anxious and trembling, Clémence got out of bed. Then, barefoot, having no dressing-gown and having no thought for the feverish state she was in, the poor woman was lucky enough to open the communicating door without making it creak. She saw her husband, pen in hand, asleep in an armchair. The candles had burnt down to their sockets. She moved slowly forward, and read on an envelope already sealed: THIS IS MY LAST WILL AND TESTAMENT.

She knelt down as if in front of a tomb and kissed her husband's hand. He woke abruptly.

'Jules, my dear,' she said, looking at him with eyes kindled with love and fever, 'criminals condemned to death are allowed a few days. Your innocent wife only asks you for two. Leave me free for two days and wait. After that I shall die happy, for at least you will be sorry to lose me.'

'Clémence, I grant you them.'

And, as she kissed her husband's hands with touching and heartfelt impulsiveness, Jules, fascinated by this cry of apparent innocence, took her to him and kissed her brow, even though he was quite ashamed still to be under the influence of her noble beauty.

The next day, after taking a few hours' rest, Jules entered his wife's room, automatically adhering to his habit of not going out without seeing her. Clémence was asleep. A beam of light passing through the topmost chinks in the curtains was falling on to the face of this stricken woman. Already grief had wrought some ravage on her brow and the bright redness of her lips. A lover's eye could not be mistaken at the sight of some deep lines and the unhealthy pallor which had replaced both the even tones of her cheeks and the matt whiteness of her complexion: two pellucid backgrounds against which the feelings of this lovely soul were so naïvely visible.

'She is suffering,' Jules said to himself. 'Poor Clémence! God help us!'

He gently kissed her forehead. She awoke, saw her husband and grasped the situation. But she could not speak. She took his hand and her eyes became wet with tears.

'I am guiltless,' she said as she emerged from her dream.

'You won't be going out?' Jules asked.

'No indeed. I feel too weak to get up.'

'If you change your mind, wait till I come back,' said Jules. And he went down to the lodge.

'Fouquereau, you will keep a careful watch on the door. I want to know what people come to this house and what people leave it.'

Then Monsieur Jules flung himself into a cab, had himself driven to the Maulincour mansion and asked for the baron. He was told that he was ill. Jules insisted on being admitted and gave his name. If he could not see Monsieur de Maulincour, he demanded to see the vidame or the dowager baroness. He waited for some time in the old lady's salon. She came to him and told him that her grandson was much too unwell to see him.

'I know, Madame,' Jules replied, 'the nature of his sickness through the letter you did me the honour to write me, and I beg you to believe . . . '

'A letter from me . . . to you?' the dowager lady burst in. 'I wrote no such letter. And what am I supposed to have said in this letter?'

'Madame,' Jules replied, 'having intended to come to Monsieur de Maulincour's house this very day and return you this letter, I thought I had better keep it in spite of its final injunction. Here it is.'

The dowager rang for her double-strength spectacles and, as soon as she had scanned the letter, she manifested the greatest surprise.

'Monsieur!' she said, 'this is so perfect an imitation of my handwriting that, except for something that has happened recently, I should have been taken in myself. My grandson is ill, Monsieur: that is true. *But his reason has not been affected to the slightest extent.* Some ill-disposed person or persons are making game of us; but even so I cannot guess with what purpose this impertinence has been committed . . . You shall see my grandson, Monsieur, and you will recognize that he is perfectly sane.'

Thereupon she rang again to find out if the baron was able to receive Monsieur Desmarets. The valet returned with an affirmative answer. Jules went upstairs to Monsieur de Maulincour's rooms, and found him sitting in an armchair at the corner of the hearth. Too weak to stand up, he saluted him with a melancholy gesture. The Vidame de Pamiers was with him.

'Monsieur le Baron,' said Jules. 'I have something to say to you of so private a nature that I wish we might be alone.'

'Monsieur,' Auguste replied, 'Monsieur le Commandeur knows all about this matter, and you may speak in his presence without fear!'

'Monsieur le Baron,' Jules continued in grave tones, 'you have disturbed and almost destroyed my happiness without having any right to do so. Until the moment comes when we shall see which of us must demand reparation of the other or grant it to the other, it is your business to guide my footsteps along the dark path which you are making me tread. So I come to ask you to give me the present address of the mysterious being who is exercising so fateful an influence on our destinies and seems to have supernatural power at his command. Here is the letter I found awaiting me at home yesterday, after receiving your warning.' He handed him the spurious letter.

'This Ferragus, alias Bourignard, alias Monsieur de Funcal, is a demon,' Maulincour exclaimed after reading it. 'What fearful labyrinth have I stepped into? And where am I making for? I have done wrong, Monsieur,' he said with a look at Jules. 'But death is certainly the gravest of expiations and I am near to death. You may therefore ask me anything you wish. I am at your command.'

'Monsieur, you certainly know where this unknown man lives. I absolutely must get to the bottom of this mystery, even if it costs me all I have. And when one is up against so cruelly intelligent an enemy, every minute is precious.'

'Justin will tell you everything,' the baron replied. At these words, the commander fidgeted in his chair. Auguste rang.

'Justin is not at my house,' the vidame exclaimed with a precipitancy which was only too fraught with meaning.

'Well,' Auguste sharply retorted, 'our servants know where he is: one of them will go and fetch him, on horseback. He's in Paris, is he not? He can be found.'

The commander was visibly upset. 'Justin will not come, my friend,' the old man said. 'He is dead. I wanted to keep the news of this accident from you, but . . . '

'Dead?' cried Monsieur de Maulincour. 'Dead? When? How?'

'Last night. He went out to supper with some old friends, and no doubt he got drunk. His friends, as much the worse for wine as he was, must have left him lying down in the street, and a big carriage ran over him.'

'So the convict didn't miss him. Got him first shot!' said Auguste. 'He wasn't so lucky with me: he needed four shots!'

Jules took on a sombre and pensive demeanour. 'So I shall remain ignorant,' he exclaimed after a long pause. 'It may be that your servant was deservedly punished. Did he not go beyond your orders in slandering Madame Desmarets, thus poisoning the mind of a certain *Ida*, and arousing jealousy in her in order to unleash it against us?'

'Oh, Monsieur, I was so angry that I delivered Madame Jules over to his tender mercies.'

'Sir!' the husband exclaimed in extremely irritated tones.

'Oh!' the officer replied. 'Now, Monsieur' – he raised his hand to impose silence – 'I am ready to make any amends. You can do no more than what has been done already, and you can tell me nothing that my conscience has not already told me. This very morning I am awaiting the most eminent expert in toxicology in order to learn what fate holds in store for me. If I am to expect excessive suffering, my mind is made up: I shall blow my brains out.'

'Don't talk so childishly!' cried the commander, appalled by the calm tone with which the baron had pronounced these words. 'Your grandmother would die of grief.'

'It appears then, Monsieur,' said Jules, 'that there are no means of knowing in what quarter of Paris this extraordinary man lives?'

'I believe, sir,' the old man replied, 'that I heard my poor Justin say that Monsieur de Funcal was lodging at the Portuguese or Brazilian embassy. Monsieur de Funcal is a nobleman who belongs to both of those countries. As for the convict you speak of, he is dead and buried: your persecutor, whoever he may be, appears to me to be powerful enough for you to accept him in the new shape he has assumed until you have found the means to confound and overwhelm him. But act with prudence, my dear sir. If Monsieur de Maulincour had taken my advice, nothing of this would have happened.'

Jules coldly but politely withdrew, without knowing what he could do to get through to Ferragus. At the moment when he returned home, his concierge told him that Madame had gone out to post a letter in the box opposite the Rue de Ménars. Jules felt humiliated when he took note of the prodigious understanding with which his concierge espoused his cause and the adroitness with which he thought out means of serving him. The eagerness of underlings and their particular aptitude for compromising their masters once the latter have compromised themselves were well known to him; he had weighed up the danger of enlisting their complicity in any matter whatsoever; but he had been unable to think of his personal dignity until he found himself so suddenly brought low. What a triumph it was for a slave incapable of rising to his master's level to bring his master down to his own level! Jules was abrupt and harsh: yet another mistake – but he was suffering so much! His life, up to that point so straightforward, so pure, was becoming tortuous; he now had to resort to ruse and prevarication; Clémence also was doing the same thing. The realization of this filled him with disgust. Plunged deep in bitter thoughts, he came automatically to a halt at the door of his house. At one instant, giving way to ideas of despair, he wanted to take flight and leave France, carrying away with him all the illusions of uncertainty regarding his love. An instant later, not questioning that the letter posted by Clémence was addressed to Ferragus, he pondered over means of intercepting the answer that this mysterious being would send. At another moment he set about analysing the singular chances which had come his way since his marriage, and wondered if the calumny for which he had exacted vengeance was not founded in truth. Lastly,

reverting to the reply that Ferragus might send, he wondered: 'But will this profoundly clever man, so logical in his
slightest acts, who sees, foresees, calculates and even divines
our thoughts, will he even answer the letter? Is he not likely
to employ methods consonant with the power he wields?
Will he not send his reply through the agency of some clever
scoundrel, or perhaps in a jewel-case brought to her by some
honest man who has no idea what he is carrying, or in the
wrappings of shoes which a shopwoman will very innocently
deliver to my wife?' He was full of mistrust and was roving
over the limitless fields, the shoreless ocean of suppositions.
Then, after for some time drifting between a host of contrary decisions, he concluded that he would be in a stronger
position in his own house than anywhere else. He resolved to
keep watch there like an ant-lion at the bottom of its spiral in
the sand.

'Fouquereau,' he said to his concierge, 'I am out for
anyone who calls. If anyone asks to speak to Madame or
brings her anything, you will ring the bell twice. Also you
will show me all the letters addressed to this house, no matter
to whom.'

'In this way,' he thought as he returned to his study on the
mezzanine floor, 'I shall be forestalling Master Ferragus's
subtleties. If he sends an emissary crafty enough to ask for
me in order to find out if Madame is alone, at least I shall
not be taken in like a simpleton.'

He glued his face to the window of his study, which looked
out on to the street, and, resorting to a final ruse inspired by
jealousy, he resolved to make his chief clerk go in his carriage
to the Stock Exchange as his substitute, with a letter for a
friendly stockbroker detailing his sales and purchases and asking him to act for him. He postponed his most difficult transac-
tions to the following day, caring nothing for bulls and bears
or any rise or fall in European funds. Such is the privilege
which love enjoys! Everything blanches and falls down before
it: altar, throne and gilt-edged securities! At half past three,
just at the time when the Stock Exchange is feverishly busied
with contangos, profit-takings, options, firm stock, etc.,

Monsieur Jules saw Fouquereau come into his study, beaming.

'Monsieur, an old woman has just turned up; she's fairly spruce and looks to be all there. She asked to see Monsieur and seemed put out not to find him in; she gave me this letter for Madame.'

A prey to feverish anguish, Jules unsealed the letter; but before long he fell back in his chair completely nonplussed. The letter made no sense from one end to the other: it was written in cipher and could not be read without a key.

'You may go, Fouquereau.' The concierge went out. 'It's a deeper mystery,' Jules said to himself, 'than the sea is when no plummet can sound it. Oh! It must be a love affair. Only a lover could be as shrewd, as ingenious as the writer of this letter. My God! I will kill Clémence!'

At that moment a happy inspiration came to him so forcibly that it was almost like a physical illumination. In the days before his marriage, when he was struggling to make ends meet, Jules had acquired a true friend, one who was halfway to being a Péméja.[2] The extreme tact with which he had spared the susceptibility of this poor and modest friend, the respect he had shown him, the ingenious adroitness with which he had nobly forced him to share his resources without making him feel ashamed had done much to deepen their friendship. This man, named Jacquet, remained faithful to Desmarets in spite of the latter's opulence.

Jacquet, a man of probity, hard-working and austere in his mode of life, had slowly made his way in that department of state which at one and the same time takes the maximum expenditure of knavery and of probity: he had a post in the Ministry of Foreign Affairs, and was in charge of the most delicate section of the archives. In this ministry Jacquet was a sort of glow-worm throwing, at appropriate moments, a glimmer upon secret correspondences by deciphering and classifying dispatches. More highly placed than the average civil servant, he occupied, in the Ministry of Foreign

2. The Marquis de Péméja. A real person brought into Mme de Staël's *Corinna* (1804). A model of devoted friendship.

Affairs, the highest among subaltern ranks, and lived in a happy obscurity which insured him against reverses. He was satisfied to pay his small contribution to the well-being of his country. Born to be the deputy mayor of his own *arrondissement*, he enjoyed, to talk journalese, all the consideration which was due to him. Thanks to Jules, his position had been improved by a good marriage. A self-effacing patriot, a ministerialist in point of fact, he contented himself with lamenting at his fireside over the way government was carried on. For the rest, Jacquet was an easy-going monarch in his own house, the man with the umbrella,[3] a man who provided his wife with a horse and carriage but never used it himself. Finally, to complete the sketch of this *unwitting philosopher*,[4] he had not yet suspected and was never to suspect all the advantage he might have drawn from his position – having a stockbroker as his intimate friend and being in daily contact with state secrets. This man, as sublime as the unknown soldier who died for Napoleon by shouting *Who goes there?*, lived on the Ministry premises.

Jules reached the archivist's office in ten minutes. Jacquet offered him a chair, methodically laid his green taffeta eyeshade on the table, rubbed his hands, took his snuff-box, stood up cracking his shoulder-blades, raised his thorax and asked: 'What chance brings you here, M'sieu Desmarets? What do you want of me?'

' Jacquet, I need you to find out a secret, a secret of life and death.'

'It's not concerned with politics?'

'I wouldn't ask you a secret of that sort. No, it's a domestic matter about which I ask you to keep absolutely silent.'

'Claude-Joseph Jacquet, a mute by profession: that's me! You know it,' he added with a laugh. 'Discretion is my middle name.'

Jules showed him the letter and said: 'I want you to decipher this letter for me. It is addressed to my wife.'

---

3. i.e. a typical bourgeois. See above, p. 56.
4. A reference to a play of 1765 by Michel Sedaine: *Le philosophe sans le savoir*.

'The devil, the devil! A bad bit of business,' said Jacquet, scrutinizing the letter in the same way as an usurer examines a negotiable bill. 'Ah! It's a stencil-cypher. Wait a minute.'

He left Jules in his study, and returned quite promptly.

'Child's play, my friend. It's written with an old-fashioned stencil as used by the Portuguese ambassador under the Duc de Choiseul, at the time when the Jesuits were banished. Look, here you are . . .'

Jacquet superimposed a piece of perforated paper, regularly designed like the patterned paper which confectioners put over their *dragées*, so that Jules could easily read the sentences which remained uncovered.

Don't worry any more, dear Clémence. Our happiness will no longer be disturbed by anyone, and your husband will shed his suspicions. I cannot come to see you. Ill though you are, you must have the courage to come here. Try and find the strength to do it in your love for me. My affection for you has forced me to undergo the most cruel of operations, and it is impossible for me to leave my bed. Yesterday evening some moxas[5] were applied to the nape of my neck from one shoulder to the other, and it was necessary to leave them burning quite a long time. You understand? But I was thinking of you and did not suffer too much. In order to baffle all Maulincour's ferretings – he will not persecute us much longer – I have left the protective roof of the Embassy and am safe from all pursuit at No. 12, Rue des Enfants-Rouges, at the house of an old woman named Madame Étienne Gruget, the mother of that Ida who is going to pay dearly for her stupid indiscretion. Come tomorrow at nine in the morning. I am in a room which can only be reached by an inside staircase. Ask for Monsieur Camuset. Till tomorrow then. I kiss your forehead, my dear.

Jacquet regarded Jules with a sort of honest terror fraught with true compassion. He uttered his favourite expletive 'The devil! The devil!' on two different tones.

'That looks clear to you, doesn't it?' said Jules. 'And yet in my heart of hearts there is a voice pleading for my wife, and more loudly than all the pangs of jealousy. Until tomor-

5. An antiquated process of cauterization by the use of the dried leaves of a plant.

row I shall be suffering the most horrible torture; but at last, tomorrow, between nine and ten, I shall know all, and shall be happy or unhappy for the rest of my life. Think of me, Jacquet.'

'I'll come for you tomorrow at eleven. We'll go there together, and I'll wait for you, if you like, in the street. You may be running some risk and may need a devoted friend near you who can size up the situation and who you may be certain will help you. Count on me.'

'Even if it came to the point of helping me to kill someone?'

'The devil! The devil!' said Jacquet with keen concern, keeping, so to speak, on the same musical note. 'I have a wife and two children ...'

Jules clasped Claude Jacquet by the hand and went out, but only to hurry in again. 'I forgot the letter,' he said. 'And that's not all. I must seal it up again.'

'The devil! The devil! You opened it without taking the impression of the wax. But fortunately the seal is cleanly broken. Leave the letter to me. I'll return it to you intact.'

'At what time?'

'At half past five.'

'If I'm not back home by then, just give it to the concierge and tell him to take it up to Madame.'

'Do you want me with you tomorrow?'

'No. Good-bye.'

Jules got quickly to the Place de la Rotonde du Temple, left his cab there and went on foot to the Rue des Enfants-Rouges, where he studied the house in which Madame Étienne Gruget lived. There the mystery on which the fate of so many people depended was to be cleared up; there Ferragus was, and all the threads of this intrigue led to Ferragus. Was not a meeting between Madame Jules, her husband and that man the Gordian knot of this already bloody drama, soon to be cut by the sword which severs the most inextricable tangles?

The house in question was one of those belonging to the kind called *cabajoutis*. This very significant name[6] is given by

6. 'Significant' because it suggests an etymology (dubious) to Balzac: noun *cab*(*ane*) (hut) verb + *ajouter* (to add).

the populace of Paris to a certain kind of patchwork housing. Almost always they are either originally separate habitations, joined together through the whims of the different owners who have successively extended them, or houses which have been begun, abandoned, taken up again and finished; unfortunate houses which, like certain peoples, have passed under the sway of several dynasties of capricious masters. Neither storeys nor windows make a whole, to borrow a term from painting; everything clashes, even external adornments. The *cabajoutis* is to Parisian architecture what the glory-hole is to a suite of rooms, a genuine lumber-room into which a jumble of most discordant objects have been flung.

'Madame Étienne,' Jules asked of the portress. This woman was lodged underneath the main door, in a sort of chicken-coop, a little wooden hut mounted on rollers, similar enough to the shelters put up by the police at all cab-ranks.

'Eh, what?' said the portress, putting aside the stocking she was knitting.

In Paris the different types contributing to the physiognomy of any portion of that monstrous city harmonize admirably with the character of the *ensemble*. Thus the concierge, door-keeper or hall porter, whatever the name given to this essential nerve-system in the Parisian monster, always conforms to the quarter in which he functions, and often sums it up. The concierge of the Faubourg Saint-Germain, wearing braid on every seam, a man of leisure, speculates in Government stocks; the porter of the Chaussée-d'Antin enjoys his creature comforts; he of the Stock Exchange quarter reads his newspapers; porters in the Faubourg Montmartre work at a trade; in the quarter given over to prostitution the portress herself is a retired prostitute; in the Marais quarter she is respectable, cross-grained and crochety.

On seeing Monsieur Jules, the portress in question took a table-knife in order to stir the almost extinct peat in her footwarmer and then said: 'You are asking for Madame Étienne: do you mean Madame Étienne Gruget?'

'Yes,' said Jules Desmarets, looking passably annoyed.

'The maker of *passementerie*?'

'Yes.'

'Well, Monsieur,' she said, emerging from her cage, putting her hand on Monsieur Jules's arm and leading him to the end of a long and narrow passage with a vaulted roof, 'go up the second staircase at the bottom of the courtyard. Do you see the windows with boxes of gillyflowers? That's where Madame Étienne lives.'

'Thank you, Madame. Do you think she's alone?'

'Why shouldn't she be? She's a widow.'

Jules skipped up a very dark staircase whose treads had lumps of caked mud left on them by the boots of comers and goers. On the second floor he saw three doors but no 'gillyflowers'. Fortunately, on the greasiest and brownest of the three doors, he saw a message scrawled in chalk: 'Ida will be here at nine this evening'. 'That's it,' Jules said to himself. He tugged at an old, completely blackened doe's-foot bell-pull and heard the muted ring of a cracked bell and the yelping of a wheezy little dog. The particular kind of resonance inside the flat indicated that it was encumbered with objects which stifled any possible echo: a characteristic feature of working people's lodgings, small as they are and lacking both space and air. Jules's eye roved round mechanically in quest of the 'gillyflowers' and eventually found them on the outside ledge of a sash window sliding between two filthy lead grooves. There were the flowers in a 'garden' two feet long and six inches wide; there he saw sprouting grains of wheat; there he saw a whole life in résumé; but there also he saw all the miseries of life. Opposite these sickly flowers and soaring cornstalks a sunbeam, falling from the sky as if by Heaven's grace, threw into relief the dust, grease, the indescribable drabness peculiar to Paris hovels, the thousand varieties of filth which provided a frame for, gave age and tarnish to, the dark walls and worm-eaten balusters of the staircase, to the disjointed window-frames and the once red-painted doors. Before long an old woman's cough and the heavy tread of one trailing along in list slippers announced the mother of Ida Gruget. This old woman opened the door, came out on to the landing, raised her head and said: 'Ah! You are Monsieur Bocquillon ... No you're not! But I must say you're the very image of Monsieur Bocquillon. Maybe you're his brother? What can I do for you? Come in Monsieur.'

Jules followed this woman into the first room, where he saw a wholesale assemblage of bird-cages, household utensils, stoves, various pieces of furniture, little earthenware dishes filled with mash or water for dogs or cats, a wooden clock, blankets, engravings by Eisen, a stack of pieces of old iron, a jumble of objects which together made a really grotesque picture: a truly Parisian glory-hole – even a few numbers of the *Constitutionnel* were not lacking.[7]

In a prudent frame of mind, Jules paid no heed to the widow Gruget when she said to him: 'Please come right in, Monsieur, and warm yourself.' Fearful of being overheard by Ferragus, Jules was wondering whether it would not be better to remain in this first room in order to conclude the bargain he wished to propose to the old woman. A hen which came out cackling from a loft put an end to his ponderings. He had made up his mind. And so he followed Ida's mother to the room with a fire, accompanied by the wheezy little pug-dog who, without any further barking, climbed on to an ancient stool. Madame Gruget had been betraying all the fatuousness of near-poverty when she talked of warming up her visitor; her stockpot completely covered two half-burned logs which were not even touching each other. The skimming-ladle was lying in the hearth with its handle in the cinders. The mantelpiece, adorned with a wax Jesus under a square glass case edged with dirty blue paper, was encumbered with balls of wool, spools and tools required for *passementerie*. Jules examined all the furniture in the flat with very interested curiosity and involuntarily manifested his secret satisfaction.

'Well now, Monsieur, have you taken a fancy to my bits of furniture?' the widow asked him as she sat down in an easy chair of yellow reed which she seemed to use as her headquarters. There she kept pell-mell her kerchief, her snuff-

7. The organ of a leftist political party. Balzac gibes at it as if it were superannuated, since by now he had committed himself to the Right.

box, her knitting, some half-peeled vegetables, her spectacles, her calendar, livery braiding in its early stages, a greasy pack of cards and two volumes of novels, the whole of it making a hollow in the seat. This article of furniture, which the old woman occupied as she 'drifted down the stream of life', looked like the voluminous holdall which a woman carries on her travels, which contains her household goods in miniature, from her husband's portrait to the melissa cordial for her fainting-fits, sweets for her children and English taffeta for her cuttings-out.

Jules studied everything. He attentively scrutinized Madame Gruget's yellow face, her grey, lashless, listless eyes, her toothless mouth, her blackly shaded wrinkles, her red tulle bonnet with its even redder frills, her calico petticoats, full of holes, her worn-out slippers, her table littered with dishes, scraps of silk, cotton and woollen work, with a bottle of wine standing up in the middle. Then he said to himself: 'This woman has some obsession, some secret vices. I can buy her.'

'Madame,' he said out loud, making a gesture of connivance, 'I have come to order some braid of you ...' Then he dropped his voice. 'I know,' he continued, 'that you have in your house an unknown person who goes by the name of Camuset.' The old woman gave him a quick look without showing the slightest sign of astonishment. 'Tell me, can he overhear us? Realize that you can make a good thing for yourself out of this.'

'Monsieur,' she replied, 'Speak freely. I have no one here. But even if there were anyone up aloft he would find it quite impossible to overhear you.'

'Ah! The cunning old woman!' Jules thought. 'She knows her way about. We shall be able to come to terms.' So he continued: 'Don't bother to lie, Madame. And in the first place, just understand that I neither wish you any harm, nor your sick tenant with his moxas, nor your daughter Ida, the corset-maker, Ferragus's mistress. You can see that I'm in the know about everything. Don't be alarmed. I don't belong to the police, and I don't want you to do anything against your conscience. A young lady is coming here tomorrow, between nine and ten, to talk with your daughter's lover. I want to be within reach, to see and hear everything without being either seen or heard by them. You will make this possible, and I will requite this service with a lump sum of two thousand francs and an annuity of six hundred francs. My notary will draw up the donation this evening in your presence. I will hand over the money to him and he will deliver it to you tomorrow, after the talk which I wish to overhear, in the course of which I shall acquire proof of your good faith.'

'Might that not do harm to my daughter, my dear Monsieur?' she asked, looking at him with the glance of a distrustful cat.

'By no means, Madame. In any case it looks as if your daughter is treating you very badly. Loved as she is by a man so rich, so influential as Ferragus, it should be easy for her to put you in a much happier position than you appear to be in.'

'Indeed, my dear Monsieur: not so much as a miserable theatre ticket for the Ambigu or the Gaieté, where she goes as often as she likes. It's a crying shame! A daughter for whom I sold my silver plate – and here I am now, at my age, eating out of German silver – so as to pay for her apprenticeship and have her taught a trade at which she could make lots of money if she chose. In fact, as far as that goes, she takes after me and is as spry as a pixie with her fingers, I must say that for her. Anyway, she might just as well hand on to me her old silk dresses, for I'm very partial to silk. Not a bit of it! She goes to the Cadran-Bleu where dinner costs fifty francs a head, flaunts about in a carriage like a princess and doesn't care a rap for her mother. Good God, Monsieur! What a mess we've made of our children! We ought to be ashamed of ourselves. I've been a good mother to her, Monsieur, got her out of her scrapes and always had her on my hands, let her sponge on me and given her everything she wanted. Some good that! They come along, give you a hug and a "Good-day, Ma!" And that's all they do for them that brought them into the world. Let 'em drag along anyhow! But she'll have children as well one day or another and then she'll see what a bad bargain they are. And yet we love them!'

'What? She does nothing for you?'

'Oh no, Monsieur, I don't say that. If she did nothing that would be the limit! She pays my rent, keeps me in wood and gives me thirty-six francs a month. But you tell me, Monsieur: at my age, fifty-two, suffering chronic from eye strain every evening, for why should I still have to work? Is she ashamed of me? Why don't she say so straight out? God's truth! You might as well get yourself dead and buried for these dratted children who've forgotten you before they've closed the door behind them.' She pulled her handkerchief from her pocket. A lottery ticket came out and fell to the floor. 'Well I never!' she said. 'That's the receipt for my rates.'

Jules swiftly guessed the reason for the wise parsimony which the mother was complaining about, and was all the more certain that Widow Gruget would acquiesce in the bargain he was about to propose.

'So then, Madame, why not accept what I am offering you?'

'So you said, Monsieur, two thousand francs on the nail and six hundred francs a year?'

'I have changed my mind, Madame. I promise you only three hundred francs' annuity. But I will give you five thousand francs in cash. Isn't that a better bargain?'

'Right enough it is, Monsieur.'

'You'll be more comfortably off and can go to the Ambigu-Comique or the Olympic Circus, or anywhere you like – and take a cab.'

'Oh, I don't like the Olympic Circus. There's no talking there. But the reason why I accept, Monsieur, is that it will be better for my child. I shan't be living on her any longer. After all, poor little thing, I don't begrudge her a bit of fun. Youth has to have its fling, Monsieur! So what? Are you sure I shan't be doing anybody in the eye?'

'Nobody,' Jules replied. 'But tell me, how are you proposing to arrange it?'

'Well, sir, if I give Monsieur Ferragus a little infusion of poppy heads this evening, he'll sleep sound, bless him! He needs it because of his sufferings; for he *does* suffer, and you'd be sorry for him. All the same, can you tell me what sort of idea it is for a healthy man to burn his back in order to get rid of a neuralgia which only worries him once in two years? Well, to come back to our business, I've got my neighbour's key. She lives over me and her room has a party wall with Monsieur Ferragus's bedroom. She's away in the country for ten days. So, if I make a hole tonight in the party wall, you'll hear them and see them quite comfortably. I'm friendly with a locksmith, a very nice man who can spin you a fine tale. He'll do it for me, and nobody will be any the wiser.'

'Here are a hundred francs for him. Come this evening to the house of Monsieur Desmarets, the notary: here is his address. At nine o'clock the deed will be ready, but ... not a word to anyone!'

'Good enough, Monsieur. Not a whisper! So long, Monsieur.'

Jules returned home, almost calm now because he was sure of knowing everything the next day. When he arrived, his porter gave him the letter, perfectly sealed up again.

'How are you feeling?' he asked his wife, despite the kind of chill there was between them. Affectionate habits are so hard to abandon!

'Not too bad, Jules,' she answered in affectionate tones. 'Will you dine with me?'

'Yes,' he replied, offering the letter. 'Look, Fouquereau gave me this for you.'

Clémence turned from pale to deep red at the sight of the letter, and this quick blush caused her husband the most acute pain.

'Is this change of colour due to joy?' he asked with a laugh. 'Is it due to expectation?'

'Oh, it might be due to many things,' she said as she looked at the seal.

'I will leave you, Madame.' And he went down to his study, and there he wrote a letter to his brother stating his intentions with regard to settling an annuity on Widow Gruget. When he returned, he found his dinner prepared on a little table near Clémence's bed. Joséphine was there ready to serve it up.

'If I were on my feet, how gladly would I serve you!' Clémence said when Joséphine had left them alone together. 'On my knees even,' she added, running her pale hands through Jules's hair. 'Dear heart, noble heart, you were very kind to me and very gracious a little while ago. The trust you showed in me did me more good than all the doctors in the wide world could do with their prescriptions. Your gentle tact – *your* love is like that of a woman – poured such a soothing balm into my heart as made me almost well again. There is a truce between us, Jules. Bring your head towards me that I may kiss it.'

Jules could not deny himself the pleasure of kissing Clémence, but not without a sort of heartfelt remorse: he felt belittled in the presence of this woman, whom he was still inclined to regard as innocent. She was showing a sad kind of joy. Through the grief expressed on her face a chaste hope was shining. Both of them seemed equally unhappy at being forced to deceive each other: one more caress and, yielding to their grief, they would have told each other everything.

'Tomorrow evening, Clémence.'

'No, husband. At midday tomorrow you will know all and you will get down on your knees before your wife. Yet no! You shall not humble yourself! No, you are completely forgiven. No, you have done me no wrong. Listen to me: yesterday you almost broke my heart; but perhaps my life would not have been complete without the anguish I felt: it will turn out to have been a cloud passing over heavenly days to come.'

'You are casting a spell upon me!' Jules exclaimed. 'You will make me ashamed of myself.'

'My poor darling, destiny is stronger than we are and I am not in control of my destiny. I shall be going out in the morning.'

'At what time?'

'Half past nine.'

'Clémence,' Monsieur Desmarets replied. 'Look after your health. Consult Dr Desplein and old Haudry.'

'I shall consult only my heart and my courage.'

'I leave you free to do as you like, and will not come to see you before noon.'

'Won't you give me your company a bit this evening? I'm feeling better now.'

Once he had made his various arrangements, Jules returned to his wife, incapable as he was of resisting the attraction she exerted on him. His passion was stronger than all the grief that was vexing him.

4

Where should one choose to die?

THE next day, at about nine o'clock, Jules slipped out of his house, hurried to the Rue des Enfants-Rouges, climbed the stairs and rang at Madame Gruget's door.

'Ah! You're as punctual as the dawn! Come in, Monsieur,' the old braid-embroiderer said as she recognized him. 'I've made you a cup of coffee and cream; in case . . . ' she continued when the door was closed. 'Yes, coffee with real cream: a little pot that I myself saw milked and skimmed off at the dairy we have in the Enfants-Rouges market.'

'Thank you, Madame, but I won't have anything. Take me...'

'Very well, my dear Monsieur. Come this way.'

The widow led Jules to a room which was over hers, and there she triumphantly showed him a hole as big as a two-franc piece, drilled out during the night at a place corresponding to the highest and darkest rosettes on the wallpaper in Ferragus's room. In both rooms the hole was over a wardrobe. Thus the slight damage done by the locksmith had left no traces either side of the wall, and in the shadow it was very difficult to espy this kind of loop-hole. And so Jules was obliged, in order to maintain his position and see clearly through, to remain in a very tiring position by perching on a pair of steps which the widow had had the forethought to bring.

'He has a gentleman with him,' the old woman said as she withdrew.

Jules in fact perceived a man engaged in dressing a series of sores produced by quite a lot of burns inflicted on Ferragus's shoulders. He recognized the latter's head by the description given him by Monsieur de Maulincour.

'How soon do you think they will be healed?' he was asking.

'I can't say,' the unknown man replied. 'But, going by what the doctors say, you'll need seven or eight more dressings.'

'Very well. I'll see you this evening,' said Ferragus, offering his hand to the man, who had just applied the outer bandage of the dressing.

'Yes, this evening,' the other man replied, giving Ferragus a hearty handshake. 'I would like to see you free from pain.'

'To end the matter, Monsieur de Funcal's papers will be handed over to us tomorrow and Henri Bourignard will be dead and done with,' Ferragus continued. 'The two fatal letters[1] which have given us so much trouble will no longer exist. So I shall become a social person again, a man among men, and shall be worth just as much as the sailor the fishes ate! God knows it's not for my own sake that I'm posing as a count.'

'Poor Gratien, you, our best brain, our cherished brother. You are the Benjamin of the band, as well you know.'

'Good-bye. Keep an eye on the wretched Maulincour.'

'Trust me for that.'

'By the way, marquis,'[2] the ex-convict cried.

'Yes?'

'Ida is capable of anything after last night's scene. If she has thrown herself into the Seine, I certainly will not fish her out again. That way she'll keep the secret of my name much more easily, and that's all she knows about me. But look after her, for after all she's a good girl.'

'Right.'

The unknown person withdrew. Ten minutes later Jules heard, not without a shudder, the swish of a silk dress and almost recognized his wife's footsteps.

'Well, father,' said Clémence, 'dear father, how are you? How brave you have been!'

---

1. The letters T. F. (*travaux forcés*: penal servitude): those branded on a criminal's shoulder. Ferragus has just had his removed by cauterization.

2. Evidently the Marquis de Ronquerolles, who has already figured as a member of the Thirteen.

'Come in, my child,' Ferragus replied, tendering his hand. Clémence offered him her forehead to kiss.

'Now then, poor little girl, what's the matter? What's vexing you now?'

'I have vexations, father, likely to cause the death of the daughter you love so much. As I told you in my yesterday's letter, your brain is fertile in ideas, and you absolutely must find some way of getting into contact with my poor Jules: this very day. If you knew how good he's been to me, in spite of his suspicions, apparently so well justified. Father, my love is my life. Do you want to see me die? Oh! I've already suffered so much! And I feel that my life is in danger.'

'To think of losing you, my darling,' said Ferragus, 'of losing you through the inquisitiveness of a wretched Parisian! I could burn down Paris itself! Oh, you know what a lover's like. You don't know what a father's like!'

'Father, you frighten me when you look at me like that. Don't compare two such kinds of feeling. I had a husband before I knew that my father was still alive.'

'Your little forehead, my dear, was moist with my tears before it received your husband's kisses ... Set your heart at rest, Clémence, and speak your mind. I love you enough to be happy knowing that you are happy, even though your father has scarcely any place in your heart, whereas you occupy the whole of his.'

'Dear God! Such words give me great consolation. They make me love you more, so that I feel that I am robbing Jules of something. But, dear, kind father, try and realize that he is in despair. What am I to say to him two hours from now?'

'Child, did I wait for a letter from you before saving you from the unhappiness threatening you? Have you not seen what comes to people who presume to tamper with your happiness or to put themselves between us? Have you never realized that a second providence is looking after you? Do you not know that twelve powerful and intelligent men are forming a train round your life and your love and will stop at nothing to preserve them? Did you not have a father who risked death when he went to see you being wheeled out in your pram, when he came at night to your mother's room in order to adore you in your cot? A father to whom only the memory of your childish caresses gave strength enough to live on at a time when a man of honour ought to have committed suicide in order to escape from infamy? In short, could anyone but I, to whom you are the breath of life, I who see only through your eyes and feel only through your heart, could I fail to defend you with the claws of a lion, the passionate love of a father, you, my only treasure, my very life, my daughter?[3] But since the death of the angel who was your mother I have dreamt of one thing only: the happiness of acknowledging you were my daughter, of holding you in my arms in defiance of God and man, of casting the slough of the *convict*.' He paused a moment. 'Of giving you a father, of being able without shame to clasp your husband's hand, of living without fear in your hearts, of looking at you and proclaiming to all and sundry: "This is my child!" In short, of being your father as I long to be!'

'Oh my father, dear father!'

'After many tribulations, after searching throughout the globe,' Ferragus continued, 'my friends have found a human skin to cover me with. A few days hence I shall be the Portuguese count Monsieur de Funcal. Realize this, beloved daughter: at my age few men would have the patience to learn both Portuguese and English, which the diabolic sailor, Funcal, knew perfectly!'

'Dear, dear father!'

'All is settled, and in a few days' time His Majesty John VI of Portugal will be my accomplice. All you need therefore is a little patience – your father has needed much. But it was all very simple for me: what would I not do to reward your devotedness during the last three years? You who with such filial affection came to console your old father and endanger your conjugal happiness!'

3. This passionately paternal adoration undoubtedly shows that Balzac was already well on to the way to *Old Goriot* (1834–5), in which paternal infatuation is most powerfully portrayed.

'Dear father!' Clémence took hold of Ferragus's hands and kissed them.

'Come, take courage for a little longer, Clémence. We must keep this fatal secret to the end. Jules is certainly no ordinary man. But yet do we know if his staunch character and intense love might not rouse in him a measure of disesteem for the daughter of a . . .?'

'Oh!' Clémence exclaimed. 'You have read the heart of your child . . . That is my sole fear,' she added in heart-rending tones. 'That is a thought that chills me. But think, father. I have promised he shall have the truth in two hours' time.'

'Very well, my daughter. Tell him to go to the Portuguese Embassy to meet the Comte de Funcal, your father. I shall be there.'

'But what about Monsieur de Maulincour who has talked to Jules about Ferragus? My goodness, father, must I go on deceiving him? I can't stand it!'

'Nor can I! But in a few days' time no one in the world will be able to give me the lie. For that matter Monsieur de Maulincour will scarcely be in a state to remember what has happened. Come, silly darling, dry your tears, and think . . . '

At that instant a terrible cry rang out in the room in which Jules Desmarets was hiding.

'My daughter, my poor daughter!'

This shriek could be heard through the little hole which had been made above the wardrobe: it terrified Madame Jules and Ferragus, who said: 'Clémence, go and see what's the matter.'

Clémence dashed down the little staircase, found the door of Madame Gruget's flat wide open, heard the cries resounding through the upper storey, ran upstairs and, drawn thither by the sound of sobbing, penetrated to the fatal room where, even before she entered, the following words reached her ears: 'You, Monsieur, you with all your schemings are the cause of her death.'

'Hold your tongue, wretched woman!' said Jules, stuffing his handkerchief into the mouth of Widow Gruget who was shrieking: 'Help! Murder!'

At that instant Clémence came in, saw her husband, gave a cry and fled away.

'Who will save my daughter?' Widow Gruget asked after a long interval of time. 'You have murdered her.'

'How could *I* have done that?' Monsieur Jules mechanically asked; he was stupefied at being recognized by his wife.

'Read this, Monsieur,' the old woman shouted before bursting into tears. 'Can any annuities make up for this?'

Good-bye, Mother. I leave you all I've got. Forgive me for wot i've done rong and for the last sorro I'm giving you by putting an end to it all. I love Henri more than myself, and he's told me I spoiled his life. And seeing he's given me the push and I've no chance of getting settled I'm going to drown myself. I shall do it below Neuilly so as not to be put in the Morgue. If Henri don't hate me more after I've done myself in, ask him to look to the burying of a poor girl who only lived for him and let him forgive me because I was rong in messing about with things which had nothing to do with me. See he gets his moxas proper. They've made his life a misery, poor blighter. But I'll be just as brave as he was doing myself in as he was burning himself. See that the corsets I finished go to the customers. And ask God's mercy for

Your daughter,

IDA

'Take this letter to Monsieur de Funcal, the man down there. If there's still time, only he can save his mistress.'

And Jules dashed away like a man who had committed a crime. His legs were trembling. The blood was pounding into his swelling heart and racing back from it more hotly and copiously than ever in his life before. The most contradictory ideas were swirling to and fro in his mind, and yet they were dominated by a single thought: he had not behaved loyally with the person he most loved, and it was impossible for him to come to terms with his own conscience, whose voice, the more strident on account of the wrong he had done her, was of equal resonance with the inner cries his passion had wrung from him during the excruciating hours of doubt which had previously tormented him. He wandered aimlessly around Paris for the greater part of the day, not daring to return home. This upright man trembled at the idea of gazing on the immaculate brow of the woman he had misunderstood. The reprehensibility of a man's actions is proportionate to the purity of his conscience and a deed which, for some persons, would scarcely be a matter for self-reproach, assumes the dimensions of a crime for certain guileless souls. Has not the word 'guilelessness' in fact a celestial connotation? And does not the slightest stain imparted to the white garment of a virgin turn it into something as vile as the rags on a beggar's back? Between two such extremes the only difference is that which lies between a misfortune and a misdeed. God never measures out repentance or divides it into portions: as much of it is needed to wipe out a spot as to obliterate the memory of a whole life. Reflections like these were bearing with their whole weight on Jules, for the passions are not readier to condone than human law, and they reason more justly: for are they not based on their own special conscience, as infallible as any instinct can be? In despair, Jules went home, pallid, overwhelmed with the consciousness of the wrong he had done; but giving some manifestation, in spite of himself, of the joy he felt over his wife's innocence. He went to her room with palpitating heart, found her in bed in a feverish condition, came and sat by her bed, took her hand, kissed it and bathed it with his tears.

'Dear angel,' he said once they were alone. 'I am weeping out of repentance.'

'For what?' she asked.

As she said this, she leaned her head back on her pillow and lay still, saying nothing of what she was suffering so as not to alarm her husband: a maternal, angelic, essentially womanly expression of delicacy. There was a long silence. Jules, believing Clémence to be asleep, went to question Joséphine on the state of her mistress's health.

'Madame was in a state of collapse when she came in, Monsieur. We sent for Dr Haudry.'

'He came, did he? And what did he say?'

'Nothing, Monsieur. He didn't look pleased, ordered that

no one should go to Madame except the nurse and said he would return sometime this evening.'

Monsieur Jules went quietly back to his wife's bedroom, sat down in an armchair in front of the bed, and remained there without moving, his gaze fixed on Clémence. When she raised her eyelids she saw him immediately, and from under her sorrowful lashes came a tender, passionate glance, free from reproach or bitterness, a glance which fell like a shaft of fire on the husband magnanimously pardoned and still beloved by the creature he was killing. Each of them was struck with the presentiment that death lay between them. Their regards were united in one common anguish, just as formerly their hearts had been united in one common love, equally felt and equally shared. No questions passed between them, but only a horrible certainty. Perfect generosity in the wife; fearful remorse in the husband; and, deep down in both of them, an identical prevision of the end, an identical feeling of fatality.

There was a moment when Jules, thinking his wife to be asleep, softly kissed her forehead, and after gazing lengthily at her, said: 'Dear God, leave this angel with me long enough for me to win absolution by a long adoration for the wrong I have done her ... As a daughter, she is sublime; as a wife, what words would be sufficient to praise her?'

Clémence closed her eyes. They were full of tears.

'You are hurting me,' she said with a weak voice.

It was late in the evening. Dr Haudry came and asked the husband to withdraw while he examined her. When he came out of the bedroom, Jules did not ask a single question: a gesture was all he needed.

'Get a second opinion from any colleagues of mine in whom you have the greatest confidence. I could be mistaken.'

'Doctor, tell me the truth. I am a man. I can take it. Moreover, I have the greatest interest in knowing it so that I can settle certain accounts.'

'There is no hope for Madame Jules,' the doctor replied. 'There is some moral complication which has gone very far and makes the physical condition more complex; this is dangerous already, but it is rendered still more grave by her imprudent actions: walking about barefoot at night; going out when I had forbidden it; leaving the house yesterday on foot and today in her carriage. She was bent on killing herself. However, my verdict is not irrevocable. She is young and has an astonishing reserve of nervous strength ... One might have to stake everything on some nervous reagent, but I will never take it upon myself to prescribe it, and would even advise against it if I were consulted. I would in fact object to its being used.'

Jules re-entered the room. For eleven days and nights he stayed at his wife's bedside, sleeping only during the day, with his head leaning against the foot of the bed. Never did any man carry jealous care and fanatical devotion further than Jules. He would not allow anyone else to render the slightest service to his wife; he was for ever clasping her hand in his as if he were thus trying to transfuse life into her. There were times of uncertainty, moments of ill-founded joy, good days, improvements, crises, in short the horrible changes for worse or better with which death, hesitant, wavering this way and that, strikes men and women down. Madame Jules always mustered enough strength to give her husband a smile: she was sorry for him, well knowing that soon he would be alone. It was a two-fold agony: both life and love in the throes; but life was draining weakly away while love was waxing in strength. There was one terrible night when Clémence passed through the delirium which always precedes death with young creatures. She spoke of her happy love, she spoke of her father, told Jules of the revelations her mother had made to her on her death-bed and the obligations her mother had imposed on her. Clémence was at odds, not with life, but with her passionate attachment to Jules which she was unwilling to renounce.

'Dear God,' she said, 'don't let him know that I would prefer that he should die with me.' – Unable to endure all this, Jules was in the neighbouring room at that moment and did not hear this avowal; otherwise he would have made it come true.

This crisis passed over and Madame Jules recovered strength. The next day she was once more beautiful and calm. She chatted, was hopeful, decked herself out as sick people do. Then she wanted to be alone for a whole day and insisted on her husband's absence with the urgent beseeching to which one accedes as one accedes to the pleas of children. For that matter, Monsieur Jules needed some respite that day. He went to see Monsieur de Maulincour to demand the duel to the death to which they had recently agreed. He had great difficulty in reaching the author of all these troubles; but when the Vidame de Pamiers realized that an affair of honour was in question he yielded to the prejudices which had governed his whole life and let Jules have access to the baron. Monsieur Desmarets looked round, perplexedly, for the Baron de Maulincour.

'This is he,' said the commander, pointing to a man sitting in an armchair near the fire.

'Who is this Jules?' the dying man asked in quavering tones.

Auguste had lost the only faculty which keeps us alive: memory. Monsieur Desmarets recoiled at the sight of him. He could not recognize the elegant young man in a thing which has no name in any language, to borrow Bossuet's phrase. He was in fact a corpse: white hair, bones poking through wrinkled, parched, desiccated skin; blank, unthinking eyes; a hideously gaping mouth, like those of idiots or rakes killed by their excesses. No trace of intelligence remained either on his forehead or in any of his features; nor was there, in his flaccid flesh tints, any flush or semblance of blood in circulation. In short, he was a man in reduced and shrunken condition, one who had degenerated to the condition of monsters pickled in jars of alcohol and preserved in a museum. Over his face Jules imagined he saw the fearsome face of Ferragus: vengeance incarnate putting even hatred to flight. The husband of Clémence found pity in his heart for the dubious debris of what had once been a young man.

'The duel is over,' said the commander.

Jules replied in anguish: 'He has brought about the death of many people.'

'Also people dear to him,' the old man added. 'His grand-mother is dying of grief. I don't suppose I shall be long following her to the grave.'

The day after this visit, Madame Jules grew hourly worse and worse. She took advantage of a moment of renewed energy to remove a letter from under her bolster, offered it impetuously to Jules and made a gesture which he easily understood. She tried to give him a last kiss with her dying breath; he took it as she died. Jules fell down in a dead faint and was taken to his brother's house. There, as he was lamenting, in tears and delirium, the fact of having been away from his wife's bedroom the day before, his brother informed him that this separation had been keenly desired by Clémence, who had not wished him to witness the religious rites, so terrifying to the imagination of tender souls, which the Church practises as it administers the last sacraments to the dying.

'You wouldn't have got over it,' his brother said. 'I couldn't stand it myself and everybody was in tears. Clémence was like a saint. She had gained strength enough to say good-bye to us, and it was heart-rending to hear the last accents of her voice. When she asked forgiveness for the pain she might have given involuntarily to those who had tended her, there was a cry mingled with sobs, a cry . . . '

'Tell me no more,' said Jules. 'No more.'

He wanted to be alone to read the last thoughts of this woman who had been admired in society, this woman who had faded like a flower.

My beloved. This is my last will and testament. Why should there not be testaments for the treasures of the heart as well as for worldly goods? Was not my love all that I had to bequeath? My love is here my sole concern: all your Clémence possessed, and all she can leave you as she dies. Jules, you still love me and I die happy. The doctors may explain my death in their own way. I alone know the true cause of it, and I will tell it you, even though it will grieve you. I would not wish to carry away in my heart – entirely yours – an undivulged secret, seeing that I myself die the victim of a secret which I was obliged to keep.

Jules, I was born and brought up in the deepest solitude, far from the vice and deceit of the world, by the good woman you knew. Society did justice to her conventional qualities, those by which a woman gains approval in society. But I myself was privileged to enjoy communion with a celestial soul and cherish a mother who gave me a childhood of unalloyed bliss – and I was well aware why she was so dear to me. Was not this a truly reciprocal love? Yes, I loved her, feared her, respected her; but none of that weighed on my heart, neither respect nor fear. She was all in all for me, I was all in all for her. For nineteen years – happy, carefree years – my soul, solitary in the midst of society rumbling around me, reflected only the purest image, my mother's image, and my heart only beat through or for her. I was scrupulously pious and took pleasure in remaining pure in God's sight. My mother encouraged the growth of all noble and proud feelings in me. Oh Jules, what pleasure it gives me to confess what I now avow to you: I came to you as a virgin-hearted girl. When I came out of the deep solitude in which I had lived; when for the first time I brushed out my hair and decked it with a garland of almond blossom; when with some self-complacency I added a few satin knots to my white dress, thinking of the society I was about to enter, and was curious to enter, well, Jules, this innocent and modest coquetry was for you because, at my *début* in society, you were the first person my eyes lit upon. I saw your face. It stood out among all other faces. I liked the look of you. Your voice and manner gave me a favourable promise. And when you came and spoke to me, blushingly and with trembling voice, it was a moment the memory of which still thrills me as I write to you today, now that I am thinking of it for the last time. Our love consisted at first in the liveliest fellow-feeling, and we soon divined it in each other; then it was immediately shared, just as since then we have both of us equally shared the innumerable pleasures it gave. From that time onwards my mother took second place in my heart. I told her so, and she smiled, adorable woman that she was! Then I became yours, all yours. That has been my life, the whole of it, dear husband. And this is what I still have to tell you. One evening before my mother died she told me, shedding hot tears the while, the secret of her life. I have loved you very much more since I learned, before the priest was called to give absolution to my mother, that there existed passions condemned by society and the Church. But surely God could not be severe with regard to the sins committed by such tender souls as my mother. The trouble was that the dear angel could not bring herself to repentance. She was very loving, Jules; she was love incarnate. And so I have prayed for her every day and forborne to judge her. It was then that I understood the cause of her passionate maternal tenderness. Then only did I learn that there was a man in Paris who had devoted all his life and love to me; that he liked you and had made your career; that he was a social exile, that he bore a branded name, and that this distressed him more for my sake and for your sake than his own. My mother was his sole consolation, and she was dying: I undertook to take her place. Ardent of soul and uncorrupted in feeling, I thought of nothing else than the happiness of sweetening the bitterness which was souring my mother's last moments, and therefore I promised to go on with this secret work of charity, the charity which flows from the heart. The first time I saw my father was when he was sitting beside my mother's death-bed. When he raised his tear-filled eyes, it was to me he looked to rekindle the hopes that were dying with her. I had sworn, not to lie, but to keep silence: would any woman have broken this silence? That, Jules, was the mistake I made, and I must pay for it with my life. I had not enough faith in you. But it is natural for a woman to be afraid, and more so still for a woman who knows all she stands to lose. I trembled for my love. I thought that the secret about my father would put an end to my happiness. The more I loved you the more I feared. I did not dare confess this feeling to my father: it would have caused him excruciating pain in such a situation. But he shared my fears without telling me so. His paternal heart was as concerned for my happiness as I was myself; but he dared not speak, thanks to the same delicacy as that which sealed my lips.

Yes, Jules, I thought that the day might come when you might no longer love the daughter of Gratien as much as you loved your Clémence. If I had not been haunted by this profound terror, would I have hidden anything from you, from you who reigned in the innermost recesses of my heart? The day when that miserable, that odious officer spoke to you, I was forced to lie. That was the second day in my life when I knew what it was to suffer, and this suffering has gone on increasingly until now, when I am talking to you for the last time. What does my father's situation matter to me now? You know everything. With my love helping me, I could have overcome sickness, endured all sufferings: but never could I have stifled the voice of doubt. Could not your knowledge of my antecedents adulterate, weaken, diminish the purity of your love? Nothing henceforward can relieve me of this fear.

This, Jules, is the cause of my death. I could not live in constant fear of hearing a certain word, of receiving a certain look: a word that perhaps you will never utter, a look that you will never give; but none the less I should fear they might come. What consoles me is that I shall die still loved. I have learnt that, during the last four years, my father and his friends have almost over-turned society in order to hoodwink it. In order to provide me with status, they bought a dead man, a reputation, a fortune – and all that in order to revive a living person, all that for you, for us. We were not supposed to know anything about it. Well, no doubt my death will spare my father this piece of fraudulence: it will die with my death. Good-bye then, Jules; I have laid my heart bare to you. To unfold my love in the innocence of its terror, is not this indeed giving my soul to you? I had not the strength to talk to you of all this, but I have had the strength to write it. I have just confessed to God the misdeeds of my life. I have cer-tainly vowed to think henceforth only of the King of Heaven; but I could not deny myself the bliss of confessing also to the person who, for me, is everything on earth. Who for pity's sake would not forgive this last sigh from one who is passing from life as it is to the life which is to come? Good-bye then, my beloved Jules, I am going home to God, in whose presence love is for ever unclouded, to whose presence you too will come one day. There, at the foot of his throne for ever united, we shall love each other for all eternity. This hope is my only solace. If I am worthy of being there before you, from there I shall watch you throughout your life, my soul will keep company with yours and be wrapped around you – for you will still be here below. Let your life then be saintly so that you may be sure of returning to me. You can do so much good on earth! Is it not an angelic mission for one who suffers to spread joy around him and to give what it does not itself possess? I bequeath you to those who are unhappy on earth. I shall not be jealous of their smiles and tears. We shall find great charm in such sweet beneficence. Shall we not be able still to live together as one if you associate my name, your Clém-ence's name, with the good you do? After having loved as we have loved, God alone remains, my Jules. God lies not nor deceives. That henceforth you should adore Him alone is what I wish. Worship Him in all people who suffer, give solace to the aching limbs of His body the Church. Good-bye, dear soul whose soul

I have filled. I know you well: you will not love a second time.
So then I shall die happy with the thought that makes all wives
happy. Your heart will be my shrine. Ever since my childhood,
which I told you about, has not my life slid by in your heart?
When I am dead you will never banish me from it. I am proud
to live on in this way. You will have known me only in the flower
of youth: I leave you regret, but not disenchantment. This, Jules,
is a happy death.

You who have understood me so well, allow me to recommend –
no doubt this is superfluous – the satisfaction of a woman's whim,
of a jealous desire to which we are subject: I beg you to burn
everything which has belonged to us in common, to destroy our
bedroom, to annihilate anything which may subsist as a souvenir
of our love.

Once more adieu, a last adieu, brimming over with love, as my
last thought and dying breath will be.

When Jules had finished reading this letter, his heart was
seized with the kind of frenzy whose violent attacks it is
impossible to describe. Any access of grief is personal and its
effect is subject to no fixed rule. Some men stop up their ears
so that they may hear nothing more. Some women shut their
eyes so that they may see nothing more; but there are great
and magnificent souls who plunge into grief as they might into an abyss. Despair may manifest itself in many different ways.
Jules fled from his brother's house, returned home wishing
to spend the night beside his wife and gaze on this celestial
creature till the last possible moment. As he walked along
with the listlessness of people who have reached the ultimate
degree of unhappiness, he understood why, in Asia, the laws
ordain that husbands and wives shall not survive one another.
He wanted to die. He was not yet completely overwhelmed
but was in a fever of grief. He managed to get back home and
walked upstairs to the sacred room, and there he saw his
Clémence on her death-bed, beautiful as a saint, her hair
parted down the middle, her hands joined, wrapped in her
shroud. A priest was praying in the light of the candles.
Joséphine, on her knees, was weeping in a corner, and near
the bed were two men. One was Ferragus. He was standing
upright and still, contemplating his daughter with dry eyes.

One would have thought his head was a bronze; he did not see Jules. The other was Jacquet, Jacquet to whom Madame Jules had been unfailingly kind. He had felt for her one of those respectful friendships which bring, not agitation, but joy to the heart, which are a mild sort of passion: love minus its lusts and storms; and he had come piously to pay his debt of tears, to say a long farewell to his friend's wife, to imprint a first kiss on the icy forehead of a creature he had tacitly treated as a sister. The silence was complete. It was neither death with its terrors as in a church, nor death in its pomp as it proceeds through the streets. No, it was death gliding under the domestic roof, death at its most touching; the funeral rites of the heart, tears concealed from all outsiders. Jules sat down beside Jacquet and pressed his hand; and without saying one word to one another, all the actors on this stage remained thus until morning. When the candlelight paled in the light of day Jacquet, foreseeing the painful scenes which were bound to ensue, took Jules into the next room. At this moment the husband looked at the father and the father looked at Jules. The two kinds of grief questioned and probed each other, fathomed each other with a look. A passing gleam of fury lit up Ferragus's eyes.

'You it is who have killed her,' he was thinking.

'Why could you not have trusted me?' the husband seemed to be replying. The scene was like one which might be enacted by two tigers recognizing the uselessness of combat after glaring at each other for a hesitant moment, without even roaring.

'Jacquet,' asked Jules, 'have you seen about everything?'

'Everything,' the civil servant replied. 'But in every matter I was forestalled by a man who ordered and paid for everything.'

'He is snatching his daughter from me,' the husband cried out in a violent fit of despair.

He rushed into his wife's bedroom, but the father had left. Clémence had been placed in a lead coffin and undertakers were about to fasten down the lid. Jules ran out, horrified at the sight of this, and the noise of the men hammering made him burst spontaneously into tears.

'Jacquet,' he cried, 'one idea remains in my head after this terrible night: one sole idea, but one I want to carry out at all cost. I don't want Clémence to remain in a Paris cemetery. I want to have her cremated, to gather her ashes and keep them. Don't say a word to me about this matter: just make the necessary arrangements. I am going to shut myself up in *her* room until it's time to go. You alone will come in there to tell me what steps you have taken ... Go, spare no effort or expense.'

In the course of that morning Madame Jules, after being exposed in a mortuary chapel at the door of her house, was taken to Saint-Roch. The church was completely draped with black. The kind of luxury displayed for this service had brought a crowd together, for in Paris everything provides a spectacle, even the most heartfelt grief. There are people who stand at their windows in order to see how a son weeps as he walks behind his mother's corpse, just as there are people who like to be conveniently placed in order to see a head chopped off. No nation in the world has ever had more avid eyes. But curious people were particularly surprised to see the side-chapels in Saint-Roch also draped with black. Two men in mourning apparel were attending a requiem mass in every one of these chapels. The only attendants in the sanctuary were Monsieur Desmarets, the notary and Jacquet; and then, outside the enclosure, the servants. The sightseers in the church found something inexplicable in so much ceremony and so few relatives present. Jules had wanted no casual persons to be present. High Mass was celebrated with the sombre magnificence which characterizes funeral masses. In addition to the ordinary Saint-Roch celebrants there were thirteen priests from various other parishes. In consequence, never perhaps did the *Dies Irae* produce on chance worshippers, fortuitously assembled through curiosity but avid for emotion, a more profound effect, one more chilling to the nerves, than the impression created by this hymn at the moment when the voices of eight cantors, accompanied by those of the priests and the choristers, sang it in alternate verses. From six side-chapels twelve other choirboys' voices rose shrill with grief and mingled their lamentations with those of the rest. From every part of the church religious awe surged up; everywhere murmurs of anguish responded to murmurs of terror. This frightening music told of grief unknown to the world and of secret friendships mourning for the dead woman. Never, in any religion of mankind, have the fears which assail the soul when violently torn from the body and tempestuously tossed into the presence of the fulminating majesty of God been so vigorously rendered. Before this clamour of clamours artists and their most impassioned compositions must bow down in humility. Nothing can compete with this great canticle which sums up human passions, galvanizes them into life beyond the coffin and brings them, still palpitating, before the living and avenging God. These cries of infancy mingling with the grave tones of maturity to embrace all stages of human life in this canticle of death, recalling the sufferings of the cradle, swelling in volume with all the pains of succeeding ages in the broad accents of grown men, the quaverings of old men and priests: does not all this strident harmony, resonant with thunder and lightning, speak compellingly to the most intrepid imaginations, the iciest of hearts – and even to philosophers! As one listens, it seems as if this is the thunder of the Almighty. The vaults of no church are unresponsive: they shudder, they speak, they pour forth fear through all the mighty resonance of their echoes. It is as if you saw the numberless dead standing forth and lifting their hands: not merely a father, a wife, a child under the black pall, but all mankind emerging from the dust. You cannot judge the Catholic, Apostolic and Roman religion until you have experienced the profoundest of griefs by weeping for the beloved person lying under the pall, until you have run the gamut of all the emotions then filling your heart, translated into this hymn of despair, these soul-shattering cries, this religious terror which increases as one strophe succeeds another, which swirls up to heaven, which appals, shrivels and yet lifts the soul and leaves the realization of eternity in your soul at the moment when the last line comes to an end. You have been at grips with the grandiose idea of eternity: a great silence fills the church. No further word is spoken; even incredulous people are nonplussed. The Spanish genius alone was capable of conceiving such unheard-of majesty for the most unheard-of griefs.

When the last rite was accomplished, twelve men in deep mourning emerged from the six chapels and gathered round the coffin in order to listen to the song of hope which the Church sings to the Christian soul before committing the human body to the grave. Then each one of these men climbed into a carriage draped in black; Jacquet and Monsieur Desmarets took the thirteenth one; the servants followed on foot. An hour later, the twelve unknown persons[4] were standing on the summit of the cemetery popularly known as Père-Lachaise in a circle around a grave into which the coffin had been lowered in the sight of an inquisitive crowd which had gathered from every direction in this public garden. After a few short prayers the priest threw a handful of soil on the remains of this woman. Then the gravediggers, having asked for their gratuity, hurriedly filled up the grave in order to proceed to another one.

*

Here, it might seem, ends our story. But it would perhaps remain unfinished if, after giving a slight sketch of Parisian life or if, after we have followed its whimsical twists and turns, we forgot to record what follows after death.

Death in Paris is not like death in any other capital. Few people know what a fight real grief may have to wage with 'civilization', that is to say with the administrative authorities of Paris. Besides, Monsieur Jules Desmarets and Ferragus XXIII may have interested the reader enough for him not to be indifferent about what happened to them after this catastrophe. Many people indeed like to clear everything up and would wish, as the most ingenious of our critics has said, to know by what chemical process the oil burns in Aladdin's lamp. Jacquet, being a public functionary, naturally applied

4. Evidently members of the Thirteen – Ferragus being the thirteenth.

to the authorities for permission to exhume Madame Jules's body for cremation. He went to the Prefect of Police, whose business it is to take the dead under his wing. This official required a formal petition. A sheet of stamped paper had to be produced and private grief had to be provided with an administrative formula. Bureaucratic jargon had to be used in order to express the wishes of a broken-hearted man who had no words at his command; it was necessary to make a cold translation of and add a marginal note to the object of the petition:

'The petitioner requests that his wife's remains may be cremated.'

Whereupon the official whose business it was to make a report to the Councillor of State, the Prefect of Police, said, when he read this apostil in which the object of the request was (in accordance with his recommendation) clearly expressed: 'But this is a serious question! It will take a week before my report is ready.'

Jules, whom Jacquet was obliged to inform of this postponement, now understood the phrase which Ferragus had used: 'I would burn down Paris!' Nothing seemed to him more natural than to annihilate this repository of monstrosities.

'But,' he said to Jacquet, 'you must go to the Home Secretary and get your Minister to talk to him.'

Jacquet went to the Home Secretary and asked for an audience, but was only granted it a fortnight hence. Jacquet was a persistent man. And so he plodded from bureau to bureau and got through to the private secretary of the Minister, to whom the case was put by the private secretary of the Minister for Foreign Affairs. With the aid of these important personages he obtained a furtive audience for the following day, having provided himself with a note written by the autocrat for Foreign Affairs to the Pasha of the Home Office. Jacquet hoped to carry the position by storm. He prepared his case, marshalled some irrefutable arguments – with others to fall back on – but to no avail.

'It's no business of mine,' said the Minister. 'It's a matter for the Prefect of Police. In any case, there's no law which grants husbands the ownership of their wives' bodies or fathers those of their children. It's a serious matter! Also there are considerations of public utility which require that the question be well looked into. The interests of the city of Paris might be involved. In short, even if the matter depended immediately on me, I could not make a *hic et nunc* decision: a report would have to be drawn up.'

A 'report' in present administrative procedure is like 'limbo' in Christian mythology. Jacquet was well up as regards the report mania, and on previous occasions had complained of this bureaucratic absurdity. He well knew that, since the 'report' had made its way into affairs – an administrative revolution which had been consummated in 1804 – there had been no Minister who had taken it upon himself to form an opinion, to make the slightest ruling without that opinion or ruling being winnowed, riddled, sifted by the scribblers, pen-pushers and sublime intelligences operating in his bureaux. Jacquet (a kind of man worthy to have had Plutarch as his biographer) recognized the fact that he had gone about this business in the wrong way and ruined the case by following normal procedure. What he should have done was to deliver Madame Jules over to one of Desmarets's country estates, where he could have had his friend's grief satisfied under the indulgent authority of a village mayor. Constitutional and administrative legality yields no results;[5] it is a sterile monster for peoples, monarchs and private interests, but peoples are only able to spell out principles which are written in blood; nowadays the misfortunes produced by legality will always be pacific ones; legality simply irons out a nation. Jacquet, himself a champion of liberty, came away on that occasion with a mind conscious of the benefits of arbitrary rule, for man judges laws only in the glimmer shed by his passions. Then, when he found himself in Jules's presence, he had no option but to deceive

5. Balzac had a great contempt for the kind of constitutional government which the accession of Louis-Philippe in 1830 had ushered in, and also for the bureaucratic administration which, in his estimation, it implied.

him, and the unhappy man, taken with a violent fever, remained two days in bed. That very evening, at a Ministerial dinner, the Minister spoke of the whimsy a Parisian had had to have his wife burnt in Roman manner. As a result of this, social circles in Paris became momentarily interested in antique funerals. Ancient things were coming into fashion, and a few people thought it would be a fine thing to re-establish the funeral pyre for great personages. This opinion had its detractors and its defenders. Some said that there were too many great men, that such a practice would send up the price of firewood, that with a people so inclined to ambulatory whims as the French, it would be ridiculous to see, on every important occasion, a procession of forefathers being carried about in their urns; and also that, if these urns had any value, there was a likelihood that, being full of venerable ashes, they might be put under distraint by creditors, people who have acquired the habit of respecting nothing. The opposite side answered that ancestors thus stowed away would be in greater security than at Père-Lachaise, for the time would come when the city of Paris would be obliged to order a Saint Barthelemy massacre of its dead who were invading the countryside and threatening sooner or later to encroach on the territory of Brie. In short, there occurred one of those futile and witty Paris discussions which, only too often, inflict penetrating wounds. Happily for Jules, he knew nothing of the conversations, witticisms and epigrams which his grief was providing for people in Paris. The Prefect of Paris was shocked because Monsieur Jacquet had dragged the Minister into this in order to avoid the delays and circumspection of the Highways Department – for indeed Madame Jules's exhumation was a matter pertaining to that department. In consequence the Police Bureau worked for a terse response to be given to the petition: it is sufficient for a request to be made for the administrative machine to be brought into action, and once that has happened, there's a long way to go. The administration can take any question as far as the Council of State, another machine which it is difficult to set in motion. The second day, Jacquet intimated to his friend that he would have to abandon his project; that in a city where a levy was imposed even on the number of tears embroidered on funeral palls, where the law sanctioned seven classes of burials, where soil for the dead cost its weight in silver, where grief was exploited at every turn, where the prayers of the Church cost dear, where the parish council intervened to claim payment for a thin trickle of voices added to the *Dies Irae*, anything departing from the administrative track was impossible.

'It would have been,' said Jules, 'a consolation in my misery. I had planned to die far away from here and yearned to hold Clémence in my arms in the grave. I did not know that bureaucracy could thrust its tentacles even into our coffins.'

Then he tried to find out if there was any room for him by his wife's side, and so the two friends betook themselves to the cemetery. On arriving, they found, as at the doors of theatres or the entry to museums or stage-coach stations, cicerones who offered to guide them through the labyrinth of Père-Lachaise. Neither of them, to their infinite distress, could find out where the body of Clémence lay. They went and consulted the cemetery porter. For the dead have a concierge and there are certain times when they are 'not at home'. One would have to upset all major and minor police regulations to obtain the right to go at night, in silence and solitude, to weep at the tomb where a loved one lies. There are regulations for summer and regulations for winter. Assuredly, of all Paris porters, the one at Père-Lachaise is the luckiest. To begin with, there is no bell-rope to pull. Secondly, in lieu of a lodge, there is a house, an establishment which is not altogether a civil service office, although it contains a large number of civil service and government employees, and although this governor of the dead draws a salary and wields a tremendous authority of which no one can complain: he can be arbitrary *ad libitum*. Nor is his lodge a business centre, although it has its offices, its accountancy, receipts, expenses and profits departments. This man is neither door-keeper, concierge nor porter; the door through which the dead are admitted is always gaping wide; moreover, although he has custody of monuments, he is not a custodian; in short he is an undefinable anomaly, an authority who has a hand in everything and yet is nothing, an authority situated, like the death it feeds on, outside the normal run of things. Nevertheless this exceptional man is answerable to the city of Paris, itself a chimerical being like the ship which serves as its emblem, a chimerical creation moving along on its thousand feet though rarely in one direction, with the result that its employees are practically irremovable. So the cemetery-keeper is a concierge who has risen to the status of a civil servant, and dissolution cannot dissolve him. Moreover his post is no sinecure. He allows nobody to be buried without a licence. He has to keep account of his dead. He marks out in this vast graveyard the six square feet into which you shall one day sink everything you love, everything you hate: a mistress? a cousin? Know this in fact: all kinds of sentiment in Paris reach his lodge in the end and there they are administrationalized! This man has his registers in which to lay his dead to rest: they lie both in their tombs and in his filing cases. He has under-keepers, gardeners, gravediggers and their assistants at his command. Weeping relations cannot speak with him directly. He only puts in an appearance in serious cases: one dead person confused with another, one who has been murdered, an exhumation, a resuscitation. The reigning king's bust stands in his hall, and perhaps he keeps older busts – royal, imperial, quasi-royal – in some cupboard, a sort of Père-Lachaise for fallen régimes. Lastly, he's a public man, an excellent man, a kind father and good husband, no matter what the epitaphs say. But so many diverse sentiments have filed along before him in the guise of a funeral procession; he has seen so many tears, true or false; he has gazed on grief in so many aspects and putting on so many faces; he has taken stock of millions of expressions of eternal grief! For him, grief means nothing more than a tomb-stone one inch thick, four feet high and two feet wide. As for *regrets*, they are his occupational vexations; he never lunches or dines without passing under a shower of inconsolable lamentation. As concerns all other afflictions he is kind and tender. He will weep over some hero of drama, over Monsieur de Germeuil in *L'Auberge des Adrets*, the man in the butter-yellow breeches murdered by Robert Macaire. But his heart has become ossified with regard to real dead people. They are just numbers for him. It is his trade to put death in order. All the same, three times in one century a situation occurs in which his role becomes sublime, continuously sublime: in times of pestilence!

When Jacquet accosted him, this absolute monarch was giving vent to something like rage.

'I had given orders,' he was saying to his subordinates, 'for flowers to be strewn from the Rue Masséna to the Place Regnault de Saint-Jean-d'Angély! A lot of notice you took, the pack of you! Dammit! If the relations take it into their heads to come along this fine day, I shall get the blame. They'll cry out like scalded cats, say horrible things about us and our names will be mud!'

'Monsieur,' Jacquet said to him, 'we wish to know where Madame Jules is buried.'

'Which Madame Jules?' he asked, 'we've had three Madame Jules in the last week.'

'Ah!' he said to an assistant, breaking off and looking through the gate. 'Here comes Colonel de Maulincour's funeral procession. Go and ask for the burial licence ... a fine procession, my word,' he continued. 'He followed close on his grandmother. There are some families in which they come rolling down as if they'd made a bet. They get so worked up, these Parisians.'

'Monsieur,' said Jacquet tapping him on the arm, 'the person I am talking about is Madame Jules Desmarets, the stockbroker's wife.'

'Ah yes,' he answered with a look at Jacquet. 'Wasn't it a funeral with thirteen mourning carriages and only one relation in each of the twelve first ones? It was so queer we were struck by it.'

'Take care, Monsieur. Monsieur Jules is with me and he might hear you. What you are saying is not very tactful.'

'Beg pardon, Monsieur. You are right. Excuse me. I took you for the heirs.'

'Monsieur,' he went on, consulting a plan of the cemetery. 'Madame Jules is in the Rue du Maréchal Lefebvre, alley No. 4, between Mademoiselle Raucourt of the Comédie-Française and Monsieur Moreau-Malvin, a hefty butcher. They've ordered a white marble stone for him, and it will certainly be one of the finest in the cemetery.'

'Monsieur,' said Jacquet, interrupting the porter. 'We are no wiser than before.'

'True enough,' he replied, looking all round him. 'Jean,' he shouted to a man whom he had sighted, 'take these gentlemen to the grave of Madame Jules, the stockbroker's wife. You know – near Mademoiselle Raucourt, the grave with a bust over it.'

The two friends walked along under the guidance of one of the keepers, but they did not reach the steep path leading to the upper alley of the cemetery without suffering from twenty propositions made to them with honied unctuousness by stone-masons, iron-smiths and monument-sculptors. 'If the gentleman wished to have some little construction put up, we could give him a very cheap estimate . . .'

Jacquet managed to spare his friend such phrases, which are excruciating to bleeding hearts, and they arrived at Clémence's resting-place. Seeing the recently removed earth in which masons had thrust pegs in order to mark the place for the stone blocks needed for the setting of the railing, Jules leaned on Jacquet's shoulder, but straightened up now and then in order to gaze lingeringly on this patch of clay into which he had had to consign the remains of the being in and through whom he was still living.

'What a horrible place for her to be in!' he said.

'But she's not there,' Jacquet replied. 'She lives in your memory. Come along, old friend. Leave this odious cemetery where the dead are dolled up like women at a ball.'

'Suppose we took her away?'

'Could it be done?'

'Anything could be done!' Jules exclaimed. And then he

added, after a pause. 'I suppose I shall come here. There's room enough.'

Jacquet succeeded in coaxing him away from this enclosure divided like a draught-board by bronze grilles, by elegant compartments in which were confined funereal monuments all enriched with palms, inscriptions, tears as cold as the tombstones which heartbroken people had used for the sculpturing of their regrets and lamentations. There you will find epigrams in black engraving aimed at inquisitive sightseers, *concetti*, witty farewells, rendezvous for the future which only one person would wish to keep, hypocritical biographies: tinsel, tatters, spangles. Here are thyrsi, there lance-heads, and further off Egyptian urns; here and there cannons; everywhere are the emblems of a thousand professions; also every variety of style: Moresque, Grecian, Gothic; friezes, ovolos, paintings, urns, genies, temples; a large number of faded everlasting flowers and dead rose-trees. An infamous piece of pretension! Paris again with its streets, shop-signs, industries and mansions as seen through diminishing spectacles: a microscopic Paris reduced to the tiny dimensions of shades, ghosts, dead people – a humankind which has nothing great left in it but its vanity. After that Jules perceived at his feet, in the long valley of the Seine, between the slopes of Vaugirard and Meudon, those of Belleville and Montmartre, the real Paris, wrapped in the dirty blue veil engendered by its smoke, at that moment diaphanous in the sunlight. He threw a furtive glance over its forty thousand habitations and said, sweeping his arm over the space between the column of the Place Vendôme and the gilded cupola of the Invalides: 'There it is that she was stolen from me, thanks to the baneful inquisitiveness of this crowd of people which mills and mulls about for the mere pleasure of milling and mulling about.'

*

Four leagues away, on the bank of the Seine, in a modest village squatting on one of the slopes dependent on the long hilly enclosure in the midst of which great Paris stirs its limbs like a baby in its cradle, a scene of death and sorrow was being enacted: but it was one from which all the pomp normal to Paris was missing: no torches or tapers, no draped carriages, no Catholic prayers: death in all its simplicity. Early one morning a girl's body had been washed up on the bank of the Seine in its mud and reeds. Workmen extracting sand had noticed it as they climbed into their fragile skiff.

'Look,' said one of them. 'Here's fifty francs for us.'

'True enough,' said the other. They rowed over to the dead woman.

'It's a very good-looking girl.'

'Let's go and report it.' The two sand-workers, after throwing their jackets over the dead body, went to the village mayor, who felt quite embarrassed at having to report this discovery.

The news of this event spread round with the telegraphic promptitude peculiar to those districts where the grapevine functions uninterruptedly; where slander, gossip, calumny and the chatter society feeds on flow on from one end to the other. People coming to the *mairie* immediately relieved the mayor of all embarrassment. They reduced the official report to a simple statement of decease. Thanks to their testimony, the girl's body was recognized as being that of Mademoiselle Ida Gruget, corset-maker, domiciled in the Rue Corderie-du-Temple, No. 14. The judicial police intervened, and Widow Gruget, mother of the deceased, came forward, armed with her daughter's last letter. In the midst of the mother's wailings, a doctor diagnosed asphyxia caused by the invasion of black blood into the pulmonary system, and that was it. After these inquiries and reports, authorization was given for the young woman to be buried at six o'clock that evening. The priest refused to allow her body into the church and to pray for her. And so Ida Gruget was wrapped in a shroud by an old peasant woman, put into a common deal coffin and taken to the cemetery by four men followed by a few inquisitive peasant women who chattered about this death with a mixture of surprise and commiseration. Widow Gruget was charitably held back by an old lady who prevented her from following her daughter's funeral procession. A man with three functions: bell-ringer, verger and gravedigger, had dug a grave in the half-acre cemetery behind the church. It was a usual sort of church, adorned with a square tower with slate-covered pointed roof, supported from outside by angular abutments. Behind the rounded apse was the cemetery with decrepit walls around it, a graveyard full of hillocks: no marble monuments, no visitors, but undoubtedly each mound recorded real tears and regrets. Ida Gruget could have no part in these. She was thrown into a corner in the middle of brambles and tall weeds. When the coffin was let down into the grave so poetic in its simplicity, the gravedigger suddenly found himself alone as night fell. As he filled in the grave, he stopped every now and then to look along the path above the wall. A moment occurred when, as his hand leaned on his pick, his glance wandered over the Seine which had carried this corpse to him.

'Poor girl!' exclaimed a man who had suddenly come into view.

'You startled me, Monsieur,' said the gravedigger.

'Was no service held for the woman you are burying?'

'No, Monsieur. The Curé refused. She is the first woman not belonging to the parish to be buried here. Here everybody knows everybody else. Does Monsieur ... ? Well I'm blowed, he's gone!'

*

Some days had elapsed when a man in black presented himself at the house of Monsieur Jules and, without engaging him in speech, placed in his wife's bedroom a large porphyry urn. On it Jules read the following inscription:

INVITA LEGE,
CONJUGI MOERENTI
FILIOLAE CINERES
RESTITUIT
AMICIS XII JUVANTIBUS
MORIBUNDUS PATER[6]

6. 'In defiance of the law, a dying father, with the aid of twelve friends, has restored the ashes of his beloved daughter to her mourning husband.'

'What a man!' said Jules, melting into tears. Within a week the stockbroker had complied with his wife's last wishes and set his affairs in order. He sold his practice to the brother of Martin Falleix and left Paris while the civic authorities were still debating whether a citizen could legitimately dispose of his wife's dead body.

CONCLUSION

Which of us has not met on the boulevards of Paris, under the arcades of the Palais-Royal, or at any other spot where chance may take him, a human being of either sex at the sight of whom a host of confused ideas come to the mind? As we look at him or her our interest is suddenly aroused either by features whose quaint structure bespeaks agitated life or by the curious *ensemble* resulting from gestures, demeanour, gait or clothing, or from a depth of gaze or some other indefinable characteristics which make an immediate and strong impression on us without our being able to explain very precisely the cause of our emotion. Then, the very next day, other thoughts and other Parisian figures sweep away the fleeting dream. But if we meet the same person again, passing by perhaps at a fixed time like a town-hall clerk who spends eight hours a day officiating at marriage ceremonies, or wandering through the promenades like the people who seem to be part of the street furniture of Paris and are always to be found in public places, in the theatres on first nights or in the restaurants to which they lend adornment, then this creature takes up a permanent abode in your memory and stays in it like the first volume of a novel whose ending you do not yet know. We are tempted to question this individual and ask him: 'Who are you? Why are you wandering about? What right have you to a pleated collar, an ivory-headed cane and a faded waistcoat? Why those blue spectacles with double lenses? Or why do you wear such an outmoded cravat?' Among these itinerant creatures, some belong to the species of Terminus, the Roman boundary god; they have no meaning for us; they are just simply there – why, no one knows. They are figures like those which serve sculptors as types for the four Seasons, for Commerce and Abundance. Others, retired solicitors, one-time merchants, decrepit generals, look as if they are moving off, are on the way somewhere but always seem to have been stopped short. Like half-uprooted trees on the bank of a river they never seem to be part of the rushing stream of Paris, nor of the young and active Paris crowd. It is impossible to tell if someone has forgotten to inter them, or if they have slipped out of their coffins; they have reached a virtually fossil state.

One of these wandering Melmoths of Paris had in recent days started mingling with the quiet withdrawn population which, on sunny days, inevitably occupies the space enclosed between the south railings of the Luxembourg and the north railings of the Observatoire, a space in Paris which has no sex or gender. There, in fact, Paris has ceased to be; and yet Paris is still there. This place smacks at one and the same time of the city square, the street, the boulevard, the fortification, the garden, the avenue, the highway, the province and the capital; certainly it has something of all that but is nothing of all that: it is a desert. Around this nameless spot rise many buildings: the Foundling Hospital, the Maternity Hospital, the Cochin Hospital, the Capuchin Friars, the La Rochefoucauld Almshouse, the Deaf-and-Dumb Hostel, the Val-de-Grâce Hospital; in short, all the ills and vices of Paris have their sanctuaries there; and in order that nothing shall be lacking to his philanthropic precinct, Science is there studying tides and longitudes; Monsieur de Chateaubriand has installed there the Marie-Thérèse Infirmary and there the Carmelites have founded a convent. The great predicaments of life are represented there by bells which are for ever ringing in this desert: for the mother brought to bed and the child she bears, for vice breathing its last, for the dying workman, the praying virgin, the shivering old man and the erring genius. Also, a few yards away is the Montparnasse cemetery which from hour to hour draws to it the poverty-stricken funeral processions of the Faubourg Saint-Marceau. This esplanade overlooking Paris has been taken over by the bowls players: grey old figures, very good-natured honest folk who continue the traditions of our forefathers and whose physiognomy can only be compared with that of the public which watches them and the moving gallery which follows them.

A man who had moved a few days ago into this sparsely inhabited quarter was an assiduous watcher of these games of bowls and could assuredly pass for the most outstanding creature among those groups who, were one permitted to assimilate Parisians to the different zoological species, would be allotted to the mollusc genus. This newcomer walked sympathetically along with the 'jack', a smaller ball at which the players aim and which is therefore the central point of interest. He used to lean against a tree when the jack came to a halt. Then, with the same attention a dog gives to his master's gestures, he watched the bowls bounding through the air or rolling along the ground. You would have taken him for a creature of fancy – the genie of the jack. He never spoke, and the bowlers, greater fanatics than any you might find in any religious sect, had never asked him to account for this obdurate silence; a few cynics merely supposed that he was deaf and dumb. On occasions when the variable distances between the bowls and the jack had to be determined, this unknown man's walking-stick became an infallible gauge; the bowlers then came and took it from the old man's icy hand without so much as a 'by your leave' and even without any friendly gesture. The loan of his stick was a kind of feudal service to which he had given negative consent. When there came a shower of rain he stayed near the jack, the slave of the bowls, the guardian of the game in progress. Rain did not take him aback any more than fine weather; he was like the players themselves, an intermediary species between the least intelligent Parisian and the most intelligent animal. Moreover, being pale and withered, careless of his person, absent-minded, he often came along bare-headed, showing his white hair and his square-shaped, yellowish, fairly denuded cranium, which looked like a pauper's knee showing through a hole in his trousers. He held his mouth open, he had a vacant look, and he tottered rather than walked along. He never smiled, never looked upward, but kept his eyes continually lowered towards the earth and seemed always to be searching for something in it. At four o'clock an old woman turned up to take him somewhere or other, towing him along by the arm like a girl dragging a wilful goat who still wants to go on grazing when it is time for it to go to its shed. This old man was really quite a distressing sight.

One afternoon Jules, by himself in a travelling barouche which was being smartly driven along the Rue de l'Est, came out on to the esplanade of the Observatoire just as this old man, leaning against a tree, was handing over his walking-stick amid the cries of a few mildly irritated bowlers. Thinking that he recognized the man's face, he wanted to stop, and indeed his carriage did stop. In fact his postilion, with hand carts hemming him in, did not demand that the insurgent bowlers should make way for him: he was too respectful towards rioters, this postilion.

'It is he,' said Jules, realizing in the end that this piece of human wreckage was Ferragus XXIII, chief of the *Dévorants*. 'How he loved her!' he added after a pause ... 'Drive on, postilion!' he cried.

Paris, February 1835

THE DUCHESSE DE LANGEAIS

To Franz Liszt

I

Sister Thérèse

In a Spanish town situated on a Mediterranean island, there
is a convent of Discalced Carmelites in which the rule of the
Order instituted by Saint Teresa has been preserved in all
the primitive austerity of the reform which this illustrious
woman carried out. This is a true fact, extraordinary as it may
seem. Although the religious houses both of the Peninsula
and the Continent were almost all destroyed or overturned
by the outbreak of revolution in France and the Napoleonic
wars, since that island had been continuously protected by
the British navy its wealthy convent and peaceful inmates
remained sheltered from the general disorders and spoliations.
So then the storms of all kinds which disturbed the first
fifteen years of the nineteenth century spent their force against
this rock, one which is quite near to the coast of Andalusia.
If the Emperor's name echoed even on these shores, it is
doubtful whether the fantastic pageantry of his glory and the
flamboyant majesty of his meteoric life were ever comprehensible to the saintly virgins kneeling in their cloister.
Through the Catholic world this house was remembered as a
sanctuary in which conventual austerity had been subjected to
no modification whatsoever. In consequence the purity of its
rule drew to it, from the remotest corners of Europe, saddened women whose souls, released from all human bonds,
yearned for the lingering suicide to be accomplished here in
the bosom of God. No other convent indeed was more favourable to the complete detachment from the things of this world
that the religious life demands. None the less, on the Continent, a great number of such houses are to be found, magni-
ficently designed to meet the purpose for which they had been
constituted. Some of them lie buried in the depths of the most
solitary valleys; others hang over the sheerest mountains or

cling to the verge of precipices. In every case man has craved for the poetry of the infinite and the awesome solemnity of silence. Everywhere he has striven to reach as near as possible to God. He has sought Him out on the heights, in the depths, on the edge of beetling cliffs. He has found Him everywhere. But nowhere more surely than on this rock, half European, half African, could so many varying harmonies have been brought so perfectly into conjunction in order to elevate the soul, to cool its most burning fevers, bring relief to its sharpest anguish and guide its griefs into a deep, calm channel.

This convent stands at the extremity of the island, at the very summit of the cliff, which, thanks to some great terrestrial cataclysm, is cut off sheer on the seaward side, where at every point it presents the sharp ridges of its surfaces, slightly eroded at water-level, but unscaleable by man. This rock is protected from assault by perilous reefs which stretch out far into the sea and on which the bright Mediterranean dashes its foamy billows. So then only from the open sea can one discern the four sections of the square building, whose shape, height and apertures had been meticulously prescribed by conventual regulations. On the town side the church entirely conceals the squat structures of the cloister, whose roofs are covered with broad tiles which completely shield them from wind, tempest and parching sun.

The church, donated by a generous Spanish family, looks over the town. Its bold, elegant façade imparts a great and noble physiognomy to this little maritime citadel. It presents a spectacle imprinted with all the sublime beauty that earth can offer: a town whose serried roofs, mostly grouped to form an amphitheatre facing a pretty harbour, are dominated by a magnificent west front with Gothic triglyph, turrets and spires cut out against the sky: religion dominating life, ceaselessly offering man a goal and the means to achieve it – and all this in a completely Spanish setting! Transport this scene to the heart of the Mediterranean under a burning sky. Add a few palm-trees, a few stunted evergreens mingling their waving tufts of verdure with the sculptured foliage of immobile architecture. Watch the waves fringing the reefs with white foam standing out against the sapphire blue of the waters. Admire the galleries and terraces built over the roof of each house to which the occupants climb up in order to breathe the flower-scented air rising through the tree-tops of their little gardens. There will be a few sails in the harbour. And lastly, in the serene calm of early night, listen to the strains of organ music, the chanting of vespers and the marvellous peal of the bells reaching out over the sea. Everywhere sound, but calm also; calm above all.

The church inside was divided into three dark and mysterious naves. The fury of the waves having doubtless discouraged the architect from building out those flying buttresses which adorn almost all cathedrals and provide space for chapels, the walls flanking the two lateral naves and supporting the shell of the church shed no light at all. These stout walls, seen from outside, showed off their greyish masses supported at intervals on enormous abutments. The great nave and its two small lateral galleries therefore drew their light solely from the stained-glass rose-window, worked in with meticulous artistry above the west front portal, so favourably laid out as to allow the luxury of stone tracery and those details of ornamentation peculiar to the style which is improperly called gothic. The greater part of the three naves was appropriated to the townsfolk who came there to attend mass and other services. In front of the choir was a screen behind which hung a brown curtain with ample folds, slightly parted in the middle so as to allow the faithful the mere view of the altar and the officiating priest. This screen was divided at equal intervals by pillars which held up an inner gallery containing the organ; a construction which, in harmony with the general ornamentation of the church, continued in sculptured wood the little columns of the galleries supported by the pillars of the great nave. And so it would have been impossible for an inquisitive person, even if he had been bold enough to climb to the narrow balustrade of these galleries and look down into the choir, to see anything more than the long, octagonal stained-glass windows rising at regular distances above the high altar.

At the time when the French expeditionary force invaded Spain in order to re-establish the authority of Ferdinand VII, after the capture of Cadiz, a French general who had come to this island in order to enforce recognition of the royal government prolonged his stay there so that he might visit the convent. He even managed to obtain admittance, which was certainly a delicate enterprise. But a man of passion, a man whose life had been, so to speak, nothing but a series of poems in action, a man who had always acted out romances in preference to writing them, a man of deeds above all, was naturally tempted to undertake something apparently impossible. How could he legally contrive that the gates of a convent should be opened to a man? Not even the Pope or the metropolitan archbishop would have sanctioned it. Any recourse to cunning or force, if indiscreetly carried out, would lose him his status, all his military prestige, and result in failure. The Duc d'Angoulême was still in Spain, and of all the improprieties which a man on favourable terms with the generalissimo could have committed with impunity, that one alone would have been pitilessly condemned. The general in question had asked to be sent on this mission in order to satisfy a secret curiosity, although no curiosity ever had less hopes of satisfaction. But it was a matter of conscience for him to make this last attempt. This Carmelite establishment was the only Spanish convent which had eluded his researches. As he crossed over from the mainland – a matter of less than an hour – a favourable presentiment came to him. Moreover, although he had seen nothing of this convent except its walls, had not even caught a glimpse of the nuns' habits and had only heard them singing their offices, he discerned in these walls and the monastic chantings some slight indications which justified a modicum of hope. In short, insubstantial as surmises so oddly grounded might be, never was human passion more violently stirred than was the general's curiosity at that moment. Where the heart is concerned there are no insignificant events: it magnifies all things. It puts on the same scales the fall of an empire and the drop of a woman's glove: in fact the glove is usually found to weigh more than the empire. Let us unveil the facts of this case in all their positive simplicity. After the facts shall come the emotions involved.

One hour after the general had landed on this little isle the royal authority was re-established there. A few of the Spanish constitutionalists, who had taken refuge there the night after the capture of Cadiz, embarked upon a ship that the general allowed them to charter in order to escape to London. So there was neither resistance to nor reaction against this small island restoration. It was celebrated by a mass which both of the companies commandeered for the expedition were obliged to attend. Now the general, not knowing how strictly the rule of enclosure was observed in the Carmelite Order, had hoped to obtain, while attending the ceremony, some information about the resident nuns, one of whom might well turn out to be a woman dearer to him than life itself and more precious even than honour.

At the beginning his hopes were cruelly disappointed. The mass was, in truth, sung with great pomp. In honour of this solemn occasion, the curtains normally concealing the choir were drawn open and allowed one to see the rich ornaments, the priceless paintings and the shrines encrusted with precious stones whose splendour surpassed that of the numerous *ex-votos* in gold and silver which the sailors of the harbour had fastened to the pillars of the central nave. The nuns had all withdrawn to the organ-loft. And yet, despite this initial check, during the mass of thanksgiving an ample drama was being unfolded, one as interesting in its secret peripeteias as ever troubled the heart of man.

The sister playing the organ roused such lively enthusiasm in the congregation that none of the soldiery regretted having come to the service. Even the rank and file enjoyed it, while all the officers were in transports. The general for his part remained apparently cold and unmoved, but his feelings as he listened to the various voluntaries played by the nun are to be counted among the small number of things which human speech is powerless to express and which like certain concepts – death, eternity and God – can only be evaluated in relation

to the slender point of contact they have with man. By a
strange chance this organ music apparently belonged to the
school of Rossini, that composer who, more than any other,
has made music the medium for the expression of human
passion and whose works will one day inspire, by their
number and breadth of range, the respect due to the Homers
of this world. Among the scores due to this fine genius, the
nun at the organ seemed to have given particular study to
Moses in Egypt, no doubt because in this work the feeling
for sacred music finds its supreme expression. Perhaps two
spirits, one so gloriously European, the other unknown,
had come together in the intuitive perception of one single
poetic truth. This at any rate was the idea which occurred to
a couple of officers, true *dilettanti* though they were and no
doubt regretting that Spain could offer them no comic opera
equivalent to that of the Theâtre Favart. But when the *Te
Deum* came, it was impossible not to discern a French flavour
in the character which the music suddenly took on. The
triumph of his Most Christian Majesty[1] quite evidently
evoked the liveliest joy in the heart of this so unmistakably
French nun. Very soon she yielded to an impulse of patriotic
feeling which spurted forth like a sheaf of light as the organ
responded antiphonally in themes redolent of all the delicacy
of Parisian taste and with which were vaguely intermingled
reminiscences of our most beautiful national airs. A Spanish
touch could never have imparted to this graceful tribute paid
to victorious arms the warmth of feeling which gave the
final revelation of the organist's nationality.

'So then one finds France everywhere one goes?' a soldier
asked.

The general had left the church during the *Te Deum*: he
could not bear to listen to it. The organist's style of execution
was identifying her as a woman he had madly loved, one
who had buried herself so deep in the bosom of religion and
so carefully concealed herself from the eyes of the world that
so far she had eluded obstinate researches skilfully carried out

1. Ferdinand VII of Spain, recently restored to absolute authority by a
French expeditionary force.

by men who possessed both great power and superior intelligence.[2] The hopes awakened in the general's heart were well-nigh justified by the vague appeal of a deliciously melancholy air, that of *Fleuve du Tage*, a ballad whose prelude he had often heard played in a Paris boudoir by the person he loved. The organist had just utilized it in order to convey, in contradistinction to the triumphal song of the victors, the yearning of a woman in exile. A terrible experience! To hope for the resurrection of a lost love, to find it again but beyond recall, to have mysterious glimmerings of its presence after five years during which passion has become fevered through lack of sustenance and intensified by the uselessness of the efforts made to satisfy it!

Who has not, at least once in a lifetime, turned his house and home and papers upside down and impatiently ransacked his memory to think where he has left a precious article, before experiencing the ineffable pleasure of finding it again after wasting several days in vain searches; after suffering the alternations of hope and despair; after fuming over this tremendous trifle to the point of impassioned exasperation? Well now, extend this rabid quest over a period of five years; for the trifle in question substitute a woman, a woman's heart, a woman's love. Raise this passion to the highest realms of feeling. Then imagine a man of fiery spirit, a man with the heart and proud dignity of a lion, one of those imposing, imperious men who excite terror and respect in all who look on them! This perhaps will help you to understand the general's abrupt exit during the *Te Deum*, at the moment when the prelude to a ballad to which he had once listened with delight under gilded, panelled ceilings rang out through the nave of this church on the cliffs.

He hurried down the hilly street which led away from the church and only stopped when the swelling tones of the organ no longer reached his ears. His thoughts were wholly taken up with his love, a volcanic eruption setting his heart aflame; and the French general only realized that the *Te Deum* was over when the Spanish congregation came flooding

2. The Thirteen, whom the general had called to his assistance!

down the slope. Feeling that his behaviour and demeanour might appear absurd, he resumed his place at the head of the procession, telling the alcalde and the city governor that a sudden indisposition had forced him to go out for fresh air. Then, wishing to prolong his stay on the island, he all at once thought that he might take advantage of the pretext which at first he had only unthinkingly put forward. On the grounds that he was feeling worse, he refused to preside over the banquet offered by the island authorities to the French officers, took to his bed, and wrote to the major-general to inform him of the temporary sickness which obliged him to hand over the command of his troops to a colonel. This commonplace but natural ruse freed him of all military duties during the period he needed for the accomplishment of his purpose. Playing the part of a loyal Catholic and royalist, he inquired about hours of services and affected the greatest attachment to religious observances: in Spain such piety would cause no surprise whatsoever.

The very next day, while his soldiers were moving off, the general attended vespers at the convent. He found the church void of citizens, who, despite their piety, had gone down to the harbour to watch the troops embark. Happy to be alone in the church, the Frenchman took care to make the clink of his spurs resound under the echoing vaults. He walked along noisily, coughing and talking out loud to himself in order to let the nuns, and above all the organist, know that, although the French were leaving, one remained behind. Was this singular intimation heard and understood? The general thought so. At the *Magnificat*, the organ seemed to convey a reply which was carried to him in the vibrations of the air. The soul of the nun sped towards him on the wings of the notes she touched, was borne to him in the very movement of the sounds. The music surged forth in all its power and filled the church with warmth. The joyful canticle, adopted into the sublime liturgy of Roman Christendom in order to express the soul's exaltation as it contemplates the splendours of the ever-living God, became the expression of a heart almost terrified with its own happiness as it confronted the splendour of a perishable but persistent love which still perturbed her beyond the tomb – the spiritual tomb in which women are buried only to rise again as the brides of Christ.

The organ is beyond question the finest, the most daring, the most magnificent of all musical instruments created by human genius. It is an orchestra in itself from which a skilled hand can demand all things and by which it can express all things. Is it not as it were a springboard from which the human spirit leaps into space when, taking wing, it strives to sketch a thousand pictures, to paint man's life, and to explore the infinity which separates earth from heaven? The more a poet listens to its titanic harmonies, the more readily he conceives that, between man kneeling in adoration and the God hidden behind the dazzling rays of the sanctuary, only the hundred voices of this terrestrial choir can fill in the distances, are the only interpreters powerful enough to transmit human prayers to heaven in the omnipotence of their modes and the diverse moods of their melancholy, with the varied tints of their meditative ecstasies, the impetuous spurts of their repentances and the innumerable fantasies of human creeds.

Indeed, under these lofty vaults, melodies brought by the genius of sacred things rise to unheard-of grandeurs, are decked and fortified with them. The dim light, the deep silence, the chants alternating with the thunder of the organ are like a veil behind which the luminous attributes of God Himself shine forth. Yet now it seemed as if all these sacred treasures were being flung like a grain of incense on to the fragile altar of earthly love rather than being offered before the eternal throne of a jealous and avenging God. In fact the nun's joy had not the character of grandeur and gravity consonant with the solemnities of the *Magnificat*; it added rich and graceful developments whose varying rhythms were indicative of human gaiety. Her improvisations had the brilliancy of the cadences of a great singer trying to give expression to love; its carols had the buoyancy of a bird flitting beside its mate. Then at moments her inspiration darted back into the past to sport or lament in it turn by turn.

Her changes of mood had something spasmodic about them, like the agitation of a woman who is happy because of her lover's return. Then, after this fantastic recognition had worked out its marvellous effects in supple and ecstatic fugues, the soul thus speaking turned in upon itself. The organ-player forsook the major for the minor key and suddenly began to relate her long bouts of melancholy and depicted to her listener the slow progress of moral sickness, showing how each day she had mortified a sense, each night suppressed some thought and by degrees reduced her heart to ashes. After a few soft modulations the music sobered down little by little to tones of profound sadness. Soon torrents of grief echoed through the church. And finally, suddenly, disparately, the high notes gave forth a concert of angelic voices, as if to tell the lost but unforgotten lover that henceforth their two souls had nothing but the blessed hope of meeting again in Heaven. Then came the *Amen*, and now neither joy nor tears, neither melancholy nor regret resounded through the air. This *Amen* was a return to God, and the last chord was grave, solemn and terrible. The organist revealed the nun in the sombre garb of her vocation, and when the last rolling thunder of the bourdons had sent a shudder through the listener's whole being, she seemed to have sunk back into the tomb from which she had for a moment emerged. As the swell and throb of the organ died away, it was as if the church until then luminous with music had once more plunged into profound darkness.

The general had quickly been carried away by the course of this powerful genius and had followed her through the regions she had swept over. He took in the full meaning of the images which abounded in that burning symphony and its harmonies reached far into his soul. For him, as for the Carmelite, it was a poem embracing future, present and past. Is not music, even the music of opera, for tender and poetic souls, for suffering and wounded hearts, a text which they develop at the bidding of things remembered? If a poet's heart is needed to make a musician, are not poetry and love needed for one to listen to and understand great works of music?

Are not religion, love and music the threefold expression of one fact: the craving for a fuller existence which works as a leaven in all noble souls? These three forms of poetry all lead to God, who unravels the tangles of all earthly emotions. Thus this holy trinity in the human sphere has its part in the infinite greatness of God, to whose likeness our imagination can never lend shape without enveloping Him in the flames of love, the golden cymbals of music, light and harmony. Is He not the beginning and end of all our strivings?

The Frenchman divined that, in this lonely spot, on this sea-girt rock, the nun had seized on music in order to unburden her soul of the abounding passion with which it was consumed. Was she thus sacrificing her love before the altar of God, or did this represent the triumph of love over God? Who should answer such a question? In any case the general no doubt felt that he could revive in this heart which had died to the world as ardent a passion as burned in his own. When vespers had finished, he went to the alcalde's house where he was staying. Content to savour the multiple joys springing from a long-awaited and at first painfully sought-for satisfaction, he could see nothing beyond that. He was still loved. In this woman's heart love had been intensified by solitude as much as it had been in his own by the successive barriers she had erected between herself and him but which he had succeeded in surmounting. This spiritual elation ran its natural course.

Then the desire returned to see this woman again, to grapple with God for possession and wrest her from Him: a rash project but one which appealed to this audacious man. After the evening meal he went to bed to evade questioning, to be alone, to be free to think undisturbed, and he plunged into deepest meditation until morning. He only got up in time to go to Mass. He went to the church and stood at the choir screen, his forehead touching the curtain. He wanted to tear it apart, but he was not alone. Out of politeness his host had accompanied him, and any imprudent act might have compromised and ruined his revived hopes. The organ pealed forth, but other hands were playing it. She who had played for the last two days was no longer at the manuals. It all sounded now pale and cold to the general. Had the woman he loved been overwhelmed by the same emotions as had been almost too much even for a man's stout heart? Had she to such an extent shared and understood his loyal and yearning love that she was lying inert on her bed in her cell? At the moment when a thousand reflections of this sort were rising in the Frenchman's mind, he heard, echoing close by, the voice of the person he adored, recognizing it by its silvery tone. This voice, affected by a slight quaver that lent it all the grace which maidenly shyness confers on young girls, stood out from the chorus of chanting like that of a *prima donna* from the harmony of a final chorus. It produced the same effect on the soul as a silver or gold thread in a dark-coloured frieze does on the eye. So it was she! Still a Parisian, she had not entirely lost her will to charm, although she had discarded worldly adornment for the headband and the bombazine of the Carmelites. After confessing her enduring love the previous evening in the midst of praise addressed to her Maker, she still seemed to be telling her love: 'Yes, it is I. I am here and I still love; but I am screened from love. You will hear my voice. My soul will envelop you. Yet I shall stay under the sombre shroud of this choir from which no power will snatch me. You will never see me more.'

'It is certainly she!' the general said to himself, raising his forehead from his hands on which it had been resting; for at first he had not been able to stand against the overwhelming emotion which had swept through his heart when the voice he knew so well had vibrated through the arches and blended with the murmur of the waves. There was a storm raging outside but calm reigned in the sanctuary. Her voice, so rich, still fell on his ear with all its endearing charm, soothed her lover's fevered heart and so embalmed the air that one could wish to take deeper breaths in order to inhale the emanations of a soul breathing out love in the language of prayer.

The alcalde came and rejoined his guest, found him melting into tears at the Elevation hymn which the nun was

singing, and took him back to his house. Surprised at meeting
with such devotion in a French soldier, the alcalde had invited
the convent chaplain to supper and informed the general, to
whom no news could have given greater pleasure. During
the supper the chaplain met with much attention from the
Frenchman, and the respectful interest showed him confirmed
the Spaniards in the high opinion they had formed of his
piety. He soberly inquired how many nuns there were and
asked details about the revenues and wealth of the convent
like a man who desired courteously to converse with the
worthy old priest on topics which were of the greatest concern to him. Then he inquired about the life these pious
ladies led. Were they permitted to leave their cloister? Was
it possible to visit them?

'Señor,' the venerable cleric replied, 'the rule is severe.
Permission is required from the Holy Father for a woman to
go into a Carthusian monastery. Here there is the same strict-
ness. No man may enter a convent of Discalced Carmelites
unless he is a priest and has been seconded by the archbishop to the service of the House. No nun can go outside.
As an exception, the great saint, Mother Saint Teresa,
often left her cell. Only the Visitor or a Mother Superior can
allow a nun, with authorization from the archbishop, to see
strangers, notably in cases of sickness. Now this is one of the
chief houses of the Order and consequently has a resident
Mother Superior. Among other foreigners we have a French-
woman, Sister Thérèse, who is in charge of the chapel music.'

'Ah!' the general answered, feigning surprise. 'She must
have been pleased at the triumph won by the arms of the
House of Bourbon.'

'I told them what the mass was for. They are always a bit
curious.'

'But Sister Thérèse may have some interests in France.
She might perhaps like to send some message there or ask
for news.'

'I don't think so. She would have made inquiries through
me.'

'As a fellow-countryman of hers,' said the general, 'I should quite like to see her ... If that is possible, if the Superior consents, if ... '

'At the parlour grille, and even in the presence of the Reverend Mother, no interview would be possible for anyone. But in favour of a liberator of the Catholic throne and our holy religion, despite the Reverend Mother's strict adherence to rule, it might be relaxed for a moment,' said the convent confessor with a wink. 'I'll inquire about it.'

'How old is Sister Thérèse?' he asked, while not daring to question the priest about her beauty.

'Age no longer counts with her,' the worthy man replied with a simplicity which sent a shudder through the general's frame.

The next morning, before taking his siesta, the chaplain came to inform the Frenchman that Sister Thérèse and the Mother Superior were ready to receive him at the parlour grille before vespers. After the siesta, during which the general whiled away the time walking round the harbour in the midday heat, the priest came to find him and admitted him to the convent. He led him along a gallery which ran alongside the cemetery and where several springs, green trees and a number of arcades preserved a coolness which was in harmony with the prevailing silence. When they had reached the end of this long gallery, the priest introduced his companion into a hall divided into two parts by a grille draped with a brown curtain. In that part of it which was more or less public, where the chaplain left the general, there was a wooden bench running along the wall; some chairs, also of wood, stood near the grille. The ceiling consisted of exposed beams of green, unsculptured oak. The only daylight reaching this hall came through two windows let into the part reserved for the nuns: light poorly reflected by dark oak panelling and scarcely strong enough to show up the great black crucifix, the portrait of Saint Teresa and a picture of the Virgin which decorated the grey walls of the parlour. That is why the general's feelings, violent as they were, took on a melancholy colouring. From this domestic calm he acquired some calm himself. An impression of grandeur took hold of him as he stood under the chilly roof-timbers: a grandeur like that of the tomb, its eternal silence, its profound peace, its intimations of infinity. Furthermore, the quietude and settled thought of the cloister, a thought which glides through the air, permeates the half-lights, seeps everywhere and leaving nowhere any visible trace, is yet further magnified by the imagination: that impressive phrase 'the peace of Our Lord' forces its way imperiously into the minds of the least pious people.

It is not easy to understand why men take to the monastic life. In a monastery a man seems bereft of strength: he is born for action, to carry out a task in life from which he withdraws if he retires to a cell. But in a woman's convent what a blend there is of steady purpose and pathetic fragility! Many different sentiments may thrust a man into the depths of an abbey – he hurls himself into it as into an abyss. But one sole motive brings a woman to the cloister: in no way does she change her nature, she becomes the spouse of God. You may say to the monk: 'Why did you not struggle on?' But for a cloistered woman the struggle – a sublime one – continues. Indeed, the general detected the persistence of his own presence in the silent parlour of this sea-girt convent. Love rarely rises to transcendental heights; but the love he had inspired, still faithful in the bosom of God, had some character of transcendence, much more so than a man had a right to hope in the nineteenth century with its relaxed morality. The general was fully capable of responding to the infinite grandeur of this situation. He had in fact sufficient elevation of soul to forget politics, worldly honours, his duties in Spain, Parisian society, and rise to the topmost pitch of feeling consonant with this grandiose conclusion to their drama. For that matter, what could be more truly tragic? What a turmoil of emotions contributed to the situation in which these two lovers found themselves: alone, reunited on a granite ledge in the middle of the sea, but separated by an idea, an impassable barrier! Look at this man as he asks himself: 'Can I triumph over God in her heart?'

A slight rustle made him tremble as the brown curtain was

drawn aside. Then the light enabled him to discern a woman who was standing, but whose features were hidden from him by the veil draped about her head and falling over her face: in accordance with the community rule, she was clothed in the brown habit whose colour has become proverbial. He was unable to see the nun's bare feet which would have borne testimony to her appalling thinness. However, despite the numerous folds of the coarse habit which covered without adorning this woman, he divined that tears, prayer, passion and solitude had already dried her in the leaf.

An icy hand, no doubt that of the superior, still held the curtain; and the general, scrutinizing the indispensable witness of this interview, encountered the dark searching gaze of an aged nun who must have been approaching her century. Yet this gaze was bright and youthful, and belied the numerous wrinkles which furrowed her pale face.

'Madame la duchesse,' he asked, in a very moved tone of voice, of the nun who listened with bowed head, 'does your companion understand French?'

'There is no duchess here,' the nun replied. 'You are speaking to Sister Thérèse. She whom you call my companion is my spiritual mother, my Superior here below.'

These words, so humbly pronounced by a voice which formerly had been attuned to the luxury and elegance of a milieu in which the speaker, a queen of fashion in Paris, had lived, coming from a mouth whose parlance had once been so light, so mocking, struck the general like a thunderbolt.

'The Reverend Mother speaks only Latin and Spanish,' she added.

'I know neither language. My dear Antoinette, please apologize for me.'

Hearing her name so softly pronounced by a man who had formerly treated her so harshly, the nun experienced a lively emotion betrayed by the slight quivering of her veil, on which the light was fully falling.

'My brother,' she said, lifting her sleeve underneath her veil, perhaps in order to wipe tears away, 'my name is Sister Thérèse.'

Then she turned to the Mother Superior and spoke to her in Spanish the following words which the general perfectly understood. He knew enough Spanish to follow the meaning, and even perhaps to speak.

'Dear Mother, this gentleman offers you his respects, and begs you to excuse him for not being able himself to lay them at your feet; but he knows neither of the two languages you speak.'

The old woman slowly lowered her head and her features took on an expression of angelic sweetness which was none the less set off by her consciousness of authority and dignity.

'You know this gentleman?' the Mother asked her with a penetrating regard.

'Yes, Mother.'

'Return to your cell, my daughter!' the Superior said in an imperious tone.

The general swiftly withdrew behind the curtain so that his face might not betray the strong emotions which were stirring within him; even in the shadows he felt the Mother Superior's eyes boring into him. This woman, who had at her mercy the fragile and transitory bliss which he had been at such great pains to obtain, had aroused fear in him, and he trembled: he whom a triple row of cannons arrayed against him had never dismayed. The duchess was making for the door, but she turned round. 'Mother,' she said, in an impressively calm tone of voice, 'this French gentleman is one of my brothers.'

'Stay then, my daughter,' the old woman replied after a pause.

The casuistry of the nun's reply gave proof of so much love and so many regrets that a man of less robust constitution than the general would have felt his spirits fail on experiencing such keen pleasure in the midst of such immense peril, one which was quite new to him. Of what value indeed were words, looks, gestures in a scene in which love had to evade lynxes' eyes and tigers' claws? Sister Thérèse returned.

'You see, my brother, how far I dare to go in order to

talk to you for a moment about your salvation and the prayers I address to heaven every day on your behalf. I am committing a mortal sin. I have lied. How many days of penance will it cost me to wipe out this falsehood! But it is for you that I shall be suffering. You do not know, my brother, the joy of living with a heavenly love, of avowing one's feelings once religion has sanctified them, transported them to the highest realms so that we are free to live only on the spiritual plane. If the teaching and the spirit of the saint to whom we owe this sanctuary had not lifted me far beyond terrestrial miseries into a sphere – much lower certainly than the one in which she resides, but well above the cares of this world – I would not have seen you again. But I am able to see you, hear you and still remain calm . . . '

'Well then, Antoinette,' exclaimed the general, breaking in. 'Let me look on you, you that I now love madly, passionately, as you formerly wished that I should love you.'

'Do not call me Antoinette, I beg you. Memories of the past do me harm. Look on me only as Sister Thérèse, a creature who trusts in the mercy of God, and,' she added after a pause, 'control your feelings, my brother. Our Mother would separate us without compunction if worldly passions were visible on your face or if you let tears fall from your eyes.'

The general bowed his head as if to collect his thoughts. When he raised his eyes again to the grille, he perceived, between two bars, the pale, emaciated, but still ardent face of the nun. Her complexion, once blooming with all the loveliness of youth and the happy contrast of pure white with the tint of a Bengal rose, had taken on the warm tone of a porcelain cup through which a soft light faintly glowed. The lovely head of hair of which she had been so proud had been shorn. A headband was drawn round her forehead and enveloped her face. Her eyes, circled with dark shadows thanks to the austerity of her life, darted forth fitful and feverish gleams, and the steady calm they showed was but a veil. To sum up, nothing remained of this woman except her soul.

'Oh, you shall quit this tomb, you who have become my

very life! You belonged to me, you were not free to give
yourself away, even to God. Had you not promised to sacrifice everything to my slightest command? Now you will
perhaps deem me worthy to hold you to that promise,
once you know what I have done for you. I have sought you
the wide world over. For five years you have been every
instant in my thought and taken up my whole life. My friends,
very powerful friends as you know, have with all their might
helped me to search the convents of France, Italy, Spain,
Sicily and America. My love burned more brightly when every
quest proved vain. I often undertook long voyages spurred
on by false hopes. I have spent my life, and my heartbeats
have been strongest, round the dark walls of many cloisters.
I will not tell you of my boundless fidelity, for what is that?
A trifle in comparison with the infinite devotion of my love.
If formerly you were sincere in your remorse, you cannot
hesitate to follow me today.'

'You forget that I am not free.'

'The Duc de Langeais is dead,' he swiftly replied.

Sister Thérèse reddened.

'May Heaven open its gates to him,' she said with lively
emotion, 'He was generous to me. But I was not speaking
of such bonds. One of my sins was to have been ready to break
them without scruple for your sake.'

'You are referring to your vows,' the general exclaimed
with a frown. 'I did not believe that anything weighed more
with you than your love. But do not doubt this, Antoinette:
I will obtain from the Holy Father a brief which will relieve
you of those vows. I will certainly go to Rome and will
entreat every power on earth. If God Himself could come
down to earth, I would . . .'

'Do not blaspheme.'

'But have no anxiety about God! Ah! Tell me rather that
you are ready to cross these walls for me; that this very evening you are ready to leap into a boat at the foot of the rocks.
We would go to the world's end, anywhere, and be happy!
And at my side you would recover life and health under the
wings of love.'

'Do not say such things,' Sister Thérèse replied. 'You do not know what you now mean to me. I love you far better than I ever loved you before. Every day I pray to God for you and no longer see you with the eyes of the body. If only you knew, Armand, the happiness of being able to give one-self over without shame to a pure friendship which God protects! You don't know how happy I am to call down Heaven's blessings upon you. I never pray for myself: God will deal with me as He pleases. But you, I would wish, at the price of my eternal life, to have some certainty that you are happy in this world and that you will be happy in the next one for ever and ever. My eternal life is all that misfor-tune has left me to offer you. Now, I have grown old in tears and am no longer young and beautiful. Moreover, you would despise a nun who reverted to womanhood, whom no feeling, not even motherly love, would absolve . . . What words can you find to weigh against the innumerable re-flections which have piled up in my heart for the last five years, which have changed it, eroded it, withered it? Oh, I ought to have given it to God with more alacrity!'

'What words can I find, dear Antoinette? These: I love you. Affection, love, true love, the happiness of living in a heart that belongs to you wholly, entirely, without reserve, is so rare and difficult to meet with, that I doubted you and sub-jected you to rude tests. But today I love you with all the might of my soul: if you flee into solitude with me, I will never more listen to any voice other than yours. I will never again look on any face other than yours . . . '

'Quiet, Armand! You are cutting short the only instant during which we shall be allowed to see each other here below.'

'Antoinette, will you come away with me?'

'But I am not leaving you. I shall live in your heart, but moved by no interest of worldly pleasure, vanity, selfish enjoyment. I am living here for you, pale and withered, in the bosom of God! If He is just, you will be happy.'

'That's nothing but talk! And suppose I want you, pale and withered as you may be? Suppose I can only be happy possessing you? You will never then think of anything but duty in your lover's presence? Will he never come first and foremost in your heart? In former times you preferred society and goodness knows what to him; now you prefer God or my salvation. In Sister Thérèse I still recognize the duchess ignorant of the joys of love and always adamant under an appearance of sensibility. You do not love me, you have never loved . . .'

'Oh, my brother!'

'You don't want to leave this sepulchre, you love my soul, you say. Well, you will destroy it for ever, this soul, for I shall kill myself . . .'

'Reverend Mother,' Sister Thérèse cried out in Spanish, 'I lied to you. This man was my lover!'

Immediately the curtain fell. The general, dumbfounded, scarcely heard the inner doors being slammed together.

'Ah! She still loves me!' he exclaimed, realizing what sublimity there was in the nun's cry. 'I must get her away from here.'

He left the island, returned to headquarters, made a pretext of ill-health, asked for leave and promptly went back to France.

We will now relate the adventure which had brought about the situation in which these two persons found themselves involved.

2
Love in the parish of
Saint Thomas Aquinas

WHAT in France goes by the name of the Faubourg Saint-Germain is neither a quarter of Paris, nor an institution, nor anything clearly definable. The Place Royale, the Faubourg Saint-Honoré and the Chaussée-d'Antin also possess mansions in which the atmosphere of the Faubourg Saint-Germain prevails. Thus the Faubourg is not strictly confined to its own territory. People born far beyond its sphere of influence can feel it and be part and parcel of this world, whereas certain others born inside it may be for ever excluded from it. The manners, speech, in a word the Faubourg Saint-Germain tradition, has been in Paris, during the last forty years, what the Court formerly had been, what the Hôtel Saint-Paul[1] had been in the fourteenth century, the Louvre in the fifteenth, the Palais, the Hôtel Rambouillet, the Place Royale in the sixteenth, then Versailles in the seventeenth and eighteenth centuries. In every phase of history the Paris of the upper classes and the nobility has had its own centre, just as plebeian Paris will always have its own special quarter. This separatism with its periodic variations offers ample material for reflection to those desirous of studying or depicting the different social zones, and perhaps we ought to research into causes not only in order to give plausibility to the episode we are about to recount, but also in order to serve certain grave interests which may affect the future even more than the present – unless it be that experience is as meaningless to political parties as it is to youth.

1. The term *hôtel*, in the diction of the time, applies to the town-house of the aristocracy and the rich, and has nothing to do with its modern, commercial sense. The Hôtel Rambouillet was an important social and cultural centre in the seventeenth century.

Great lords and plutocrats – the latter will always ape the former – have at all times kept their residences away from populous districts. If the Duc d'Uzès, in the reign of Louis XIV, built himself the fine mansion at whose gate he set the fountain of the Rue Montmartre, a beneficent act which enhanced his reputation for benevolence and made him such an object of popular veneration that the whole district followed his hearse to the cemetery, this corner of Paris was at that time waste ground. But as soon as the fortifications were razed to the ground and houses were built on the marshy swamp beyond the boulevards, the Uzès family abandoned this fine residence which in our time a banker inhabits. Then the nobility, finding itself in the middle of a shop-keeping area, vacated the Place Royale and the environs of central Paris and moved across the Seine to go and breathe more freely in the Faubourg Saint-Germain, where, already, palaces had been erected round the town-house built by Louis XIV for the Duc du Maine, the Benjamin among his legiti-mized bastards. For people accustomed to the splendours of life, can there in fact be anything more degrading than the tumult, mud, clamour, stench and narrowness of these teeming streets? Are not the prevailing habits in a shop-keeping or manufacturing district continually at variance with those of the great ones of this world? Commerce and labour are going to bed at the hour when aristocracy is thinking of dining; the former are bustling about when the latter are taking to their beds. Their budgets have nothing in common: receipts on the one side, expenditure on the other. Hence two diametrically opposed ways of living. This is not a snobbish observation. An aristocracy in some sense represents the thought of a society, just as the middle and working classes are the organic and active side of it. Hence there are different centres of operation for these forces, and from the apparent antagonism between them there results a seeming antipathy produced by a diversity of movement which never-theless works for a common aim. These social discords are the logical result of paper constitutions, and the liberals most inclined to complain about them, as if they constituted an attack on the sublime ideas under which the ambitious members of the lower classes dissimulate their designs, would find it prodigiously absurd for the Prince de Montmorency to live in the Rue Saint-Martin at the street corner which bears his name or Monsieur le Duc de Fitz-James, the descendant of the royal Scottish race, to have his mansion in the Rue Marie-Stuart, at the corner of the Rue Montorgueil.[2] *Sint ut sint, aut non sint*: these fine pontifical words may serve as a motto for the grandees of all countries. This fact, palpable in all periods and always accepted by the common people, carries reasons of state within itself: it is at once an effect and a cause, a principle and a law. The masses possess a fund of common sense which they only renounce at the moment when people of bad faith stir their passions. It is based on verities of a general order, as true in Moscow as in London, as true in Geneva as in Calcutta. Everywhere, when you assemble families of unequal fortune in a given area, you will see upper circles being formed – patricians, then first, second and third social orders. Equality may perhaps be accepted as a *right*, but no power on earth will convert it into a *fact*. It would be well for the happiness of France if this truth could be brought home to the people. Even to the least intelligent masses the benefits accruing from political harmony can be made clear. Harmony is the poetry of order, and all peoples feel an imperious need for order. Now is not the cooperation of all things with one another, unity in a word, the simplest expression of order? Architecture, music, poetry, every art in France leans, more than in any other country, on the principle which for that matter is written into its clear and pure language – the language will always provide a nation with its most infallible formula. That is why you see the people of France taking to itself the most poetic and best modulated tunes; seizing hold of the simplest ideas; preferring incisive themes in which the greatest number of ideas are concentrated. France is the only country in which a chance phrase may cause a great revolution. The French masses have never

2. The Rue Saint-Martin had become essentially middle class. The Rue Marie-Stuart was a bawdy-house area.

revolted except in order to try and bring men, interests and principles into harmony. Now no other nation is more sensible of the idea of solidarity which must exist in aristocratic life, perhaps because no other has a more realistic notion of political necessities: history will never find her lagging behind in this respect. France is often deceived, but as a woman is deceived – by generous ideas, by a warmth of feeling whose range it is at first impossible to estimate.

Thus already, as its foremost characteristic feature, the Faubourg Saint-Germain possesses the splendour of its mansions, its great gardens and their silence, formerly in harmony with the magnificence of its territorial fortunes. Surely this distance set between one class and an entire capital is a material consecration of the moral distance which ought to separate them? In all things created the head has its place marked out. If by chance a nation fells its leader to the ground, it sooner or later perceives that it has committed suicide. Thereupon, since every nation is loath to die, it furnishes itself with a new head. When a nation is no longer strong enough to do this it perishes, as Rome, Venice and so many other communities perished. The distinction created by the difference of manners between the upper sphere and the other spheres of social activity necessarily implies real merit, of capital importance, in the high reaches of aristocracy. Once in any state, whatever the form of government may be, patricians fail to maintain a status of complete superiority, they lose their driving power and the common people immediately cast them down. The people always wants to see them holding in their hands, their heart and their head, fortune, authority and action: speech, intelligence and glory. Without this triple might, all privilege vanishes. The popular classes, like women, love to see strength in those who govern them. Where they do not respect they cannot love. They will not accord obedience to those who cannot impose it. An aristocracy in low esteem is like a *roi fainéant*, a husband in petticoats; it passes from nullity to nothingness. Thus, the fact of the grandees forming a class apart, the sharp distinction in their way of life, in a word the total accoutrement of the patrician castes, is at once the symbol of a real power and the cause of their destruction when they have lost that power. The Faubourg Saint-Germain allowed itself to be momentarily knocked on the head because it refused to recognize the obligations on which its existence depended at a time when it was still easy to perpetuate it. It should have had the good faith to realize in time, as the English aristocracy did, that institutions have their climacteric years when terms change their meaning, when ideas put on a new garb and the conditions of political life assume a totally new form without the basic substance being affected. These ideas call for a development which appertains essentially to the adventure here being recounted: it relates to it both as a definition of causes and as an explanation of the facts.

The grandeur of aristocratic châteaux and palaces, the luxury of their details, the unvarying sumptuousness of their furnishings, the *orbit* in which, unconfined and unencumbered, the fortunate landowner moves, born as he is with a silver spoon in his mouth; also the habit of never stooping to calculation of the petty interests of daily life, the time he has at his disposal, the superior education he is able precociously to acquire; and finally the patrician traditions which provide him with a social power for which his adversaries can scarcely compensate by dint of study, determination and tenacity of vocation: all of this ought to elevate the soul of the man who, from tender infancy, enjoys such privileges, ought to imprint in him that lofty self-respect which should at the very least create in him a nobility of heart consonant with the nobility of his name. That does happen in some families. Here and there, in the Faubourg Saint-Germain, fine characters are met with, exceptions which prove the rule notwithstanding the general egoism which has caused the downfall of this segregated society.

The above advantages have accrued to the French aristocracy as they do to all patrician efflorescences, which will blossom forth on the surface of nations so long as their existence is based on *domain*, whether it be real estate or capital – the only solid foundation for a well-regulated society. But these advantages are retained by patricians of all sorts only in so far as they abide by conditions on which the people allows them to enjoy them. They are, one might say, *moral* fiefs whose tenure involves obligations to the sovereign, and in this case the sovereign today is certainly the people. Times have changed, and with them the armoury of weapons. The banneret for whom it was formerly sufficient to wear the coat of mail and hauberk, to wield his lance adroitly and display his pennon, must today show proof of mental ability. Whereas all that then was needed was a doughty heart, in our days a capacious skull is called for. Art, science and wealth form the social triangle within which is inscribed the shield of power and from which modern aristocracy must emerge. A fine theorem has as much value as a noble name. The Rothschilds, like the Fugger firm in the sixteenth century, are princes in their own right. A great artist is as good as an oligarch: he represents a whole century and almost always asserts himself as a law. Likewise, the eloquence of the orator, the high-pressure machines of the writer, the genius of the poet, the sturdy persistence of the merchant, the driving power of the statesman who concentrates in himself a thousand dazzling qualities, the sword of the general, all these personal conquests carried off by a single individual against society in the aggregate in order to levy tribute on it: of all these the aristocratic class should today strive to secure the monopoly, just as in olden times it had the monopoly of brute strength. Those who wish to remain at the head of a country must always be worthy of leading it; they must constitute its mind and soul in order to control the activity of its hands. But how can a people be led except by those who possess the qualities of leadership? What would a marshal's baton be worth without the intrinsic strength of the captain who wields it? The Faubourg Saint-Germain has made great display of its batons, believing that in them resided all the power. It had reversed the very conditions safeguarding its existence. Instead of jettisoning insignia obnoxious to the people while quietly holding on to the power, it allowed the middle class to lay hands on the power, and with fatal obstinacy clung to the insignia, and consistently forgot the laws imposed on it by its numerical weakness. An aristocracy which by a count of hands scarcely constitutes a thousandth part of a society, must today, as in former times, multiply its means of action in order that in times of great crisis it may exert a weight equal to that of the masses. In our days means of action lie in positive strength and not in historic memories. Unfortunately the French Restoration nobility, still swollen with pride at the thought of its now vanished power, had provoked against itself a kind of prejudice against which it was difficult for it to defend itself. That is perhaps a national defect. A Frenchman is unique in this respect: he never looks beneath him but tries to step upward. He rarely pities the unfortunates over whom he steps, but he always groans when he sees so many lucky people rising above himself. He may be a man of much heart, but only too often he lets his head take charge. The national instinct which always drives Frenchmen forward, the vanity which gnaws away at their fortunes and rules them as absolutely as thrift rules the Dutch, has for three centuries dominated our nobility, which in this respect has behaved in an eminently French way.

The denizen of the Faubourg Saint-Germain has always inferred that his material superiority made him intellectually superior. Everything that has happened in France has convinced him of this, because, since the establishment of the Faubourg Saint-Germain, an aristocratic revolution which began the day the monarchy quitted Versailles, the Faubourg has always, except for a few lapses, leaned on the governmental power, which in France will always more or less stand by the Faubourg Saint-Germain. Hence its defeat in 1830. At that period it was as it were an army operating without a base. It had not taken advantage of the peace in order to implant itself in the heart of the nation. It erred through ignorance and a complete lack of vision concerning its overall interests. It was destroying a future on which it could count in favour of a very dubious present. We may perhaps suggest a motive for this mistaken policy:

The material and moral distance which these people of

rank tried to maintain between themselves and the rest of the nation has inevitably led, for the last forty years, to the fostering of individual sentiment in the topmost class while destroying caste exclusiveness. Formerly, at a time when the French nobility was great, rich and powerful, noblemen were able, when danger faced them, to choose themselves leaders and obey them. Reduced in stature, they showed themselves unamenable to discipline; and, as in the Byzantine Empire, each one of them wished to be Emperor. They saw that they were all equal in weakness, but each of them fancied himself individually superior. Each family, ruined by the Revolution, ruined by the equal division of property, thought only of itself instead of thinking of the great aristocratic family, and it seemed to them that, if they all enriched themselves, the party itself would be strong. They were wrong. Even money is only a symbol of power. All these families, composed of persons who kept up the high traditions of good manners, true elegance, cultured speech, a reserve in pride appropriate to nobility and consonant with its way of life, but paltry once they have become the ruling principle in an existence to which they should only be accessory – all these families possessed a certain intrinsic value which, envisaged at its surface value, was nothing more than nominal. Not one of these families had the courage to ask themselves: are we capable of wielding power? They pounced upon it like the barristers in 1830. Instead of assuming a protective role like the great lords of the seventeenth century, the Faubourg Saint-Germain displayed all the avidity of *parvenus*. From the day when it was made clear to the most intelligent nation in the world that the restored nobility was organizing power and finance for its own profit, that day it fell mortally ill. It wanted to be an aristocracy when it could be no more than an oligarchy: two very different systems, as any man will understand who is clever enough to read and mark the ancestral names of the lords of the Upper Chamber. Certainly the royal government had good intentions, but it was constantly forgetting that the people has to be drilled to form its own desires, even its desire for happiness, and that France, femininely capricious, wants to be a happy or an ill-treated wife as the fancy takes her. If there had been many Ducs de Laval, whose modesty made him worthy of his name,[3] the throne of the elder Bourbons would have become as irremovable as that of the House of Hanover. In 1814, but more so still in 1820, the French nobility had to establish its ascendancy over the most enlightened generation, the most aristocratic middle class and the most feminine nation in the world. The Faubourg Saint-Germain could very easily have led and humoured a middle class intoxicated with public honours, enamoured of art and science. But the petty-minded leaders of this great epoch, when intelligence was at a premium, all hated art and science. They were not even able to endow religion, so desperately needed, with a poetic colouring which might have endeared it to the populace. When Lamartine, Lamennais, Montalembert and a number of other talented writers were imparting a golden poetic glow, a new glamour and grandeur to religious ideas, the muddlers on top were making religion harsh and unpalatable. Never was a nation more amenable; France was like a woman who is weakening and ready to yield; but no government ever committed more blunders. France, like a true woman, prefers misconduct to blunders!

In order to regain its prestige, in order to found a great oligarchic government, the nobility of the Faubourg ought in good faith to have ransacked its pockets in an effort to muster some Napoleonic small change; it should have tried to draw out from its own entrails a constitutional Richelieu. Or, if it could bring forth no such genius, it should have gone to look for it where it languished in some cold garret and assimilated it to itself, just as the English House of Lords constantly assimilates those nature's gentlemen whom chance throws up. Then it should have commissioned such a man to be implacable, to prune away rotten boughs, to

3. A word-play on the meaning of *val* as a common noun: 'valley'. This man, Adrien de Montmorency, was one of the more intelligent supporters of Charles X before 1830. The 'elder Bourbons' are of course those who were driven out in 1830.

pollard the tree of aristocracy.[4] But, firstly, the great system of English Toryism was too vast for little minds, and secondly the importation of it would have been too slow a process for the French, for whom a merely gradual success is equivalent to a fiasco. Moreover, far from adopting the saving policy which seeks strength wherever God has put it, these conceited little people despised any strength which did not emanate from themselves. Finally, far from seeking rejuvenation, the Faubourg Saint-Germain rushed into old age. Etiquette, an institution of secondary necessity, might have been maintained if it had been kept for great occasions. But it became a source of daily wrangling, not over questions of art or sumptuary display, but over the possession of power. Not only did the throne lack the kind of counsellor capable of rising to circumstances, but the aristocracy lacked above all that comprehension of its general interests which might have made up for all other deficiencies. It shied at the marriage of Monsieur de Talleyrand,[5] the only man with one of those brains cased in steel in which those political systems are forged anew which bring nations back to a glorious renascence. The Faubourg made scorn of the ministers who were not of noble birth, but produced no men of noble birth with talent enough to be ministers. It might have done real service to the country by raising justices of the peace to gentle status, by interesting itself in agricultural improvement, by building roads and canals and playing its part as an active power in the land. But it sold its lands in order to speculate on the Stock Exchange. It might have filched from the bourgeoisie its men of action and talent whose ambition was undermining the government – by opening its ranks to them. It preferred to fight them – but without weapons, for now it possessed only as a tradition what it had once possessed in reality. Unfortunately for this nobility it only retained just enough of its diverse fortunes to maintain its pride of caste. Content to live on its past, not one of these families seriously

4. Balzac certainly imagined himself as capable of fulfilling such a role.
5. With an English adventuress. The French nobility could not stomach this.

thought of making their eldest sons take up a career among the many openings which the nineteenth century was making available to the public. The young nobles, thus excluded from public affairs, danced at Court balls instead of continuing in Paris – using the talents they possessed, young as they were, conscientious, inheriting no guilt from Republic or Empire – the work which the heads of each family could have initiated in the *départements*, winning recognition of their claims by standing up continuously for local interests, conforming to the spirit of the age and remodelling their caste to suit the requirements of their century.

But the aristocracy, huddled up in its Faubourg Saint-Germain, where the spirit of the ancient feudal rivalries still survived, mingled with that of the court of the *ancien régime*, having little solidarity with royalty at the Tuileries, was easy to vanquish since its existence was centred in a single point and more so still because its status in the Chamber of Peers was, constitutionally speaking, ill-defined. As part of the texture of the country, it would have been indestructible; but, cornered in its *faubourg*, leaning back against the royal palace, spreadeagled over the Budget, one stroke of the axe was enough to cut the thread of its ebbing life. The commonplace figure of a little barrister came forward to deal the blow. Despite the admirable speech of Monsieur Royer-Collard, the hereditary peerage, with its estates in tail, succumbed to the pasquinades of a man who boasted of having adroitly cheated the executioner of several heads but clumsily murdered some great institutions of France.[6] Here are to be found examples and instruction for the years to come. If the French oligarchy had no prospect of a future life, it would be inconceivably cruel to put its dead body to the torture: what need would there be except to provide for its burial? But though the surgeon's scalpel is painful to endure, it sometimes brings dying people back to life. The Faubourg Saint-Germain may still find itself more powerful

6. Allusions to the events of 1830, elucidation of which would not be of much importance. The essential fact is that in 1830 the hereditary peerage was abolished.

under persecution than it was when it triumphed – if only it is ready to choose for itself a leader and a system.[7]

We may now easily sum up this semi-political glimpse at facts. A failure to take the broad view; a vast accumulation of petty mistakes; the commonly shared concern to restore the great fortunes confiscated during the Revolution; the imperative need for religion as a basis for political action; a craving for pleasure which militated against religion and necessitated hypocrisy; the partial resistance of some loftier and clear-sighted spirits frustrated by Court jealousies; a provincial nobility, often of purer race than the court nobility but which was so often snubbed that it became disaffected: – all these factors combined to give the Faubourg Saint-Germain a confusion of discordant manners. It was neither compact in its system nor consequent in its acts; it was neither completely moral nor frankly licentious, neither corrupt nor corrupting. It would not cease from raising issues which worked to its disadvantage, nor would it adopt ideas which might have saved it. In fine, poorly supplied though the royalist party was with strong personalities, it had none the less armed itself with all the great principles which constitute the life of nations. What then ailed it for it to have perished in full vigour?

It was exacting in its choice of persons presented to it; it had nicety of taste and elegance in its disdains; but certainly there was nothing brilliant or chivalric in the manner of its fall. Patriotic sentiment had played its part in the emigration of 1789; the 'internal' emigration of 1830 was dictated purely by self-interest. Yet a number of features on the credit side – the possession of some illustrious men of letters and illustrious orators, Monsieur de Talleyrand's statesmanship at the European congresses, the conquest of Algiers and certain great names recovering their glory on the field of battle – reveal to the aristocracy of France the means at its disposal to reinstate itself as a national institution and re-gain possession of its titles. Will it deign to do so?

In all organized beings a process takes place which makes

7. What leader? Balzac's friend the Duc de Fitz-James or Balzac himself?

for internal harmony. Is a man slothful? His sloth becomes apparent in every movement he makes. Likewise the physiognomy of a class of men conforms to the general spirit, to the soul animating the whole body. Under the Restoration the woman of the Faubourg Saint-Germain displayed neither the proud audacity with which the court ladies of former times committed their indiscretions, nor the modest grandeur of the late-found virtues with which they expiated their faults and which put so bright a halo round their heads. There was nothing specifically virtuous about her. Her passions, with a few exceptions, were a matter of make-believe: one might say that she struck a compromise with the enjoyment they offered. Some of these families led a middle-class life like the Duchess of Orleans, whose conjugal bed was so absurdly displayed to gapers who came to visit the Palais-Royal. Two or three of them at the most continued the moral standards of the Regency and inspired a measure of disgust in more adroit women. The new kind of great lady exerted no influence on manners; nevertheless several possibilities were open to her, and if all else failed she might have adopted the imposing attitude of the English gentlewoman. But she stupidly hesitated between old-established traditions, became devout willy-nilly and concealed every quality she had, even her good ones. Not one of these Frenchwomen was capable of founding a salon in which the socially eminent might come to take lessons in taste and elegance. Their voice, once so authoritative in literature, that living expression of social life, had now no influence at all; and when a literature has no general system to support it lacks solidity and fades out with the age to which it belongs.

Whenever, at any time, there exists in the midst of a nation a people apart thus constituted, the historian almost always meets with a principal figure who sums up in himself the virtues and defects of the group to which he belongs: Coligny among the Huguenots, the Cardinal de Retz in the bosom of the Fronde, the Maréchal de Richelieu in the reign of Louis XV, Danton during the Reign of Terror. This identity of physiognomy between a man and his historical milieu belongs to the nature of things. In order to lead a party must one not fall in with its ideas? In order to shine in any period must one not represent it? From this constant obligation, imposed on the sage and prudent heads óf parties, to yield to the prejudices and extravagances of the masses which trail along after them derive the actions for which certain historians blame the party leaders when, being themselves remote in time from the terrible popular ebullitions, they coldly judge those passions which are the most necessary for the conduct of great secular struggles. What is true in the historic comedy of the centuries is equally true in a narrower sphere: the fragmentary scenes in the national drama of *manners*.

At the beginning of the ephemeral life of the Faubourg Saint-Germain during the Restoration, a life to which, if the preceding considerations are valid, it failed to give any consistency, one young woman was for the time being the most complete type of the nature, at once superior and feeble, great and petty, of her caste. She was a woman artificially educated but in reality ignorant: full of lofty sentiments but lacking ideas to coordinate them; expending the rich treasures of her soul in obedience to convention; ready to brave society but hesitant; so addicted to scruples as to fall into artifice; having more stubbornness than strength of character, more effusiveness than enthusiasm, more head than heart: sovereignly feminine, sovereignly coquettish; eminently Parisian; loving ostentation and festivities; never reflecting, or reflecting too late; of an imprudence that rose on occasions to poetic heights; ravishingly insolent, though humble in her heart of hearts; making a show of rigidity like a stiff-standing reed, but, like a reed, liable to bend under a forceful hand; talking much of religion without loving it, but ready to accept it in the last resort. How shall I explain so many-sided a creature? Capable of heroism, but forgetting to be heroic for the sake of making some malicious remark; young and suave; not old in heart but aged by the maxims of those around her; understanding their selfish philosophy but never applying it; having all the shortcomings of a courtier and all the nobility of adolescent femininity; sceptical in all things and yet sometimes going to the extremes of credulity. No finished portrait could ever be made of this woman: she was one in whom the most iridescent hues clashed while yet producing a poetic confusion, because there was in them a divine luminosity, a brilliance of youth which gave this profusion of traits a perceptible *ensemble*. From gracefulness came unity. There was no pretence in her. Passions and semi-passions, fitful aspirations to grandeur contrasting with an only too palpable pettiness, frostiness of mood and outbursts of warm feeling, all this was natural in her and came as much from her personal situation as from the caste to which she belonged. She thought of herself as a creature apart, and proudly set herself above the world under the shelter of the name she bore. She had the self-assertiveness of Corneille's Medea, like the aristocracy itself, which was passing languidly away without trying either to rise from its bed of sickness or seek help from a physician in the political sphere; unwilling to touch or be touched, so feeble and moribund it felt itself to be.

The Duchesse de Langeais – such was her name – had been married for about four years when the Restoration came to its peak, that is to say in 1816: the period when Louis XVIII, enlightened by the revolution of the Hundred Days, came to understand his situation and his century, in spite of his entourage which none the less later got the better of him – a Louis XI minus the executioner's axe – once infirmity struck him down. The Duchesse de Langeais belonged to the ducal family of the Navarreins which, since the time of Louis XIV, had made it a principle not to relinquish its name and title in the alliances it made. The daughters of this house were destined sooner or later to have, like their mother, the privilege of the 'folding stool', that is to say the right of being seated in the presence of the king and queen. At the age of eighteen, Antoinette de Navarreins emerged from the profound retreat in which she had lived, in order to wed the eldest son of the Duc de Langeais. At that time both families were living in isolation from the world; but the invasion of France by foreign troops convinced the royalists that only the return of the Bourbons could save the country from the disaster of further war.

The Duc de Navarreins and the Duc de Langeais had stood faithful to the Bourbons; they had nobly resisted all the seductions of Napoleonic glory, and in the circumstances in which they found themselves at the time of this union, they perforce conformed to the long-settled policy of their families. And so the lady Antoinette de Navarreins, beautiful and poor as she was, espoused Monsieur le Marquis de Langeais, whose father died a few months after the wedding. When the Bourbons returned to France, the two families reassumed their rank, offices and court dignities and moved back into the social swim from which so far they had kept aloof. They took their place, a brilliant one, at the head of this new political world. In this period of treachery and false conversions, the public conscience was pleased to recognize in these two families the untarnished fidelity and the harmony between private life and political action to which all parties involuntarily render tribute. But, thanks to a misfortune frequent enough in times of compromise, the persons with the purest motives, those who, by their lofty views and sage principles, could have brought France to believe in the generosity of a new and bold policy, were thrust aside from public affairs, so that these fell into the hands of people whose interest it was to push principles to their logical extreme in order to give proof of their own devotion. The Langeais and Navarreins families remained at the summit of court life, were condemned to the ceremony of etiquette, to the reproaches and sneers of the liberals, and were accused of gorging themselves with honours and riches, whereas in fact their patrimony did not increase and the liberalities of the Civil List were consumed in the expenses of official entertainment which are indispensable in any European monarchy, even one with republican inclinations. In 1818, Monsieur le Duc de Langeais commanded a military division, and the duchess, as lady-in-waiting to a princess, occupied a position which authorized her remaining in Paris, far away from her husband, without scandal. Moreover the duke held, in addition to his military command, a court function which he discharged during his duty period, leaving an adjutant in control. So then the duke and duchess lived quite apart both factually and sentimentally without society realizing this. This conventional marriage had fared much as such family pacts usually do. Two inconceivably incompatible characters had been brought together, had imperceptibly bruised and wounded each other and become for ever estranged. Then both of them had followed their own bent while adhering to convention. The Duc de Langeais, phenomenally methodically-minded, methodically delivered himself over to his tastes and pleasures, and left his wife free to follow hers, after recognizing in her an eminently haughty spirit, a cold heart, great submissiveness to society usages, and a youthful loyalty which had to remain unsullied in the eyes of her grandparents under the floodlight of a prudish and pious court. So then he coldly played the part of an eighteenth-century *grand seigneur*, leaving to her own devices a woman of twenty-two, one who was conscious of having suffered a grave offence and whose character included one fearful trait, that of never forgiving an offence once all her feminine vanity, her self-love, perhaps even her virtue, had been impugned or secretly slighted. When a woman suffers a public outrage she is willing to condone it: it gives her an opportunity to be magnanimous and show a woman's clemency. But women will never forgive secret wrongs: they hate anything to be secret: either betrayal, virtue or amorous relationships.

Such was the position, unknown to the world, in which Madame la Duchesse de Langeais found herself, and on which she was wasting no reflection, when the festivities occasioned by the marriage of the Duc de Berry occurred. At that moment the Court and the Faubourg Saint-Germain emerged from their apathy and reserve. That was really the beginning of the unprecedented splendour which so much deluded governments of the Restoration epoch. It was then that the Duchesse de Langeais, whether through calculation or vanity, never appeared in society without being surrounded or accompanied by three or four women as distinguished in name as in fortune. As the queen of fashion, she had her ladies-in-waiting to reproduce her wit and manners in other salons, and she had cleverly chosen them from among a few persons who as yet were on close terms neither with the Court nor the élite of the Faubourg Saint-Germain but nevertheless were aspiring to reach that goal: in the language of the angelic hierarchy, they were simple 'dominations' desirous of mounting towards the throne and mingling with the seraphic 'powers' inhabiting the high sphere known as *the little château*. Adopting such a posture, the duchess was stronger, more dominant, more secure. Her ladies defended her from calumny and helped her to play the odious role of a woman of fashion. She was free to mock at men and passions as she liked, excite them, win the homage on which all feminine nature feeds and yet remain mistress of herself. In Paris, even in the highest social circles, a woman is always a woman: she thrives on incense, flattery and attentions. Of what avail is beauty, however unchallengeable, or a graceful figure, however admirable, if it is not admired? To have a lover and to be fawned upon gives proof of power. And what is power if unattested? Nothing. Imagine the prettiest of all women languishing alone in the corner of a salon: could she be anything but sad? When therefore one of these beauties finds herself at the centre of social magnificence, she wants to reign over all hearts, and often enough because she cannot reign as a happy sovereign in one single heart. All this dressing up, all these frills and fineries were aimed at the poorest beings imaginable, witless fops, men whose sole merit lay in their good looks and for whom all the women compromised themselves unprofitably, mere gilded idols of wood who, despite a few exceptions, had neither the antecedents of the coxcombs of the time of the Fronde,[8] nor the stalwart valour of the Napoleonic heroes, nor the wit and manner of their grandfathers, but wanted more or less to resemble them without paying the price; who were brave as French youth is, would no doubt have shown ability had they been

8. An anti-monarchical, pseudo-democratic movement of the mid-seventeenth century.

put to the test, but could not prove their worth under the reign of the old men who kept them on the leash. It was a cold, shabby, unpoetic period. Perhaps much time is needed for a restored monarchy to become a genuine one.

For the last eighteen months the Duchesse de Langeais had been leading this shallow life, exclusively occupied with balls and the visits they entail, with empty triumphs, ephemeral passions begun and ended in a single evening. When she arrived at a salon all eyes were turned to her; she reaped a harvest of fulsome compliments, a few asseverations of passion which she encouraged with a gesture or a glance and which never dipped below the surface. Everything about her – tone and manner – denoted authority. She lived in a fever of vanity and a giddy round of pleasure-seeking. She was passably daring in conversation, listened to slanderous talk and allowed depravity, so to speak, to ripple the surface of her heart. Back home again, she often blushed at things which had made her laugh, at scandalous stories the details of which had aided her in discussing theories of love, of which she knew nothing, and the subtle distinctions of modern passion as expounded by complaisant hypocrites of her own sex; for women, being completely outspoken with one another, bring more of their companions to perdition than men can ever corrupt. There came a time when she realized that to be beloved is the only guarantee a woman can have that her beauty and wit will be universally recognized. What does it prove to have a husband? That before marriage a woman had a rich dowry or was well-bred, had a clever mother or satisfied her suitor's ambitions. But a lover furnishes an inexhaustible catalogue of one's personal qualities. Madame de Langeais learnt, while still young, that a woman could allow herself to be loved ostensibly without sanctioning or approving of it, without satisfying it otherwise than with the most meagre pittance of reciprocity; and more than one coy hypocrite showed her how to play this dangerous kind of comedy. And so the duchess had her court, and the number of those who worshipped or wooed her was a warranty for her virtue. She was flirtatious, amiable, seductive until the fête, ball or soirée was over; then, once the curtain was down, she became once more her solitary, cold and uncaring self; none the less she lived again the following day for other equally superficial emotions. There were one or two young men who were completely duped and really fell in love with her. She mocked them with total callousness, and would tell herself: 'I am loved, he loves me!' The certainty of this satisfied her. Like a miser content to know that he can indulge a whim if he wants to, she perhaps no longer even allowed herself to toy with a desire.

One evening she was at the house of one of her closest friends, Madame la Vicomtesse de Fontaine, a humble rival who hated her cordially but always went about with her: the sort of armed friendship which everyone distrusts and in which confidences exchanged are adroitly discreet and sometimes perfidious. After having distributed little protective, affectionate and disdainful greetings with the air natural to a woman who knows the full value of her smiles, her regard fell on a man completely unknown to her, whose frank and grave countenance took her by surprise. As she looked at him she experienced an emotion very similar to fear.

'My dear,' she asked of Madame de Maufrigneuse, 'who is that newcomer?'

'A man you have no doubt heard about, the Marquis de Montriveau.'

'Ah, so that's who he is.' She raised her eyeglass and examined him with impertinent appraisal, as she might have scanned a portrait, something to be looked at but which cannot look back in return.

'Introduce him to me. He must be amusing.'

'No one could be more boring or gloomy, my dear; but he's very much in fashion.'

Just then Monsieur Armand de Montriveau was, unwittingly, an object of general curiosity, but he deserved it more than any of the temporary idols Paris craves for and becomes momentarily enamoured of in order to satisfy the passion for infatuation and make-believe enthusiasm with which it is periodically tormented. Armand de Montriveau was the only son of General de Montriveau, one of those *ci-devant* aristocrats who nobly served the Republic and was killed in action at Novi side by side with Joubert. The orphan had been sent through the care of Bonaparte to the school of Châlons and placed, like several other sons of generals who had perished on the battlefield, under the protection of the French republic. After emerging from this school with no money to his name he entered the artillery and at the time of the Fontainebleau disaster was still only a battalion-commander. The armed service to which Armand de Montriveau belonged had offered him few chances of promotion. In the first place, the number of officers is smaller than in any other corps; secondly, the liberal, almost republican opinions professed by the artillery, and the fears inspired in the Emperor by a collection of scientifically-minded men accustomed to thinking were an obstacle to the military advancement of most of them. And so, contrary to what is usual, officers who had risen to be generals were not always the most gifted members of that service, because, being mediocre, they roused few fears. The artillery formed a corps apart in the army and really only belonged to Napoleon on the field of battle. To these general causes explaining the slow advancement of Armand de Montriveau's career were added others inherent in his person and character. Alone in the world, flung at the age of twenty into the tempestuous crowd of men who surrounded Napoleon, having no interests outside himself, taking his life in his hands every day, he had grown accustomed to living only by virtue of self-respect and the consciousness of duty accomplished. He was by habit taciturn as all shy men are; but his shyness by no means sprang from a lack of courage – it was a sort of modesty which barred him from any display of vanity. There was no ostentation in his intrepidity on the battlefield: he had an eye to everything, gave calm and sound instructions to his troops, and did not flinch before the cannon-balls though he stooped at the right moment in order to avoid them. He was kind-hearted, but his demeanour gave an impression of haughtiness and severity. Mathematically strict in everything, he allowed of no hypocritical compromise either with the duties of a situation or the consequences of a fact. He lent himself to nothing shameful and never asked anything for himself. In short, he was one of those unknown great men, philosophical enough to be scornful of glory, who live without laying great store by life because it gives them no opportunity to develop their powers of mind or heart to their full extent. He was feared, esteemed, but little loved. Our fellow-men certainly allow us to rise above them, but they never forgive us for not stooping to their level. And so the respect they accord to great characters is not unaccompanied by a modicum of hatred and fear. To reap too much honour is a tacit censure of themselves which they pardon neither in the living nor the dead.

After Napoleon made his farewells at Fontainebleau, Montriveau, though a titled noble, was put on half-pay. His old-fashioned integrity alarmed the Ministry for War, where his loyalty to the oath he had sworn to the imperial eagles was well known. When the Hundred Days came he was commissioned Colonel of the Guard and was wounded on the field of Waterloo. His wounds having kept him in Belgium, he did not serve with the army of the Loire; but the royal government would not recognize grades conferred during the Hundred Days and Armand de Montriveau left France. Carried away by his genius for daring enterprise, by a loftiness of mind which, hitherto, the hazards of war had satisfied, and fired by an instinctive idealism which urged him towards projects of great usefulness, General Montriveau embarked upon the design of exploring Upper Egypt and the unknown parts of Africa, the central regions above all, which today excite so much interest among scholars. He had collected precious notes destined to resolve the geographical or industrial problems which have inspired so much research, and, in the teeth of many obstacles, he had reached the heart of Africa when treachery brought him into the power of a savage tribe. He was stripped of everything he had, enslaved and for two years dragged through the deserts, threatened with death continuously, and treated worse than an animal which has become the plaything of pitiless children. His physical endurance and constancy of soul enabled him to bear all the horrors of captivity; but he spent almost all his energy in contriving a miraculous escape. He reached the French colony of Senegal, half-dead and in rags, and retaining nothing more than confused recollections of his adventures. The tremendous privations he had undergone, the study he had made of African dialects, his discoveries and observations had all been useless. One single fact will show how much he suffered. For several days the children of the sheikh of the tribe which had enslaved him amused themselves by using his head as a target in a game which consisted of hurling the huckle-bones of a horse at it and making them stick.

Montriveau returned to Paris about the middle of 1818: ruined, having no protectors and seeking none. He would have suffered twenty deaths before soliciting any favour, even recognition of the rights he had acquired. Adversity and pain had developed his energy even in small matters, and the habit of preserving his dignity as a man in face of that moral entity we call the conscience gave value in his eyes to apparently insignificant acts. However, his relationship with the chief scientists in Paris and a few military men of culture caused both his merit and his adventures to become known. The details of his captivity, escape and journey back to civilization bore witness to so much self-possession, intelligence and courage that he acquired unwittingly the temporary celebrity so lavishly accorded by the salons of Paris, although it calls for unheard-of efforts on the part of artists in particular when they wish to perpetuate it. Towards the end of that year his position suddenly changed. From poor he became rich, or at any rate he came to enjoy all the external advantages of wealth. It was then that the royal government, seeking to recruit men of merit in order to strengthen the army, made some concessions to former officers whose loyalty and character offered guarantees of fidelity. Monsieur de Montriveau was put back on the active list, regained his rank, received his arrears of pay and was admitted to the Royal Guard. These favours came to him one by one without his having made the slightest solicitation. Some friends of his spared him from taking such personal steps as he would have refused to take.

Then, contrary to his habits, which he suddenly modified, he went into society, where he was favourably received and met with marks of high esteem in every quarter. He seemed to have reached a turning-point in his life; but all this took place in his own breast and was shown by no exterior signs. In society he maintained a grave and thoughtful, quiet and cold bearing. He had much social success for the very reason that he stood out strongly from the conventional figures with which the Paris salons are crowded, and indeed was quite unique. He had the curtness of speech characteristic of solitaries and savages. His shyness was mistaken for haughtiness and went down well. He was both strange and grand, and the women were the more generally taken with this novel person because he eluded their adroit flatteries and the wiles with which they circumvent the men of strongest will and soften up the most inflexible of minds. Monsieur de Montriveau understood nothing of these little Parisian affectations and his soul could only respond to the ringing vibrations of genuine feeling. He would have readily been dropped at that point had it not been for the glamour resulting from his life and adventures and the triumph of *amour-propre* awaiting the woman who succeeded in capturing his attention. And so the Duchesse de Langeais's curiosity was as lively as it was natural. By a stroke of chance, this man had aroused her interest the evening before when she had heard related an episode of his travels likely to make the most vivid impression on a woman's excitable imagination.

During an expedition to investigate the sources of the Nile, Monsieur de Montriveau had had with one of his guides the most extraordinary conflict of wills ever known in the annals of travel. There was a desert to cross, and he could only go on foot to the place he wanted to explore. Only a single guide was capable of taking him there. Up to then no traveller had succeeded in penetrating into that region, one in which the intrepid officer supposed that he might well find the solution to various scientific problems. In spite of the representations made to him both by the old men of the country and his guide, he undertook this terrible journey. Armed with all his courage – it had been whetted by the announcement of fearful difficulties to be vanquished – he set off one morning. After a whole day's march, he camped out that night unusually tired thanks to the softness of the sand which seemed to slip away at every step he took, knowing that at dawn next morning he would have to start off again: but his guide had promised that he would reach his objective at about midday. This promise gave him courage and new energy, and despite his sufferings he resumed his march, though not without some animadversions against science! But, thinking it shameful to complain in his guide's presence, he refrained from displaying his discomfort. He had already been walking for a third of the day when, feeling his strength exhausted and his feet bleeding after so much tramping, he asked if they would soon be there. 'In an hour,' the guide replied. Armand felt he could last out for another hour and went on. The hour ran out without his perceiving, even on the horizon – a horizon of sand as endless as that of the open sea – the palm trees and the mountains whose ridges were to show him the end of his journey. He stopped, threatened the guide, refused to go any farther and reproached him for deceiving him and leading him to his death. Tears of rage and fatigue rolled down his burning cheeks. His back was bent under the incessant pain of walking and his throat was parched with the thirst only the desert brings. His guide, motionless, listened to his complaints with an ironic air whilst he studied, with the apparent indifference of Orientals, the imperceptible undulations of the sand, almost as dark in colour as burnished gold. 'I have made a mistake,' he coolly remarked. 'It is too long since I followed this route for me to be able to recognize the tracks. We are on the right road, but we have to walk for two more hours.'

'The man is right,' thought Monsieur de Montriveau. Then he set off again, painfully following in the track of the pitiless African to whom he felt as if he were tied by an invisible tether, as a condemned criminal is to the hangman. But the two hours dragged on, the Frenchman had drained off his last drops of energy, and the horizon was still clear: no date-palms and no mountains were in sight. Unable any longer even to cry out or groan, he lay down on the sand to wait for death; but the look in his eyes would have terrified the most doughty of men, for it seemed to announce that he did not intend to die alone. To this glance his guide, demoniacally unperturbed, replied with one which was calm and full of power. He let him lie there, being careful to keep as distant from him as to evade a desperate assault from his victim. Finally Montriveau summoned up enough strength to voice one last imprecation. The guide came nearer, looked him in the eyes, quelled him into silence and said:

'Did you not insist against our advice on going where I am taking you? You blame me for deceiving you. If I had not done so, you would never have got so far as here. Do you want to know the truth? This is it: we have another five hours' march in front of us, and it is too late to turn back. Think it out, and if you cannot face it, here is my dagger.'

Surprised by this appalling alliance between pain and human endurance, Monsieur de Montriveau could not bear to prove inferior to a barbarian. Drawing a new dose of courage from his pride as a European, he got up to follow his guide. When the five hours had elapsed, Monsieur de Montriveau could still see nothing. He turned a dying eye towards his guide. Thereupon the Nubian took him on his shoulders, lifted him up several feet, and showed him, a hundred yards away, a lake surrounded with verdure and an admirable forest bathed in the red fire of the setting sun. They had come to within a short distance of a vast shelf of granite, beneath which this gorgeous landscape lay as it were buried. Armand felt as if recalled to life; his guide, a titan in intelligence and courage, ended his labour of devotion by carrying him across the smooth and burning tracks marked out over the granite. On one side was the inferno of the sands, on the other an earthly paradise: the most beautiful oasis which these deserts contained.

The duchess, already struck with the appearance of this poetic personage, was still more impressed on learning that he was no other than the Marquis de Montriveau of whom she had dreamed the night before. For a woman of her nature, to have been with him in imagination in the burning sands of the desert and shared his nightmares, was this not a delightful promise of entertainment? Never did any man better betray his character by his physiognomy or more justly challenge attention than Armand. His large, square head was most characteristically set off by an enormous and abundant shock of black hair which so framed his face as perfectly to recall that of General Kléber whom he resembled by the vigour outlined in his forehead, the cut of his profile, the quiet audacity of his glance and the fiery impetuosity expressed in his strongly marked features. He was small, broad in the chest and as muscular as a lion. When he walked, his carriage, stride, his slightest gesture betrayed an indefinable but impressive self-assurance and even a suggestion of despotic authority. He looked as if he knew that nothing could stand against his will – perhaps because he never willed anything that was other than just. None the less, like all men of really strong character, he was mild of speech, simple of manner and by nature kind. And yet all these attractive qualities seemed likely to disappear when grave circumstances arose, those which make a man implacable in his feelings, immovable in his resolutions and terrible in his actions. Moreover, an observant person might have discerned in the set of his lips an upward curl, etched in by habit, which betrayed an inclination to irony.

The Duchesse de Langeais, knowing what temporary prestige the conquest of this man could confer upon her, resolved, during the minute or two it took for the Duchesse de Maufrigneuse to bring him for introduction, to have him as one of her suitors, to allot him precedence over all the others, to attach him to her person and give him the benefit of all her coquettish charms. It was a whim, the pure caprice of a duchess, like the one which inspired Lope de Vega in his *Dog in the Manger*. She intended that he should belong to no other woman than herself, though she had no idea of belonging to him. Nature had endowed her with the qualities needed for playing the role of a coquette, and her manner of education had brought her to perfection in this. Women had good reason for envying her and men for loving her. She lacked none of the charms which can inspire, justify and perpetuate love. Her style of beauty, manners, diction and pose combined to endow her with a natural coquetry which, in a woman, seems identical with the consciousness of her own power. She had a good figure and perhaps exploited this fact too complacently in her movements – and this was the only palpable affectation with which one could reproach her. Everything about her was harmonious, from the least gesture to her special turn of phrase and the charming hypocrisy of her glances. The predominant trait in her physiognomy was an elegant, noble dignity which the entirely French mobility of her personality did nothing to destroy. Her ever-changing attitudes were prodigiously attractive to men. One would have sworn that she would be the most delicious of mistresses after shedding her corset and the other paraphernalia of social display. In fact all the joys of love existed in embryo in the free promise of her glances, the caressing modulations of her voice and the gracefulness of her speech. It was plain to see that there were in her the makings of a noble courtesan and that her religious practices gave the lie to this in vain. Whoever sat near her during a reception found her now gay, now melancholy without it appearing that these moods were assumed. She could be at whim affable, scornful, impertinent or confidential. She seemed and indeed was kindly. In a situation like hers she was under no compulsion to stoop to spitefulness. At different moments she showed herself trustful or wily, movingly tender, then harsh and hard enough to break one's heart. But in order to depict her faithfully one would have to make a list of all opposing traits in a woman: in a word she was whatever she wanted to be or to seem. Her face was a trifle too long, but there was grace in it, a certain subtlety, a certain minuteness reminding one of medieval figures. Her skin was pale with delicate rose tints. In fact, if she had a blemish it was excess of delicacy.

Monsieur de Montriveau obligingly allowed himself to be introduced to the Duchesse de Langeais, and she, with the exquisite taste which steers clear of the commonplace, received him without overwhelming him with questions or complaints, but with a certain respectful graciousness likely to flatter a superior man; for superiority in a man implies that he possesses to some extent the tact which enables a woman to divine his capacity for feeling. If she manifested any curiosity at all, it was by dint of the looks she gave him. If she paid him any compliments, it was merely by her manner. And she displayed that feline flattery of speech, that subtle desire to charm at which she excelled. But the whole of her conversation was as it were the text of a letter she might have written: what really mattered had to be conveyed in the postscript. When, after half an hour of desultory chatting in which tone and smiles alone had any meaning, Monsieur de Montriveau made as if to withdraw discreetly, the duchess held him back with an expressive gesture.

'Monsieur,' she said to him, 'I don't know if the few moments during which I have had the pleasure of chatting with you have offered you sufficient attraction to justify my inviting you to my house. I fear it may be too great selfishness on my part to wish to welcome you there. If happily this were agreeable to you, you would always find me at home in the evening up to ten o'clock.'

She said this with such blandishment that Monsieur de Montriveau could do no less than accept the invitation. When he fell back among the groups of men standing some distance away from the women several of his friends congratulated him, half-seriously, half-mockingly, on the extraordinary welcome given him by the Duchesse de Langeais. Decidedly, they said, he had made a difficult, an illustrious conquest, and the glory of this accrued to the artillery of the Guard. It is easy to imagine the pleasantries in good and bad taste that this topic, once taken up, prompted in that type of Paris salon, where diversion is the order of the day and opportunities for raillery are so short-lived that everyone makes the most of them while he may.

This nonsense flattered the general without his being aware of it. From the standpoint he had adopted, his attention was attracted to the duchess by much vague musing; nor could he refrain from admitting to himself that of all the women whose beauty had captured his regard, none had offered him a more delicious expression of the virtues, defects and harmonies that the most juvenile French imagination might look for in a mistress. What man of whatever rank has not felt an ineffable spiritual elation on finding in a woman on whom his choice has fallen – if only in his dreams – that triple perfection, spiritual, physical and social, which enables him to look upon her for ever as the realization of all he desires? Even if it is not an incentive to love, so gratifying a combination of qualities is assuredly one of the most effective vehicles for sentiment. 'Without vanity,' said a profound eighteenth-century moralist, 'love lacks robustness.' Undoubtedly, for men as for women, the superiority of the beloved person is a treasure-house of delight. It is much, it is everything perhaps, to know that our self-esteem will never be wounded through her, that she is of too high birth ever to suffer the humiliation of a slighting glance, that she is rich enough to live on as brilliant a scale as the ephemeral potentates of finance, witty enough never to let herself be worsted in an exchange of subtle sarcasms, and beautiful enough to outvie all her sex.

It takes a man no time to make reflections of this sort. But if the woman who sets him thinking on these lines simultaneously offers him, for the future of his incipient passion, the varying charms of feminine graciousness, the ingenuousness of a virgin soul, the thousand folds and pleats of coquettish adornment, the perils attendant upon love, would not all this stir the heart of the coldest man? That is the situation in which, at that moment, Monsieur de Montriveau found himself with regard to the opposite sex, and the circumstances of his past afforded some explanation of its singularity. Flung in adolescence into the tumult of the French wars, having spent his life on the battlefield, he knew no more about women than what a hurried traveller moving from inn to inn can know of the country he passes through. He might perhaps have said of his life what Voltaire at eighty said of his, and had he not thirty-seven follies to blame himself for? He was, at his age, as new to love as a young man who has just read a licentious novel surreptitiously. He knew everything about women but nothing about love; and consequently his virginity of sentiment aroused quite novel desires in him. A certain number of men, absorbed in activities which poverty, ambition, art or science has forced them to undertake, just as Monsieur de Montriveau had been swept away by war and personal vicissitudes, are cognizant of this singular situation but rarely admit the fact. In Paris every man is deemed to have loved. No woman in Paris wants a man if no other woman has wanted him. From the fear of being taken for an innocent proceed the boasts put forward by the fops in France, where to be reckoned an innocent is to be reckoned a foreigner.

And so, at that juncture, Monsieur de Montriveau was at one and the same time seized with a violent desire, a desire which the heat of the deserts had intensified, and with a surge of passion whose burning grip he had never before experienced. As strong as he was violent, he succeeded in stifling his emotion; but while chatting with her about insignificant matters he had been withdrawing into himself and had sworn that he would possess this woman. This was the only way for him to embark upon a love affair: the desire became an oath after the manner of the Arabs with whom he had lived and for whom an oath is a contract made between themselves and their destiny, the whole of which they forthwith subordinate to the successful execution of the oath, counting the risk of death merely as giving them an additional chance of success. One young man would have said to himself: 'How I would like to have the Duchesse de Langeais as my mistress!' Another would have said: 'The man whom the Duchesse de Langeais loves will be a lucky fellow!' But the general said: 'Madame de Langeais shall be my mistress.' When a man, virgin in heart and for whom love is becoming a religion, conceives such an idea, he little knows into what an inferno he is stepping.

Monsieur de Montriveau left the salon abruptly and returned home burning for the first time with the fever of love. If a man, as he nears middle age, still cherishes the beliefs and illusions, the candour and impetuosity of childhood, his first gesture as it were is to stretch forth his hand in order to grasp the thing he covets. Then, when he has gauged the almost unbridgeable distance that separates it from him, he is seized, as children are, with a kind of astonishment or impatience which enhances the value of the object desired: he trembles or he weeps. And so it was with Armand de Montriveau. The next day, after the stormiest reflections that had ever ravaged his soul, he found himself under the domination of emotion intensified by the fact of being genuinely in love. The woman he had so cavalierly decided should be his the night before had now become the most sacred and awesome power in the world: from henceforth she was indeed the whole world, life itself to him. The liveliest joys and most excruciating pains of his past life were as nothing compared to the mere recollection of the emotion she had stirred up in him. The most rapid reversals of fortune disturb only a man's interests, whereas the onset of passion revolutionizes his whole way of feeling. For those whose life is guided by feeling rather than self-interest, for those who have more heart and blood than mind and lymph, real love changes the whole course of existence. And so, at a single stroke, with a single reflection, Armand de Montriveau effaced his entire past.

After asking himself a score of times, like a child: 'Shall I go? Shall I not go?' he dressed, came to the Langeais residence about eight in the evening, was admitted to the presence of the woman – or rather the idol he had seen the evening before under a blaze of light as a fresh and pure girl in a filmy veil of gauze and lace. He went in impetuously with the intention of declaring his love like a commander bringing up his cannon to the battlefield. Poor neophyte! He found his nebulous sylph wrapped in a peignoir of brown cashmere, skilfully flounced, and languidly reclining on a divan in a dimly-lit boudoir. Madame de Langeais did not even rise to her feet, and showed only her head, with her hair dishevelled though caught up in a veil. Then, with a hand which, in the half-light produced by the flickering gleam of a single candle placed some distance away, seemed to his eyes as white as a hand of marble, she signed to him to sit down and said, in a voice as soft as the candlelight itself: 'Had it been anyone but you, Monsieur le Marquis, had it been a friend whom I could have treated unceremoniously, or a casual visitor in whom I was only slightly interested, I should have sent you away. I am feeling frightfully ill.'

Armand thought, 'I'd better go away.'

'But,' she continued, darting at him a glance whose brightness the ingenuous soldier attributed to fever, 'I don't know whether this is due to a presentiment of your kind visit – I am extremely touched by your promptitude in paying it – but for the last few moments my head has been feeling better.'

'So I may stay?' Montriveau asked her.

'Indeed I should be very sorry to see you go. I was telling myself this morning that I could not have made the slightest impression on you, that you had doubtless taken my invitation for one of those meaningless phrases casually lavished by Parisian hostesses; and I forgave you in advance for your ingratitude. A man back from the Sahara is not bound to know how selective our *faubourg* is in the friendships it accords.'

These gracious words, half whispered, dropped one by one, laden as it were with the pleasurable feeling with which they appeared to be spoken. The duchess had wanted to make the most of her migraine and her calculation met with complete success. The naïve soldier really did feel for her in her feigned suffering. Like the valiant Crillon who, when listening to the story of Christ's passion, exclaimed: 'Why wasn't I there?' he was ready to draw his sword to kill her headache. How then could he dare to tell this fragile divinity of the love she inspired in him? Armand realized that it would be absurd to fire his love, point-blank like a pistol, at so superior a being. A single flash of thought instructed him in the niceties of feeling and the delicate exigencies of spiritual communication. To love is to plead one's cause, to entreat, to be patient. Now that he was feeling such love, was it not his duty to prove it? He discovered that his tongue was stilled and chilled by the conventions of the aristocratic *faubourg*, by the majestic prestige of migraine and by the timidity of true love. But no power on earth could veil what his eyes conveyed: the torridity, the infinitude of the desert. His gaze was as steady as that of a panther, and only at rare intervals did his eyelids droop. She was thrilled by this fixed regard which bathed her with light and love.

'Madame la duchesse,' he answered. 'I fear I shall imperfectly express the gratitude I feel for your kindness. At this moment I have but one desire: to be able to dispel your sufferings.'

'I find it too warm now, allow me to remove this;' she said, gracefully throwing off the cushion covering her feet, which she now displayed in all their attractiveness.

'Madame, in Asia your feet would command a price of some ten thousand sequins.'

'A globe-trotter's compliment!' she said with a smile.

In spritely mood, she took pleasure in drawing the rugged Montriveau into a conversation full of nonsensical and platitudinous trivialities, during which, if we may use a military term, he manoeuvred as the Archduke Charles would have done when at grips with Napoleon. She took a mischievous delight in gauging the extent of his incipient passion by the number of silly remarks she extracted from this inexperienced wooer whom she was enticing step by step into a hopeless maze in which she intended to leave him ashamed and confused. The length of a first visit is often a flattery, but Armand had no lot or part in this. The celebrated traveller had been in this boudoir for an hour, chatting on all subjects without having said anything, feeling that he was merely an instrument in the hands of the woman who was playing on him, when she bestirred herself, sat up, drew about her neck the veil which had covered her head, leaned on her elbows, did him the honour of a complete recovery from her indisposition and rang for the lights to be lit. To a long phase of immobility followed one of most graceful movement. She turned to Monsieur de Montriveau and, in reply to a confidence she had just wrung from him and which she seemed to find vividly interesting, she said to him: 'You are mocking at me by trying to convince me you have never loved. That's what men always pretend. We take their word for it, but purely out of politeness. Don't we know from our own experience what the truth really is? Find me a man who through all his life has not had occasion to fall in love. But you like to deceive us, and we let you do it, poor sillies that we are, because all the same the deceits you practise on us are the tributes you pay to the nobility and delicacy of our feelings.'

This last sentence was uttered with an accent so full of haughtiness and pride that the neophyte lover felt like a ball hurled to the bottom of an abyss and saw the duchess as an angel soaring upwards to her own special sphere in heaven.

'The devil!' Armand de Montriveau exclaimed to himself. 'By what means can I manage to tell this unapproachable being that I love her?'

Actually he had told her twenty times, or rather the duchess had twenty times read it in his eyes and anticipated that the passion of a truly great man would be a distraction for her and bring some interest to her dull life. She was already therefore very skilfully preparing to throw up round herself a series of barriers which he had to carry by assault before he obtained entry to the citadel of her heart. He was to be a plaything for her whims; he was to surmount one obstacle after another while making no advance, like an insect which, teased by a child, hops from one finger to another in the belief that it is getting away, while its malicious tormentor keeps it stationary. None the less, the duchess recognized with inexpressible pleasure that this sterling character was not misrepresenting the facts: he had indeed never loved before.

He was about to withdraw, dissatisfied with himself and

even more dissatisfied with her. But she was glad of this sullenness, for she knew she could dispel it with a word, a look, a gesture.

'Will you come tomorrow evening?' she asked him. 'I am going to a ball and will wait for you until ten o'clock.'

Montriveau spent most of the next day sitting at his study window smoking an indeterminate number of cigars. He was thus able to kill time before dressing and going to the Hôtel de Langeais. To those who knew the noble worth of this man it would have been a pitiable experience to see him so dwarfed, so unsure of himself, to know that a range of thought capable of embracing the whole wide world was now confined to the limits of a fashionable lady's boudoir. But he himself felt so fallen from happiness that not even to save his life would he have confessed this love to one of his closest friends. There is perhaps always, in the diffidence which takes hold of man when he loves, an element of shame, and perhaps it is in this sense of belittlement that a woman glories. In fact there might be a multitude of motives of this kind – they do not bother to sort them out – which impel almost all women to be the first to let out the secret of their love, a secret which perhaps has become irksome to them.

'Monsieur,' said the footman, 'Madame la Duchesse cannot see you yet. She is dressing, and begs you to wait for her here.'

Armand strolled round the drawing-room and took note of the good taste displayed in every detail. He admired Madame de Langeais in admiring whatever came from her and revealed her habits, as a preliminary to comprehending her personality and her ideas. After about an hour, the duchess glided silently from her bedroom. Montriveau turned round, saw her walking forward with the lightness of a sylph and was startled. She came towards him without seeming to ask him, as a woman of the bourgeoisie might have done, 'How do I look?' She was sure of herself, and her steady glance told him: 'I have dressed to please you.' Only the fairy godmother of some unrecognized princess could have draped round the throat of this delicate creature the filmy gauze in whose folds the warm tones were further enhanced by the flush of a satiny skin. The duchess was dazzling. The light blue of her gown, whose floral designs were repeated in her head-dress, seemed by its richness of colour to lend substance to her slight and now quite ethereal form; for her swiftly smooth approach towards Armand caused the ends of the sash which hung at her sides to flutter, so that our gallant soldier perforce compared her in his thoughts to the pretty blue insects which flit over ponds amid the flowers with which they appear to mingle their colours.

'I have kept you waiting,' she said with the tone that women readily adopt for the man they wish to please.

'I would wait in patience for all eternity to find so lovely a divinity. But it is no compliment to speak to you of your beauty: you can accept nothing but adoration. Permit me then simply to kiss your scarf.'

'Indeed no!' she said with a stately gesture. 'I esteem you well enough to offer you my hand.' And she held out her still moist hand for him to kiss. A woman's hand, just after she has come out of a perfumed bath, retains a kind of dewy freshness, a velvety softness which transmits a tender tingling from the lips to the soul. In the case of a man in love whose senses are as pleasurably aroused as his heart is enamoured, such a kiss, seemingly chaste, may excite considerable turmoil.

'Will you always offer it to me like this?' the general humbly asked as he respectfully kissed that dangerous hand.

'Yes, but we shall go no further than that,' she said with a smile. She sat down and appeared to find difficulty in replacing her gloves, which seemed too tight for her fingers to slip into them; meanwhile she was stealing glances at the marquis, whose admiration was divided between the duchess and the gracefulness of her reiterated gestures.

'I am delighted,' she said. 'You are punctual. I like punctuality. His Majesty calls it the politeness of kings. But, between ourselves, I look upon it as the most respectful of compliments. Don't you think so yourself?' Then she gave him another sidelong glance expressive of deceptive friend-liness, seeing that he was speechless with pleasure and charmed with these trifling attentions. Indeed the duchess was wonderfully adept in feminine tactics. She knew exactly how to bolster up a man's self-esteem and how to recompense him with hollow flatteries at every downward step he took into the inanities of sentimentality. '

'You will never forget to come at nine o'clock?'

'No. But will you be going to a ball every evening?'

'I really don't know,' she replied with a childish shrug as if to confess that she was an impulsive creature and that an admirer had to accept the fact. 'In any case, does that matter? You shall take me.'

'For this evening,' he said, 'it would be difficult. I am not correctly dressed.'

'It seems to me,' she replied with a haughty look, 'that if anyone should take exception to your dress, it should be I. But learn this, gentle traveller, the man whose arm I take is always superior to fashion and impervious to criticism. I see that you are not familiar with the ways of society, but I like you the better for that.'

Thus she was already throwing him into the petty niceties of the world by trying to initiate him into the vanities of a lady of fashion.

'If she is ready to commit a solecism for me,' thought Armand, 'I should be a great fool to prevent her. She no doubt likes me, and she certainly doesn't despise society more than I do myself. So here goes for the ball!'

No doubt the duchess thought that no one who saw the general following her in boots and black cravat would hesitate to believe that he was passionately enamoured of her. The general, happy to see the queen of elegant society willing to compromise herself for him, found his wit rising as his hopes increased. Confident of his powers to please, he gave full rein to his ideas and feelings, freed henceforth from the constraint which had made him reticent the evening before. Had this more substantial and animated conversation, full of first avowals as sweet to utter as to hear, really charmed

Madame de Langeais, or had she contrived this ravishing exchange of coquetries? In any case when midnight struck she threw a mischievous glance at the clock.

'Oh! You've made me miss the ball!' she said, expressing surprise and vexation at having forgotten the time. Then she forgave herself for having changed one enjoyment for another with a smile which made Armand's heart leap.

'I promised Madame de Beauséant I would be there,' she added. 'Everybody's expecting me.'

'Very well, go.'

'No,' she said. 'Continue. I'm thrilled by your adventures in the East. Tell me the whole story of your life. I love to share the privations of a man of courage – for indeed I do share them!' She was playing with her scarf, twisting it and tearing at it with impatient tugs which seemed to indicate inward dissatisfaction and deep reflection. 'We women are of no use,' she continued. 'We are unworthy, selfish, frivolous. All we can do is to bore ourselves to death with amusements. No one of us has any sense of mission. In the old France women were beacon lights and lived to console those who wept, to encourage outstanding virtue, to give artists their reward and inspire them with noble thoughts. If the world has become so petty, it is our fault. You make me hate society and its ballrooms. No, I'm not making much of a sacrifice in staying here with you.' She ended by tearing her scarf into shreds, as a child playing with a flower ends up by pulling out all its petals. She rolled it up, threw it away from her, and was thus able to display her swanlike neck.

Then she rang. 'I shall not go out,' she told her footman. Then, shyly, she turned her long blue eyes on Armand, so shyly as to make him feel, by the timidity they expressed, that the order she had given was an avowal, a first and great favour. 'You have passed through many tribulations,' she said after a thoughtful silence and with the tenderness a woman can often put into her voice without feeling it in her heart.

'No really,' Armand replied. 'I never knew what happiness was until today.'

'So now you know what it is?' she asked, looking at him from beneath her lashes with bewitching hypocrisy.

'Henceforward, for me, happiness means just to see you, hear you. Up to now I have merely endured; only now do I realize what unhappiness might mean ...'

'No more for now,' she said. 'You must be going, it is midnight. Let us respect the proprieties. We must not make people talk. Good-bye. I don't know what excuse I shall give, but migraine is a kind friend that never lets us down!'

'Is there a ball tomorrow?' he asked.

'You'll get used to them, I think. Yes indeed, and we will go to it.'

Armand went away the happiest man in the world. Every evening he called on Madame de Langeais at the time which, by a kind of tacit agreement, she reserved for him. It would be wearisome and, for many young people who have sweet memories of such occasions, superfluous to let our story creep on at a slow pace, as did the poem of these secret conversations, their course speeded up or slowed down at a woman's whim, through a dispute over words when feeling moves too fast, or through a complaint over feeling when words no longer respond to thought. And so, perhaps, in order to mark the stages on the growth of this Penelope's web, we should confine our attention to material gauges of sentiment. Thus, several days after these two first met, the persevering general had acquired the exclusive right of kissing the insatiable hands of the lady he was wooing. Wherever Madame de Langeais went, there was Monsieur de Montriveau to be seen; some jesting persons called him the duchess's orderly. Armand's position had already given rise to envy, jealousy and enmity. Madame de Langeais had achieved her aim. The marquis had taken his place among her numerous admirers and, by giving him precedence in public over all others, she used him as a means for humiliating those who preened themselves on being in her good graces.

'Decidedly,' said Madame de Sérisy, 'Monsieur de Montriveau is the man whom the duchess distinguishes the most.'

There is no mistaking what it means in Paris to be 'distinguished' by a woman: everything therefore was deemed to be perfectly settled. The tales told about the general's prowess made him so redoubtable that prudent young men tacitly abandoned their claims to the duchess's favour and only remained within her orbit so as to avail themselves of the importance their presence in it gave them and in order by using her name and person to make the best possible terms with certain secondary divinities who were enchanted to filch admirers from Madame de Langeais. The duchess was keen-eyed enough to take note of these desertions, and her self-pride did not allow her to be duped by any pacts thus made. And, as Prince Talleyrand, who was fond of her, said, she was well able to exact double vengeance by the two-edged sarcasms she directed against these 'morganatic nuptials'. Her disdainful raillery contributed not a little to making her feared and establishing her as an extremely witty person. She thus consolidated her reputation for virtue while deriving amusement from other people's secrets without letting her own be guessed at. Nevertheless, after receiving two months of assiduous attentions from him, she felt deep down within her a vague apprehension when she saw that Monsieur de Montriveau was impervious to the subtleties of Faubourg Saint-Germain coquetry and took Parisian affectations seriously. 'That man, my dear duchess,' the old Vidame de Pamiers had told her, 'is first cousin to the eagles. You won't tame him, and he'll carry you off to his eyrie if you don't look out.' The evening after the wily old man had made this remark, which Madame de Langeais feared might turn out to be a prophecy, she tried to make herself odious and showed herself hard, exacting, irritable and detestable to Armand; but he responded with an angelic gentleness which she found disarming. She was so unfamiliar with the generous kindliness of noble characters that she was deeply impressed by the graceful good humour with which her plaintiveness was received from the start. Here she was, picking a quarrel, and meeting only with proofs of affection! But she persisted.

'How,' Armand asked her, 'can a man who idolizes you have managed to displease you?'

'You don't displease me,' she answered, and she suddenly became meek and submissive. 'But why do you want to compromise me? You can only be a *friend* to me. Don't you realize that? I wish I could discover in you the instinct, the tactfulness of true friendship, so that I need lose neither your esteem nor the pleasure that I feel in having you near me.'

'Only be a *friend* to you!' exclaimed Monsieur de Montriveau, and the sound of this terrible word ran through him like an electric shock. 'Putting my faith in the delightful hours you grant me, I wake and sleep in your heart! And today, without motive, you take gratuitous pleasure in killing the secret hope by which I live. After making me promise so much constancy, after claiming to feel so much horror for women who follow their mere caprices, are you trying to tell me that, like all other women in Paris, you have passions but no love? Why then have you asked my life of me? And why have you accepted it?'

'I did wrong, my friend. Yes, a woman is wrong to be swept off her feet by such intoxicating declarations when she cannot and must not reward them.'

'I see ... You have merely been indulging in a little coquetry.'

'Coquetry? I hate coquetry. To be a coquette, Armand, is to promise oneself to many men and give oneself to none. To give oneself to all is to be a libertine. That is the conclusion I draw from our way of life. But to be melancholy with the moody, and gay with the carefree, to talk politics with ambitious men, to listen admiringly to chatterboxes, to discuss war with military men, to be passionately patriotic with philanthropists, to spoon out to all and sundry their little dose of flattery, all that seems to me as necessary as putting flowers in our hair, wearing diamonds, gloves and pretty clothes. Conversation is the moral equivalent to self-adornment: it is taken up or laid aside like a fashionable hair-style.

'Is that what you call coquetry? But I have never treated you as I treat the world at large. With you, my friend, I am sincere. I have not always agreed with your ideas, but when you have convinced me in a discussion, have you not seen how happy I have been? In short, I love you, but only in the way a pure and religious-minded woman should love. I am married, Armand, and although my mode of life with Monsieur de Langeais leaves me free to dispose of my heart as I please, the laws and conventions of society withhold from me the right to dispose of my person. Whatever her rank in life, a dishonoured woman is exiled from society, and so far I have never heard of a man aware of the obligations to which such a sacrifice commits him. I will go further still: the breach which everyone foresees between Madame de Beauséant and Monsieur d'Ajuda who, they say, is marrying Mademoiselle de Rochefide,[9] has proved to me that sacrifices of this kind are almost the precise reason why men abandon women. If you love me sincerely, you will give up seeing me for a certain time, and I myself, for your sake, will forgo all worldly vanity. Is not that something? What do they not say of a woman to whom no man devotes himself? That she is heartless, witless, soulless, and, above all, devoid of charm. Oh! the coquettes will spare me nothing; they will rob me of the very qualities they are so vexed to find in me. But so long as my reputation is intact, what does it matter to me for any advantages I may possess to be contested by my rivals? They can certainly not inherit them from me. I beg you, my friend, give something to me who sacrifices so much to you! Come here less often. I shall love you no less for it.'

'Ah!' Armand replied with the profound irony of a wounded heart. 'Love, according to the scribblers, feeds only on illusions! I now see that nothing is more true. I must just persuade myself that I am loved. But believe me: there are certain thoughts, as there are certain wounds, from which there is no recovery. I placed my faith in you as in a last resort. I now perceive that here below there is nothing but falsity.'

She broke into a smile.

'Yes,' Montriveau continued in a faltering voice. 'Your Catholic faith to which you are trying to convert me is a lie people tell one another. Hope is a lie looking forward to the future. Pride is a lie we tell one another. Pity, wisdom,

9. Recounted in *Old Goriot* and *A Deserted Mistress*.

terror are lying calculations. So then my happiness must also be an illusion: I must cheat myself and always be ready to barter gold for silver. If it's so easy for you to do without seeing me, if you will not acknowledge me either as friend or lover, you have no love for me. And I, poor fool that I am, tell myself all that. I know it's true, and still I love you.'

'But good heavens, dear Armand. You're going beyond all limits.'

'Going beyond all limits?'

'Yes, you're imagining that everything is in question just because I'm saying we must be prudent.'

At heart she was delighted to see such anger blazing in her lover's eyes. At present she was teasing him; but she was also sizing him up and noting his every change of countenance. Had the general been so unlucky as to be generous without demur – as unsophisticated souls often are – he would have been for ever put beyond the pale: tried and convicted for incapacity to love. Most women like to feel themselves morally violated: it is part of their self-flattery to yield only to force. But Armand's education was not complete enough for him to perceive the trap so cleverly laid. Strong men in love have still so much of the child in them!

'If all you want is to save appearances,' he naïvely said, 'I am ready to . . .'

'To save appearances?' she broke in impetuously. 'But what sort of idea have you of me? Have I ever given you the slightest right to suppose that I could belong to you?'

'Why then, what is all this about?' Montriveau asked.

'But Monsieur de Montriveau, you appal me! No, forgive me, I thank you, Armand,' she continued in a chilling tone of voice. 'You are warning me in time of an imprudence I certainly did not intend to commit, believe me, my friend. You are used to suffering, you say. I too shall learn how to suffer. We shall give up these meetings. Then, when we have both had time to calm down a bit, well, then we will think how to arrange for ourselves a kind of happiness which society can accept. I am young, Armand. A man without delicacy might make a woman of twenty-four do many stupid and reckless things. But *you* will be a friend to me. Promise me that.'

'A woman of twenty-four,' he answered, 'is old enough to work things out.' He sat down on the divan and remained there with his head in his hands. 'Do you love me, Madame?' he asked, raising his head again and showing a face full of resolution. 'Speak frankly: yes or no.'

The duchess was more frightened at this question than she would have been at a threat of murder, a commonplace ruse which impresses few women of the nineteenth century now that men no longer carry swords. But there are certain visible signs in eyelids and eyelashes, frowning looks and quivering lips which are vividly, magnetically communicative of terror.

'Ah!' she replied. 'If I were free, if . . . '

'What? It's only your husband who's in our way?' the general joyously cried, taking great strides up and down the boudoir. 'My dear Antoinette, I possess a power which is more absolute than that of the autocrat of all the Russias. I have struck a bargain with Fate. Socially speaking, I can advance or retard a man's fate at my whim, just as one does with a watch.[10] In order to control destiny in our political machine one merely has to understand how it works. Before long you will be free. Will you then abide by your promise?'

'Armand, what do you mean? Great God! Do you think that I can be the reward for such a crime? Do you wish for my death? Have you not a shred of religion in you? I fear God. Although Monsieur de Langeais has given me the right to hate him, I wish him no harm.'

Monsieur de Montriveau, who was automatically drumming with his fingers on the marble of the chimney-piece, contented himself with looking calmly at the duchess.

'My friend,' she continued, 'respect him. He does not love me, he does not treat me well, but I have my duty towards him. There is nothing I would not do to shield him from the misfortunes you threaten him with.

'Listen,' she resumed after a pause. 'There shall be no more

10. A probable allusion to the hidden power of the Thirteen.

talk of parting. You will come here as in the past and you shall have my forehead to kiss. If sometimes I have refused you this, it was pure coquetry, I admit. But let us be clear about this,' she said as she saw him approaching her. 'You will allow me to increase the number of those who pay court to me, to receive in the mornings even more than I did in the past. I shall be twice as frivolous. I shall pretend to treat you harshly and make it look as if we are breaking apart. You will come slightly less often. But then, afterwards . . .'

As she spoke these words, she let him put his arm round her waist and hold her tightly. It appeared as if she felt the extreme pleasure which most women feel at such pressure and which seems like a foretaste of all the pleasures of love. No doubt also she was desirous of drawing some discreet avowal from him, for she rose on tiptoe in order to bring her forehead to Armand's burning lips.

'After this,' Montriveau rejoined, 'never again mention your husband. Think no more of him.'

Madame de Langeais remained silent.

'At any rate,' she said after an expressive pause, 'you will do everything I wish, without grumbling or bad temper, will you not, dear friend? Were you not trying to frighten me? Come now, own up – you are too kind ever to harbour criminal thoughts. But can it be that you have secrets unknown to me? How can you possibly control fate?'

'Now that you have confirmed the gift that you had already made me of your heart, I am too happy to be quite sure what answer I should make to you. I trust you, Antoinette; I will nurse neither suspicion nor false jealousy. But if chance sets you free, we shall be united . . .'

'Chance, Armand,' she said with a pretty toss of the head of the sort which seems to be fraught with meaning and which women of her kind throw off as lightly as an opera-singer scatters her trills. 'Chance alone,' she continued. 'Understand this: if through your agency some misfortune happened to Monsieur de Langeais, I would never be yours.'

They parted in mutual satisfaction. The duchess had made a pact which allowed her to prove to the world, by word and deed, that Monsieur de Montriveau was not her lover. As for him, the wily creature purposed to tire him out by granting him no other favours than those he could snatch during the playful struggles which she provoked or cut short as she pleased. She was so charmingly skilful at revoking one day the concessions she had made the day before, she was so seriously determined to remain physically virtuous that she saw no risk for herself in preliminary skirmishes which only a woman far gone in love might find dangerous. In fact, a duchess separated from her husband offered little leverage to love by sacrificing to it a marriage which for long since had meant nothing. On his side Montriveau, quite happy to have obtained the vaguest of promises and to have thrust aside for ever the objections which a married woman makes on the grounds of marital fidelity in order to repulse an offer of love, congratulated himself on having advanced yet a little further. And so, for some time, he abused the rights of usufruct which he had found it so difficult to acquire. More of a child than he had ever been, he indulged in all the childish absurdities which make first love the springtime of life. He regressed to infancy by pouring out his soul and all the frustrated energy which passion aroused in him on this woman's hands, her blond hair whose soft curls he kissed and the peerless brow which seemed to him so pure.

The duchess, inundated with love, overcome by the magnetic effluvium issuing from so strong a passion, was loath to provoke a quarrel which might part them for ever. She was more of a woman than she thought, this fragile creature, in her efforts to conciliate the claims of religion with the recurrent impulses of vanity and the semblances of pleasure on which the women of Paris dote. She never missed mass or any other offices on a Sunday. But when evening came, she submerged herself in the intoxicating voluptuousness which repressed desire procures. Armand and Madame de Langeais were like the Hindu ascetics who are rewarded for their chastity by the temptations it provokes. Perhaps also the duchess had reached the point of identifying love with these almost fraternal caresses which doubtless would have appeared innocuous to all and sundry, but to which the extravagance of her ideas attributed excessive depravation. How otherwise could we explain the impenetrable mystery of her perpetual fluctuations? Every morning she thought of closing her door to the Marquis de Montriveau. Then every evening, at the appointed hour, she allowed his charm to operate. After a weak defence she would become more accommodating. Her conversation became sweet and gracious as befits two lovers together.

The duchess used to display her most scintillating wit and practise her most captivating courtesies. Then, when she had sharpened her lover's senses and sensibilities beyond breaking point, if he clasped her in his arms, she was not unwilling to yield to a modicum of violence, but she assigned a *ne plus ultra* to his passion. When it reached a critical stage and it appeared as if he might press on too far, she grew angry. Yet no woman dares without motive refuse herself to love, nothing being more natural than to yield to it. And so Madame de Langeais soon girded herself with a second line of fortification, more difficult to take by storm than the first had been. She invoked the terrors of religion. Never did the most eloquent father of the Church better plead a holy cause. Never did the vengeance of the Almighty find better justification than from the duchess's lips. She used neither sermonizing phraseology nor rhetorical developments. No, she had her own particular style in oratory. To Armand's most ardent supplications she responded with a tearful look and a gesture which depicted a fearful plenitude of feeling. She silenced him by imploring mercy of him: one more word she could not bear to hear, she would give way. Better death than the enjoyment of guilty happiness.

'Is it then a light matter to disobey God?' she would ask, recovering her voice weakened by inward conflict – this charming actress seemed now, with difficulty, to be regaining momentary control of it. 'Men and the whole world I would willingly sacrifice to you: but it is very selfish of you to ask me to give up my eternal happiness for a moment of pleasure. Come now, are you not happy?' she added, putting her hand into his; she was displaying herself in a négligé which assuredly offered her lover consolations of which he always took the best advantage he could.

If, in order to keep her hold on a man whose ardent passion furnished her with unaccustomed emotions; or if, out of weakness, she allowed him to snatch a rapid kiss, she immediately made a show of fear, blushed and banished Armand from her sofa, since their proximity on it seemed to be becoming dangerous.

'The pleasures I allow you are sins which I have to expiate, Armand,' she would exclaim. 'They cost me penitence and remorse.'

When Montriveau was himself thus removed to a distance of two chairs from this aristocratic daughter of Eve, he took to blasphemy and cursed God. Then the duchess became angry.

'My friend,' she said, curtly. 'I don't understand why you refuse to believe in God, for it's impossible to believe in men. Hold your tongue. Don't say such things. You have too great a soul to accept the stupidities of liberalism, which claims to do away with God.'

Theological and political discussions were as good as cold showers for cooling Montriveau's ardour, for he was incapable of returning to the theme of love when she excited his wrath and removed him a thousand leagues away from her boudoir by trotting out absolutist theories which she defended marvellously well. Few women are daring enough to be democratic, for that puts them into too great a contradiction with the despotism they like to exercise in the realm of sentiment. But also often the general shook his mane, thrust politics aside, growled like the lion he was, lashed his tail, pounced on his prey, and then returned to his mistress in a rage of love, incapable as he was of keeping his heart and his thought for long in flagrant opposition. If she then felt pricked with a fancy which might provoke her enough to compromise her, she knew the moment was ripe to leave her boudoir. She withdrew from its desire-laden atmosphere, went to her salon, sat down at her piano, sang the most delightful melodies of modern music, and in this way cheated the sensual love which sometimes gave her no quarter but which she was still strong enough to overcome. At such moments Armand thought her sublime: there was no pretence but only truth in her, and the fond lover believed he was loved in return. Her egoistical resistance made him take her for a saintly and virtuous creature. He grew resigned and talked of platonic love: he, a general of artillery! When Madame de Langeais had played long enough on the religious note in her own interest, she did it in Armand's interest: she wanted to bring him back to a Christian way of thinking. She adapted *Le Génie du Christianisme*[11] for military consumption. Montriveau lost patience and felt that his yoke was heavy. Whereupon, out of sheer perversity, she belaboured him with God in order to see if God would rid her of a man who was driving towards his goal with a persistency which was beginning to frighten her. Moreover, she took pleasure in prolonging any dispute which helped to keep the conflict on an intellectual plane, for it was succeeded by a much more dangerous physical conflict.

But if the resistance offered in the name of the marriage laws represented the *civil* phase of this sentimental war, this could be said to constitute the *religious* phase, and, like the former, it reached a climax after which its rigour was bound to abate. One evening Armand, having by chance come early, found the Abbé Gondrand, Madame de Langeais's spiritual director, settled in an armchair in the chimney corner, looking like a man in the process of digesting his dinner and his penitent's charming sins. The sight of this man with his fresh complexion and placid composure, with his serene forehead, his ascetic mouth, his maliciously inquisitorial glance, a man with a real clerical dignity in his demeanour and already a touch of episcopal purple in his garb, brought a singularly dark frown over the countenance of Montriveau, who gave no salute and remained silent. Except in the domain of love, the general was not lacking in perception. And so, as he

11. Chateaubriand's lengthy work of 1802 which did a lot to bring Christianity back into credit in France.

exchanged a few glances with the predestined bishop, he divined that this man was the source of the difficulties which provided the duchess with arms against her love for him. A scheming cleric interfering and thwarting the happiness of a man of Montriveau's calibre! The very thought made him boil with rage, clench his fists, stand up, stride and stamp about. Then, when he returned to his chair with the intention of making a scene, a single look from the duchess sufficed to calm him down. Madame de Langeais, in no way embarrassed by her lover's black silence, which would have put any other woman out of countenance, went on chatting in spritely fashion with Monsieur Gondrand about the need to re-establish religion in its former splendour. She explained much more cleverly than the abbé could have done why the Church needed to be both a temporal and a spiritual power, and was sorry that the House of Peers did not yet have its 'Bishops' bench' as in the English House of Lords. None the less the abbé, knowing that when Lent came he would get his own back, gave way to the general and left. The duchess scarcely even rose to return the humble reverence that she received from her confessor, so much was she puzzled by Montriveau's attitude.

'What's wrong, my friend?'

'Just this: your abbé is more than I can stomach.'

'Why didn't you take up a book?' she asked, not caring whether she was heard or not by the abbé as he closed the door behind him.

Montriveau remained speechless for a moment, for the duchess's question was accompanied by a gesture which made it even more impertinent.

'My dear Antoinette, I thank you for giving Cupid precedence over the Church. But allow me, I beg you, to put a question to you.'

'A question? Why not?' she continued. 'Are we not friends? I can certainly show you what is deep down in my heart. There is only one picture in it.'

'Do you talk about our love to this priest?'

'He's my confessor.'

'Does he know that I love you?'

'Monsieur de Montriveau, you do not ask, I hope, to probe into the secret of my confessions?'

'And so that man knows of all that is between us and my love for you . . .?'

'Not "that man", Monsieur! Say rather: God.'

'God! God! I must reign alone in your heart. Leave God in peace, wherever he is, for the love of him and myself. Madame, you will go no more to confession, or else . . . '

'Or else?' she asked, smiling.

'Or else I shall never come here again.'

'Leave me, Armand. Good-bye, good-bye for ever.'

She rose and went to her boudoir without throwing a single glance at Montriveau. He remained standing, with one hand leaning on a chair. How long he stayed like that he never himself knew. The soul has a mysterious power of expanding as well as contracting time and space. He opened the boudoir; it was dark inside. A weak but petulant voice gathered strength to say: 'I did not ring. Besides, why do you come in without my bidding you? Leave me, Suzette.'

'Are you unwell then?' Montriveau called out.

'Pray leave this room, Monsieur,' she replied, ringing for her servant, 'at least for a moment.'

'Madame la Duchesse is asking for the lights,' he said to the footman, who came into the boudoir and lit the candles.

When the two lovers were alone, Madame de Langeais continued to recline on her sofa, still and silent, absolutely as if Montriveau had not been there.

'Darling,' he said in a moving tone of grief and gentleness. 'I was wrong. I would certainly not wish you to give up your religion.'

'It's a good thing,' she retorted in a harsh voice and without looking at him, 'that you do recognize the claims of conscience. I thank you on God's behalf.'

At this point the general, cast down by the inclemency of a woman who at will could become either a stranger or a sister to him, stepped towards the door in despair and was about to leave her for ever without a further word. He was suffering, and the duchess was inwardly laughing at his suffering caused by a spiritual torture more cruel than the judicial torture of old times. But he was not free to go as he pleased. In any kind of crisis a woman is, so to speak, pregnant with a certain quantity of words and so long as she has not delivered herself of them she experiences a sensation of incompleteness. Madame de Langeais had not yet had her full say. She began again.

'We do not share the same convictions, general. It grieves me. It would be fearful for a woman not to believe in a religion which allows people to love one another beyond the grave. I will say nothing of real Christian feeling, for you do not understand it. I will merely talk of the proprieties. Would you wish to exclude a woman of the Court from the Holy Table when it is the accepted thing to prepare oneself for it at Easter-tide? Yet one must be ready to do something for one's own party. You liberals will never destroy religious sentiment, however much you want to. Religion will always be a political necessity. Would you take the risk of ruling a people of rationalists? Even Napoleon was not so daring: he persecuted the Ideologues. If you want to stop people arguing you must appeal to their feelings. Let us therefore accept the Catholic Church and all that proceeds from it. If we want France to go to mass, we must set an example by going to mass ourselves. Religion, Armand, as you can see, is what binds conservative principles together, and they it is that make it possible for the rich to live in tranquillity. Religion and property are closely linked. It is certainly a finer thing to lead peoples by moral ideas than by erecting scaffolds, as during the Terror: the only device your execrable Revolution could think of to ensure obedience. Priest and king: but they are you and I and my next-door neighbour the princess; in a word, all the interests of honest folk personified. Come, deign to belong to your own party, you who could become its leader if you had the slightest ambition. As for me, I know nothing of politics – feeling guides my arguments. All the same I know enough about it to guess that society would be turned topsy-turvy if its foundations were continually being called into question.'

'If that's the way your Court and government think, I pity you,' said Montriveau. 'The Restoration, Madame, must say to itself what Catherine de Medici said when she thought that the battle of Dreux was lost to the Protestants: "Ah well, we shall have to listen to Huguenot rantings." 1815 was your battle of Dreux.[12] Like the monarchy in those days, you won the battle *de facto*, but lost it *de jure*. Political protestantism has prevailed, morally speaking. If you refuse to make an Edict of Nantes;[13] or if you make it and then revoke it; if one day you are accused and condemned for repudiating the Charter, which is only a warranty pledging the mainten-ance of revolutionary interests, the Revolution will rise again in all its terror and strike you down with one single blow. It is not the Revolution which will quit the soil of France: it *is* the soil of France. Men may be killed, but not causes. My God, what do France, the throne, legitimate monarchy, the whole world matter to us all? Set against my happiness, all that is balderdash. Reign or be overthrown, what do I care? ... Where am I? ... '

'My friend, you are in the boudoir of Madame la Duchesse de Langeais.'

'No, no, no. No duchess, no Langeais. I am with my dear Antoinette!'

'Will you do me the pleasure of staying where you are?' she said, laughing and pushing him gently back.

'So you have never loved me!' he exclaimed, his eyes flashing with rage.

'No, my friend.'

This 'no' was as good as a 'yes'.

'What a great fool I am!' he replied, kissing the hand of this terrible queen who was now a woman once more.

'Antoinette,' he went on, leaning his head on her feet, 'you are too chaste and tender to tell anyone in the world of our happiness.'

12. A battle of 1562 won by Catholics against the Huguenots, though for some time the issue remained undecided.
13. An uneasy compromise between Catholics and Protestants (1598).

'Ah indeed you *are* a great fool!' She stood up with a lively but graceful movement, and ran into the salon without another word.

'What's amiss now?' asked the general, quite unable to divine the powerful commotion which his fevered brow had communicated, like an electric shock, from his mistress's feet to her head.

Just as he reached the salon, frantic, he heard celestial strains of music. The duchess was sitting at her piano. Men of science or poetry who are able to understand and simultaneously enjoy, without reflection intervening to spoil their pleasure, are aware that the notes and phrases of music are the composer's means of expressing himself, just as are the performer's instruments, his woods and brasses. For them there exists a music apart underlying the double expressiveness of the sensuously spiritual language. *Andiamo mio ben* may extract tears of joy or pitying laughter according to the singer who renders it. Often, here and there in the world, a girl expiring under the load of a hidden grief, or a man with passion plucking at his heart-strings, may take up a musical theme and be reconciled with Heaven or commune with himself or herself through the medium of some sublime melody, a sort of fugitive poem. At that moment the general was listening to some such poem, as strange as the solitary plaint of a bird dying alone in a virgin forest can be.

'Heavens! What is that you are playing?' he asked in a moved tone.

'The prelude to a ballad which is called, I believe, *Fleuve du Tage*.'

'I didn't realize how exquisite piano music could be,' he replied.

'Oh my friend,' she said, for the first time giving him the look of a woman in love, 'you don't realize either that I love you and that you cause me horrible suffering, or that I have to find a way of complaining without making my meaning too clear – otherwise I should surrender ... But you are blind to all that.'

'And you refuse to make me happy!'

'Armand, I should die of grief the day after.'

The general left abruptly; but once in the street he wiped away the tears which, in her salon, he had the strength to hold back.

Religion held sway for three months. After that the duchess, bored with repeating herself, delivered God over, bound hand and foot to her lover. Perhaps she was afraid that, with all her talk of eternity, she might perpetuate the general's love in the next world as well as this. To vindicate this woman's honour, one needs to believe that she was virgin even in heart; otherwise her conduct was horribly cruel. Being still far from the age at which man and woman mutually find themselves too near to a sterile future to waste time cavilling about their enjoyments, she was no doubt at the stage, not of first love, but of first dalliance. Having insufficient experience to compare the good with the evil, without the knowledge of suffering which would have taught her the value of the treasures being poured at her feet, she toyed with them. Ignorant of the entrancing splendour of light, she was satisfied to linger in darkness. Armand, who was acquiring some understanding of this strange situation, was putting his hopes in the primary promptings of nature. Every evening, as he left Madame de Langeais's house, he told himself that a woman did not for seven months accept the attentions of a man and the most tender and delicate proofs of love, did not yield to the surface exigencies of a passion in order to cheat it at one fell stroke; and he was waiting patiently for the summer season to set in, not doubting that he would then be able to pick the fruit as soon as it ripened. He had perfectly appreciated her wifely and religious scruples. Indeed he rejoiced at them. He put down to pure-mindedness what was really heartless coquetry. He would not have had things otherwise. And so he liked to see her inventing obstacles: was he not by degrees getting the better of them? And did not each victory increase the modest sum of amorous familiarities for a long time refused and then conceded by her with every semblance of love? But he had sipped so appreciatively at the disputed, hard-won sweets on which shy lovers feed that they had become a matter of habit for him. And so as far as obstacles were concerned he now had only his own terrors to conquer, for he could no longer see any other impediment to happiness than the whims of her who allowed herself to be called Antoinette.

He then resolved to demand more, to demand everything. Embarrassed like a still youthful lover who dares not believe that his idol will humble herself, he hesitated for a long time and went through all those painful reactions of the heart, the firm resolutions which one word annihilates and the decisions taken which expire as one arrives at the threshold of the beloved's door. He despised himself for not having the strength to utter a word, and yet he did not utter it. Nevertheless one evening, in a mood of sombre melancholy, he formulated a fierce demand for his illegally legitimate rights. The duchess did not need to await her slave's request before guessing the desire which prompted it. Can a man ever disguise his desires? Do not women intuitively know all there is to know about the emotions which are written on a man's countenance?

'What! Can it be that you wish our friendship to cease?' she asked, interrupting him at his first word and casting on him a glance made lovelier by a divine flush which suffused her limpid complexion. 'To reward me for the generosity I have shown you, you would rob me of my honour. Reflect a little – I have reflected a lot, and I always think of us *both*. A woman has her integrity, which must be respected no less than you men must respect your honour. I for my part am not ready to be a cheat. If I gave myself to you, I could henceforth no longer be in any sense the wife of Monsiur de Langeais. And so you are demanding that I should sacrifice my position, my rank, my life for a dubious love which has not stood the test of seven months' patience. What! You would already wrest from me the free disposition of myself. No, no, speak no more to me like this. No, say no more. I will not, I cannot listen to you.' At that point Madame de Langeais took her hair in her hands in order to push her thick locks back and cool her forehead, and gave every sign of agitation.

'You come to visit a frail creature with very firm intentions and you tell yourself: "She will talk to me for a certain time of her husband, then of God, then of the inevitable consequences of love. But I will use and abuse the influence I shall have gained. I will make myself necessary to her. I shall have in my favour the bonds of habit and assumptions already arrived at by the public; and finally when society has come round to accepting our liaison, I shall obtain the mastery of this woman." Be frank: that is what you are thinking ... Fie! You make these calculations and you call that love! You are in love. Oh yes, I believe you! You want me, you want to have me as your mistress: it's as simple as that.

'Well, you are wrong. The Duchesse de Langeais will not sink so low. Let naïve bourgeois women fall for your wiles; I will not. Nothing assures me of your love. You talk of my beauty. I might become ugly in six months' time, like my dear neighbour the princess. My wit delights you and my gracefulness. My goodness! You would get accustomed to it, just as you would get accustomed to the pleasures of love. Have you not, during the last few months, got used to the favours I have been weak enough to grant you? Once I am lost, one day, you will not give me any other reason for your betrayal than the decisive word: "I no longer love you." Rank, fortune, honour: the Duchesse de Langeais will be immersed in a disappointed hope. I shall have children to attest to my shame, and ... '

She broke off with a gesture of impatience. 'Why now, it's too kind of me to explain what you know better than I do. So then, let us go no further. I am only too happy still to be able to snap the bonds which you think are so strong. Is there after all anything so very heroic in having come to the de Langeais house every evening to spend a few moments with a woman whose chatter you found pleasing and with whom you played as with a toy? Why, several young fops come here between three and five o'clock as regularly as you come in the evenings. They are, we must conclude, very generous. I make fun of them, they very placidly put up with my caprices, my impertinences, and make me laugh. Whereas you, to whom I accord the most precious treasures of my soul, you want to bring me to ruin and inflict a thousand griefs upon me. – Enough, say no more,' she exclaimed as he tried to speak, 'You have no heart, no soul, no delicacy. I know what you want to tell me. Very well, yes. I prefer you to think of me as a woman who is cold, insensible, incapable of devotion, heartless even, rather than to pass in the eyes of society for a common woman, than to be condemned to everlasting punishment after being condemned to your supposed pleasures, of which you will certainly tire. The selfish love you offer is not worth so many sacrifices . . . '

These words only imperfectly record those which the duchess whispered forth with the volubility of a barrel-organ. Certainly, as she went on talking, poor Armand was only able to respond to this torrent of fluty pipings by a silence fraught with grim misgivings. Only now, for the first time, had he some conception of feminine coquetry, and instinctively divined that devoted love, love really shared, would not calculate or reason thus in the heart of a sincere woman. Then he felt a kind of shame when he remembered that he himself had indeed, though involuntarily, made the calculations whose odious motives had been imputed to him. Then, examining his conscience with a candour worthy of the angels, he found nothing but selfishness in his words, his ideas and the answers he had thought of making but had left unexpressed. He felt that he himself was in the wrong and, in desperation, thought of throwing himself out of the window. The thought of human egoism tortured him. What indeed can one say to a woman who does not believe in unselfish love? – 'Let me prove how much I love you.' Always the *I*. Montriveau was unable, unlike the boudoir gallants in similar circumstances, to imitate the matter-of-fact logician who just went on walking in order to refute the Pyrrhonians' [14] contention that movement is impossible.

14. Followers of Pyrrho of Elis (c.360–c.270 B.C.), founder of the Sceptic school of philosophers. Actually the possibility of movement was questioned by an earlier school, Parmenides (c.540–c.450 B.C.) and his disciple Zeno (born c.490 B.C.), as a means of refuting the Pythagorean theory of matter. Zeno invented the famous argument of Achilles and the tortoise in support of his contention.

Montriveau was a man of audacity, but he just happened to lack the audacity normally possessed by lovers versed in the formulae of feminine algebra. If so many women, even the most virtuous, fall an easy prey to practised seducers, it may be because the latter have much skill in *demonstration* and because love demands, despite its delicious poetry of feeling, more geometry than we imagine. Now the duchess and Montriveau were alike in this: that they were equally inexpert in love. She had an inkling of the theory but knew nothing of the practice: thought only, and so far not feeling, was involved. Montriveau had little practical experience, knew nothing of the theory and felt too strongly to be able to think. Both of them therefore were suffering from the strain of this anomalous situation. At this critical moment Armand's tumult of thoughts might well be reduced to these words: 'Give yourself to me.' Distressingly egoistical words for a woman for whom they could evoke no memory and recall no picture. Nevertheless an answer had to be given to her accusations. Although his blood was boiling as a result of the little barbed phrases, sharp, cold and stinging, which she had shot off one after another, Montriveau was forced also to conceal his fury in order not to lose everything by losing control of himself.

'Madame la Duchesse, I am in despair to think that God invented no other way for a woman to confirm the gift of her heart than by adding to it the gift of her person. The high price you attach to yours shows me that I myself must attach no lesser one. If you give me all your soul and feelings as you say you do, what then does the rest matter? Anyhow, if making me happy entails so painful a sacrifice for you, let us say no more about it. But you will pardon a man with some self-respect for feeling humiliated when he sees himself treated like a spaniel.'

The tone with which this last sentence was uttered would perhaps have excited fear in any other woman; but once anyone in petticoats has set herself on a pinnacle and become a divinity, no power is as vainglorious as she can be.

'Monsieur le Marquis, I am in despair to think that God

invented no nobler way for a man to confirm the gift of his heart than by the manifestation of such prodigiously vulgar desires. Whereas we, when we yield our person, become slaves a man commits himself to nothing by taking us to himself. Who will assure me that I shall always be loved? The love that I should be expected to manifest at every moment in order to bind you closer to me would perhaps become a motive for you to desert me. I do not intend to be a second Madame de Beauséant.[15] Does one ever know what keeps you men by our side? A woman's continued coldness is the secret of the continued passion some of you feel for us. Other men must enjoy perpetual devotion, unremitting adoration; others must have kindness, others tyrannical treatment. No woman has yet been able to read your hearts.' She paused for a moment, and then her tone changed.

'In short, my friend, you cannot prevent a woman from trembling at the question: "Shall I always be loved?" Hard as my words may be, they are dictated to me by the fear of losing you. Believe me, dear one, it is not I who speak, but reason. And yet how comes reason to exist in a person as far gone in folly as I am? Truly, I just don't know.'

To hear this reply, which had begun with the most cutting irony and ended with the most melodious accents ever used by a woman to depict love in all its simple truth, was to rise in a twinkling from torment to felicity. For the first time in his life Montriveau turned pale and fell on his knees before a woman. He kissed the hem of her dress, her feet, her knees. But, for the honour of the Faubourg Saint-Germain, let us not lift the veil of what may happen in its boudoirs, where everything was demanded of love except the ultimate proof of it.

'Dear Antoinette!' Montriveau exclaimed in the delirium of joy into which he was plunged by her entire self-surrender to the adoration which the duchess believed herself generous in accepting. 'Yes, you are right, I don't want you to have any doubts left. Here and now I also tremble at the thought

15. See above, p. 220.

of being abandoned by the angel of my life. I wish I could invent indissoluble bonds for us two.'

'Ah then!' she whispered, 'You see I am right.'

'Let me finish,' Armand went on. 'With a single word I am going to dissipate all your fears. Listen to me: if I abandoned you I should deserve a thousand deaths. Be wholly mine, and I will give you the right to pronounce my death sentence if I betray you. I will myself write a letter in which I shall lay bare certain motives for suicide; it will in fact contain my last will and testament. You will hold this document which will legitimize my death, and in this way you will be able to avenge yourself without having anything to fear from God or man.'

'Do I need such a letter? If I had lost your love, what use would life be to me? If I wanted to kill you, should I not find a way to follow you? No, I thank you for the thought, but I don't want such a letter. Might it not make me believe that you remained faithful only out of fear? Or might not the risk arising from infidelity be an attraction for a man thus jeopardizing his life? Armand, the only thing I ask for is hard for you to do.'

'What is it you *do* want?'

'Your obedience and my freedom.'

'My God!' he cried. 'You treat me like a child.'

'A wilful and very spoilt child,' she said, stroking the thick hair of his head, which she still kept on her lap. 'Oh yes! Much better loved than he thinks, and yet very disobedient. Why not keep things like this? Why not sacrifice to me desires which offend me. Why not accept what I grant seeing that it is all that I can honourably grant? Are you not happy then?'

'Yes indeed. I am happy when I have no doubts. When one loves, Antoinette, is not to doubt to die?'

And he suddenly showed himself to be what he was and what all men are when inflamed with desire: eloquent and ingratiating. After tasting the pleasures which no doubt only an unspoken and casuistical ukase could have sanctioned, the duchess felt all the mental excitement the habit of which had made Armand's wooing as necessary to her as were society, the ball and the opera-house. To see herself adored by a man whose superiority, whose character inspired fear in others; to make a child of him; to play with him as Poppaea did with Nero: many women, some wives of Henry VIII, for instance, paid for this perilous happiness with the blood of their veins. A curious presentiment came to her while she was letting him caress her lovely light hair through which he loved to pass his fingers and feeling the pressure exerted by the small hand of this truly great man; while herself toying with the black locks of his hair, in this boudoir in which she reigned, the duchess was saying to herself: 'This man is capable of killing me if he perceives that I am fooling him!'

It was two in the morning before Monsieur de Montriveau left his mistress who, from this moment onwards, seemed to him to be neither a duchess, nor a Navarreins. Antoinette had carried disguise to the point of posing as a woman. During this delicious evening, the sweetest prelude that any woman of Paris has ever given to what society calls a *fault*, the general was permitted to see in her, despite her affectations of simulated modesty, all the charm of a young maiden. He had cause for believing that so many whimsical quarrels were the veils in which an angel's soul was wrapped, and that they had to be lifted one by one, like the material veils with which her adorable person was enveloped. In his eyes the duchess was the most naïve, the most ingenuous of mistresses, and he made her the unique woman of his life. He went away blissful at having at last brought her to the point of giving so many pledges of love that it seemed impossible that he should not henceforward be her husband in secret, chosen with the approval of God.

Having this thought in mind, with the simple-mindedness of those who are conscious of all the obligations of love as they savour its pleasures, Armand slowly returned home along the Seine quayside in order to gaze at the widest possible space of sky; with his own heart so swollen, he wanted to see the firmament and nature broadened to infinity. His lungs seemed to be taking in more air than they had the previous evening. As he walked along he questioned himself and promised to love this woman with such religious zeal that she might every day find absolution for her social faults in constant happiness. Sweet agitations of a life fulfilled! Men strong enough to steep their souls in one unique sentiment experience infinite joys as, intermittently, they contemplate a whole life of undying ardour; just as certain votaries reach ecstatic contemplation of the light divine. If love did not believe in its own perpetuity it would be nothing at all; it is magnified by constancy. Thus it was that Montriveau, as he walked along in rapture, came to an understanding of passion. 'So we belong to each other for ever!' To him this thought was a talisman which was making all his wishes come true. He did not ask himself if the duchess would change, if their love would last. He was filled with faith, one of the virtues without which there is no future for Christians; but perhaps it is even more vital for human societies. For the first time he conceived of life as lived through feeling, he who hitherto had lived only by virtue of the unstinting expenditure of human strength, the almost exclusively corporal self-devotion of the soldier.

The next day Monsieur de Montriveau went early to the Faubourg Saint-Germain. He had an appointment in a house near the de Langeais mansion where, once his business was over, he betook himself as one betakes oneself to one's own house. He was walking along with a man for whom he made a show of aversion when he met him in the salons. It was the Marquis de Ronquerolles,[16] a man who was to acquire a great reputation in the boudoirs of Paris; a man of wit, talent and above all courage, who set the tone for all the young dandies of Paris; a gallant whose successes and experience were a matter for equal envy, who lacked neither fortune nor birth, those two commodities which add so much lustre to the qualities of fashionable people.

'Where are you going?' Monsieur de Ronquerolles asked of Montriveau.

'To call on Madame de Langeais.'

'Ah! Just so. I was forgetting that you have let yourself

16. One of the Thirteen, hence hand in glove with Montriveau.

get caught in her toils. The love you are wasting on her could be much better employed elsewhere. I could have provided you in banking circles with a dozen women who are worth more than that titled courtesan, who does with her head what other more straightforward women do with . . . '

'Mind what you say, my friend,' Armand broke in. 'The duchess is an angel of innocence.'

Ronquerolles burst out laughing.

'If that's how it is with you, old boy,' he said, 'I ought to enlighten you. But just one question, of no consequence between you and me. Are you on intimate terms with the duchess? If so, I've nothing more to say. Come, make a clean breast of it. It's just to save you from wasting your time grafting that noble soul of yours on to an ungrateful stock which will stultify your hopes of fruitful produce.'

When Armand had naïvely given an account of things and revealed in minute detail what lover's rights he had so painfully obtained, Ronquerolles went off into so cruel a burst of laughter as would have cost any other man his life. But to judge by the way these two looked at and spoke to each other, standing alone at the angle of a wall, as far removed from other men as they could have been in the middle of the Sahara, it was obvious that they were united in boundless friendship and that no human interest could set them at variance.

'My dear Armand, why didn't you tell me you were involved with the duchess? I would have given you some helpful advice for bringing the affair off. Learn this first of all: the women of our *faubourg*, like all other women, like to take a bath of love; but they like to possess without being possessed. They have made a compromise with nature. Parish-church discipline has permitted them almost everything short of actual adultery. The dainties to which your duchess treats you are venial sins which she washes off in the waters of penance. But if you had the impertinence seriously to desire to commit the capital mortal sin, to which naturally you attach the highest importance, you would see with what profound disdain she would promptly close to you the door of her boudoir and her house too. The tender Antoinette would have forgotten everything and you would be less than nothing to her. Your kisses, dear friend, would be wiped off her brow as nonchalantly as a woman wipes off her powder and paint; the duchess would sponge love off her cheeks just as she sponges off her rouge. This kind of woman, the Parisienne pure and simple, is well known. Have you ever seen a *grisette* tripping along the streets? A pretty picture on top: a pretty bonnet, fresh cheeks, smart hair-style, fetching smile. But she takes precious little trouble over the rest. Now isn't that the spit and image of your Parisienne? She knows people will only look at her head. Therefore all care, adornment and vanity go to the head. Well, your duchess is just a headpiece: she feels only with her head, stores her heart in her head. Her voice is in her head and her tastes are of the head. This poor creature is defined as an intellectual Laïs. She's playing with you like a child. If you doubt that, you may have proof of it this evening, this morning, this instant. Go to her, just try asking, imperiously demanding what she is refusing you. Go to it as the last Maréchal de Richelieu went to it. Nothing doing.'

Armand was dumbfounded.

'Do you want her so much that you've lost your wits?'

'I want her at any price,' Montriveau exclaimed in desperation.

'Right. Listen. Be as implacable as she herself will be. Do your best to humiliate her, to prick her vanity, to appeal, not to the heart or soul but to the nerves and lymph of this woman – she's both nervous and lymphatic. If you can rouse a desire in her, you're there. But give up your beautiful childish ideas. If, after clutching her in your eagle's claws you yield or retreat, if you so much as flick an eyelid, if you let her think she can still dominate you, she'll slip out of your talons like an eel and get away once and for all. Be as inexorable as the law. Show no more charity than the hangman. Strike. And when you have struck, strike again. Go on striking as if you were giving her the knout. Duchesses are tough, my dear Armand, and women of her kind only soften up with blows. Suffering gives them a heart, and it's an act of charity to hit them. So hit away. Oh yes! Once pain has made their sinews tender and softened the fibres which you think are already soft and yielding; once it has started a dried-up heart beating again – under this treatment it will regain elasticity – when the brain has capitulated, passion will perhaps find its way into the metallic springs of this machine devised for the production of tears, pretence, swoons and melting phrases; and, if so be that the chimney catches fire, you will witness the most magnificent of conflagrations. This steel contraption of female manufacture will become as red-hot as a blacksmith's forge! That's a more durable heat than any other, and such an incandescence will perhaps turn into love.

'But I doubt it.

'Anyway, is the duchess worth so much trouble? Between ourselves, she would need as a preliminary to be licked into shape by a man like me. I would make a charming woman of her, for she's a thoroughbred, whereas the two of you won't get beyond the ABC of love. But you're in love, and at present I can't expect you to share my views on this matter . . . Have a good time, children,' Ronquerolles added with a laugh and after a pause. 'I have myself declared in favour of easy women: at least they're affectionate, they make love in a natural way without all the seasoning of social snobbery. My poor boy, why bother with a woman who puts the price up, who merely wants to *inspire* love? Why, one should possess a woman as one possesses a prize horse. One should look upon the combat between the confessional and the couch, the white and the black, the queen and the jester, scrupulosity and pleasure, as a very diverting game of chess. A man who knows the game and has a few tricks at his command makes it *mate* in three moves, just as he wants. If I went in for a woman of her kind, I should make this my aim . . . '

He whispered in Armand's ear and left him abruptly so as to hear no reply.

Montriveau bounded into the courtyard of the Hôtel de Langeais and went up to the duchess's rooms. Without having himself announced he marched straight into her bedroom.

'But that isn't done,' she said, hastily folding her dressing-gown over. 'Armand, you are an abominable man. Please leave me. Go out. Wait for me in the salon. Go.'

'Dear angel,' he said, 'has a consort no rights?'

'But it is detestably bad form, monsieur, for either a consort or a husband to burst in on his wife this way.'

He went up to her, took hold of her and clasped her in his arms. 'Forgive me, my dear Antoinette, but my heart is tortured with a thousand dark suspicions.'

'Suspicions? For shame! For shame!'

'Suspicions which are well-nigh justified. If you loved me, would you have made such a fuss? Would you not have been pleased to see me? Would you not have felt your heart leap a little? I'm not woman myself, but the mere sound of your voice puts me in a tremble. Often the impulse to throw my arms around your neck takes me in the middle of the ball-room.'

'Oh! If you're going to be suspicious just because I don't leap to your neck in front of all and sundry, obviously I'm going to be suspected my whole life long! Compared with you, Othello was a babe in arms!'

'So then,' he exclaimed in despair. 'I am not loved.'

'Just agree that at this moment you are not lovable.'

'So I still fall short of pleasing you.'

'It certainly looks like it. Come,' she said with an imperious little air, 'leave me. *I* am not like you: I still try to please you.'

Never did any woman know better than Madame de Langeais how to instil so much grace into so much impertinence. It was a way of doubling its effect. Also it was enough to put the coolest of men into a rage. At this moment her eyes, tone of voice and attitude betokened an assertion of perfect freedom such as never exists in a woman who loves when she finds herself in the presence of the man whom she has but to look on to feel her heart moved. His intelligence awakened by the Marquis de Ronquerolles's counsels and helped still more by the rapid power of absorption with which the least sagacious beings are momentarily endowed through passion

but which is so complete in the case of men of strong character, Armand divined the terrible truth which the duchess's
ease of manner betrayed, and a storm surged up in his heart
as in a lake ready to burst its bounds.

'If you meant what you said, my dear Antoinette, be mine!'
he cried. 'I want . . . '

'To begin with,' she said, thrusting him back forcibly
and calmly when she saw him advancing, 'do not compromise
me. My chambermaid might hear you. Please show me some
respect. To be on familiar terms with you is all very well in
the evenings in my boudoir. Here not at all. Secondly, what
does "I want" mean? "I want!" No one has said that to me
before. It sounds ridiculous to me, perfectly ridiculous.'

'You will make no concession to me on this point?'

'Ah! You call the free disposal of ourselves a point? A very
capital point in fact. Will you allow me to make my own mind
up on this point?'

'Suppose that, relying on your promises, I were exigent?'

'Ah! Then you would be proving to me that I had made a
mistake in making you the slightest promise. I would not
be such a fool as to keep the promise, and should beg you to
leave me in peace.'

Montriveau turned pale and was about to rush forward.
The duchess rang, and when her chambermaid appeared,
said to him with a mockingly gracious smile, 'Be so good
as to return when I am ready to be seen.'

Only then did Armand de Montriveau feel the hardness of
this cold-hearted woman, as chilly and cutting as steel and
crushingly contemptuous. In one instant she had severed
bonds which only her lover had felt to be strong. The duchess
had read on Armand's brow the unavowed exigencies behind
this visit, and had deemed that the moment had come to
make this Empire soldier realize that duchesses might lend,
but not give, themselves to love; and that the conquest of
them was more difficult to carry out than the conquest of
Europe had been.

'Madame,' said Armand, 'I have not the time to wait. I
am, as you yourself have said, a spoilt child. When I come

to want seriously what we were talking about just now, I shall have it.'

'You will have it?' she said with an air of *hauteur* not unmingled with surprise.

'I shall have it.'

'Oh! Then do me the great pleasure of wanting it. Out of pure curiosity, I should be charmed to know how you would set about it.'

'I am delighted,' Montriveau replied, with a laugh which frightened the duchess, 'to be able to provide you with an interest in life. Will you allow me to call for you this evening to take you to the ball?'

'I give you a thousand thanks, but Monsieur de Marsay forestalled you, and I promised him.'

Montriveau gave a solemn bow and withdrew.

'Ronquerolles is right then,' he thought. 'Now we are going to have a game of chess.'

From then on he hid his emotions under a mask of complete calm. But no man has the strength to support changes of this kind, which rapidly transport the soul from sheer bliss to dire misery. Had he only caught a glimpse of a happy life the better to feel the emptiness of his previous existence? A terrible storm was raging within him. But he was inured to suffering, and he stood up to the assault of his tumultuous thoughts as a rock of granite stands up against the angry ocean waves.

'I wasn't able to say anything. In her presence my wits fail me. She doesn't know how vile and despicable she is. No one has dared to bring this creature face to face with herself. No doubt she has duped many men. I will avenge them all.'

For the first time perhaps in the heart of a man, love and vengefulness were so equally blended that it was impossible even for Montriveau to know which of the two, love or vengeance, would win the victory. That evening he attended the ball at which he knew that the Duchesse de Langeais would be present, and almost despaired of reaching through to this woman to whom he was tempted to ascribe some demoniacal quality: she showed herself gracious to him and greeted him with agreeable smiles, no doubt not wanting the world to think that she had compromised herself with Monsieur de Montriveau. Coldness between two persons can be a sign of love. But did not the fact that the duchess betrayed no change of manner when the marquis was sombre and downcast make it clear that Armand had obtained nothing from her? Society people are well able to divine the unhappiness of men disdained and certainly do not confuse it with the tiffs that certain women order their lovers to affect in the hope of concealing their mutual love. And everyone mocked at Montriveau, who, not having taken further counsel of Monsieur de Ronquerolles, remained dreamy and afflicted; whereas Ronquerolles would have perhaps prescribed that he should compromise the duchess by opposing impassioned demonstrations to her fickle display of friendship. Armand left the ball holding human nature in horror but as yet scarcely able to believe that people could be so completely perverse.

'Since there are no public executioners for crimes of that sort,' he said as he looked up at the illumined windows of the salons in which the most seductive women of Paris were dancing, chatting and laughing, 'I will take you by the nape of the neck, Madame la Duchesse, and you shall feel a blade that is keener than that of the guillotine. Steel for steel: we will see which of us can inflict the deeper wound.'

3
The real woman

FOR about a week Madame de Langeais looked forward to seeing the Marquis de Montriveau again. But Armand was content to send his card every morning to the Hôtel de Langeais. Every time this card was handed over to the duchess, she could not repress a shudder, assailed as she was with sinister thoughts though they were as indistinct as a presentiment can be. When she read his signature, at one moment she seemed to feel the powerful hand of this implacable man running through her hair; at another moment his name conveyed a threat of vengeance which her volatile spirit told her would be atrocious. She had studied him too closely not to fear him. Would she be murdered? Would this man with the neck of a bull gore her and toss her over his head? Would he trample her underfoot? When, where and how would he lay hands on her? Would he inflict much suffering, and what sort of suffering would it be? She was in repentant mood. At certain times, had he come to her, she would have flung herself into his arms with complete abandon.

Every night when she went to sleep she saw Montriveau's features under some new aspect. Now she saw his bitter smile, now the Jove-like contraction of his eyebrows, his leonine stare; or some disdainful shrug would make him terrible to look at. The next day the visiting-card seemed covered with blood. She lived agitated by the name on it more than she had been by the impetuous, persistent, exigent lover. Then her apprehensions grew greater as his silence persisted: she saw herself having to prepare, without outside help, for a terrible conflict of which she could speak to no one. Her proud, hard soul was more sensible of the pricks of hatred than it had been formerly to the caresses of love. Indeed, if the general could have seen his mistress, with heavily knitted eyebrows, plunged in bitter thought in the recesses of the boudoir in which he had savoured so many joys, perhaps great hope would have been renewed in his heart. Pride is, after all, one of the human sentiments which can give birth to none but noble actions. Although Madame de Langeais kept her thoughts to herself, we may suppose that Monsieur de Montriveau no longer sensed indifference in her. Is it not an immense achievement for a man to monopolize a woman's thoughts? In her innermost self there must necessarily be progress in one or another direction. Put the fragile creature under the hoofs of a maddened horse, or face to face with some fearsome animal; she will certainly drop to her knees and wait for death. But if the animal calms down and refrains from killing her, she will love it – horse, lion or bull – and will talk quite happily about the experience. The duchess felt that she was at the lion's feet: she trembled, but did not hate. These two persons, so singularly pitted against each other, met three times that week in social gatherings. Each time, in response to coquettish questions, the duchess received from Armand respectful salutations and smiles imprinted with such cruel irony that they confirmed all the apprehensions which the morning visiting-card had inspired. Life is nothing but what our feelings make of it, and feelings had hollowed out a deep abyss between these two persons.

At the beginning of the following week, the Comtesse de Sérisy, sister of the Marquis de Ronquerolles, was giving a great ball at which Madame de Langeais was to be present. Armand was the first person she saw as she arrived. This time Armand was waiting for her – so at any rate she thought. They exchanged a look. A cold sweat suddenly issued from every pore of her skin. She had believed that Montriveau was capable of some unheard-of vengeance proportionate to their station in life; its nature was already decided on, was ready, hot and seething. The betrayed lover's eyes darted lightning flashes at her and his face was radiant with satisfied hatred. And so, despite the duchess's determination to be cold and provocative, there was no challenge in her glance. She went and sat beside the Comtesse de Sérisy, who could not help asking her: 'What's the matter, my dear Antoinette? You're looking dreadful.'

'A quadrille will put me right again,' she replied as she gave her hand to a young man who was approaching her.

Madame de Langeais began to waltz with a sort of fury and frenzy which was redoubled under Montriveau's heavy gaze. He stood in advance of those who were amusing themselves by watching the dancers. Each time his mistress passed in front of him his eyes were fixed on her spinning head like those of a tiger sure of its prey. When the waltz was over the duchess sat down again by the countess and the marquis continued to gaze at her while chatting with a stranger.

'Monsieur,' Montriveau was saying to him, 'one of the things which struck me most during my stay in England . . .'

The duchess was all ears.

' . . . was the words which the guide at Westminster, as he shows you the axe with which, so they say, the masked executioner cut off the head of Charles I, quotes in memory of that king, who spoke them to an inquisitive person.'

'What were they?' asked Madame de Sérisy.

'*Touch not the axe*,'[1] Montriveau replied in a tone of voice which had a menacing note in it.

'In truth, Monsieur le Marquis,' said the Duchesse de Langeais, 'you are looking at my neck with so melodramatic an air as you repeat that old story, known to all who visit London, that I seem to see you with an axe in your hand.'

These last words were uttered with a laugh, although a cold shudder passed through the duchess.

'But in present circumstances this story is quite a new one,' he replied.

'How is that? In what respect, I beg you to tell me.'

'In this respect, Madame: You have touched the axe,' Montriveau told her in a whisper.[2]

---

1. We have seen (Introduction, p. 13) that this was the original title Balzac gave to the novel. The actual words were: 'Hurt not the axe that may hurt me.'

2. The meaning of the metaphor is clear. A more usual way of putting it would be that she had been playing with fire.

'What a delightful prophecy!' she rejoined, with a strained smile. 'And when is my head to fall?'

'I do not wish to see your pretty head fall, Madame. But I do feel that some great misfortune may happen to you. Supposing you came to be shorn, would you not regret the loss of that dainty head of fair hair which you use to such good advantage?'

'But there are some persons to whom women like to make sacrifices of that sort, and often even to men who are incapable of overlooking a moment of bad temper.'

'I agree. Well, suppose that, by some chemical process, a practical joker robbed you of your beauty and made you look as if you were a hundred, whereas to us you look no more than eighteen.'

'But, Monsieur,' she broke in, 'smallpox is a woman's Waterloo. When we have lost that battle we know who they are that really love us.'

'Would you not regret losing that lovely complexion which . . . '

'Indeed, I should much regret it; but less for my own sake than for him who rejoiced in it. And yet, if I were still greatly and sincerely loved, what would beauty matter to me? What do you say, Clara?'

'You're making a dangerous speculation,' Madame de Sérisy replied.

'Might I ask his Majesty the King of the Sorcerers,' Madame de Langeais went on, 'when I committed the misdeed of touching the axe, I who have never yet been in London?'

'That I cannot tell you,' he said, with a mocking laugh.

'And when will the execution take place?'

At that point Montriveau coldly pulled out his watch, looked at the time and said with really terrifying conviction:

'This day will not end without an appalling calamity overtaking you.'

'I am no child to be easily frightened. Or rather, I'm a child ignorant of danger,' said the duchess, 'and I shall dance without fear on the edge of the precipice.'

'I am delighted, Madame, to know that you are so courageous,' he replied as he saw her going to take her place in a quadrille.

In spite of her seeming disdain for Armand's dire predictions, the duchess was a prey to genuine terror. Scarcely had the moral, almost physical oppression under which her lover had held her ceased its grip when she left the ballroom. Nevertheless, after for a moment enjoying the pleasure of breathing more freely, she noticed with some surprise that she was regretting the emotion of fear, so avid is female nature for the extremes of sensation. This regret was not identical with love, but it certainly belonged to the order of feelings which lead to love. Then, as if the duchess had felt once more the effect that Monsieur de Montriveau's attitude had had on her, she recalled the air of conviction with which he had looked at his watch. Thoroughly frightened, she withdrew. It was about midnight. The manservant who was in attendance on her helped her into her pelisse and walked ahead of her in order to hail her carriage. Then, once in it, she fell quite naturally into a reverie provoked by Monsieur de Montriveau's prediction. Arriving at a courtyard, she entered a vestibule almost identical with the one in her own house: but all of a sudden she failed to recognize the staircase. Then, just as she was turning round to call for her lackeys, a number of men pounced upon her, stuffed a handkerchief into her mouth, bound her hands and feet and carried her off. She tried to scream.

'Madame, we have orders to kill you if you cry out,' someone whispered to her.

The duchess was so terrified that she was unable to make out how or in what direction she was being transported. When she came to her senses she found that her feet and wrists were tied with silver cords and that she was lying on a couch in a bachelor's room. She could not hold back a cry when her eyes met those of Armand de Montriveau, who was sitting calmly in an armchair, wrapped in his dressing-gown and smoking a cigar.

'Do not cry out, Madame la Duchesse,' he said, coolly

removing the cigar from his mouth. 'I have a migraine. In any case I am going to untie you. But listen attentively to what I have the honour to tell you.' He delicately loosened the cords binding the duchess's feet. 'What would be the use of calling out? Nobody can hear you. You are too well-bred to make a fuss uselessly. If you didn't keep quiet, if you tried to struggle with me, I would tie up your hands and feet again. I believe that, all things considered, you will have sufficient self-respect to remain on that couch as if you were at home on your own: and still frigid, if you feel that way . . . On this sofa you have made me shed many tears that I hid from all eyes.'

While Montriveau was speaking, the duchess glanced about her in that typically feminine, furtive way which takes everything in while appearing to notice nothing. She very much liked this room which looked so like a monk's cell. It was pervaded with the very mind and soul of its occupant. No ornament detracted from the greyness of its bare walls. A green carpet covered the floor. A black divan, a table covered with papers, two large armchairs, a commode with an alarm clock on it, a very low bed on which was spread a red coverlet with a Grecian border betokened in their *ensemble* the habits of a life reduced to its most simple expression. A three-branched candlestick standing on the mantelpiece recalled, by its Egyptian form, the immensity of the deserts in which this man had wandered for so long. Between the bed – whose feet, carved in the shape of enormous sphinxes' paws, protruded from under the folds of the coverlet – and one of the lateral walls, there was a door concealed by a green curtain with red and black fringes, suspended from the curtain poles on large rings. The door through which her kidnappers had entered had a similar curtain, but it was held up by a loop. At the last look she cast at these two curtains in order to compare them, she perceived that the door by the bed was open and that reddish gleams glowing in the room beyond were perceptible under the lower fringe. Her curiosity was naturally excited by this sombre illumination: she could just pick out certain mysterious shapes in the darkness.

But at that moment it did not occur to her that danger might threaten her from that direction, and she attempted to satisfy a more imperious curiosity.

'Monsieur, would it be an indiscretion to ask you what you are proposing to do with me?' she asked with pert and biting sarcasm.

The duchess felt that the words Montriveau had spoken revealed an overwhelming love: after all, one only abducts a woman when one worships her.

'Nothing at all, Madame,' he replied as he gracefully blew out his last puff of cigar smoke. 'You are here for only a short time. I want first of all to explain to you what you are and what I am. When I see you striking attitudes on your divan in your boudoir I fall short of words. Also, in your house, at the slightest thought you find displeasing you pull your bell-rope, utter an indignant cry and show your lover the door as if he were the worst of reprobates. Here I am free to think. Here no one can throw me out. Here you will be my victim for a moment or two, and you will have the extreme goodness to listen to me. Have no fear. I have not abducted you in order to utter insults or to obtain from you by violence what I was not able to obtain by merit or what you were unwilling to grant me of your good grace. That would be an indignity. Maybe you can conceive of rape: I cannot.'

With an abrupt movement he threw his cigar in the fire. 'Probably, Madame, you dislike tobacco smoke.'

Immediately he got up, took an incense-burner from the hearth, set fire to perfumes in it in order to purify the air. The duchess's astonishment was only comparable to her humiliation. She was in this man's power, and this man was not intending to abuse his power. His eyes, once aflame with love, were now as calm and steady as stars. She trembled. Then the terror Armand was inspiring in her was increased by a kind of petrifying sensation analagous to the motionless convulsions of a nightmare. She lay transfixed with fear, for it seemed to her that the glimmer of light behind the curtain was growing in intensity as a pair of bellows blew on it. Suddenly the gleams, now quite bright, lit up the figures of three masked men. But this hair-raising sight faded out so quickly that she took it for an optical illusion.

'Madame,' Armand continued, gazing at her with contemptuous coldness, 'one single minute will suffice for me to strike at you through every moment of your life on earth; not being God, I cannot reach into eternity. Listen to me attentively,' he said, making a pause in order to add solemnity to his words. 'Love will always come at your bidding; you have unlimited power over men; but remember that one day you bade love come to you, and it did come: as pure and sincere as love can be on this earth, as respectful as it was violent, as caressing as the love of a devoted woman or that of a mother for her child, so great indeed that it amounted to madness. You committed the crime of trifling with this love. Any woman has the right to reject a love which she feels she cannot share. The man who loves without being loved in return has no cause for complaint and no right to be pitied. But, Madame la Duchesse, to lure by a pretence of feeling an unhappy man who has no other love in his life, to give him a foretaste of happiness in all its plenitude and then to snatch it from him; to cheat him of a blissful future; to kill him, not merely for a brief space of time, but for the eternity of his life by poisoning his every hour and his every thought, that is what I call an appalling crime.'

'Monsieur . . .'

'I still cannot yet permit you to answer me. So please listen to me still. In any case I have certain rights over you, but I claim only those which a judge exercises against a criminal, in order to rouse your conscience. If you no longer had a conscience I would not appeal to it. But you are so young! I like to think that there are still some stirrings of life in your heart. Even though I believe you are depraved enough to have committed a crime unpunished by the law, I do not hold you to be so degraded as not to understand the drift of my words. So I continue . . .'

Just then the duchess heard the hoarse wheeze of a pair of bellows, with which the unknown men whom a moment since she had glimpsed were no doubt again blowing up the

fire, the brightness of which was projected on to the curtain;
but the lightning flare in Montriveau's gaze compelled her to
face him, with fast-beating heart and staring eyes. However
great her curiosity, the fire in his words absorbed her interest even more than the crackling of the mysterious
flame.

'Madame,' he said after a pause, 'when, in Paris, the executioner has to lay his hand on a wretched murderer and strap
him to the plank on which the law stipulates that a murderer
must be laid for his head to be cut off . . . you are aware that
the newspapers inform rich and poor, so that some of them
may sleep undisturbed and others may be told to take care if
they wish to remain alive. Well, you who have pious leanings,
you have masses said for that man. You belong to the family,
but to the older branch of it, which can lord it in peace and
lead a happy and carefree existence. Spurred on by poverty or
fury, your convict brother has merely killed a man, while
you have killed happiness in a man, all that was most beautiful
in his life, his dearest hopes. The other has waylaid his victim
in all simplicity of mind and has killed him reluctantly for
fear of the scaffold. But you . . . you have marshalled all the
arts of feminine fragility against rugged masculine strength;
you have tamed your victim's heart the better to devour it;
you have baited your hook with kisses; you have omitted
not one of those caresses which might lure him into imagining,
dreaming of and yearning for the delights of love. You have
demanded all possible sacrifices of him in order to refuse
him any reward for them. You have set a dazzling light before
his eyes before gouging them out. What admirable courage!
Such infamies are a luxury which the bourgeois women you
mock at would never comprehend. They can yield and forgive;
they can love and suffer. They show us how small we are by
the grandeur of their devotion. High as one may climb up
the social ladder, one finds as much mud as down below;
but higher up it grows harder, gilded though it may be. Yes,
in order to reach the ideal in baseness, you need a fine education, a noble name, you need to be a beautiful woman,
a duchess. To fall to the lowest level you must rise to the

highest one. I express my thoughts badly because I still smart too much from the wounds you have given me.

'But don't think I am complaining. No, what I am saying is the expression of no personal hope and contains no bitterness. Know well, Madame, that I pardon you, and that this pardon is complete enough for you not to complain that you were forced to come and seek it. *But*: you might abuse other hearts as infantile as mine, and I reckon it my duty to spare them grief. So then you have inspired me with a mission of justice. Atone for your crime here below, and God will perhaps forgive you: I wish it may be so. But He is inexorable and will smite you.'

At these words, the duchess's eyes filled with tears: she felt humbled and lacerated.

'Why weep? Remain true to your nature. You had no qualms while you watched the tortures of the heart you were breaking. No more tears, Madame, console yourself. I am now beyond suffering. Others will tell you that you have brought them to life. I have the exquisite pleasure of telling you that you have brought me to annihilation. It may occur to you that I do not belong solely to myself, that I also have to live for my friends, that it is my lot to endure simultaneously the coldness of death and the tortures of life. Would you be capable of so much altruism? Could you behave like the tigers of the desert, who, after inflicting the wound, lick it?'

The duchess melted into tears.

'Pray spare those tears, Madame. If I believed they were real I should still distrust them. Are they, or are they not, one of your tricks? After all the tricks you have played, how could I possibly imagine that there is anything sincere in you? Nothing coming from you has henceforth any power to move me. Can I say more?'

Madame de Langeais rose to her feet with a movement full of dignity, but also of humility.

'You have the right to treat me harshly,' she said, proffering him a hand which he did not take. 'Your words are still not harsh enough, and I deserve the punishment you are giving me.'

'Punishment, Madame? To punish one must love. Do not expect anything like feeling from me. I could in my own cause appoint myself prosecutor and judge, pass sentence and carry it out. I will not. Presently I shall fulfil a duty, but in no wise satisfy a desire for vengeance. In my view the most cruel vengeance possible is to disdain to exact it. Who knows? Perhaps I shall be the minister of your pleasures. Perhaps, as you wear, elegantly, the sad stigma with which society brands its criminals, you may be forced to be as honest as they are. Maybe then you will really love someone!'

The duchess was listening with a submissiveness which was no longer simulated or coquettishly calculated. She only took to speech after an interval of silence.

'Armand,' she said. 'It seemed to me that in resisting love I was obedient to a woman's every instinct for chastity, and it is not from you that I should have expected such reproaches. You pounce on all my weaknesses and make out they are crimes. Why has it not occurred to you that I might have been carried off my feet by all the curiosity which love incites, and that the next day I might be vexed and distressed to have gone too far? Alas! My sin was one of ignorance. I swear to you that there was as much good faith in the concessions I made as in the remorse which followed. And there was much more love in my obduracy than in the kindnesses I showed you. For that matter, what are you complaining about? The giving of my heart was not enough for you. You made a brutal demand for physical possession.'

'Brutal?' exclaimed Monsieur de Montriveau. But he said to himself: 'I am lost if I get involved in a war of words with her.'

'Yes. You came to my house as to that of a woman of evil life, without either the respect or any of the attentions paid to love. Had I not the right to reflect? Well, I did reflect. The impropriety of your conduct is excusable: it has its basis in love. Let me believe that so that I can justify you in my own eyes. Very well, Armand. At the very moment when you were prophesying misfortune for me, I myself believed we could be happy. Yes, I had confidence in the noble, proud character of which you have given me so many proofs ...

And I was entirely yours,' she added, bending to Montriveau's ear. 'Yes, I had an indescribable desire to give happiness to a man so violently tested in the crucible of adversity. If I had to have a master, I wanted him to be a great man. The more exalted I felt myself to be, the less I wished to descend. Having confidence in you, I foresaw a whole lifetime of love at the very instant when you were threatening me with death. Strength is not unalloyed with goodness. My friend, you are too strong to be vindictive to a poor woman who loves you. If I have done you wrong, can I not repair it and obtain pardon? Repentance is the grace of love, and for you I would wish to be full of grace. How should I have been the only woman to share the uncertainty, the fear, the timidity which one so naturally feels when one commits oneself for life, knowing that you men find it so easy to sever such ties? The bourgeois women to whom you compare me give themselves up – but not without a struggle. Well, I have struggled. But here I am ... My God, he isn't listening to me,' she cried out, breaking off her discourse. She wrung her hands and exclaimed: 'But I love you! I am yours!' She fell down at Armand's feet: 'Yours, yours, my one and only master!'

'Madame,' said Armand as he tried to raise her to her feet, 'Antoinette is no longer able to save the Duchesse de Langeais. I no longer believe in either of you. You may well give yourself today and refuse yourself tomorrow. No power in heaven or earth could give me the sweet guarantee of your fidelity in love. Any pledges of this belong to the past. The past is over for us.'

At this instant a gleam of light shone so vividly that the duchess could not help turning her head towards the door-curtain: she again distinctly saw the three masked men.

'Armand,' she said, 'I would not wish to think ill of you. What are these men doing here? What are you plotting to do against me?'

'These men are as discreet as I myself shall be as regards what is about to happen here,' he said. 'They represent my action and purpose. One of them is a surgeon ...'

'A surgeon!' she exclaimed. 'Armand, my dear, uncertainty is the most cruel of pains. Speak then, tell me if you want my life. You shall not take it. I will give it to you.'

'So you have not understood?' Montriveau retorted. 'Did I not talk to you of justice? I am going,' he coolly added, taking a lump of steel which lay on the table, 'in order to settle your apprehensions, to explain to you what I have decided to do with you.'

He showed her a cross of Lorraine fitted to the end of a shaft of steel.

'Two of my friends are at present heating red-hot a cross modelled after this one. We shall apply it to your forehead, there, between your eyes, so that you will not be able to conceal it with a diamond tiara and thus escape the questionings of society. You will in fact bear on your brow the ignominious brand which is applied to the shoulder of your brothers the convicts. There will be little pain, but I did fear there might be some nervous reaction or resistance . . .'

'Resistance,' she said, clapping her hands with joy. 'No, no, I would at this moment wish to see the whole world witnessing this scene. Oh my Armand, brand, brand your creature quickly as a poor little chattel which belongs to you! You were asking for some pledges of my love. Here they are reduced to a single one. Oh, I see nothing but kindness and forgiveness and everlasting happiness in the vengeance you are exacting . . . When you have thus designated a woman as your property, when you have a soul in bondage with your red cipher upon her, why, you will never be able to cast her aside, you will belong to me for ever. By setting me apart on earth you will be responsible for my happiness under penalty of proving yourself a coward. But I know that you are noble and great! But a woman who loves always brands herself. Come, gentlemen, come in and brand me, brand the Duchesse de Langeais. She belongs for ever to Monsieur de Montriveau. Come in quickly, all of you: my forehead burns hotter than your branding-iron.'

Armand turned round quickly to avoid seeing the duchess on her knees and quivering with emotion. At a word from him his three friends disappeared. Women accustomed to life in the salons are skilled in the use of mirror reflections, and so the duchess, interested in reading deep into Armand's heart, was all eyes. Armand, not suspecting that his mirror might betray him, swiftly wiped tears from his eyes. The duchess's entire future was involved in these tears. When he turned round again to draw Madame de Langeais to her feet he found her already upright. She was sure that he loved her, and so her heart almost stopped when she heard Montriveau saying to her, with the firm tone which she herself had formerly been so ready to adopt when she was trifling with him:

'You have my free pardon, Madame. Believe me, this scene will be as if it had never been enacted. But here and now let us say good-bye. I like to believe that you were sincere in your boudoir when playing the coquette, and that you are sincere here and now in your emotional outpourings. Good-bye, I have lost faith. You would torture me again and always play the duchess. And ... but good-bye, we should never reach an understanding.

'What do you wish to do now?' he asked, assuming the air of a master of ceremonies. 'Return home, or go back to Madame de Sérisy's ball? I have done everything I could to leave your reputation intact. Neither your servants nor society can know anything about what has happened between us during the last half-hour. Your servants think you are still at the ball; your carriage is still in Madame de Sérisy's courtyard; your coupé is still perhaps in your own courtyard. Where do you wish to be?'

'What is your opinion, Armand?'

'Armand no longer exists, Madame la Duchesse. We are strangers to each other.'

'Then take me to the ballroom,' she said, being still curious to put Armand's power to the test. 'Fling back into the social inferno a creature who was suffering in it and must continue to suffer in it if henceforth no happiness is possible for her. And yet, my friend, I do love you, just as the bourgeois women you talked about love. I love you enough to throw my arms round you even in the ballroom. The world, vile as it is, has not corrupted me. See, I am young and have just become younger still. Yes, I'm a child, your child, you have just brought me into the world. Oh! Don't cast me out of Eden!'

Armand made a gesture.

'Ah! If I leave here, at any rate let me take something away, some trifle! This, to rest on my heart this evening,' she said, taking possession of Armand's cap, which she rolled up in her scarf.

'No,' she continued. 'I do not belong to the world of depraved women. You have no knowledge of it, and therefore you cannot assess me. Learn this then: some give themselves for money; some are won over with presents; all is infamy there. Ah! I would rather be a simple member of the bourgeois or a working woman if you prefer to have a woman beneath you, than a woman in whom devotion goes hand in hand with human greatness. Ah! my Armand, there really are noble, great-hearted, chaste and pure women among us, and they are exquisite. I wish I possessed every sort of noble quality in order to sacrifice them all to you. For my misfortune I am a duchess; I wish I were more – a royal princess – but merely in order to give it all up for you. I would be a *grisette* for you and a queen for everyone else.'

As he listened he was moistening his cigars.

'When you are ready to go,' he said, 'you will let me know.'

'But I want to stay . . . '

'That's a different matter!' he said.

'Look, that one was badly trimmed!' she cried, taking up a cigar and devouring what Armand's lips had left on it.

'You wish to smoke?'

'I would do even that to give you pleasure!'

'It would please me if you went, Madame.'

'I obey,' she said, bursting into tears.

'You must veil your face so as not to see the streets you will be passing through.'

'I am ready, Armand,' she said, bandaging her eyes.

'Can you see through the scarf?'

'No.'

He silently knelt at her feet.

'But I can hear you!' she said with a most captivating gesture, for she believed that his severity was feigned and was about to cease.

He made as if to kiss her lips. She moved towards him.

'But you can see, Madame.'

'I can't help feeling curious.'

'So you are still making a fool of me?'

'Oh!' she exclaimed, furious at this misinterpretation of her generous impulse. 'Remove this handkerchief, Monsieur, and take me home. I will keep my eyes shut.'

Hearing this cry, Armand felt sure that the duchess would keep her word and led her away. She nobly kept her promise but, as he kept a paternal hand on her to guide her upwards and downwards, Montriveau could not but notice the quickened heartbeats of this woman who had so swiftly given in to genuine love. Madame de Langeais, happy for the opportunity of talking to him, tried to make a complete avowal; but he remained inflexible, and when the duchess made a mute interrogation with the touch of her hand, his hand remained unresponsive. Finally, after they had gone some considerable distance together, Armand told her to step forward. She did so, and noticed that he was preventing her dress from brushing against the walls of what no doubt was a narrow opening. Madame de Langeais was touched by this attention, which indicated some residuum of love. But this was more or less Montriveau's way of saying good-bye, for he left her without a further word. The air was warm around her. She opened her eyes and found she was alone in front of the fire in the boudoir of the Comtesse de Sérisy. Her first concern was to repair the disorder of her appearance; she quickly adjusted her dress and restored the poetry of her hair.

'Why, my dear Antoinette, we have been looking for you everywhere,' said the countess, opening the boudoir door.

'I came to get a breath of air here,' she replied. 'The heat in the salons is intolerable.'

'We thought you had left, but my brother Ronquerolles

told me he had seen your servants still waiting for you.'

'I'm tired out, my dear. Let me rest here a moment.' And the duchess reclined on her friend's divan.

'But what's the matter? You're trembling.'

The Marquis de Ronquerolles came in.

'I fear, Madame la Duchesse, that some accident may happen to you. I have just come upon your coachman, and he's as drunk as a lord.'

The duchess made no reply. She was looking at the chimney-piece and the mirrors in an effort to discover how she had got where she was. Also she felt extraordinarily puzzled at finding herself back in the middle of ballroom gaiety after the terrible scene which had just altered the course of her life. She was seized with a fit of trembling.

'My nerves are on edge thanks to the prophecy which Monsieur de Montriveau made to me here. No doubt it was a joke, but I'm going to see if the Whitehall axe will disturb me even in my sleep. Good-night then, my dear. Good-night, Monsieur le Marquis.'

She passed through the suites of rooms where her progress was halted by compliments which, she felt, were of pitiable value. She found the social milieu of which she had been the queen very petty since she herself had been made to feel so humiliated. Anyway, what worth had these men compared with the man she now really loved, whose character had regained the gigantic proportions of which she had momentarily robbed it and which now, perhaps, she was over-estimating? She gave a close look at the manservant who had accompanied her. He was sound asleep.

'You have not been away from here?' she asked him.

'No, Madame.'

As she climbed into her coach, she indeed perceived that her coachman was in a state of intoxication which would have frightened her in any other circumstance; but the great shocks of life rob fear of its everyday pabulum. In any case she reached home without mishap. But once there she found that her whole outlook had changed and that she was a prey to completely different sentiments. Henceforward only one man meant anything to her, only one man for whom she wished to be accounted of value. Physiologists perhaps are able to give an *ad hoc* definition of love by confining themselves to the laws of nature. Moralists are much more embarrassed to explain it when they apply themselves to considering it in all the developments society has given to it. Yet there exists, despite the heresies of the thousand sects into which the church of love is divided, a sharp dividing line between the different doctrines, a straight line which no amount of discussion will ever cause to swerve. Its inflexible application explains the crisis in which the Duchesse de Langeais, like almost all other women, was plunged. As yet she did not love: she had a passion.

Love and passion are two different states of soul which poets, men of the world, philosophers and boobies continually confound. Love entails a mutuality of sentiment, the certainty of unfailing joys, a reciprocity of pleasure and a oneness of feeling that are too complete to allow room for jealousy. So that possession is a means and not an end; infidelity hurts but does not separate; the soul is neither more nor less ardent or stirred; it is incessantly happy. In short, desire, which a divine exhalation spreads over the immensity of time from one extremity to the other, stains it for us with an identical tint: life is like the purest of blue skies.

Passion is but the presentiment of love and its infinitude, to which all yearning souls aspire. Passion is hope, but hope may be disappointed. Passion means both suffering and mutability; when hope dies passion comes to an end. Both men and women may feel more than one passion without dishonour, since it is so natural to reach out impetuously towards happiness! But in life there is only one love.

All discussions about feeling therefore, written or verbal, can be summed up in a single question: is this love or passion? Since love cannot exist without intimate experience of the joys which perpetuate it, the duchess could only be under the yoke of passion. And so she experienced all the fever and agitation, all the involuntary calculations and parching desires, in short the very essence of passion; namely, *suffering*.

Mingled with these emotional perturbations there were the eddies of vanity, self-love, pride and haughtiness: all of them varieties of egoism which are very closely related. She had said to a man: 'I love you. I am yours!' Was it conceivable that a Duchesse de Langeais should proffer such words in vain? She either had to be loved or abdicate her social sovereignty. She then tossed and turned in her luxurious but lonely bed in which she had never enjoyed the warmth of voluptuous pleasure, and kept on saying to herself: 'I *will* be loved!' And the faith she still had in herself gave her good hope of succeeding. The duchess in her was piqued, the vain Parisienne was humiliated, the genuine woman in her envisaged the prospect of happiness and her imagination, seeking compensation for time wasted, delighted in conjuring up a vision of the unextinguishable flames of amorous pleasure. She was indeed not far from experiencing the emotions of true love, for, stung as she was by the doubt whether she was loved, she derived some satisfaction from telling herself: 'I love him!' She felt like trampling God and human society underfoot. Henceforth Montriveau was her religion.

She spent next day in a state of moral torpor, but with this went a physical restlessness difficult to describe. She wrote many letters and tore them all up; she let her imagination run wild in impossible speculations. At the time when Montriveau usually came, she still counted on his arriving, and eagerly awaited him. She concentrated solely upon her sense of hearing. Sometimes she closed her eyes and tried to listen through space. Then she longed for the power to eliminate all obstacles between herself and her lover in order to obtain the absolute silence which permits the reception of sound at enormous distances. When she was so withdrawn into herself the ticking of her clock became intolerable to her; it was a kind of sinister chatter and she silenced it. The clock in her salon struck midnight.

'My God!' she said to herself. 'To have him here would be happiness. And yet he used to come here under the spur of desire.' Her voice echoed through her boudoir. 'And now: nothing!'

Recalling the scenes of coquetry which she had acted and thereby driven him away, tears of despair streamed from her eyes for hours and hours.

'Madame la Duchesse,' her chambermaid said to her, 'does not perhaps realize that it is two in the morning. I feared that Madame was not feeling well.'

'You are right, I am going to bed. But remember, Suzette,' said Madame de Langeais, wiping away her tears, 'never to let anyone in without my orders. I shall not tell you this a second time.'

For a whole week, Madame de Langeais went to all the houses in which she might hope to meet Monsieur de Montriveau. Contrary to her custom, she would arrive early and leave late. She played cards instead of dancing. Useless efforts! She could get no sight of Armand, whose name she no longer dared pronounce. However, she said one evening to Madame de Sérisy, with as much indifference as it was possible for her to affect: 'Have you fallen out with Monsieur de Montriveau? I no longer see him at your house.'

'He no longer comes here,' the countess replied with a laugh. 'For that matter, one never sees him anywhere now. No doubt he is giving his attention to some woman or other.'

'I thought,' the duchess continued in a soft tone of voice, 'that the Marquis de Ronquerolles was one of his friends . . . '

'I have never heard my brother say even that he knew him.'

Madame de Langeais gave no answer. Thereupon Madame de Sérisy thought that she might with impunity castigate Antoinette's friendship with Montriveau, which, though discreet, had for a long time embittered her. She therefore pursued the topic.

'So you miss that gloomy creature? I have heard monstrous things about him. Hurt his feelings and he never comes back and never forgives. Love him and he will put you in chains. Whatever I have said about him, one of those who laud him to the skies has always given me the same reply: 'He knows how to love.' They never stop saying that he has a noble nature and will give up everything for a friend. Bah! Society has no use for such magnanimity. Men of that ilk are good enough among themselves. Let them keep their own company and leave us to our selfish little ways. Don't you think so, Antoinette?'

Despite her social self-possession, the duchess seemed put out, but none the less she replied with a naturalness which deceived her friend. 'I am sorry to see him no more. I took much interest in him and felt sincere friendship for him. Think me silly, dear friend, if you like, but I like people of strong character. To give oneself to a fool: is not that a clear admission that one lives only by one's senses?'

Madame de Sérisy had never singled out other than commonplace men: at this time a handsome nonentity, the Marquis d'Aiglemont, was paying court to her.

The countess cut her visit short, as you may well believe. Then Madame de Langeais, seeing some grounds for hope in Armand's total withdrawal from society, instantly wrote him a humble and conciliatory letter which, supposing that he still loved her, should have brought him back to her. She sent it to him the following day by her manservant, and on his return asked him if he had delivered it into Armand's own hands. On hearing that he had done so she could not repress a start of joy. So Armand was still in Paris, alone, in his own house, and paying no social visits. So then he loved her!

She waited a whole day for his answer. No answer came. As one access of impatience succeeded another, Antoinette imagined excuses for this delay: Armand was embarrassed and his reply would come by post; but when evening came she could no longer delude herself. It had been a frightful day: a mixture of pleasurable suffering, devastating shocks and exhausting emotional strain. The next day she sent Julien to Armand to ask him for his answer.

'Monsieur le Marquis sent word that he would come to see Madame la Duchesse,' Julien replied. She ran to her boudoir to hide the joy she felt and fell back on her sofa in order to savour her first emotions.

'He is coming!' The very thought of it rent her soul. Unhappy indeed are those beings who are insensitive to the anguish and the bliss of expectation with its stormy surges and moments of jubilation, for they lack the flame which lights up the vision of things and gives nature a dual meaning by attaching our attention as much to the pure essence as to the objective appearance of reality. When one loves, to wait is to be incessantly draining the cup of confident hope and yet baring one's shoulders to the terrible flail of passion, passion which is still happy because it has not yet come up against the disenchantment of truth. Might we not say that such expectation, a continuous effluence of force and desire, is to the human soul what their exhalations of perfume are to certain kinds of flowers? We quickly turn from the gaudy but scentless coreopsis or tulip to inhale the fragrant essence of the orange-blossom or the volkameria, two flowers which in their country of origin have been spontaneously likened to enamoured young brides, lovely in their past and lovely in their future.

It was by savouring these scourgings of love to the point of intoxication that the duchess had a foretaste of joys to come in the new existence she hoped for. Then she changed her point of view and discovered other purposes and a fuller meaning in life. She rushed to her bathroom and realized what refinements of self-adornment and the minutest care of one's person can mean when they are motivated by love instead of vanity. Already the attention she was giving to her personal appearance was helping her to endure the slow dragging-on of time. But once she had completed her toilet she fell back into the excessive agitation and nervous excitement induced by that dread power which puts all ideas into a state of ferment although it is perhaps no more than a malady which one loves for the pain it inflicts.

The duchess was ready at half-past two. By half-past eleven in the evening Monsieur de Montriveau had still not arrived. To explain the anguish suffered by this woman – one who might justly have passed for a spoilt child of civilization – would be like trying to compute the number of poems the heart can concentrate in a single thought, to estimate the expense of emotion the ring of a door-bell may occasion or to measure the dejection and despondency which ensue when a carriage rattles past one's door without stopping.

Midnight struck. 'Is he playing with me?' she asked herself.

She turned pale, her teeth chattered and she struck her hands together as she leapt up from her sofa in this boudoir in which formerly, as she remembered, he used to appear without being summoned. But she resigned herself. Had she too not made him turn pale and leap to his feet under the stinging shafts of her irony? Madame de Langeais now realized how miserable is the destiny of women who, deprived of all the means of action which men possess, can only wait when they love. To take the initiative with the man one loves is a fault which few men will condone. A celestial flattery: but most men think of it as a degradation. Yet Armand was great of soul and ought surely to be counted among the small number of men generous enough to reward such excess of love with undying devotion?

'Well then, I will go to him,' she said to herself as she tossed over and over in bed without finding sleep. 'I will go to him and offer him my hand. I will never tire of offering it him. An exceptional man sees in every step a woman takes towards him a promise of love and constancy. Yes indeed: angels must descend from heaven to come to men. I want to be an angel for him.'

The next day she wrote him the sort of letter in which the ten thousand Sévignés now flourishing in Paris show their mettle. And yet, to be able to complain without demeaning oneself, fly with the full sweep of one's wings without trailing humbly along, scold without giving offence, show gracefulness in rebelling, forgive without compromising one's personal dignity, say everything and admit nothing: in order to write such a delightful note one had to be the Duchesse de Langeais and have been brought up by Madame la Princesse de Blamont-Chauvry. Julien set off with it. Like all footmen, Julien became the victim of the marches and countermarches of love.

'What answer did Monsieur de Montriveau give you?'

she asked with as much nonchalance she could assume when Julien returned to give account of his mission.

'Monsieur le Marquis desired me to tell Madame la Duchesse that her letter was duly received.'

Fearful reaction of the soul upon itself! To have one's heart put to the torture in the presence of inquisitive witnesses, to make no murmur and to be forced to silence! One of the thousand pains the wealthy have to suffer!

On twenty-two successive days Madame de Langeais wrote to Monsieur de Montriveau and received no reply. In the end she had to plead sickness so as to be dispensed from her obligations, either towards the princess to whom she was attached or towards society in general. She received no one but her father the Duc de Navarreins, her aunt the Princesse de Blamont-Chauvry, the old Vidame de Pamiers, her maternal great-uncle and her husband's uncle. These persons readily believed in Madame de Langeais's sickness on finding her day by day paler, thinner and more depressed. The undefinable fever of genuine love, the irritations caused by wounded pride, the constant sting of the only scorn to which she was vulnerable, her yearnings after pleasures perpetually longed for and perpetually denied her; in short all her vital resources, vainly summoned to action, undermined her versatile nature. She was making back payment for a misguided life.

She at last went out one day to attend a military review in which Monsieur de Montriveau was to take part. Seated on the Tuileries balcony with the royal family, the duchess enjoyed one of those festive occasions which linger long in the memory. Her appearance was one of sublime languor and she was a target for admiring eyes. She exchanged a few glances with Montriveau and her beauty was heightened by his presence. The general marched past almost at the foot of the balcony in all the splendour of military accoutrement whose effect on the female imagination is acknowledged even by the most prudish persons. For a very enamoured woman who had not seen her lover for two months, must not this rapid moment have resembled that phase of our dreams when our gaze sweeps fleetingly over a limitless horizon? Only women and young people would be able to imagine the spellbound, delirious avidity expressed in the duchess's eyes. If ever men in their youth, during the paroxysm of their earliest passion, have experienced these phenomena of nervous force, later they forget them so completely as well-nigh to deny ever having known such superabundant ecstasy – for not otherwise can we designate those magnificent intuitions. Religious ecstasy is the extravagance of thought released from its fleshly bonds, whereas, in the ecstasy of earthly love, the forces of our two natures mingle, unite and fuse together. When a woman falls a prey to the tyrannical passions which now held sway over Madame de Langeais, decisive resolutions follow each other in such rapid succession that it is impossible to keep count of them. Then one thought engenders another and they run through the mind like clouds swept by the wind across the grey background of a sunless sky. Once that stage is reached, actions speak louder than words. Let us look at what happened.

The day after the review, Madame de Langeais sent her carriage and livery-servants to wait at the Marquis de Montriveau's gate from eight in the morning until three in the afternoon. Armand lived in the Rue de Seine, a few yards away from the House of Peers where there was to be a session that day. But long before the peers repaired to their palace, a handful of people noticed the presence there of the carriage and livery-servants of the duchess. A young officer whom Madame de Langeais had disdained but whom Madame de Sérisy had welcomed, the Baron de Maulincour, was the first to recognize her armorial bearings. He went straight to the lady he was courting to give her secret news of this strange folly. Immediately the news was conveyed to every coterie in the Faubourg Saint-Germain. It got as far as the royal palace and the Elysée-Bourbon and became the sensation of the day and the sole subject of conversation from noon to night. The ladies – practically all of them – denied the fact, but in such a way as to give it credit. The men accepted it while showing the most indulgent sympathy for Madame de Langeais.

'This brute of a Montriveau has a heart of bronze. No doubt he demanded this brazen display,' said some of them, thus blaming Armand.

'Well well!' said others, 'Madame de Langeais has committed the most generous imprudence possible. To defy all Paris, to renounce for one's lover's sake society, rank, fortune and respectability is a feminine *coup d'état* as dashing as the barber's knife-stroke which so staggered Canning at the Court of Assize. Not one of the women who censured the duchess would make a manifestation so worthy of olden times. Madame de Langeais is a heroine in declaring herself so frankly. Henceforth she can love none but Montriveau. Is there not a measure of greatness in a woman who says: "I will have no other passion than this?"'

'What then will become of society, Messieurs, if you pay such honour to vice without respect for virtue?' asked the Comtesse de Grandville, wife of the Attorney-General.

While chatter went on at Court, in the Faubourg Saint-Germain and the Chaussée-d'Antin, about the collapse of the aristocratic lady's virtue; whilst eager young men rode over to make sure, by seeing the carriage in the Rue de Seine, that the duchess really was paying these visits to Monsieur de Montriveau's house, she was reclining in her boudoir with fluttering heart. Armand, who had ceased sleeping at home, walked about the Tuileries gardens with Monsieur de Marsay. Meanwhile Madame de Langeais's grandparents were visiting one another and arranging to meet at her house in order to reprimand her and think of means for putting an end to the scandal caused by her behaviour. At three o'clock that day Monsieur le Duc de Navarreins, the Vidame de Pamiers, the aged Princesse de Blamont-Chauvry and the Duc de Grandlieu were together in Madame de Langeais's salon and awaiting her appearance. The servants had told them and other inquisitive people that their mistress was not at home, and the duchess had made no exceptions from this exclusion.

The four personages named, illustrious in the aristocratic sphere whose reversions and claims the *Almanach de Gotha* annually consecrates, call for a rapid sketch without which this social picture would be incomplete.

The Princesse de Blamont-Chauvry was femininely speaking the most picturesque remnant of the reign of Louis XV, to whose appellation – Louis the Well-Beloved – in the season of her youth and beauty, she was said to have contributed her quota. Of her *ancien-régime* charms she retained nothing but a remarkably prominent nose, slender and curved like a Turkish scimitar, the principal adornment of a face now reminiscent of an old white glove, and also a modicum of crimped and powdered curls, high-heeled slippers, a lace cap with ribbon bows, black mittens and a necklace set with five diamonds. But let us do entire justice to her by adding that she had so exalted an idea of her decayed beauty that she wore long gloves and a low-necked dress in the evening, and that she still tinted her cheeks with Martin's celebrated rouge. A fearsome amiability in her wrinkled face, a prodigious flame in her gaze, a profound dignity in her entire person, a three-pronged wit in her tongue, and in her head an unfailing memory made of this old woman a power to be reckoned with. In the parchment archives of her brain she stored as much as was contained in the Cabinet des Chartes, and she could detail the marriage alliances of the princely, ducal and lesser aristocratic houses down to the last descendants of Charlemagne. Consequently no usurpations of title escaped her attention. Young men anxious to be well thought of, people of ambition and aspiring young women paid her constant homage. Hers was the ruling salon in the Faubourg Saint-Germain. Any pronouncement uttered by this female Talleyrand was final. People came to her for advice on etiquette or social usages, or to receive lessons in good taste. Indisputably no other old lady knew how to pocket her snuff-box with such panache. When she took a seat or crossed her legs she arranged her petticoats with such precision and grace that the most elegant young women were reduced to despair. For at least one third of her life she had kept her voice on its upper register, but she had not succeeded in preventing it from falling to her nasal membranes, and that gave it a strangely authoritative note. Of a very great fortune she still possessed one hundred and fifty thousand francs' worth of woodland graciously restored to her by Napoleon. And so, goods and chattels and person, she was a figure of importance.

This interesting human antique was sitting on a sofa near the fireplace and was chatting with the Vidame de Pamiers, another ruin contemporaneous with her. This old nobleman, a former commander of the Order of Malta, was a tall, tapering and slender man whose collar was always so tight as to compress his cheeks, which slightly bulged over his cravat and forced him to hold his head erect: an attitude which might have bespoken self-importance in certain people but in his case was justified by his Voltairian cast of mind. His protruding eyes seemed to miss nothing and did in fact take everything in. He kept cotton in his ears. In short his person in its totality provided a perfect model of aristocratic lines: slight and frail lines, supple and pleasing, serpentine also, for at will they can bend, rear up, glide along or become stiff as steel.

The Duc de Navarreins was walking up and down in the salon with Monsieur le Duc de Grandlieu. Both of them were fifty-five, still in the prime of life, stout, short, well-nourished, somewhat florid, with tired eyes and their lower lips already pendulous. Except for their exquisite tone of speech, their affable courtesy and their ease of manner which might well suddenly change to insolence, a superficial observer might have mistaken them for bankers. But any such error would cease once one listened to their conversation, hedged with precaution when talking to people they feared, curt or non-committal with their equals, equivocal with inferiors whom Court people or statesmen are adept at winning over by verbal tact or at wounding with unexpected sarcasms. Such were the representatives of this high nobility which was intent either on dying out or preserving its integrity, which was as worthy of praise as of blame and which will never be fairly judged until some poet has revealed it as it was: happy to obey the king by perishing under Richelieu's axe but despising the guillotine of 1789 as a base instrument of vengeance.

These four personages had one single distinctive feature: high-pitched voices, singularly harmonizing with their ideas and deportment. What is more, the most perfect equality reigned between them. A habit they had acquired at Court, that of concealing their emotions, no doubt restrained them from manifesting the vexation that their young kinswoman's indiscretion was causing them.

To prevent critical minds from taxing the opening dialogue of the following scene with puerility, it is perhaps necessary here to observe that John Locke, finding himself in the company of certain English lords renowned for their wit and as distinguished by their manners as they were by their party loyalty, maliciously amused himself by recording their conversation in a special sort of shorthand and reduced them to bursts of laughter by reading it back to them and asking them what they themselves could make of it. It is a fact that the upper classes in all countries speak a sort of scintillating jargon which, when assayed in the embers of literary or philosophic scrutiny, leaves an infinitely small yield of gold in the crucible. On all planes of social life except in a few of the Paris salons, an onlooker will find the same absurdities, differing only in the transparency or opaqueness of the varnish. Thus worthwhile conversation is an exception in social intercourse, and a dull-witted Boeotianism[3] is all that keeps talk alive in the various circles of society. In the higher social spheres there is necessarily much chatter but little thought. Thought brings fatigue and the rich like effortlessly to watch life flowing by. And so it is by comparing the basic stock of witticisms ranging upwards stage by stage from the Paris street arab to the peer of France that an observer will appreciate the aphorism of Monsieur de Talleyrand: 'Manners are everything', an apt translation of the legal axiom: 'Form takes priority over matter.' In a poet's eyes the advantage will remain with the lower classes, who never fail to impress a

3. Boeotia was a district of ancient Greece derided by the Athenians on account of the supposed stupidity of its inhabitants.

rough stamp of poetry on their thoughts. This observation will also perhaps explain the barrenness of salon discourse, its vacuity and shallowness, and the reluctance of more cultured people to embark upon an unprofitable exchange of thought with those who frequent them.

The duke suddenly halted, as if struck with a luminous idea, and said to the man by his side: 'So you've sold Thornton?'

'No, he's sick. I very much fear I may lose him. I'd be very vexed. He's a first-rate hunter . . . Do you know how the Duchesse de Marigny is getting on?'

'No, I haven't called on her this morning. I was going out to see her when you came to talk to me about Antoinette. But she was very ill yesterday. She was not expected to live and was receiving the last sacraments.'

'Will her death alter your cousin's prospects?'

'Not in the least. She disposed of her property in her lifetime and kept a pension for herself which is paid her by her niece, Madame de Soulanges, to whom she has made over her Guébriant property in return for an annuity.'

'Socially speaking, she will be a great loss. She was a good woman. Her family will have one person less whose advice and experience carried weight. Between ourselves, she was the head of the family. Her son, Marigny, is a decent man; he has some wit and can talk. Oh yes, he's all right, quite all right, no denying that. But he has no idea of proper behaviour. And yet it's strange: he's a smart man. The other day he was dining at the club with all those rich fellows of the Chaussée d'Antin, and your uncle, who always goes there for his game of cards, spotted him. Surprised to see him there, he asked him if he were a member of the club. "Yes," he said, "I've given up society. I live with the bankers." Do you know why?' the marquis asked the duke with a sly smile.

'No.'

'He's infatuated with a newly-wed bride, little Madame Keller, Gondreville's daughter, a woman who is said to be very much in fashion in that quarter.'

'Well now, Antoinette isn't bored with life, it seems,' the old vidame interpolated.

'The affection I feel for that little person is at present making me take to a peculiar pastime,' the princess replied to him as she pocketed her snuff-box.

'My dear aunt,' said the duke, ceasing his perambulation, 'I am in despair. Only one of Bonaparte's men could have demanded such unseemly conduct from a woman of society. Let us be frank; Antoinette could have made a better choice.'

'My dear,' the princess replied, 'the Montriveau family is an old and well-connected house, allied to the highest Burgundian stock. If the Rivaudoults of Arschoot, of the Dulmen branch, came to an end in Galicia, the Montriveaus would succeed to the estates and titles of Arschoot, which they would inherit through their great-grandfather.'

'Are you sure of that?'

'I am better informed than Montriveau's father, whom I saw quite a lot and whom I told about it. Although he was a knight of several orders, he ridiculed all of them: he was an Encyclopaedist. But his brother did well out of the emigration. I heard that his northern kinsmen had behaved admirably towards him.'

'That's certainly true,' said the vidame. 'The Comte de Montriveau died at St Petersburg where I met him. He was a stout man with an incredible passion for oysters.'

'What was his score in oysters?' asked the Duc de Grandlieu.

'Ten dozen a day.'

'And none the worse for it?'

'Not in the least.'

'That's a feat! And this mania gave him neither stone, nor gout, nor any other discomfort?'

'None. He enjoyed perfect health and died of an accident.'

'Of an accident! Well, Nature must have prompted him to eat oysters. He probably needed them, for up to a certain point our dominant tastes are the condition of our continued existence.'

'I agree with you,' said the princess with a smile.

'Madame, you always take a satirical view of things,' said the marquis.

'I merely wished to give you the hint that a young woman might be misled by such aphorisms.'

She cut short her own drift and said: 'But my niece, my niece!'

'My dear aunt,' said Monsieur de Navarreins, 'I still cannot believe that she really has visited Monsieur de Montriveau.'

'Pshaw!' exclaimed the princess.

'What is your opinion, vidame?' asked the marquis.

'If the duchess were an ingenuous girl, I could believe it.'

'But when a woman falls in love she becomes ingenuous, my dear vidame. Are you losing your grip?'

'Well, what are we to do?' asked the duke.

'If my dear niece has any sense,' the princess replied, 'she will go to Court this evening, since luckily today is Monday, a reception day, see that a crowd gathers round her, and have this absurd rumour belied. It can be explained away in a thousand ways, and if the Marquis de Montriveau is a gentleman he will lend himself to any explanation. We will bring these young people to their senses . . . '

'But, dear aunt, it's difficult to break a lance with Monsieur de Montriveau. He's a pupil of Bonaparte and a man of standing. You must realize he's very much to the fore, with an important command in the Guard, where he's extremely useful. And he hasn't the slightest ambition. At the first remark he doesn't like, he's the kind of man to tell the King: "Here is my resignation, leave me in peace." '

'What sort of opinions does he hold?'

'Very wrong ones.'

'For that matter,' said the princess, 'the King himself is still what he always was – a Jacobin with a fleur-de-lis in his buttonhole.'

'Oh, he doesn't go so far as that,' said the vidame.

'I assure you, I've known him a long time. The man who said to his wife, the day of their first public banquet, as he pointed to the Court, "Those are our menials!" could not be anything but a black-hearted scoundrel. The erstwhile

Monsieur[4] is perfectly recognizable in the present king.
The disloyal brother who voted so treacherously in the
Constituent Assembly is bound to come to terms with the
liberals and let them go on talking and arguing. This sancti-
monious "philosopher" will be just as dangerous for his
younger brother[5] as he was for his elder brother, for I doubt
whether his successor will be able to extricate himself from
the difficulties which this gross and stupid man has taken
pleasure in creating for him. Besides, he loathes him and
would be glad if he could tell himself on his death-bed: "He
won't reign long." '

'Aunt! He's the King; I have the honour to serve him,
and . . . '

'My dear nephew, does the office you hold rob you of the
right of free speech? You are of as good house as the Bourbons. If the house of Guise had been a little more resolute,
His Majesty of today would only be a minor noble. It's time
I left this world: the nobility is done for. Yes, all is lost for
us, my children,' she added, with a look at the vidame.
'Ought my niece's behaviour to be the talk of the town?
She has done wrong. I do not approve of her. A useless
scandal is a grave mistake, and I therefore take a poor view of
her flouting of the conventions. I brought her up, and I
know that . . . '

At this moment the duchess came out of her boudoir.
She had recognized her aunt's voice and heard Montriveau's
name pronounced. She was not yet dressed and, just as she
showed herself, Monsieur de Grandlieu, who was looking
unconcernedly out of the window, saw his niece's empty
carriage coming into the courtyard.

'My dear daughter,' the Duc de Navarreins said to her as
he took her head and kissed her brow. 'Don't you know then
what's going on?'

4. The title traditionally given to the eldest brother of the reigning
monarch. The then Louis XVIII, brother of Louis XVI, as Comte de
Provence had supported the progressive party at the outbreak of the
Revolution.

5. The Comte d'Artois, who became Charles X at his brother's death
in 1824.

'Is something out of the way going on, dear father?'

'Why, all Paris believes that you're living with Monsieur de Montriveau.'

'My dear Antoinette, you have not been out today, have you?' the princess asked as she proffered her hand which the duchess kissed with respectful affection.

'No, dear aunt, I have not been out. But,' she said as she turned round to greet the vidame and the marquis, 'I wanted all Paris to believe I was with Monsieur de Montriveau.'

The duke lifted his hands to heaven, clasped them in despair and then folded his arms.

'But don't you know what will come of this mad demonstration?' he asked at last.

The old princess had suddenly risen on her heels and was regarding the duchess, who turned red and dropped her gaze; Madame de Blamont-Chauvry drew her gently to herself and said: 'Let me kiss you, my little angel.' She kissed her on the forehead very affectionately, squeezed her hand and continued with a smile: 'We are no longer under the Valois monarchs, dear girl. You have compromised your husband and your social position. Never mind, we'll see what we can do to put things right.'

'But dear aunt, I don't want to put things right. I want the whole of Paris to believe or to say that I went to see Monsieur de Montriveau this morning. To destroy this belief, ill-founded as it may be, would be to do me extreme harm.'

'So then, dear girl, you want to ruin your reputation and bring distress to your family?'

'My father and my family, by sacrificing me to family interests, involuntarily condemned me to irreparable unhappiness. You can blame me for trying to alleviate it, but you will certainly feel sorry for me.'

'That's what comes of taking infinite pains in order to make a decent settlement for your daughters!' Monsieur de Navarreins mumbled to the vidame.

'Dear child,' said the princess, shaking off the grains of snuff that had fallen on to her dress, 'be happy if you can. We don't want to spoil your happiness, but to bring it into line with convention. All of us here know that marriage is an imperfect institution which has to be tempered with love. But, when you take a lover, must you really make your bed in the public thoroughfare? Come, dear, be reasonable, listen to us.'

'I am listening.'

'Madame la Duchesse,' said the Duc de Grandlieu, 'if uncles were obliged to look after their nieces, they really would have their work cut out. Society would owe them honours, rewards and emoluments such as are given to those who serve the King. Consequently I have not come here to plead on behalf of my nephew, but to talk of your own interests. Let us figure things out. Are you anxious to make a clean break with your husband? I know that fellow fairly well and don't like him much. Langeais is something of a miser and devilishly self-interested. He will agree to a separation, but will keep your fortune, leave you in poverty and consequently without social standing. The hundred thousand francs' income which you recently inherited from your maternal great-aunt will go to pay for the pleasures of his mistresses, and you will be bound fast, garotted by the laws and obliged to say Amen to these adjustments. Now suppose that Monsieur de Montriveau leaves you! God help us, dear niece, don't get angry. No man will abandon you while you're young and beautiful. Nevertheless we have seen so many pretty women left in the lurch – princesses included – that you will permit me to make a supposition which is, I concede, almost absurd: what then will become of you, no longer having a husband? So then keep on reasonable terms with your husband in the same way that you take care of your beauty, which is, after all, a woman's sheet-anchor, just as her husband is. Now, supposing that you stay happy and beloved – ruling out any untoward events. Even so, fortunately or unfortunately, you may have children. What name will you give them? Montriveau? Well, they won't inherit the bulk of their father's fortune. God knows nothing could be more natural than that you will want to leave them all yours and that he will want to leave them all his. But you'll find yourself

up against the laws of inheritance. How many law-suits have
we seen brought by legitimate heirs against love-children!
The echo of them rings through law-courts the wide world
over. Suppose you put the matter in the hands of a trustee?
If you are betrayed by the man in whom you have put your
trust – and you may be sure that human justice will not take
cognizance of this – your children will be brought to ruin.

'So then pick your way carefully. See what a maze you'll
be in. In any case your children will be sacrificed to your
emotional whimsies and deprived of their position in society.
My God, while they're small they'll be charming. But one day
they'll blame you for thinking of yourselves more than of
them. We old noblemen know all about that. Children grow
into men, and men are ungrateful. Did I not hear young De
Horn, in Germany, saying one evening after supper: "If
my mother had been an honest woman I should be a reigning
prince"? But we have heard commoners saying that "If" all
our lives, and that's what caused the Revolution. And
when men can accuse neither their father nor their mother
they blame God for their bad lot in life. In short, dear child,
we are here to enlighten you. I sum up with a remark on
which you should ponder: a wife should never put her husband in the right.'

'Uncle, I too calculated until I fell in love. Then, like you,
I saw self-interest in operation. Now all that matters to me is
feeling.'

'But, my dear child, life is quite simply a mix-up of self-
interest and feeling,' the vidame retorted. 'And in order to be
happy, above all in your present position, one must try to
reconcile feeling and self-interest. A shop-girl takes love as
she chooses, that's understandable. But you have a tidy fortune, a family, a title, a place at Court, and they're not things
to be thrown overboard. To come to the heart of the matter,
what are we asking of you? To manoeuvre carefully round
convention instead of flouting it. God bless me, I'm nearly
eighty, and I have no memory of ever in any regime having
come upon a love worth the price you wish to pay for
that of this lucky young man.'

The duchess silenced the vidame with a look; if Montriveau had been able to see it he would have forgiven her completely.

'All this would make a fine scene in a play,' said the Duc de Grandlieu, 'but it's meaningless when it comes to the question of the rights you retain by your marriage contract, your position and independence. You're ungrateful, dear niece. You won't find many families having the courage to bring the lessons of experience and the language of common sense to idiotic young heads. Renounce the hope of salvation in a couple of minutes if you want to be damned: be it so! But give a lot of thought to it when it comes to renouncing your revenues. I know of no confessor who will absolve you from the sin of poverty. I believe I have the right to talk to you in this way because, if you come to perdition, I alone can take you under my wing. I am practically Langeais's uncle, and I alone have the right to put him in the wrong.'

'Daughter,' said the Duc de Navarreins, stirring himself up from a doleful meditation, 'since you are talking of feeling, let me observe that a woman bearing your name is bound to a quality of feeling different from that of the common people. Do you really want to ensure victory for the Liberals, Robespierre's Jesuits, who are making every effort to bring the nobility to contumely? There are certain things that a Navarreins could not do without disgracing her whole house. You yourself would not be the only person to be dishonoured.'

'Come now,' said the princess. 'Now we're talking of dishonour. Children, don't make so much fuss over the direction taken by an empty carriage, and leave me alone with Antoinette. You will all three come and dine with me. I undertake to sort things out appropriately. You men are bunglers in such matters. You are already putting too much acerbity into your words, and I don't want to see you falling out with my dear girl. So be so good as to take your departure.'

The three noblemen no doubt guessed the princess's intentions and took leave of their kinswomen. Monsieur de Navarreins kissed his daughter's brow and said to her: 'Dear child, be sensible. If you will, there's still time.' The vidame asked as they went downstairs: 'Couldn't we find some good fellow belonging to the family who would pick a quarrel with Montriveau?'

*

'My jewel,' said the princess, motioning her pupil to sit down beside her on a little low chair. Once they were alone she said: 'I know nothing that is more calumniated in this wicked world than God and the eighteenth century, for, as I recall the experiences of youth, I do not remember a single duchess trampling convention underfoot the way you have just done. The reign of Louis XV has been decried by novelists and scribblers. Don't believe them. The Dubarry woman, my dear, was at least of as good family as Widow Scarron and personally more attractive. In my day a woman was capable of keeping her dignity in spite of all her love-affairs. It is our indiscretions that have brought about our ruin; hence all the trouble. The "philosophers", those nobodies we admitted to our salons, had the ingratitude and the indecency to requite the kindness we showed them by making an inventory of our feelings, decrying us wholesale and retail and railing against the century. The common people, who are in no position to judge anything whatsoever, have looked into the bottom of things but not discerned their shape. But in those times, my love, men and women were every bit as remarkable as in any other period of the monarchy. Not one of your Werthers, not one of your notabilities so-called, not one of your men in yellow gloves who wear trousers to conceal the spindliness of their legs, would travel across Europe disguised as a pedlar in order to go and shut himself up in the dressing-room of the Regent's daughter at the risk of his life and braving the daggers of the Duke of Modena's hirelings. Not one of your little consumptives with tortoise-shell spectacles would hide for six weeks in a wardrobe in order to inspire courage in a mistress during her confinement. There was more passion in the Marquis de Jaucourt's little finger than in all your race of logic-choppers who will leave a woman's side to go and vote for an amendment in the Chambre! See if you can find me today a page-boy who would let himself be hacked to pieces and buried under the floor merely in order to kiss the gloved hand of the Countess of Kœnigsmark. In fact it looks today as if roles are interchanged and it is for women to pay their devotions to men. These gentry are worth less and value themselves more. Believe me, my dear, all those escapades which have become public knowledge and are now used as sticks with which to belabour our good Louis XV, were originally kept secret. But for a mob of poetasters, rhymesters and moralists who consorted with our chambermaids and wrote down the scandals they were told, our period would have enjoyed a sound moral reputation in literature.

'It's the century I am defending and not its frayed fringes. There may have been a hundred women of quality who went to perdition, but those scoundrels have multiplied them to a thousand, just like war correspondents when they compute enemy casualties. For that matter, I don't know what reproach Revolution and Empire can level against us: coarse, licentious, witless times. Faugh! all that is revolting: those are the insalubrious spots in our history!

'The drift of this preamble, my dear child,' she continued after a pause, 'is this: if you're enamoured of Montriveau, there's nothing to prevent you from loving as you will and as much as you can. I myself know by experience that, short of locking you up – and today people are no longer locked up – you'll do as you please. I should have done the same at your age. Only, my treasure, I would not have abdicated the right of giving birth to Dukes of Langeais. And therefore observe the proprieties. The vidame is right: no man is worth even one of the sacrifices with which we women are idiotic enough to pay for their love. And so put yourself in a position to be able, if you had the misfortune to come to the stage of repentance, still to remain the wife of Monsieur de Langeais. When you've grown old, you'll be very glad to hear Mass at Court instead of in a provincial convent: there lies the whole question. One imprudence means an annuity, an errant life, being at the mercy of a lover; it means the mortification caused by the impertinences of women who are of less worth than you, precisely because they have been clever in a contemptible sort of way. It would have been a hundred times better to visit Montriveau in the evenings, in a cab, in disguise, than to have sent your carriage to his house in the open daylight. You are a stupid little thing, dear child. Your carriage has flattered his vanity, your person would have captured his heart. I have put the exact truth to you, but I'm not angry with you. You're two centuries behind the times with your spurious nobility of heart. Come, let us arrange the matter and say that Montriveau got your servants drunk in order to appease his self-esteem and compromise you . . . '

'In heaven's name, aunt,' the duchess cried as she leapt to her feet, 'do not slander him.'

'Oh! dear child,' said the princess, her eyes lighting up. 'If only you cherished illusions which were not disastrous! But all illusions are shattered sooner or later. My heart would be quite moved if I were not so old. Come, cause vexation to no one, neither him nor ourselves. I will take it upon myself to satisfy everybody; but promise me to take not a single step henceforth without consulting me. Tell me everything, and perhaps I shall be able to put everything to rights.'

'All right, aunt, I promise . . . '

'To tell me everything?'

'Yes, everything that can be told.'

'But, dear heart, it's just what can't be told that I want to know. Let's come to a real understanding. Now dear, let me press my lips on your lovely brow. No, let me do it; it's not for you to kiss my old bones, old people have their special courtesy . . . Now then, take me to my coach,' she added after embracing her niece.

'Dear aunt, you think I can go to his house in disguise?'

'Certainly, that's something you can always deny afterwards,' the old lady said.

The duchess had only fastened on to one idea in the princess's sermon. When Madame de Chauvry was seated in a corner of her carriage, Madame de Langeais bade her a gracious farewell and returned to her apartments beaming with happiness.

'Had I gone to him in person I should have won his heart. My aunt is right: no man can refuse a pretty woman when she knows how to make the right approach.'

That evening, at the reception of Madame la Duchesse de Berry, the Duc de Navarreins, Monsieur de Pamiers, Monsieur de Marsay, Monsieur de Grandlieu and the Duc de Maufrigneuse victoriously discredited the insulting rumours which were current about the Duchesse de Langeais. So many officers and personages bore witness to having seen Montriveau passing through the Tuileries during the morning that this stupid tale was laid to the door of chance, which accepts everything laid on its doorstep. Consequently, the next day, the duchess's reputation, in spite of the stationing of her carriage, emerged as clean and spotless as Mambrino's helmet after Sancho Panza had burnished it.[6] However, at two o'clock, in the Bois de Boulogne, Monsieur de Ronquerolles, passing beside Montriveau in a secluded alley, said to him with a smile: 'Your duchess is shaping well! Keep going,' he added, giving a meaningful flick of his whip to his mare, which shot away like a cannon-ball.

Two days after her ineffectual gesture, Madame de Langeais wrote Monsieur de Montriveau a letter which, like the previous ones, received no answer. But this time she had taken certain measures and bribed Auguste, Armand's valet. And so, that evening at eight o'clock, she was admitted to Armand's flat, into a very different room from the one in which the scene between the two of them had taken place. The duchess was told that the general would not be returning home. Had he two domiciles? The valet gave no reply. Madame de Langeais had bought her way into this room, but she had not purchased the valet's entire probity. Left alone she saw her fourteen letters lying on an antique pedestal table: none of them was either crumpled or unsealed; in fact, he had not read them. Realizing this, she sank back into an armchair and for a moment lost consciousness. She came to with Auguste holding vinegar to her nostrils.

6. An allusion to an episode in Don Quixote. Mambrino's helmet was in fact a barber's basin.

'Quick,' she said, 'get me a carriage.'

When the carriage came she ran downstairs in a convulsive rush, returned home, went to bed and refused to see anyone. She stayed in bed for twenty-four hours, allowing only her chambermaid to approach her in order to bring her cup after cup of orange-flower tea. Suzette heard her mistress giving voice to moans and saw signs of tears in her eyes, which were bright but had dark circles around them. The day after that, after pondering in tearful despair over the decision she had to take, Madame de Langeais consulted with her legal agent, whom she obviously wished to make certain preparatory financial arrangements. Then she sent for the old Vidame de Pamiers, and whilst waiting for him to appear she wrote to Monsieur de Montriveau. The vidame came promptly. He found his young cousin pale, dejected but resigned. Never had this divine creature looked more poetic than now, in all the languor of her distress.

'Dear cousin,' she said to the vidame, 'it is because you are eighty that I have asked you to come. Oh! don't smile, I beg you, at the expense of a poor woman who is desperately unhappy. You are a chivalrous man, and I like to think that your youthful adventures have inspired you with some indulgence for women.'

'Not the least indulgence,' he replied.

'You don't mean that?'

'They are lucky whatever befalls them.'

'Indeed? Well, in any case you are one of my closest kinsmen and perhaps the last friend whose hand I shall ever clasp. Do me, dear vidame, a service I could not ask either of my father, or my uncle Grandlieu, or any woman. You must surely understand me. I implore you to do as I ask and to forget you have done so, whatever the result of your action. Will you take this letter to Monsieur de Montriveau, see him, show it him, and ask him, as one man to another – you men have feelings of fair play between yourselves that you forget in your dealings with us – ask him to be kind enough to read it: not in your presence, since men like to hide certain feelings. I authorize you to say, if you judge this necessary to help him

to decide, that for me it is a matter of life or death. If he deigns
...'

'*Deigns*?' said the commander.

'If he deigns to read it,' the duchess continued with dignity,
'make one last remark to him. You will call on him at five – I
know that today he will be dining at home at that time – well,
the only answer I require of him is that he comes to see me.
If, three hours after that, if at eight o'clock he is still at home,
all will be over. The Duchesse de Langeais will have disappeared from this world. Not that I shall be dead, dear cousin.
No. But it will be beyond human power to find me again on
this earth. Come and dine with me, and at least I shall have a
friend to minister to me in my last agonies. Yes, dear cousin,
by this evening my fate will be decided. Whatever happens
can only be excruciatingly cruel. Say nothing, I beg of you.
I want to hear nothing by way either of comments or counsel.
– Let's chat, let's laugh,' she said, holding out her hand for
him to kiss. 'Let's be like two philosophical greybeards
capable of enjoying life until the instant of death. I will put on
my best and be as attractive as I can for you. It may be that
you will be the last man to set eyes on the Duchesse de
Langeais.'

The vidame made no reply, bowed, took the letter and did
his errand. He returned at five and found his kinswoman
dressed with studied elegance: she was indeed seductive.
Her salon was bedecked with flowers as for a celebration.
The meal was exquisite. To please the old man the duchess
brought into play all her brilliancy of wit and was more
fascinating than she had ever been. To begin with, the commander was inclined to see nothing but a young woman's
whimsy in this attempt to charm; but now and again the
false magic of his cousin's seductiveness lost its glamour.
At one moment he saw that she was quivering with a kind of
sudden terror; at another she seemed to be listening across
the silence. Then, if he asked her: 'What is wrong with you?'
she replied: 'Hush!'

At seven o'clock the duchess left the old man and promptly
returned, but dressed as her chambermaid might have

been for a journey. She asked her guest to conduct her, took his arm and threw herself with him into a hired carriage. By about a quarter to eight the two of them were waiting at Monsieur de Montriveau's door.

As for Armand, all this time he had been pondering over the following letter:

My friend,

I have spent a few moments in your study without your knowing, and I recovered my letters. Oh! Armand, there cannot be indifference between you and me. Hatred has other methods of procedure. If you love me, give up this cruel game. It would kill me, and later you would be in despair when you realized how much I loved you. If, unhappily, I have misunderstood you, if you have nothing but aversion for me, aversion involves both contempt and disgust. In that case I lose all hope: men never recover from such feelings. Terrible as it may be, this thought will bring some consolation to the lasting grief before me: you will never have any regrets. Regrets? If I caused you a single one, let me not know of it. If I did, I cannot tell you what havoc the knowledge would cause in me. To go on living and not to be your wife! After giving myself totally in my thoughts, to whom could I give myself except to God? Indeed, the eyes you loved for a moment will never look again on any man's face; may they be closed to everything but the glory of God! I shall listen to no other human voice after hearing yours, so sweet at first, but yesterday so terrible, for I am still living in the morrow of your vengeance. So then may I be consumed in the fire of God's word. Between His anger and yours, my friend, no room will be left to me but for tears and prayers.

Perhaps you will wonder why I am writing to you. Alas, do not blame me for clinging to a glimmer of hope, for still sighing after a life of happiness before giving up the hope of it for ever and ever. I am in a desperate situation. I already feel in me all the serenity born of a great resolve, but I still feel in my heart the last rumblings of the storm I have passed through. You told me how, in the terrible adventure which befell you and which tied me so closely to you, you moved, Armand, under competent guidance, from the desert to an oasis; but I am being dragged from oasis to the desert under your pitiless guidance. Nevertheless you alone, my friend, can understand with how great melancholy I look back on happiness; you are the only person to whom I can complain without a blush. If you listen to my prayer I shall be happy. If you are pitiless I must expiate the wrong I have done. But admit that it is natural for a woman to wish to live on, clad in all noble feeling, in the memory of the man she loves. Oh my only beloved! Allow her whom you have brought to life to leave the world in the belief that you will find some greatness in her. Your harsh treatment has brought me to reflection, and since I have come to love you so much I feel that I am less guilty than you suppose. Listen then as I make my justification, which I owe it to you to make. You also, who are all the world to me, owe me at least a moment of justice.

My own suffering has taught me how much my coquetry made you suffer. But at that time I had absolutely no idea what love meant. You yourself know the secret of the tortures love inflicts, and now you are inflicting them on me. During the first eight months you gave to me you did not succeed in making me love you. Why, my friend? I can no more tell you that than I can explain why I love you now. I was certainly flattered to be the object of your passionate wooing and the recipient of your burning gaze; yet you left me cold and void of desire. No, I was not yet a woman, and had no idea of the devotedness or the happiness of which my sex is capable. Whose fault was that? Would you not have despised me if I had tamely surrendered? It may be that the noblest quality of our sex is to give pleasure without receiving it and that there is no merit in abandoning oneself to delights we have already enjoyed and ardently desired. Alas, my friend, let me admit it, these thoughts occurred to me while I was still playing the coquette. But already I thought you so great that I did not want you to win me out of sheer pity . . .

What admission have I just made? Ah! I took back from your study all the letters I wrote you. Now I am throwing them in the fire! They are burning. Now only their ashes remain. You will never know how much love, passion, madness they contained . . . I have gone far enough, Armand, I must stop. I must tell you no more of what I have been feeling. If my yearnings have not reached from my soul to yours, I no more than you, woman though I am, could bear to owe your love to pity. I want to be loved irresistibly or ruthlessly cast aside. If you refuse to read this letter it will be burned. If, after reading it, you are not, within three hours, my one and only husband, I shall not feel ashamed to know that it is in your hands: proud despair will guard my memory from all insult, and my end will be worthy of my love. You yourself, who will never meet me again on earth though I shall still be alive, will not think without a tremor of the woman who, three hours from now, will breathe no more except to overwhelm you with her tenderness, a woman consumed with hopeless love, a woman who remains faithful, not to pleasures shared, but to feelings that went unrecognized and were cast aside.

Louise de Lavallière[7] wept for lost happiness and vanished power: the Duchesse de Langeais will be happy for the tears she has shed and will still retain power over you. Yes indeed, you will regret losing me. I have a feeling that I was not of this world, and I thank you for proving it to me. Good-bye. You will not touch my axe. Yours was the executioner's axe, mine belongs to God. Yours kills, mine saves. Your love was a mortal one and could endure neither disdain nor mockery; mine can endure everything, will never weaken, is everlasting. Ah! I feel a sombre joy in rising superior to you, you who feel so lofty, in humbling you with the tranquil and tutelary smile of the lesser angels who, as they lie at the feet of God, assume the right and might to watch over men in His name. You have had ephemeral desires: the lowly nun will unceasingly light your path with her ardent prayers and for ever spread the wings of divine love over you. I anticipate your answer, Armand, and I give you our next rendezvous: in heaven. There, dear friend, is room for both strength and weakness, both being the fruit of suffering. This thought calms the agitations of my soul as it faces its last trial. I feel such peace that I might even fear I no longer love you were it not for the fact that I am quitting the world for you.

ANTOINETTE

'Dear vidame,' said the duchess as they arrived at Montriveau's house. 'Be so good as to ask the porter if Armand is at home.'

The commander, courteously obedient in his eighteenth-century manner, left the carriage and returned with an affirmative reply which sent a shudder through her. She squeezed his hand, offered both of her cheeks for him to kiss, and begged him to go away without keeping watch on her or trying to protect her.

'But what about passers-by?' he asked.

'No one would show me disrespect,' she answered.

7. The first mistress of Louis XIV.

This was the last word of the duchess, the woman of the world. The commander went away. Madame de Langeais stood on the threshold of Montriveau's door, wrapped in her mantle, waiting for eight o'clock to strike. It struck. The unhappy woman waited for another ten minutes, a quarter of an hour. Finally she saw a new humiliation in this delay and gave up hope. She could not repress one cry: 'Oh my God!' before leaving this fatal threshold. The Carmelite had spoken her first word.

Montriveau was in conference with a group of friends. He was in a hurry for them to finish, but his clock was slow and he did not leave his house to go to the Hôtel de Langeais before the duchess, in a cold rage, was already running off on foot through the streets of Paris. She burst into tears on reaching the Boulevard Denfert. From there, for the last time, she gazed down on Paris, smoky, noisy, bathed in the red glow of its illuminations. Then she hired a cab and left the city for the last time. When the Marquis de Montriveau arrived at the Hôtel de Langeais his mistress was no longer there. He thought she had played another trick on him. So he rushed to the vidame's rooms, and was admitted just at the moment when the old man was getting into his dressing-gown and rejoicing at the thought that his pretty great-niece had found happiness. Montriveau cast at him his terrifying glance, so charged with electricity that it was capable of paralysing man and woman alike.

'Monsieur,' he cried, 'are you playing some cruel joke on me? I have just come from the Hôtel de Langeais and am told that the duchess is out.'

'It looks as if a great misfortune has happened, and no doubt through your fault,' the vidame replied. 'I left the duchess at your door.'

'At what time?'

'A quarter to eight.'

'Thank you. Good evening,' said Montriveau, and he hurried home to ask his porter if he had not seen a lady at the door in the course of the evening.

'Yes, monsieur. A beautiful lady who seemed very upset.

She was weeping like Mary Magdalen, but quietly, and standing up as straight as a pike. In the end she let out an "Oh my God!" and went away. Saving your presence, my wife and I were there without her noticing us, and it nearly broke our hearts.'

At these few words the adamant Montriveau turned pale. He despatched a short missive to Monsieur de Ronquerolles and returned to his flat. At about midnight the Marquis de Ronquerolles joined him.

'What's wrong, my good friend?' he asked as he took in the general's appearance. Armand gave him the duchess's letter to read.

'What has happened since?' Ronquerolles asked.

'She was at my door at eight, and at eight-fifteen she had gone. I have lost her, and I love her! Ah! If my life were my own I should already have blown my brains out!'

'Come come!' said Ronquerolles. 'Calm down. Duchesses don't flit away like water-wagtails. She can't do more than eight miles an hour. Tomorrow we will do sixteen.'

'But yet, confound it!' he added. 'Madame de Langeais is no ordinary woman. We must all take to horse in the morning. In the course of the day we'll find out from the police which way she's gone. She'll have to take a carriage, for they haven't wings, these angels. Whether she's on the highroad or hiding in Paris we'll find her. No need to run after her – the telegraph will catch up with her. You'll be all right. But, dear brother, you've made the mistake to which all men with energy like yours are more or less prone. They judge others by themselves and don't know when ordinary human beings reach the breaking-point. Why didn't you tip me the wink earlier? I should have told you "be punctual". – I will see you tomorrow then,' he added, shaking the mute Montriveau's hand. 'Sleep if you can.'

Nevertheless, the widest resources with which society ever invested statesmen, sovereigns, ministers, bankers, in short all human authorities, were in vain brought into play. Neither Montriveau nor his friends could find any trace of the duchess. Quite evidently she had taken refuge in some cloister. Montriveau determined to ransack or have ransacked every convent in the world. He would have the duchess even if it involved razing a city to the ground. To do justice to this extraordinary man, we must state that his passionate fury was renewed every day with equal heat and did not abate for five years. It was not until 1829 that the Duc de Navarreins learned by chance that his daughter had gone off into Spain as waiting-maid to Lady Julia Hopwood, and that she had left this lady at Cadiz without the latter having had any idea that 'Mademoiselle Caroline' was the illustrious duchess whose disappearance had aroused so much curiosity in the higher reaches of Parisian society.

The feelings of the two lovers when they met at long last at the grating of the Carmelite convent in the presence of the Mother Superior, can now be appreciated in all their intensity. Their violence, reawakened on both sides, will no doubt serve to explain the concluding events of this story.

4

. . . God disposes

THE Duc de Langeais having died in 1823, his wife was free.
Antoinette was living, wasted with love, on a reef in the
Mediterranean. However, the Pope had the power to annul the
vows taken by Sister Thérèse, and happiness bought with so
much passion might yet come into bloom for the two lovers.
This idea brought Montriveau from Cadiz to Marseilles, from
Marseilles to Paris. A few months after his arrival in France, a
merchant brig, fitted out for fighting, left the port of Marseilles
and set a course for Spain. This vessel carried several notable
men on board, mostly Frenchmen passionately in love with
oriental countries and anxious to visit them. Montriveau's
extensive knowledge of these countries made him a most
attractive travelling companion for the gentlemen concerned:
they entreated him to join them, and he consented. The
Minister for War commissioned him lieutenant-general and
placed him on the Committee of Artillery in order to facili-
tate his participation in this pleasure party.

The brig dropped anchor, after sailing for twenty-four
hours, north-west of an island within sight of the Spanish
coast. The vessel had been chosen with sufficiently slender
keel and light rigging for her to be able to anchor within
half a league of the reefs which on that side constituted a sure
defence against any attack on the island. If fishing smacks
or islanders noticed the brig at anchor, there was no conceivable reason for anxiety. For that matter it was easy to
explain why she was at anchor there. Before arriving within
sight of the island Montriveau had run up the flag of the
United States. The seamen on board were all Americans and
only spoke English. One of Monsieur de Montriveau's
companions put them all on to a longboat and took them to
one of the inns in the small town, where he kept them in a

state of inebriation which prevented them from making free use of their tongues. Then he made out that the brig had been chartered by treasure hunters, a fraternity well known in the United States for the enthusiasm they bring to their pursuit – an American writer has written the history of their adventures. In consequence, the presence of this vessel among the reefs was easy to explain. The supposed boatswain's mate put it forth that both passengers and crew were searching for a wrecked galleon which had foundered in 1778 with treasures brought from Mexico. Innkeepers and local authorities let it go at that.

Armand and the devoted friends who were assisting him in this difficult enterprise decided straight away that neither force nor ruse would avail to liberate or abduct Sister Thérèse by approaching the convent from the little town. Therefore, unanimously, these men of daring resolved to take the bull by the horns and gain access to the convent by what seemed to be a completely unapproachable route: they would get the better of natural obstacles as General Lamarque had done at the siege of Capri. In this particular case, the perpendicular granite cliffs at the end of the island offered less foothold than those of Capri had offered to Montriveau, when he had taken part in that astounding expedition. The nuns themselves seemed to him to offer a more formidable opposition than Sir Hudson Lowe had done. These men would have been ashamed to abduct the duchess with noise and violence, as they might have done by laying siege to the town and convent and, like a gang of pirates, leaving no one alive as witnesses of their victory. So then this enterprise could present only one of two aspects: either a major conflagration, some feat of arms which might startle Europe without revealing any motive for the crime, or else an aerial, mysterious witching-away which might persuade the nuns that the devil had paid them a visit. At the secret council held in Paris before they set off the latter plan was agreed on. And everything had been thought out for the success of a venture which promised real entertainment to a group of men bored with urban pleasures.

A kind of exceedingly light canoe, made at Marseilles

after a Malay model, enabled them to feel their way among the reefs to a point beyond which further navigation was impossible. Two iron wire cables, stretched more or less parallel, though inclining inwards for a distance of some feet, along which baskets, also of iron wire, were made to slide, served them for a bridge, as in China, for passing from rock to rock. The reefs were thus connected by a network of cables and baskets rather like the web which certain species of spider weave round a tree from branch to branch and use to run across: an instinctive process which the Chinese, born imitators of nature, were the first, historically speaking, to copy. No surges or caprices of the sea could upset these frail constructions. The cables had enough give in them to yield to the violence of the waves in a kind of curve, one which was studied by an engineer, the late Cachin, the memorable designer of the port of Cherbourg: a scientifically drawn line which sets a limit to the force of the angriest waves: a curve determined by a law wrested from the secrets of nature by the genius of observation – and observation constitutes well-nigh the sum total of human genius.

Monsieur de Montriveau's companions alone were on this vessel. No eye of man could reach them; the best glasses levelled from the upper deck of passing ships could not have revealed either the cables half submerged among the reefs, or the men hidden among the rocks. After eleven days' preparatory toil, these thirteen demonic workers reached the foot of the promontory rising thirty fathoms or more above the sea, a mass of rock as difficult for a man to clamber up as it would be for a mouse to climb the smooth, rounded surface of a porcelain vase. This mass of granite was fortunately cracked, and the two edges of the cleft, being perfectly straight, enabled them to drive in, at a distance of a foot apart, stout wooden wedges to which these indomitable workmen fixed iron cramps. These had been suitably shaped and were finished at one end with perforated plates on each of which they fixed steps of thin deal plank which were then fitted into notches cut into a mast of the same height as the rock-face, the base of them being embedded in the granite at the foot of the cliff. With a skill worthy of such practised artisans, one of them, a mathematician of genius, had calculated the angle at which the steps at the top and bottom of the mast should gradually be spaced so as to set in the middle of it the point from which the steps of the upper half fanned out towards the summit of the rock, while the steps of the lower half angled down towards the bottom. This marvellously light yet perfectly firm staircase took twenty-two days to make. A phosphorus match flashing in the darkness and the ebb of a tide would suffice to obliterate all of it for ever. So no tell-tale clues were possible, and any pursuit of the violators of the convent was doomed to failure.

On the summit of the rock was a platform surrounded on three sides by precipitous cliff. The thirteen intruders, examining the terrain through their telescopes from the topmast, had satisfied themselves that, in spite of some rugged surfaces, they could easily reach the gardens of the convent, where the trees were sufficiently thick to offer some cover. There, no doubt, they could make their final decision as to the best means of kidnapping the nun. After all the efforts they had made they were unwilling to jeopardize the success of their enterprise by risking discovery, and felt obliged to wait for the last quarter of the moon to expire.

Montriveau spent a couple of nights lying on the rock, wrapped in his cloak. The evening and morning convent chants filled him with inexpressible delight. He went as far as the foot of the convent wall to listen to the organ music, and tried to pick out one particular voice from the chorus of voices. But in spite of the silence around him, the distance was too great for any but the confused sounds of the music to reach his ear: soft harmonies in which even faulty execution was no longer perceptible, from which the pure thought of the musical art issued and seeped into the hearer's soul, demanding of him neither the effort of attention nor the strain of listening. Excruciating memories for Armand, whose love bloomed fresh and entire in this gentle surge of music, in which he tried to sense aerial promises of happiness. The morning after the second night, he climbed down from the rock before sunrise, after spending several hours with his eyes glued to the unbarred windows of a cell: one of those which, since they overlooked the abyss of the ocean, needed no grille. A light had gleamed from it the whole night long. An instinct of the heart, which misleads as often as it speaks truth, had cried to him: 'There she is!'

'Assuredly she is there, and tomorrow she will be mine!' he cried, mingling his joyous thoughts with the slow tolling of a bell. Strange waywardness of the heart! He far more passionately loved the nun worn down by the transports of love, wasted away in the tears, fasts and vigils of prayer, the so sorely tried woman of twenty-nine, than he had loved the light-hearted girl, the slender nymph of twenty-four! But have not men of vigorous soul a natural predilection for the sublime expression that noble grief or the impetuous surge of thought has imprinted on a woman's face? Is not the beauty of a grief-stricken woman the most arresting of all for a man who holds in his heart an inexhaustible treasure of consolation and tenderness to be lavished on a creature so graceful in her frailty but so strong in her emotions? The beauty which consists of fresh colouring, the smooth complexion, prettiness in short, is a commonplace attraction appealing to the common run of men. Montriveau was more likely to prefer the kind of face which lights up with love amid the lines of grief and the ravages of melancholy. Such a lover brings to life, by the summons of his imperious desires, a totally new being, vibrant with youth, one which for him alone bursts forth from a chrysalis which to him is still lovely though to other eyes it appears faded. He possesses two women: one who seems pale, bloodless, sad; another who lives in his heart and is invisible to everyone else: an angel for whom life is only comprehensible through feeling, who only shines out in all her glory for the solemn rites of love.

Before quitting his post, the general heard faint harmonies breathing out from the cell he had been watching: soft, thrillingly tender voices. When he returned to the base of the rock where his friends were waiting, he told them, with an economy of words instinct with the communicative but contained passion whose imposing accents men always respect, that never in his life had he heard such blissful harmonies.

The next evening, after nightfall, eleven devoted companions hoisted themselves up to the cliff-top, each of them carrying a dagger, a ration of chocolate and all the tools needed for the house-breaker's trade. When they arrived at the wall encircling the convent they climbed over it on ladders made for the purpose, and that brought them to the convent cemetery. Montriveau recognized both the long, vaulted gallery which some time ago had brought him to the convent parlour, and also the windows which ran along it. He immediately decided on a plan of action: to gain entry through that particular parlour window which gave light to the part reserved for the Carmelites; to move into the corridors; to see if names were inscribed on each cell; to find that of Sister Thérèse; to surprise and gag her while she was sleeping, to bind and carry her away. Every part of this programme was child's play for men who combined the audacity and dexterity of convicts with the specialized knowledge of men of the world: men moreover who would not hesitate to purchase silence with their daggers.

It took two hours to saw through the bars of the window. Three men stood sentinel outside and two others kept watch in the parlour. The others, bare-footed, posted themselves from point to point along the cloister on which Montriveau advanced, hiding behind a young man, Henri de Marsay, who had taken the precaution of robing himself in a Carmelite habit identical with the one worn in this convent. The clock struck three as the false nun and Montriveau reached the dormitory area. They quickly took stock of the position of the cells. Then, hearing no noise, they deciphered, with the help of a dark lantern, the names which fortunately for them were engraved on each door, decorated with the mystical devices and the portraits of male and female saints which each nun elects to inscribe as a kind of epigraph on the new phase in her life, and by means of which she reveals her ultimate ideal. When he reached the cell of Sister Thérèse,

Montriveau read this inscription: *Sub invocatione sanctae matris Theresae.* The motto was *Adoremus in aeternum.* Suddenly his companion laid his hand on his shoulder and showed him a bright gleam lighting up the flagstones of the corridor through the chinks of the door. At this moment Monsieur de Ronquerolles joined them.

'All the nuns are in the chapel and are beginning the Office for the Dead,' he said.

'I shall stay here,' Montriveau replied. 'The rest of you fall back into the parlour and close the door of this corridor.'

He glided quickly into the cell, preceded by the false nun whose veil was pulled down. They then saw, in the antechamber of the inner cell, the dead body of the duchess, laid upon the floor on the plank of her bed and lighted with two wax tapers. Neither Montriveau nor de Marsay said a word or uttered a cry; but they looked at each other. Then the general made a sign which meant: 'Let us take her away.'

'We must ourselves get away,' cried Ronquerolles. 'The procession of nuns is returning and they will spot us.'

With the magical rapidity which an urgent purpose lends to action, the dead body was carried into the parlour, slipped through the window and conveyed to the foot of the wall. Just as the abbess, with the procession of nuns behind her, arrived at the cell to take Sister Thérèse's body to the chapel, the sister whose duty it was to watch over the dead body had committed the imprudence of ransacking the cell out of curiosity, and had been so busy searching that she had heard no noise and was appalled when she returned to the antechamber and found the body gone. Before the stupefied woman could think of making any search, the duchess's body had been lowered by ropes to the foot of the cliff, and Montriveau's companions had destroyed their handiwork. By nine o'clock the next morning no trace remained of the improvised staircase or the wire bridges. Sister Thérèse's body was on board the brig. This came into port in order to embark its crew, and made off in the course of the day.

Montriveau remained alone in his cabin with the corpse of Antoinette de Navarreins, whose countenance, for several hours, was still, for him, indulgently resplendent with the sublime beauty which the calm of death sometimes bestows on mortal remains.

'Ah well!' said Ronquerolles to Montriveau when the latter reappeared on deck. 'She was a woman. Now she is nothing. We will tie a cannon-ball to each of her feet and throw her overboard. Think no more of her than we think of a book we read in our childhood.'

'Yes indeed,' said Montriveau. 'Only a poem remains.'

'That's a sensible view. From now on be content with passion. Love is an investment which we should think out cautiously. And only the last love of a woman can satisfy the first love of a man.'

Geneva, Pré-Levêque, 26 January 1834

THE GIRL WITH THE
GOLDEN EYES

To Eugène Delacroix, Painter

I

Parisian physiognomies

UNDENIABLY one of the most fearsome spectacles in Paris is the general aspect of the Parisian population: a population revolting to look on – gaunt, yellow, sallow. What is Paris other than a vast cornfield whose waving stalks are incessantly swayed this way and that by the winds of self-interest – a swirling harvest of men and women which the scythe of death cuts down more ruthlessly than anywhere else, even though it springs up again as dense as ever: a sea of faces, twisted, contorted, exuding through every pore of the skin the toxic lusts conceived in the brain? Or rather, not so much faces as masks: masks of weakness or strength, masks of misery or joy or hypocrisy, all of them drained of vitality, all of them bearing the ineffaceable mark of panting avidity. What are they striving for? Gold, or pleasure?

A few reflections on Paris as a moral entity may help to explain the reasons for its cadaverous physiognomy. Here there are only two ages of man: youth and decrepitude; a youth which is pale and anaemic, a decrepitude which paints thick in order to appear young. Foreigners, when they set eyes on this people of exhumed corpses, being under no obligation to consider what they see, are immediately moved to disgust at the sight of this vast metropolitan workshop for the manufacture of enjoyment; one from which they soon find it impossible to emerge and in which they remain to suffer voluntary deterioration. Few words are needed to assign a physiological cause to the almost infernal tones of Parisian complexions – for it is not only in jest that Paris has been called an inferno. The epithet is well deserved. There all is smoke, fire, glare, ebullience; everything flares up, falters, dies down, burns up again, sparkles, crackles and is consumed. Never in any country has life been more ardent, more intense. There, social nature, for ever in the crucible, once one task is accomplished, seems to urge itself to a new effort, like Nature herself. Like Nature herself, society concerns itself with the insects and flowers of a day, frivolities, ephemera. It is for ever vomiting fire and flame from its unquenchable crater. Perhaps, before we analyse the causes which create a special physiognomy for each category of this intelligent and mobile nation, we ought to put a finger on the generally operative cause which in greater or lesser degree robs its individual members of their colour, blanches them, turns them blue or turns them brown.

The Parisian is so interested in everything that he ends up by being interested in nothing. No dominant emotion has left its mark on his countenance over which so many emotions have skimmed, and therefore it turns grey, like the plaster of the house-fronts, overlaid with all shades of dust and smoke. Truth to tell, the Parisian, caring nothing one day for what will delight him the day after, lives like a child whatever his age may be. He grumbles at everything and puts up with everything, mocks at everything, forgets and longs for everything, likes to sample everything; he passionately takes up a cause and drops it without a further thought – royalism, foreign conquest, national glory, any idol be it of bronze or tinsel. He sheds them as he sheds his hose, hats or dreams of fortune. In Paris no sentiment can stand against the swirling torrent of events; their onrush and the effort to swim against the current lessens the intensity of passion. Love is reduced to desire, hate to a whimsy. The only family link is with the thousand-franc note, one's only friend is the pawnbroker. This general attitude of devil-may-care bears its fruit: in the salon as in the street no one is *de trop*, no one is absolutely indispensable or absolutely noxious, be he knave or blockhead, intelligent man or honest citizen. In Paris there is toleration for everything: the government, the guillotine, the Church, cholera. You will always be welcome in Parisian society, but if you are not there no one will miss you. What then are the dominant forces in this community devoid of morals, principles and genuine feeling, which yet are forces in which all feeling, principles and morals have their beginning and their end? They are gold and pleasure. Take these two words as a guiding light, and make your way through that huge stucco cage, that human beehive with black runnels marking its sections, and follow the ramifications of the idea which moves, stirs and ferments inside it. Look around you.

First of all look at the class which has no possessions. The artisan, the proletarian, the man who toils with foot, hand, tongue, back, his strong right arm or his ten fingers to gain a living. This man, who should be the first to think of sparing his vital resources, overtaxes his strength, harnesses his wife to some machine or other, and exploits his child by gearing him to a cog-wheel. The manufacturer – the intermediary string pulling and moving these puppets who with grimy hands model and gild the potter's clay, stitch coats and dresses, beat out iron, shave and plane wood, temper steel, spin and weave hemp and flax, burnish bronzes, festoon crystal with floral decorations, embroider woollens, train horses, plait and braid harness, cut out copper, paint carriages, pollard aged elms, steam-dye cotton, dry out tulle,[1] polish diamonds and metals, foliate marble, round off precious stones, give thought a graceful form in print, deck it out in colour or plain black and white – the aforesaid middleman has approached that sweating, willing, patient, industrious populace and promised it a lavish wage, either in order to cater for a city's whims or on behalf of the monster we call Speculation. Thereupon these quadrumanous mammals have set themselves to working through the night-watches, suffering, toiling, cursing, fasting and forging along: all of them wearing themselves out in order to win the gold which keeps them spellbound. Then, heedless of the future, greedy for enjoyment, relying on their muscular strength as the painter relies

1. The French is *souffler les tuls*. *Tuls* is a variant of *tulles*. *Souffler* (English technical term 'puff'): 'the drying of piece-goods by stretching to size on a frame and creating air movement by means of large paddles or "wafters". (This process has now been superseded.) The phrase has puzzled readers for about 140 years. Previous English translators have crudely substituted 'blow glass'.

on his palette, feeling – when Monday comes – as rich as lords, they fling their wages away in the taverns which surround the city as with a girdle of foulness – the girdle of the most unchaste of the daughters of Venus, undone and done up again every minute of the day – there it is that these people, as brutish in the pleasures they take as they are docile in the work they do, squander their weekly earnings as quickly as in a gambling-hell. So then, for five days in the week, there is no repose for this toiling population. They give themselves over to activities which buckle the body, give it superfluous flesh or waste it and reduce it to pallor, but break forth in a thousand spurts of purposeful creation. Then it takes its pleasure and relaxation in the form of exhausting debauchery, and emerges from it black and blue from violent quarrels, livid with drunkenness and yellow with indigestion. This lasts only two days but steals tomorrow's bread, a whole week's soup, the wife's new dress and decent wrappings for the baby.

Such men, undoubtedly born to be handsome, for all creatures have their own brand of beauty, have been enrolled from infancy under the standard of physical force, the reign of hammer, chisel and loom, and have been rapidly vulcanized. Is not Vulcan, with his ugliness and strength, the emblem of this strong and ugly race of men, superb in its mechanical skill, patient so long as it chooses to be so, terrible one day in every century, as explosive as gunpowder, primed with brandy to the point of revolutionary incendiarism, quick-witted enough in short to take fire at a captious word, which it always interprets as a promise of gold and pleasure! If we include all people who hold out their hands for alms, for lawful wages or for the five-franc piece accorded to the various kinds of Parisian prostitution, in fact for all money honestly or dishonestly earned, this population amounts to three hundred thousand souls. Would not the government be overturned every Tuesday were it not for the taverns? Fortunately, by Tuesday, these sons of toil are in a state of torpor, sleeping off their excesses and penniless: they go back to their work and dry bread, stimulated by the urge to material productivity which has become a second nature for them ... Nevertheless this race has its men of exemplary virtue, its fully accomplished men, its unknown Napoleons who typify its capacities raised to their highest expression and sum up its social potentialities in a kind of life in which mental and bodily activity are combined, less in order to infuse joy into it than to dull the effect of pain.

It may be that chance has made some workman thrifty and favoured him with the ability to think. He has looked into the future, met a woman and become a father. After some years of hard privation he sets up in a small way as a haberdasher and rents a shop. If neither sickness nor vice have held him up, if he has done well, here is a sketch of his normal progress in life:

But first of all, salute this monarch of Parisian activity who has made time and space his servants. Yes, salute this creature, this compound of saltpetre and gas who, during his strenuous nights, gives children to France and during the day does not spare himself for the service, glory and pleasure of his fellow-citizens. He solves a multifarious problem: how simultaneously to satisfy an amiable wife, the family they have brought into the world, the *Constitutionnel*,[2] the office in which he works, the Opera House, the National Guard[3] and his Maker; but in such a way as to convert the *Constitutionnel*, his office, the Opera House, the National Guard, his wife and his Maker into solid cash. Finally, salute in him an irreproachable pluralist. Up every day at five, he whips like a bird over the space which separates his domicile from the Rue Montmartre. Wind or thunder, rain or snow, he gets to the *Constitutionnel* and waits there for the batch of newspapers he has contracted to distribute. He pounces on this political pabulum and carries it off. By nine o'clock he is back in the bosom of his family, cracks a joke with his wife, gives her a hearty kiss, sips at a cup of coffee and scolds his children. At a quarter to ten he takes up his post at the town hall. There,

2. A liberal daily in Restoration times and after: an organ mostly favoured by the middle classes.

3. A militia in which, after 1830, all citizens had to serve.

poised on a stool like a parrot on its perch, kept warm at the expense of the municipality of Paris, until four o'clock, without expending either a smile or a tear, he registers the births and deaths of an entire district. The joys and woes of the quarter flow through the nib of his pen, just as, a few hours earlier, he had all the wit of the *Constitutionnel* riding on his shoulders. Nothing weighs heavy on him! He always marches straight forward, takes his patriotism ready-made from the newspaper, never contradicts, shouts or applauds with the multitude and is as lively as a cricket. He lives quite near his parish church and, when an important ceremony is toward, he can leave an assistant in charge of his office and take his place in the church choir for a requiem. On Sundays and holy days he is its finest ornament and his voice echoes through the vaults. He vigorously contorts his wide mouth as he thunders out a joyful Amen in his capacity as lay clerk. Freed at four o'clock from his administrative duties, he makes his appearance in the most popular stores in the city, there to dispense mirth and gaiety. What a happy woman his wife is! She knows he has no time to give her cause for jealousy: he is a man of action, not of sentiment. His very arrival at the emporium is a challenge to the girls behind the counter, who make play with their bright eyes to attract as many customers as possible. He revels in the fichus and fineries and the muslin flimsies fashioned by the girls' deft fingers. Or, more often still, before going home to dinner, he waits on a client, copies out a page of his day-book or delivers an overdue bill to the process-server. Every other evening at six he takes up his post at the Opera: as a permanent base in the chorus he is ready for any role – soldier, Arab, prisoner of war, aborigine or village yokel, ghost, one leg of a camel, lion, demon, genie, slave, eunuch black or white. He is always expert in miming mirth, grief, pity, astonishment, at producing conventional cries or remaining mute. He may be a huntsman, a soldier, a Roman citizen or an Egyptian slave, but at heart he is still the haberdasher. At midnight he's home again, the man, the good husband, the loving father. He slips into the conjugal bed, his imagination still aflame with the illusive visions of opera nymphs; and so he turns the depravities of the world and Taglioni's entrancing *ronds de jambe* to the profit of conjugal love. Finally, if he sleeps at all, he sleeps in a hurry, rushing through his slumbers as he rushes through his life. He is movement metamorphosed into man, space incarnate, the Proteus of civilization. He is the epitome of all things: history, literature, politics, government, religion, the military art. He is in fact a living encyclopedia, a grotesque Atlas, endlessly on the march and never taking rest, like Paris itself. He is all legs.

No physiognomy could preserve its purity when caught up in such toils. Perhaps the artisan who dies old at thirty, his liver tanned by ever-increasing doses of cognac, will be proved by a handful of well-to-do philosophers to be happier than the haberdasher. The one goes out like a light; the other dies by degrees. From his multiple occupations, from the strength of his shoulders and the use of his hands, his wife, his trade, the latter draws – as from so many leases – a number of children, a few thousand francs' income and the hardest-earned happiness that has ever rejoiced the heart of man. This small fortune and these children, or rather the children, who mean everything to him, are recruited into the class immediately above, into whose hands he commits his ducats and his daughters, or his son, who has been to a secondary school, is better educated than his father and looks above him with ambitious eye. Often enough the younger son of a small retailer aspires to a position in the civil service.

That kind of ambition brings our attention to the second[4] of the spheres of Paris. So let us mount one storey to the *entresol,* or descend from the garret and linger on the fourth floor; in short make your way into the company of those who possess something. There you will see the same result. Wholesale merchants and their staffs, government employees, small bankers of great integrity, swindlers and catspaws, head clerks and junior clerks, bailiffs', solicitors' and notaries' clerks, in short the bustling, scheming, speculating members of

4. Why not third? But Balzac regards the small retailer, just dealt with, as a working-class man who has, slightly, bettered himself.

that lower middle class which assesses demand in Paris and reckons to cater for it, makes corners in commodities, stores the retail goods made by the proletariat and takes charge of fruit from the South, fish from the sea and the wines produced on every sun-drenched hill-slope; which stretches its hands out over the Orient, buys the shawls which Turks and Persians have disdained, goes foraging as far as the Indies, bides its time for an auspicious sale and the profit it will bring, discounts bills of exchange, circulates and cashes all sorts of securities; which takes over the whole of Paris in all its requirements, supplies it with means of transport, makes provision for the fantasies of children, spies out the whims and vices of grown-ups and squeezes out dividends from their diseases.

Well now, although these people do not imbibe alcohol like the working man or go beyond the city boundaries[5] to wallow in debauch; they too, all of them, abuse their strength, put body and spirit, by reciprocal reaction, to excessive strain, are burned up with desire and let their frantic pace of living ruin their health. In their case it is the flail of self-interest, the goad of those ambitions which torture the more elevated classes of this monstrous city, that are responsible for this physical wrenching, just as, with the proletariat, it is due to the cruel and ceaseless swings of the pendulum regulating the material production demanded by an imperious aristocracy. So then in this sphere also, if one is to obey the universal tyranny of pleasure or gold, one must devour time, squeeze time, extract more than twenty-four hours from day and night, wear oneself to the bone, work oneself to death and sell thirty years of old age for two years of unhealthy ease. The difference is that the artisan dies in the infirmary when his stunted life has reached its term, whereas the *petit bourgeois* persists in living and indeed goes on living – like a cretin. You will meet him dragging himself dazedly along the boulevard, which is the girdle to his Venus, with his worn, dull, withered face, dim eyes and tottering legs. What did he want, this bourgeois?

5. See above, p. 312. The reference is to the wine-shops on the outskirts of Paris where the working classes sought amusement.

The short sabre of the National Guard, a never-failing stockpot, a respectable plot in the Père-Lachaise cemetery and, while old age lasted, a little money legitimately acquired. For him Sunday is the equivalent of the workman's Monday. His idea of repose is a drive in a hired carriage, a country outing to enable his wife and children in merry mood to gulp in clouds of dust or broil in the sun. His favourite resort outside the city wall is the restaurant whose poisonous food enjoys a good reputation. Or sometimes he will go to some family ball and swelter there until midnight.

There are some people simple enough to be astonished at the St Vitus's dance performed by the animalculae which the microscope brings into view in a drop of water. But what would Rabelais's Gargantua, that superbly audacious but badly understood figure, what would this giant fallen from celestial spheres say if he whiled away a moment contemplating the activities of this second stage of Parisian life which we are here attempting to outline? Have you come upon one of those little booths, cold in summer and in winter heated only by a small stove, situated under the vast copper dome which surmounts the Corn Exchange? Madame is there from early morning. She conducts the auction of vegetables in Les Halles, the Covent Garden of Paris and, so they say, makes twelve thousand francs at this trade. Monsieur, when Madame gets up, moves into his gloomy office where he makes short-term loans to the tradesmen in his quarter. At nine o'clock he betakes himself to the passport office, where he is one of the deputy chiefs. In the evening he sits at the box-office of the Théâtre Italien or any other theatre you care to mention. Their children are put out to nurse, and only come back home to go to a lycée or a boarding-school. Monsieur and Madame live on a third floor, their only domestic is the cook and they give dances in a drawing-room twelve feet by eight, oil-lit. But they will hand over a dowry of one hundred and fifty thousand francs with their daughter and take their ease when they reach fifty, at which age they begin to appear in the third-tier boxes at the Opera House, in a hired cab at the Longchamps races or, on sunny days, in somewhat faded clothes, on the boulevards: their espaliers have borne fruit. Monsieur is of good repute in his quarter, in good favour with the powers that be, in good relations with the higher bourgeoisie. At sixty-five he is awarded the Cross of the Legion of Honour, and his son-in-law's father, the mayor of a district, invites him to his receptions. And so a lifetime of labours brings profit to children whom this lower bourgeoisie tends inevitably to raise to the ranks of the upper bourgeoisie. Thus each social sphere projects its spawn into the sphere immediately above it. The rich grocer's son becomes a notary, the timber merchant's son becomes a magistrate. Not a cog fails to fit into its groove and everything stimulates the upward march of money.

*

Here we are then, brought to the third circle of this inferno which, one day perhaps, will find its Dante.[6] In this third circle – as it were the stomach of Paris in which the interests of the city are digested and compressed into a form which goes by the name of *affaires* – there bustles and stirs, as by some acrid and rancorous intestinal process, the crowd of lawyers, doctors, barristers, business men, bankers, traders on the grand scale. Here are to be found more causes of physical and moral destruction than anywhere else. Almost all of these men live in insalubrious offices, pestilential courtrooms, small chambers with barred windows,[7] spend their day bowed down with the weight of their affairs, get up at dawn in order to cope with them, to avoid being cheated, to gain all they can or at least not to lose anything, to get their grip on a man or his money, to set a piece of business going or to wind it up, to seize opportunity by the short hairs, to get accused men hanged or acquitted. This fever of action affects even their horses: they overwork them, ride them to death, wear out their legs – their own too – before their time. Time is

6. An early hint of the title Balzac found, round about 1840, for his vast work: *The Human Comedy*.

7. In this long tirade Balzac seems mainly to be thinking of the legal profession but not exclusively so.

their tyrant: they need more, it slips away from them; they can neither stretch nor shrink it. What soul can remain great, pure, moral, generous, and, consequently, what countenance can retain its beauty in the debasing exercise of a profession which compels a man to bear the burden of public miseries, to analyse them, weigh them, appraise them, batten on them? In what safe deposit do these people store their hearts? I cannot tell, but when they have a heart they leave it behind them before descending every morning into the abyss of sorrows which put families to the torture. For them there are no mysteries; they see the reverse side of society – they are its confessors and despise it. Now whatever befalls, either by dint of coping with corruption they conceive a horror for it and are saddened, or, out of lassitude or by an unavowed compromise, they come to terms with it. In the long run, of necessity, they become cynical about all human feeling, they whom the laws, men and institutions force to hover like birds of prey over still-palpitating corpses.

At all hours the man of money is weighing the living, the man of contracts weighs the dead, the man of law weighs the human conscience. Compelled to be always talking, they all put talk in place of thought and rhetoric in place of feeling: their soul merely functions as a larynx. They become jaded and demoralized. Neither the merchant prince, nor the judge, nor the barrister keeps his sense of rectitude; they no longer feel, they merely apply rules which particular cases stultify. Carried away in this torrent of existence, they can be neither husbands, fathers nor lovers. They skim as in a sleigh over the realities of life and live from hand to mouth, hounded on by the affairs of the great city. When at last they get home again they are required to go out to a ball, to the opera, to social entertainments where they meet new clients, new acquaintances, new patrons. They all over-eat, gamble and keep late hours; their faces fill out or flatten down or grow rubicund. For such a terrific expense of intellectual stamina, for the moral contraction so continually imposed upon them, they recoup themselves, not with pleasure, which affords too pallid a contrast, but with debauchery: a secret and terrifying debauchery, for all means are at their disposal and they set the moral pace for society. Their fundamental stupidity lies concealed under their special aptitude. They know their job but are totally ignorant about all things outside it. Therefore, to preserve their self-respect, they call all things into question and criticize without rhyme or reason. They pose as sceptics but in reality are eminently gullible and fuddle what wits they have in unending argument. Practically all of them take over the current social, literary or political prejudices in order to avoid forming their own judgements, just as they let the Civil Code, or the Tribunal of Commerce take care of their consciences. After setting off early to make their mark they sink into mediocrity and, if they reach social heights, show subservience. And so their faces present the raw pallor, the unnatural colouring, the lack-lustre eyes with rings round them, the sensual, babbling mouths by which an observant person recognizes the symptoms of the deterioration of thought, and its rotation within a narrow circle of ideas calculated to destroy the faculties of the brain and the gift for seeing things broadly, for generalizing and drawing inferences. All of them get shrivelled in the furnace of affairs. Consequently no man who has let himself get caught up in the grinding cog-wheels of this immense machine can achieve greatness. If he is a doctor, either he has had little practice or he is an exception, a Bichat who dies young.[8] If, being a great merchant, he remains personally important, he is almost a Jacques Cœur.[9] Did Robespierre ever practise as a barrister? Or Danton, an idler who waited on events? But who for that matter has ever felt envious of such figures as Danton and Robespierre, superb as they may have been?

Those who are pre-eminently men of affairs attract money to themselves and accumulate it in order to ally themselves with aristocratic families. If the workman's ambition is that of the *petit bourgeois*, here also are the same passions. In Paris vanity is the sum total of all passion. A typical member of this

8. Xavier Bichat (1771–1802), a brilliant analogist and physiologist.

9. A rich merchant and important statesman under Charles VII (early 15th century).

class might be either the ambitious bourgeois who, after a
life of effort, stress and continual planning, insinuates himself
into the Council of State as an ant passes through a crack in a
wall; or maybe a newspaper editor, a master of intrigue whom
the King makes a peer of France, perhaps in order to avenge
himself on the nobility; or else some notary who has become
mayor of his district: all of them have been flattened out
under the pressure of affairs and, if they reach their goal,
have no life left in them when they get there. In France it is
a regular practice to set old fossils on a pedestal. Only Napoleon, Louis XIV and great kings have always looked to young
men to carry out their designs.

*

Above this sphere lives the artist world. But here again you
see faces which are stamped, it is true, with the seal of originality, but still are ravaged, not ignobly, but ravaged, fatigued,
tortured. Overtaxed by the necessity of producing, over-
burdened by their costly fantasies, wearied by the genius
which devours them, avid for pleasure, the artists of Paris all
strive by excess of effort to fill in the gaps left by their idleness,
and seek in vain to conciliate mundane dalliance with the
conquest of glory and money with art. When he begins, the
artist is incessantly harassed by creditors; his needs engender
debts, and his debts take toll of his nights. After work comes
pleasure. The actor plays until midnight, cons his parts in the
morning and rehearses at noon; the sculptor's back aches as
he bends over his statue; the journalist represents thought on
the march like a soldier going to the wars; the fashionable
painter is overwhelmed with work while the uncommissioned
painter feels a gnawing at his vitals if he is conscious of
genius. Competition, rivalry and calumny are deadly enemies to
talent. Some of these men, in despair, plunge deep into
vice, others die young and unknown because they have too
early discounted their future. The faces of a few of them,
originally sublime, retain their beauty. In any case the glowing
beauty of their countenance passes unappreciated. An artist's
physiognomy is always abnormal, always above or below the

conventional lines of what fools call ideal beauty. What is the force that destroys them? Passion. All passion in Paris is resolved into two terms: gold and pleasure.

At the level you have now reached, do you not breathe more freely? Do you not feel that both air and space are purified? Here is neither toil nor trouble. The whirling spiral of gold has reached the heights. From underneath the gratings from which it begins to drain forth, from the coffers of the little shops where its current is momentarily halted, from the heart of the counting-houses and great furnaces where it is converted into bars, this gold, in the shape of dowries and inheritances, conveyed by the hands of marriageable maidens or the bony fingers of old men, finds a quick way to aristocratic centres where it will gleam, glisten and sparkle. But before we leave the four social tiers on which patrician wealth in Paris is built, should we not, having dealt with moral causes, make also some sounding about physical causes and draw attention to what one might call a subjacent pestilence whose operation is consistently visible on the face of the porter, the shopkeeper and the artisan? Should we not point out a deleterious influence whose corruptive action is equal only to that exerted by the municipal authorities who so complacently allow it to subsist? If the air of the houses in which the majority of middle-class citizens live is foul, if the atmosphere of the street spews out noxious vapours into practically airless back premises, realize that, apart from this pestilence, the forty thousand houses of this great city have their foundations plunged in filth which the authorities have not yet seriously thought of confining within concrete walls capable of preventing the most fetid mire from percolating through the soil, poisoning the wells and making the famous name Lutetia[10] still appropriate, at least underground. Half of Paris sleeps nightly in the putrid exhalations from streets, back-yards and privies.

*

But now let us take a look at the great, airy, gilded salons,

10. In Celtic, 'the town in the marshes'.

the mansions enclosed in gardens, the world of the rich, leisured, happy, moneyed people. There the faces you see are withered and consumed with vanity. There nothing is real. Is not seeking after pleasure a sure way of finding boredom? Society people have warped natures at an early age. Having nothing to do but create artificial means of enjoyment, they have been quick to misuse their senses, as the working man misuses alcohol. Pleasure is like certain medicaments: in order to keep on obtaining the same effects one has to double the doses, and death or brutishness is contained in the last one. All the lower classes pander to the rich and study their tastes in order to convert them into vices as a source of profit. How can one resist the alluring temptations which in this country are so ingeniously contrived? Thus Paris has as it were its opium-eaters, and their particular opium is gambling, the pleasures of the table, or fornication. And so you see that even in early years these people have inclinations but not passions; romantic fantasies and lukewarm loves. There impotence reigns; there ideas are non-existent: like vigour of character they have been contorted into boudoir affectations and feminine mannerisms. You will find callow youths of forty, aged pedants of sixteen. In Paris the wealthy come by ready-made wit, pre-digested knowledge and cut-and-dried opinions – and that dispenses them from any need to have wit, knowledge or opinions. The lack of good sense in this social sphere is as conspicuous as its feebleness and licentiousness. They waste so much time that they can find none to spare. Don't expect affection from them any more than ideas. Embraces are a disguise for profound indifference and politeness for unremitting contempt. There no one loves his neighbour. Shallow witticisms, indiscretions galore, slanderous gossip and, above all, platitudes: that is the basis of their talk. But these fortunate unfortunates disclaim the idea that they come together to devise and utter maxims after the manner of La Rochefoucauld. As if there did not exist a *via media*, such as the eighteenth century invented, between superfluity and utter vacuity! If a few gifted men have recourse to fine and subtle irony it is misunderstood; and soon, weary of giving without ever receiving, they stay at home and leave the blockheads to dominate the scene. This hollow existence, this perpetual waiting for a pleasure that never comes, this unrelieved boredom, this inanity of mind, heart and brain, this weariness with the unending round of Paris receptions, all leaves its mark on the features and produces those pasteboard faces, those premature wrinkles, that rich man's physiognomy on which impotence has set its grimace, in which only gold is mirrored and from which intelligence has fled.

Such a picture of Paris from the moral point of view proves that, physically speaking, Paris could not be other than it is. This city with its diadem is a queen who, always with child, is vexed with the irresistible desires of a pregnant woman. Paris is the intellectual centre of the globe, a brain teeming with genius which marches in the van of civilization; a great man, a ceaselessly creative artist, a political thinker with second sight who must necessarily have the wrinkles which go with intelligence, the defects which go with greatness, the fantasies of the artist and the disillusion of the politician. Its physiognomy implies the germination of good and evil, conflict and victory; the moral battle of 1789, whose trumpets are still resounding in every corner of the world; and also the dejection of 1814. Therefore do not expect to find more morality, more good feeling or more cleanliness than you do in the boilers of the magnificent steamships which you admire as they cleave the waves! Paris is indeed a very fine ship, carrying a cargo of intelligence. Its very coat of arms constitutes the kind of oracle which destiny sometimes condescends to emit. The *City of Paris* has its great mast of bronze with victories carved on it and Napoleon at the helm. No doubt this stout craft may pitch and roll, but she ploughs her way across the billows of humanity, fires her broadsides through the hundred mouths of her tribunes, rides proudly over the seas of science and calls out from the height of her topsails through the voices of her learned men and artists: 'Forward! March onward! Follow me!'

She carries a vast crew which delights to deck her with newly-won pennons. Her ballast is the stolid bourgeoisie, there are ship's boys and cabin boys sporting in the rigging, workmen and tarry bluejackets handling the sails; comfortable passengers recline in their cabins; neatly clad midshipmen smoke their cigars as they lean over the rails, while on the forecastle the fighting men, fired with new ideas or great ambitions, await the moment of landing on new shores, there to carry forward the bright torch of civilization. They are agog for glory – that too is a pleasure – or for love. For that too gold is required.

Hence it is that the phenomenal activity of the proletariat, the deterioration resulting from the multiple interests which grind down the two middle classes described above, the spiritual torments to which the class of artists is subjected and the surfeit of pleasure incessantly sought by the grandees, explain the normal ugliness of the Paris population. Only in the Orient does the human race offer some magnificence of face and figure; but this results from the undisturbed calm cultivated by those profound philosophers, with their long pipes, short legs and broad chests, who have nothing but scorn for perpetual motion; whereas in Paris people of all social statures, small, medium and great, run and leap and caper under the whip of a pitiless goddess, Necessity: the necessity for money, glory or amusement. And so the most extraordinary, the rarest exception is to come upon some fresh, serene, graceful and really youthful countenance. If you see one, be sure that it belongs to a young, idealistic cleric or some worthy abbé of forty with three chins; to a young person of chaste morals, such as certain middle-class families still produce; to a mother of twenty, nursing her first-born son and still full of illusions; to a young man fresh from the provinces, living under the care of a devout old lady who keeps him short of pocket-money; or perhaps to a shop assistant who goes to bed at midnight, worn out with folding and unfolding calico and rising at seven in order to drape the shop window. Often enough it belongs to a man of science or a poet who lives an ascetic existence, communes with noble thoughts and remains sober, long-suffering and pure – or even perhaps to some self-satisfied imbecile who feeds on his own folly, is bursting with health and never fails to give himself a smile of approval; or to the cheerful, easy-going species of loiterers, the only really happy people in Paris, which from hour to hour, from one quarter to another, offers them its poetry to savour.

Nevertheless, Paris contains its quota of privileged beings who draw profit from this perpetual to-and-fro of manu-facturers, interests, affairs, arts and affluence. They are the women.

Although a thousand secret causes operate on them which, there more than anywhere else, ravage their features, one finds, in the feminine world, happy little colonies which live after the Oriental mode and are able to preserve their beauty; but these women are rarely seen out in the streets on foot. They lie hidden, like rare plants which only unfold their petals at certain seasons and really are exceptional.

However, Paris is also, essentially, a region in which con-trasts occur. There true feeling may be rare, but there also, as elsewhere, noble friendships and unreserved devotion are met with. On this battlefield of interests and passions, just as in the midst of those agglomerations of men on the march in which egoism triumphs and every member has to rely on his own strength for self-defence – we call them *armies* – it seems that feeling, when it does manifest itself, is bent on achieving full expression and is sublime by way of contrast. So is it with physiognomies. In Paris, in high aristocratic circles, may sometimes be seen, here and there, a few ravishing young faces, the fruit of quite exceptional breeding and man-ners. The youthful comeliness of English stock is blended with the firmness of southern traits, the intelligence of the French race and its purity of contour. The flame in their eyes, the delectable red bloom on their lips, the glossy blackness of their silky hair, a fair complexion and a distinguished cast of countenance make lovely human flowers of them, magni-ficent to look on against the mass of other visages, leaden, wizened, distorted, grimacing. It follows that women in-stantly admire such young men with the same keen pleasure as men feel when they gaze on a pretty, modest, gracefully proportioned girl, one bedecked with all the virginal charms with which our imagination loves to embellish the ideal maiden.

If this rapid glance at the population of Paris has helped the reader to realize how rarely the eye perceives a Raphael-esque figure and what passionate admiration it inspires so soon as it is seen, the main purpose of our story will have been achieved. This had to be made clear: *quod erat demonstrandum*, if one may be permitted to apply a Euclidean formula to the science of manners.

*

On one of those beautiful spring mornings when the leaves, though uncurled, are not yet green; when the sunlight sets the roofs ablaze and the sky is blue; when the population of Paris comes buzzing forth from its hives and swarms along the boulevards – or slides like an iridescent grass-snake through the Rue de la Paix on its way to the Tuileries, hailing the hymeneal rites which earth and nature are renewing: on one of those jocund days a young man, as handsome as the day itself was fair, tastefully attired and elegant of manner – we will let out the secret and admit he was a love-child, the natural son of Lord Dudley and the celebrated Marquise de Vordac – was sauntering along the main avenue of the Tuileries gardens. This Adonis, Henri de Marsay by name, had been born in France, and to France Lord Dudley came in order to marry off the young woman who had just given birth to Henri, to an elderly nobleman named Monsieur de Marsay. This faded and almost extinct butterfly recognized the child as his own, in return for the usufruct of an income of a hundred thousand francs which was ultimately to revert to his putative son: an extravagance which Lord Dudley did not find very costly, since French government stock was then quoted at seventeen francs fifty. The old gentleman died without having known his wife. Subsequently Madame de Marsay married the Marquis de Vordac; but, prior to becoming a marquise, she had shown little concern either for her child or Lord Dudley. For one thing, the war between France and England had separated the two lovers, and fidelity come what may was not then, and never will be, fashionable in Paris. Also, her success as a pretty, elegant, universally adulated woman stifled all maternal sentiment in this Parisian lady. Lord Dudley no more concerned himself with his progeny than the mother did. Perhaps it was the speedy infidelity of a girl he had ardently loved that aroused in him some aversion for any issue of hers. Also it may well be that fathers only love the children with whom they have made ample acquaintance: a social belief of the highest importance which every bachelor should do his utmost to encourage by proving that the sentiment of paternity is a hot-house product cultivated by women, convention and the law.

Poor Henri de Marsay found a father only in that one of the two men who had no real paternal obligations towards him. Naturally, however, Monsieur de Marsay's effectual paternity proved to be very incomplete. In the natural way of things children only have a father for a few brief moments; the nobleman in question conformed to nature. The good man would not have bartered his name had he been free of vices. So, without compunction, he took his meals in gambling dens, and in other places he drank away the half-yearly interest which the Treasury paid out to its bond-holders. Then he handed the child over to his elder sister, a Demoiselle de Marsay, who took great care of him and, out of the slender allowance made to her by her brother, gave him a tutor, a penniless cleric, who took the measure of the youngster's expectations and decided to recoup himself, from the hundred thousand francs' income, for the care given to his ward; but he conceived an affection for him. This preceptor happened to be a true priest, the type of cleric cut out to be a cardinal in France or, in Italy, a Borgia candidate for the tiara. In three years he taught the child what it would have taken him ten years to learn at college. Then this great man, by name the Abbé de Maronis, finished off his pupil's education by putting him through the study of civilization in all its aspects. He gave him the benefit of his own experience, which included very little church-going (at that period churches were mostly closed). He sometimes took him to the theatre greenrooms, and more frequently still to the boudoirs of courtesans. He dissected human motives for his instruction, taught him all about political intrigue in the very salons where it was then mainly concocted, explained to him in detail the workings of bureaucratic government and did his best, out of sympathy for a well-endowed nature, rich in promise though as yet undeveloped, to mother him in a virile way – for after all the Church is the mother of orphans.

The pupil was responsive to such great care. The worthy man died in 1812, a bishop, content to have left here below a child whose heart and mind, even at the age of sixteen, had been so well moulded that he could get the better of a man of forty. Who would have expected to find a heart of bronze or a brain packed in ice beneath as seductive an exterior as ever medieval painter, with naïve artistry, gave to the serpent in the garden of Eden? But that was only a beginning. Over and above this, the good-natured bishop had obtained for his favoured pupil certain contacts in Parisian high society which, if the young man properly exploited them, might bring him a further hundred thousand francs' income. To sum up, this priest, unprincipled but politic, sceptical but learned, perfidious but amiable, frail in appearance but vigorous both of mind and body, proved to be so genuinely useful to his ward, so indulgent of his shortcomings, so able at assessing the strength of friend and foe alike, so perspicacious when it was a question of allowing for human foibles, so lusty at table, at Frascati's gaming-house, at no matter where, that by 1815 only one thing could still excite gratitude and emotion in Henri de Marsay: the sight of his dear bishop's portrait, the only item of furniture which had been bequeathed to him by this prelate, an outstanding example of the men whose genius will save the Catholic and Apostolic Church of Rome, at present compromised by the feebleness of her recruits and the age of her pontiffs; but that is how the Church likes things at present. The war in Europe prevented young de Marsay from getting to know his real father: it seems that he did not even know his name nor, as a castaway child, did he know Madame de Marsay. It goes without saying that he never mourned for his reputed father. As for Mademoiselle de Marsay, the only mother he ever knew, when she died he erected a very dainty little monument in the Père-Lachaise cemetery. My lord bishop, Monseigneur de Maronis, had guaranteed for this venerable dame one of the front seats in Heaven, so that, seeing she was happy to die, Henri shed only selfish tears over her for the loss he himself had sustained. Taking note of this grief, the abbé dried his pupil's tears, reminding him that the old lady had had a disgusting way of taking her snuff and was becoming so ugly, so deaf, so much of a bore that he ought to be grateful for her removal. The bishop gave up his tutorial charge in 1811. Then, when Henri de Marsay's mother married again, the bishop summoned a family council and from it selected an honest simpleton – whom he had submitted to the further test of the confessional – whose business it should be to administer the young man's estate, applying the income to general necessities while keeping the capital intact.

So then, as 1814 drew to a close, Henri de Marsay was under a sense of obligation to nobody and felt as free as an unmated bird. Although he had reached the age of twenty-two, he looked to be scarcely seventeen. Generally speaking, even the most critical of his rivals admitted that he was the handsomest young man in Paris. From his father Lord Dudley he had inherited the most amorously bewitching blue eyes, from his mother an abundance of black hair, from both of them pure blood, a girlish complexion, a gentle and modest air, a slender, aristocratic figure and exceptionally beautiful hands. For a woman, merely to see him was to become infatuated, to be taken with the sort of desire which grips the heart but is quickly forgotten because it has no chance of being satisfied, since normally, in Paris, women lack pertinacity. Few of them would adopt the virile motto of the House of Orange: I WILL MAINTAIN! With this bloom of life on him, despite the limpid pools of his eyes, Henri was as bold as a lion and as agile as a monkey. At ten yards' distance he could cut a bullet in half on the edge of a knife-blade, he sat a horse in such a way as to make the fable of the centaur come true; he drove a four-in-hand with consummate grace.

At such exercises he was as light as a cherub and as gentle as a lamb; but he could take on a man of the slums at the terrible games of *savate*[11] and quarterstaff. Also he played the piano with such skill that he might well have become a musical artist had he fallen on evil days; and he had a voice which any popular singer would willingly have hired from him at fifty thousand francs a season. But unfortunately all these fine qualities and attractive shortcomings were neutralized by one appalling defect: he believed neither in men nor women, God nor devil. Nature, often wayward, had conferred the basic endowments; but a priest had been his finishing school.

To make this story comprehensible, we must at this point add that Lord Dudley not unnaturally found many women ready enough to strike a few copies of so delightful a portrait. His second masterpiece of this kind was a girl called Euphémie, the daughter of a Spanish lady, brought up in Havana, conveyed back to Madrid with a young creole from the Antilles, both of them burdened with the ruinous tastes customary in the colonies. But she was luckily married to an old and phenomenally rich Spanish hidalgo, Don Hijos, Marquis of San-Real, who had come to live in Paris, in the Rue Saint-Lazare, after the occupation of Spain by French forces. As much out of unconcern as through respect for youthful innocence, Lord Dudley gave his children no information about the relationships he was creating for them here, there and everywhere. Such situations are one of the inconveniences in civilization, though the latter has so many advantages that we must shut our eyes to its defects in view of the benefits it brings. But let us finish with Lord Dudley: he came and took refuge in Paris in 1816 in order to escape from English justice, which gives its protection to nothing exotic except merchandise. The itinerant lord saw Henri one day and asked who the the beautiful young man was. On hearing his name he said: 'Ah! He's my son. What a pity!'

*

11. A French kind of boxing, in which head and feet are used as well as fists.

331

That is the antecedent history of the young man who, towards the middle of April 1815, was nonchalantly strolling up and down the broad alley of the Tuileries, with the gait of all those animals which, conscious of their strength, pace along in peace and majesty. Bourgeois women turned round naïvely to look at him after he had passed. More sophisticated women did not turn round, but waited for his return and then engraved his features in their memory so that in due course they might recall that charming face which would have done no discredit to the beauty of the fairest among them.

'What are you doing here on a Sunday?' the Marquis de Ronquerolles, passing by at that moment, asked Henri.

'There's fish in the net,' the young man replied. This communication was supplemented by two significant glances without either Ronquerolles or de Marsay seeming to recognize one another. The young man was eyeing the strollers with the swift visual and auditory appraisal peculiar to the Parisian who at first sight appears to see and hear nothing but actually sees and hears all. At that instant a young man came up to de Marsay, took him familiarly by the arm and said: 'How goes it with you, my dear de Marsay?'

'Well enough, thank you,' de Marsay replied with that air of apparent affection which, as between young Parisians, means nothing at all, either for the present or the future.

In fact, the young men of Paris are unlike the young men of any other city. They are divided into two categories: the young man who has possessions and the young man who has none; alternatively the young man who perpends and the young man who spends. But let this be clear: here there is question only of those born and bred in Paris and who follow the pleasurable round of an elegant life. Many other types of young men are to be found there, but they are as it were backward children who are very slow in understanding life in Paris and never come to terms with it. They do not speculate, they study, they *cram*, as those of the other kinds say. Finally if certain young people, rich or poor, are still to be found who take to a career and doggedly pursue it, they are rather like Rousseau's Emile, the stuff of which second-rate citizens are made, and they never figure in polite society. Diplomats impolitely call them boobies. Boobies or not, they swell the number of the mediocrities under whose weight France is sagging. They are always to hand, with the flat trowel of their mediocrity, to make a jerry-builder's mess of both public and private affairs, priding themselves on their futility, which they call morality and integrity. These social prize-winners infest the administration, the army, the magistracy, the law chambers and the courts. Under them the country is dwarfed and deflated, and in the body politic they constitute a kind of lymph which saturates it and makes it flaccid. These honest citizens call men of talent libertines and knaves. No doubt these knaves charge for their services – but they do serve, whereas the others do harm. They are respected by the mob, but fortunately for France our gilded youth constantly stigmatize them as numbskulls.

At first sight then it is natural to believe that the young men who cultivate the elegant life – an amiable corporation to which Henri de Marsay belonged – are sharply divided into two groups. But observant people who look beneath the surface are quickly convinced that the differences between them are purely moral, and that nothing is so deceptive as a decorative exterior. Nevertheless they all assert their superiority over the rest of society; they chatter, in season and out of season, of men and things; they are always conversant with the shifts and shufflings of party leaders. They will break into a conversation with some silly play on words; they make a mockery of science and scientists; they treat with contempt anything they are afraid of or know nothing about; they stand on a pedestal and set themselves up as supreme judges and arbiters in all matters. All of them would willingly make fools of their own fathers or shed crocodile tears with their heads buried in their mothers' laps. But as a rule they believe in nothing, put slander on women, or make a show of virtue while in reality they are under the thumb of a scheming courtesan or some old hag. All alike are rotten to the core through calculation, depravity and a ruthless determination to succeed at all costs. If a doctor had to treat them for the stone he would find it, not in their bladder, but in their heart.

Normally they wear a most pleasing exterior, stake their friendship at every turn and are equally enthusiastic about everything. Their jargon varies, but there is the same spirit of persiflage behind it. They aim at a certain eccentricity in dress, glory in repeating the gags of fashionable actors, and their opening gambit in any conversation is a display of scorn or impertinence in order to score the first point; but woe to him who is not ready to take one black eye in order to give his adversary two in return! They seem equally unconcerned about the calamities and disasters which beset their country. In fact they all of them resemble the dainty white froth which rides on the billows in time of storm. They dress, dine, dance and disport themselves on the day of Waterloo, during a cholera epidemic or while revolution is raging. To conclude, all of them incur the same expenses, but from this point onwards they move on parallel lines. Of this fluctuating and pleasantly squandered fortune some possess the capital; the others are still waiting for it; they go to the same tailors, but the former have to pay their bills. Also, if some of them, like so many sieves, allow all kinds of ideas to filter through their heads without retaining a single one, the others compare them and assimilate those they find good. If some of them, thinking they know something, in fact knowing nothing but professing to understand everything, lend freely to those who need nothing but offer nothing to those in need, the others make a secret study of other people's ideas and invest their money, just as they invest their follies, so as to reap a big return of interest. Some of them no longer retain a faithful image of things because their mind has become as it were a mirror tarnished by use which no longer reflects a picture; the others use their life and sensual faculties sparingly although, like the other people, they seem to be throwing them overboard. The first of these types, building on hope, gives its allegiance, though without conviction, to a system which a fair wind is carrying forward, but they promptly leap on to another political craft once their own starts drifting.

The second of these types sounds and plumbs the future, and discovers in political consistency what the English discover in commercial probity – an element of success. But whereas the young man who possesses something makes a pun or cracks a joke about a change of dynasty, the one who has nothing dips into some public intrigue or underhand roguery, and not only makes good himself but also gives his cronies a helping hand. Some of them never credit other people with any ability, think that every idea they have is original – as if the world had only been created yesterday – and have unlimited confidence in themselves; whereas in reality they are their own worst enemies. But the others value men at their true worth, mistrust them on principle and are acute enough to see one move ahead of the friends they exploit; then at night when they lay their heads on their pillows, they weigh their fellow men, as a miser weighs his gold coins. Some take offence at slights that do not matter but are willing dupes of the smooth people who make fools of them by pulling the mainstring that makes such puppets dance – that of vanity – whereas others know how to command respect and choose both their victims and their patrons. As a result, one day the have-nots have something, while the haves have nothing. The latter regard their friends who have made good as cunning and evil-hearted rogues, but they acknowledge their ability. 'He's a capable fellow!' That is the ultimate praise accorded to those who, *quibuscumque viis*, have made their way in politics, gallantry or moneymaking. Among them are found certain young men who are in debt when they embark on that career. It goes without saying that they are more dangerous than those who have nothing to start off with!

The young man who styled himself a friend of Henri de Marsay was a scatterbrain fresh from the provinces whose acquaintances, the fashionable young men of the moment, were initiating him into the art of squandering an inheritance with neatness and dispatch. But in his native province he had one last resource to fall back upon: a settled estate. He was, quite simply, an heir, who without transition had passed from a meagre allowance of a hundred francs a month to the entire paternal fortune and who, even if he lacked the intelligence to perceive that he was an object of ridicule, could count up far enough to stop short at two thirds of his capital. At the expense of a few thousand franc notes he had just discovered the exact cost of riding equipment in Paris, the art of not making gloves last too long, of listening to expert advice on the wages to be paid to servants and the most advantageous terms to be made with them. He was very anxious to use the right sort of vocabulary when talking of his horses or his Pyrenean hound, to place a woman in her social class according to her dress, style of walking and footwear; to study *écarté*, to pick up fashionable diction and acquire, by virtue of his sojourn in Parisian society, the necessary prestige for later importing into his native province the taste for tea-drinking and English silverware and gaining the right to turn up his nose at everything around him for the rest of his days. De Marsay had accepted him as a friend in order to make use of him in society as a bold speculator makes use of a confidential clerk. De Marsay's friendship, real or sham, was of social import for Paul de Manerville, who for his part gave himself much credit for in his way making the most of their close friendship. He basked in the light his friend reflected, took shelter constantly under his umbrella, trod in his footsteps and gained a lustre from the sunlight he emitted. When he struck an attitude beside Henri, and even when he strutted along beside him, he seemed to be saying: 'Put no slight upon us, we are devils of fellows.' Often he was fatuous enough to say: 'We are such friends, I have only to ask Henri to do something and he will do it.' But he took care never to ask him to do anything. He feared him, and this fear, though scarcely perceptible, impressed other people and was useful to de Marsay.

'De Marsay is a splendid person,' Paul used to say. 'Just wait and see: he'll get wherever he wants to be. It wouldn't surprise me if one day he became Minister for Foreign Affairs. Nothing will hold him back.' And then he would treat de Marsay as Corporal Trim[12] treated his cap – continually using him as a trump card so to speak. 'Ask de Marsay, he'll tell you' . . . Or, 'The other day de Marsay and I were out hunting. He wouldn't believe I could do it, but I jumped a hedge without getting thrown.' Or else, 'De Marsay and I were in the company of women, and, upon my word of honour, I was . . . etc.'

So Paul de Manerville could only be classed among the great, illustrious and puissant family of imbeciles who achieve some success. One day he was to become a deputy. De Marsay – his friend! – gave this definition of him: 'You ask me what Paul is? Paul? . . . Why, he's Paul de Manerville.'

*

'I'm surprised, old man,' he said to de Marsay, 'to see you here on a Sunday.'

'I was about to make the same remark to you.'

'An affair?'

'An affair.'

'Well now!'

'I can tell *you* that without compromising the object of my passion. In any case a woman who comes to the Tuileries on a Sunday is of no account from a social point of view.'

'Ha! Ha!'

'Keep quiet, or I say no more. You laugh too loud. People will think we have lunched too well. Last Thursday, here, on the Terrasse des Feuillants, I was strolling about thinking of nothing in particular. But as I arrived at the Rue Castiglione gate by which I was intending to leave the garden, I found myself face to face with a woman, or rather a young person who, if she refrained from throwing her arms round my neck, did so, I believe, less out of respect for convention than through one of those paralysing shocks which rob your arms and legs of movement, run right down your spine and root the soles

12. The reference is to Sterne's *Tristram Shandy* which Balzac much admired. Corporal Trim is the manservant of the central character 'Uncle Toby', and he makes much play with his Spanish hunter's (Montero) cap.

of your feet to the ground. I have often produced effects of that kind. They are due to a kind of animal magnetism which attains tremendous potency whenever the elective affinities are strong. But, my dear fellow, this was no case of stupe-faction, nor was she a common street-walker. Judging by the expression on her face, she seemed to be saying: "What! You are here, my ideal, the being I have thought of, dreamed of night and morning! How come you here? Why this morning? Why not yesterday? Take me, I am yours . . ." And so on. "Good," I said to myself, "here's one more of them!" So I looked at her closely. My dear fellow, from a physical standpoint, this incognita is the most adorably feminine woman I have ever met. She belongs to that variety of women whom the Romans classified as *fulva, flava*, the woman of fire. And what most struck me straightaway, what I still find most fascinating is her two eyes, yellow as a tiger's, a golden, gleaming yellow; living gold, brooding gold, amorous gold! The gold of your watch is nothing to it!'

'My dear chap, tell us something we don't know,' cried Paul. 'She comes along here sometimes. She's the *Girl with the Golden Eyes*. That's the name we give her. She's young: twenty-two or thereabouts. I saw her here before the Bourbons fled to Belgium, though she was with a woman a hundred thousand times more beautiful still.'

'Nonsense, Paul! No woman on earth could surpass this girl, who's like a kitten rubbing against your legs. A fair-skinned girl with ash-blond hair, of delicate appearance, but who no doubt has a satiny fleece on the third joint of her fingers; and along her cheeks a line of white down, luminous in bright daylight, runs down from the ears and fades out at the neck.'

'But the other one, de Marsay! Black eyes which have never wept and burn right through you. Black eyebrows that meet and give her an air of hardness belied by the curve of her lips, fresh and ardent lips which bear no mark of kisses; a moorish complexion in which a man may bask as in sunlight. Why now, upon my word, she takes after you!'

'How you flatter her!'

'A slender waist, the streamlined waist of a corvette built for speed, the kind which sweeps on a merchant ship with Gallic impetuosity, rams her and sinks her in a trice!'

'Anyway, my dear fellow, what do I care for a woman I have never seen?' de Marsay continued. 'Ever since I have taken an interest in women, my unknown *she* is the only one whose virginal bosom, whose ardent and voluptuous curves have realized for me the unique woman of my dreams. She is the original of that captivating painting which goes by the name of 'A Woman Fondling her Chimaera,'[13] the most fervid, the most demonic inspiration of ancient genius: a sacred poem prostituted by those who have copied it for frescoes and mosaics, or by the bourgeois herd who regard that cameo as nothing but a trinket and hang copies of it on their watch-chains. No indeed! She is the very essence of woman, an abyss of pleasures whose depths may never be sounded: the ideal woman one sometimes really finds in Spain and Italy, but scarcely ever in France. Well then, I have once more seen this girl with the golden eyes, this woman *fondling* her chimaera, I saw her here last Friday. I had had a feeling that the next day she would be here again at the same time. I was right. It pleased me to follow her without her seeing me, so that I might watch the indolent step of this woman who had nothing to do with her time but in whose every movement dormant voluptuousness could be divined. Well, she turned round and saw me again, registered adoration, trembled again and shuddered. Then I took a look at the typical Spanish duenna in charge of her, a hyena in human dress furnished by a jealous lover, a well-paid virago whose business it was to guard this sweet creature ... Oh, this duenna made me more than amorous: I became curious. On Saturday no one appeared. So here I am today, waiting for the girl

13. Balzac read about this fresco in a novel of 1829 by H. de Latouche: *Fragoletta*, in which it is described as being viewed by visitors to the Palazzo degli Studi in Naples. Balzac had already referred to it in *The Magic Skin* (1831) as 'a Latin queen lovingly fondling her chimaera'. In *Gambara* (1837) he refers to it as a 'Roman mosaic'.

whose chimaera I have become and asking for nothing better than to pose as the monster in the fresco.'[14]

'There she is,' said Paul. 'Everybody's looking round at her . . .'

The unknown girl blushed. Her eyes shone as she caught sight of Henri. She closed them and passed on.

'You say she notices you?' Paul de Manerville asked sarcastically.

The duenna looked fixedly and attentively at the two young men. When Henri and the unknown girl passed by one another again she brushed lightly against him and her hand pressed against his. Then she turned her gaze and gave him a passionate smile. But the duenna brusquely pulled her away towards the gate of the Rue Castiglione. The two young men watched after the girl, admiring the graceful curve of her neck and the firmness of the lines which joined it to her head, from which a profusion of little curls stood out in relief. The girl with the golden eyes had that shapely, dainty, high-arched foot which sensuous imaginations find so attractive. Moreover, she was elegantly shod and her dress was short. As she moved forwards she now and then gave a backward glance at Henri and seemed to be reluctant to follow the old woman, who appeared to be at once her mistress and her slave; it was obvious that she could have her flogged but that she could not get rid of her.

The two friends reached the gate. Two liveried footmen let down the steps of an elegant coupé with armorial bearings. The girl with the golden eyes stepped into it first, took her seat on the side where she could best be seen when the carriage turned round, raised her hand to the window and without the duenna seeing, waved her handkerchief, regardless of any comments curious idlers might make, and quite obviously beckoning to Henri to follow her.

'Have you ever seen a handkerchief so invitingly fluttered?' said Henri to Paul de Manerville.

Then, perceiving a cab that had just deposited a fare and

14. See footnote p. 339. The 'chimaera' in question is depicted as having the wings of a dove and the fins of a fish.

was preparing to move off again, he hailed it. 'Follow that coupé,' he said to the cabman. 'See what street and house it goes to, and I'll give you ten francs. – Goodbye, Paul.'

The cab followed the coupé. It turned into the Rue Saint-Lazare and pulled up in front of one of the finest mansions in the quarter.

2

A singular love affair

DE MARSAY was not a scatterbrain. Any other young man would have yielded to the desire to obtain immediate information about a girl who so completely embodied the most luminous ideas on women expressed in Oriental poetry; but he was too adroit thus to compromise the future of a love intrigue, and so he had told his cab driver to continue along the Rue Saint-Lazare and take him back home. The next morning he set his senior manservant, Laurent, as crafty a fellow as any valet in eighteenth-century comedy, to loaf round the house in which the strange girl lived, at the time when the post was delivered. So that he might be free to spy and prowl round the mansion, he had adopted the tactics of police detectives when they want to disguise themselves, by buying up the cast-off clothes of an Auvergnat[1] and doing his best to look like one. When the postman who that morning was on that particular round came by, Laurent pretended to be a street-porter trying to remember the name of the person to whom he was to deliver a parcel. He asked the postman. Straightway taken in by appearances, this public servant, in his picturesque uniform which clashes so much with humdrum Parisian civilization, told him that the house in which the girl with the golden eyes lived belonged to Don Hijos, Marquis of San-Real, a Spanish grandee. Naturally enough the supposed Auvergnat was not interested in the marquis.

'My parcel,' he said, 'is for the marquise.'

'She's away,' the postman replied. 'Her letters are forwarded to London.'

'So the marquise is not the young lady who . . .'

1. Auvergnat: natives of Auvergne, immigrants to Paris; they were usually water-carriers. Balzac made one of them the hero of *An Atheist's Mass* (1836).

'Ah!' said the postman, interrupting the valet and looking him straight in the eye. 'If you're a street-porter I'm a dancing-girl.'

Laurent proffered a few gold coins to the clapper-wielding public servant; the latter broke into a smile.

'Here you are. Here's the name of the quarry you're after,' he said, taking from his leather wallet a letter with a London stamp and this address:

PAQUITA VALDES,
Rue Saint-Lazare, Hôtel de San-Real, Paris

Its long, spidery characters betokened a feminine hand.

'Would you say no to a bottle of Chablis, a dozen oysters or so and a fillet steak with mushrooms?' asked Laurent, who wanted to get on useful friendly terms with the postman.

'I would say yes, after I've done my round. Where?'

'At the *Puits-sans-vin* – corner of the Rue de la Chaussée-d'Antin and the Rue Neuve-des-Mathurins.'

'Listen, friend,' said the postman when he rejoined the valet one hour after their first meeting. 'If your governor's interested in that girl he's in for a peck of trouble. I don't suppose you'll even get to see her. I've been a postman in Paris for ten years, and I've seen lots of dodges people use to guard their doors. But I can tell you this, and none of my mates will call me a liar: no door is more of a puzzle than the one that belongs to Monsieur de San-Real. No one can get into that house without some password or other, and take note that he chose a house between courtyard and garden so that it would be completely detached. The porter's an old Spaniard who can't speak a word of French. But he looks people up and down as Vidocq[2] might do to make sure you're not a thief. Well, if a lover, a robber or you yourself – no offence meant – managed to take in this first watchdog, once he got through the glazed door into the entrance hall he'd find himself up against a butler with footmen all round him, and this old joker's more savage,

2. The notorious chief of security police in Napoleonic and Restoration times: an ex-criminal on whom Balzac partly modelled his Vautrin (*Old Goriot* and *A Harlot High and Low*).

more bad-tempered than the porter. If anyone gets beyond the porter's lodge out pops the butler, waits for you at the porch and puts you through an interrogation as if you were a criminal. This has happened to me, a simple postman. He took me for a *hemisphere*[3] in disguise,' he said, laughing at his own malapropism. 'As for the servants, don't hope to get anything out of them. I believe they're dumb. No one in the quarter has ever heard them utter a word, and goodness knows how much wages they're paid for not speaking, and keeping off the drink. The fact is you can't get near them, whether they're afraid of getting shot or whether they're liable to lose an enormous packet if they open their mouths. Even if your master's enough in love with Mademoiselle Paquita Valdes to get over all these hurdles, he certainly won't get the better of Doña Concha Marialva, the duenna who goes round with her and would tuck her under her skirts rather than let her get away from her. You'd think the two women were sewn together.'

'What you tell me, praiseworthy postman,' Laurent continued after taking a sip at his wine, 'confirms the information I have just acquired. Honestly, I thought they were making a fool of me. The fruit-seller opposite told me that every night dogs were let loose in the gardens and their meat hung up at the top of stakes to prevent them from reaching up to it. So that these accursed animals may believe that people trying to get in are after their food and rend them limb from limb. You may tell me that meat-balls could be thrown down to them, but it seems they are trained to eat nothing but what the concierge gives them.'

'That in fact is what Monsieur le Baron de Nucingen's porter, the top end of whose garden adjoins that of the San-Real property, has told me,' the postman replied.

'Good,' Laurent said to himself. 'My master knows the Baron.' He gazed straight at the postman. 'Now I tell you, the master I serve is a determined man, and if he took it into his head to kiss the soles of an empress's feet she would have to put up with it. If he needed your help – for your sake I

3. i.e. 'emissary': someone sent out on a secret mission.

hope he may, for he's a generous man – can we depend on you?'

'For sure, Monsieur Laurent. My name's Moinot: Sparrow. Just like they spell the bird's name. S-p-a-r, *spar*, r-o-w, *row*.'[4]

'That's fine,' said Laurent.

'My address is 11, Rue des Trois-Frères, fifth floor. I've a wife and four kids. If what you want me to do doesn't go beyond what my conscience tells me to do and my duty as a postman, take it that I'm at your service.'

'Splendid fellow!' said Laurent, giving him a handshake.

*

When Henri's manservant told him the result of his inquiries, he said: 'I expect Paquita Valdès is the mistress of the Marquis of San-Real, a friend of King Ferdinand. Only an old Spanish mummy of eighty would be capable of taking such precautions.'

'Monsieur,' Laurent replied. 'Nobody could get into that house unless he came down into it from a balloon.'

'Idiot! Why should one get into the house in order to have Paquita? Paquita can come out of it.'

'But what about the duenna, sir?'

'We'll put the duenna into cold storage for a few days.'

'Good! So we shall have Paquita!' said Laurent, rubbing his hands.

'You scoundrel!' Henri answered. 'I'll deliver you over to the Concha if you have the insolence to talk like that of a woman before I have had her. Turn your thoughts to dressing me. I'm going out.'

For a moment, Henri remained plunged in joyous reflections. Let this be said to women's credit: he obtained any one of them he condescended to desire. What indeed would one think of a woman who, having no lover, could resist a young man armed with beauty, which is the intelligence of the body, with intelligence, which is the grace of the soul,

4. In fact the word is *moineau*.

with moral strength and wealth, which are the only two potent forces? But de Marsay, reaping such easy triumphs, was bound to find them boring; and indeed, during the last two years, he had been feeling very bored. Diving into the very depths of pleasure, he brought back more gravel than pearls. So then he had come, like sovereign princes, to the point of importuning chance for some obstacle to surmount, some enterprise calling for the deployment of his moral and physical potentialities, at present inert. Although Paquita Valdès offered a wonderful multiplicity of perfections which, as yet, he had only enjoyed piecemeal, passion itself had now almost no attraction for him. Constant satiety had weakened the faculty for love in his heart. Like old men and surfeited voluptuaries, nothing was left to him but extravagant whims, fantasies which, once satisfied, left him no pleasant memories. With young people love is the finest of sentiments; it quickens the life of the soul; like sunshine, it has the power to bring into blossom the most beautiful inspirations and the great thoughts that emanate from them, first-fruits which in every sphere of life have a delicious savour. With grown men, love becomes a craving: virility leads to abuse. With old men love turns into vice: impotence leads to extremes. Now Henri was simultaneously old, middle-aged and young. In order to recapture the emotions of true love he needed, as Lovelace needed, a Clarissa Harlowe.[5] Deprived of the magic lustre of so unattainable a pearl, all he could hope for was either passions whetted by the vanity arising from some Parisian conquest, or a wager made with himself to bring such and such a woman to such and such a stage of corruption or adventures capable of stimulating his curiosity. The report made by his valet Laurent had enormously enhanced the value of the girl with the golden eyes. Battle had to be given to his secret antagonist, as dangerous, it seemed, as he was cunning. To gain the victory all the forces at Henri's command would not be superfluous. He was about to act the eternally old, eternally new comedy with three characters: an old

5. Heroine of Samuel Richardson's novel *Clarissa* (1748), persecuted by the villainous Lovelace. This novel took Europe by storm.

man – Don Hijos – a girl – Paquita – and a suitor – de Marsay. Laurent was ready in the role of Figaro, but the duenna seemed to be incorruptible. Thus it happened that this real-life play had a more complicated plot, thanks to chance, than any Beaumarchais had ever devised. But then, chance is a dramatic author of great genius.

'This calls for careful handling,' Henri told himself.

*

'Well now,' said Paul de Manerville as he came into Henri's apartment. 'How are things going? I've come to have lunch with you.'

'So be it,' said Henri. 'You don't mind if I go on dressing in your presence?'

'Don't be silly!'

'All right. But we're taking so much from the English at present that we may as well become as hypocritical and strait-laced as they are.'

Laurent had brought out such a wealth and such a variety of elegant toilet apparatus that Paul could not help saying: 'But this will take you two hours!'

'No,' said Henri. 'Two hours and a half.'

'All right. Since we are alone and can be perfectly frank, tell me why a superior man like you – for you *are* a superior man – should make a pretence of exaggerating a foppishness which is not in your nature. Why spend two and a half hours with the curry-comb when all you need is to spend fifteen minutes in a bath, put your clothes on and give your hair a quick brushing? Tell me, what's all this about?'

'I must be very fond of you, great clod, to discourse with you in such lofty terms,' the young man replied: at this moment he was having his feet brushed with a soft brush lathered with English soap.

'Hang it! I've shown you the closest affection,' Paul de Manerville replied. 'And I'm fond of you because I know you are superior to me . . . '

'You must have noticed, if so be that you are capable of taking in moral truths, that women love fops' – de Marsay said this without giving any other response than a mere glance to Paul's declaration. 'And why do women love fops? My friend, fops are the only men who take care of their persons. Now, if one takes too great care of one's person, does not this mean that, in one's own person, one takes care of what belongs to another? The man who belongs to others than himself is precisely the man that women like to grab, since Cupid is essentially a thief.

'I'm not referring to the excessive cleanliness of which they make such a fetish. But can you name a single one of them who has ever conceived a passion for a dirty, slovenly man, however outstanding he may be? If such a thing has ever happened, we must explain it in terms of a pregnant woman's cravings: idiotic ideas which may pass through anyone's brain. On the other hand I have seen very outstanding people dropped without warning because they neglected their persons. A fop concerned only with himself is concerned with imbecilities and trivialities. But what is a woman? A triviality herself, a collection of imbecilities. Throw off a couple of ideas and you can keep her busy for four hours. She can rely on a fop giving her his attention because he has nothing important to think of. He will never neglect her in favour of glory, ambition, politics or art, those public wantons whom she reckons to be her rivals. Moreover the fops are brave enough to cover themselves with ridicule in order to please a woman, whose heart offers full rewards for a man who makes a fool of himself for love. Finally, a fop is only a fop if he has earned the title. It's the women who publish our names in that gazette. The fop is, in military terminology, a colonel in Cupid's army: he wins his victories with the women at his command!

'Dear friend, in Paris nothing is hidden, and it costs something to be a fop. You, for instance; there's only one woman in your life – perhaps rightly – suppose you tried to be a fop. You'd not only make a fool of yourself,[6] it would kill you.

6. According to Balzac's system of reappearing characters, Paul is the main character in *The Marriage Contract*, which Balzac was writing at the same time. Paul does indeed make a fool of himself through his passion for a woman.

You'd become an *idée fixe* on two legs, the sort of man inevitably condemned to go on doing the same things for ever and ever. You would stand for *stupidity* as Monsieur de Lafayette stands for the United States of America, Monsieur de Talleyrand for diplomacy, Désaugiers as a *chansonnier* and Monsieur de Ségur for balladry.[7] Remove men from their speciality and no one gives credence to what they do. That is what we are in France: always and sovereignly unjust! We might suppose that Monsieur de Talleyrand was a great financier, Monsieur de Lafayette a tyrannical ruler, Désaugiers a civil administrator. You yourself might, one year from now, boast of forty mistresses, but public repute would not allot you a single one.

'So, friend Paul, foppishness is the sign and token of the unquestioned power we have acquired over the female population. A man who wins the love of several women is credited with superior qualities. From then on it's a question as to who will snap him up, unhappy man! But, for that matter, do you think it means nothing to have the right, as you make your entry into a salon, to look down on everybody from the height of your cravat or through your monocle and be privileged to despise the most important man there if his waistcoat is out of fashion? – Laurent, you're hurting me – After lunch, Paul, we'll go to the Tuileries to look for the adorable girl with the golden eyes.'

When after making an excellent meal, the two young men had strolled up and down the Terrasse des Feuillants and the broad avenue of the Tuileries, nowhere did they meet with the sublime Paquita Valdes, on whose account fifty of the best-dressed young men of Paris, all preened and perfumed in high cravats, booted and spurred, cracking their whips, were riding or striding along, chatting, laughing, boisterous.

'Love's labours lost,' said Henri. 'But I have had a splendid

7. These allusions to political and literary reputations of the time have little significance today. Lafayette, of course, had made his name as an apostle of liberty by fighting against England in the American War of Independence. By 1830 and beyond he had become more or less a figure of fun in France, thanks to having let himself be duped into supporting Louis-Philippe.

idea. The girl receives letters from London. We must bribe the postman or get him drunk, open one of the letters, read it, slip a little *billet-doux* into it and seal it up again. The old tyrant, *crudel tiranno*, must certainly know the person who writes the letters coming from London and would not be suspicious.'

The next day de Marsay came again to sun himself on the Terrasse des Feuillants, and saw Paquita Valdès, her beauty enhanced by the passion he felt for her. He grew wildly enamoured of the sunbeam glances of her eyes, whose ardent flashes matched the perfect beauty of her voluptuous body. He burned with the desire to brush against the dress of this enchanting girl each time they crossed each other in their to-and-fro pacing, but his efforts were always in vain. Once, when he had hurried past the duenna and Paquita with the intention of being on the same side as the girl when he turned round again, Paquita, no less impatient, moved forwards impetuously; and de Marsay felt her press his hand so swiftly and with such passionate significance that it was as if the tingle of an electric current passed through him. Instantly all the emotions of youth surged up in his heart. When their eyes met Paquita seemed very shy; she looked down to avoid gazing into his again, but she did not fail to steal a glance at the figure and feet of the man whom, had she lived before the time of the Revolution, she would have referred to as her *conqueror*.

'Decidedly,' Henri said to himself, 'I will make this girl my mistress.'

As he followed her to the end of the terrace in the direction of the Place Louis XV, he perceived the old Marquis de San-Real, who was walking along on his valet's arm with the painful and faltering step of one afflicted with gout and cacochymia. Doña Concha, who had her suspicions of Henri, kept Paquita between the old man and herself.

'Oh, as for you,' de Marsay said to himself, casting a glance of contempt at the duenna, 'if we can't bring you to terms, we'll put you to sleep with a little opium. We know all about mythology and the fable of Argus.'

Before climbing into her carriage, the girl with the golden eyes exchanged with her admirer a few glances of whose meaning there could be no doubt and which ravished Henri; but the duenna intercepted one of them and spoke a few sharp words to Paquita, who flung herself into the coupé with a desperate air. For several days Paquita did not reappear at the Tuileries. At his master's order Laurent kept watch round her house and learnt from neighbours that neither of the two women nor the old marquis had been out of doors since the day when the duenna had surprised the glance between Henri and the girl committed to her charge. And so the flimsy bond between the two lovers was already severed.

Some days later, without anyone knowing by what means, de Marsay had achieved his end, he had a seal and sealing-wax absolutely identical with those used for the letters dispatched from London to Mademoiselle Valdes, writing paper similar to that used by her correspondent and all the apparatus and stamps needed for affixing the English and French post-marks. He had written the following letter, which bore all the outward appearance of one sent from London.

Dear Paquita,

I will not try to express in words the passion you have inspired in me. If, for my great happiness, you reciprocate it, I wish you to know that I have found a means of corresponding with you. My name is Adolphe de Gouges, my address 54 Rue de l'Université. I shall know by your silence if you are too closely watched to be able to write or if you have access neither to pen nor paper. And so, if between 8 a.m. and 8 p.m. tomorrow you have not thrown a letter over the wall of your garden into that of the Baron de Nucingen, where a look-out will be kept for it all day, a man who is entirely at my service will let two phials down over the wall by means of a cord, at 10 a.m. the day after tomorrow. Be walking round your garden about that time. One of the phials will contain enough opium to put your Argus to sleep – six drops will suffice. The other will contain ink. The one with ink in it is of cut glass, the other plain. Both of them are flat enough to be hidden beneath your corset. Everything I have already done in order to be able to correspond with you will surely show you how much I love you. Should you doubt this, I confess that I would give my life to be able to spend one hour with you.

'They always believe such taradiddles, poor creatures!' de Marsay thought to himself. 'But there's some justification. What should we think of a woman who refused to be beguiled by a letter which has such convincing evidence to support it?'

The letter was handed in by the postman, the worthy Moinot, at eight the following morning, to the concierge of the San-Real mansion.

In order to get nearer to the field of operations, de Marsay had come to lunch with Paul, who lived in the Rue de la Pépinière. At two, just as the two friends were laughing together over the discomfiture of a young man who had attempted to keep up an elegant mode of life without having a settled fortune, and were speculating as to how he would end up, Henri's coachman, having followed his master to Paul's house, introduced to him a mysterious personage who insisted on talking to him directly. This person was a mulatto who, had Talma met him, would certainly have provided that great actor with a model for Shakespeare's Othello. Never did an African physiognomy more graphically express grandeur in vengefulness, rapidity in suspicion, lightning speed in translating thought into action, the strength and childlike impetuosity of the Moor of Venice. His black eyes had the fixed stare of a bird of prey and, like those of a vulture, were framed in a bluish membrane devoid of lashes. His low, narrow forehead had a menacing expression. Obviously this man was the slave of one single obsessive idea. His sinewy arm was at the orders of another person.

Behind him came an individual whom the imagination of all men, from the shivering natives of Greenland to the sweltering inhabitants of New Caledonia,[8] would find adequately characterized in the phrase: 'he was a destitute man.' By this everyone will divine his condition and will sum him up in accordance with the ideas peculiar to each country. But who can imagine his wrinkled face, white but ringed with red, and his long beard? Who can visualize his dirty yellow,

8. The text says New England!

stringy cravat, his greasy shirt-collar, frayed hat, shabby green frock-coat, worn-out trousers, shrivelled waistcoat, imitation gold tie-pin and dirty shoes with muddied laces? Who will encompass him in all the immensity of his past and present poverty? No one but a Parisian. The destitute man in Paris is as destitute as a man can be, for there are still enough flashes of momentary joy in his life for him to realize how destitute he is.

The mulatto looked like an executioner of Lous XI leading a man to the gallows.

'Where have these two rogues been fished out from?' asked Henri.

'Devil only knows!' Paul answered. 'One of them makes my flesh creep.'

'Who are you, my man?' Henri asked of the destitute-looking man. 'You don't look such a heathen as your companion.'

The mulatto stood staring at the two young noblemen like someone quite at sea, but trying to guess what they were saying by observing their gestures and the movement of their lips.

The other man spoke: 'I'm a scrivener and interpreter. Poincet by name. My address is the Palais de Justice.'

'Right. But what about that fellow?' Henri asked Poincet, pointing to the mulatto.

'I don't know. He only talks a kind of Spanish dialect. He brought me along to get on terms with you.'

The mulatto pulled from his pocket the letter Henri had written to Paquita. He handed it over, and Henri tossed it into the fire.

'Well, well, things are beginning to develop,' Henri thought to himself, 'Paul, leave us a moment.'

'I translated this letter for him,' the interpreter continued once they were alone. 'When it was translated he went off somewhere or other. Then he came back to ask me to bring him here, promising me a couple of louis.'

'Hey, blackamoor, what do you want of me?' Henri asked.

'I left out "blackamoor",' said the interpreter as he waited for the mulatto's answer.

'He says this, sir,' the interpreter replied after listening to what the other man said. 'You are to wait tomorrow evening, at half-past ten, at the Boulevard Montmartre near the café. There you will see a carriage, and you will climb into it after saying to the man waiting to open the door: *cortejo*. – That's a Spanish word meaning "lover",' Poincet added, with a congratulatory glance at Henri.

'Good.'

The mulatto offered two louis to the interpreter, but de Marsay intercepted and himself rewarded the man. Whilst he was paying him, the mulatto uttered a few words.

'What is he saying?'

'He's warning me,' the interpreter replied, 'that if I let anything out about this he will strangle me. He's a nice specimen and looks quite capable of doing it.'

'I'm sure of that,' said Henri. 'He'd be true to his word.'

'He also says,' the interpreter continued, 'that the person who sent him implores you, for your sake as well as hers, to behave with the utmost prudence, because the daggers held over your heads would strike into your hearts without any human agency being able to save you.'

'He said that? So much the better. We shall have all the more fun.' He shouted to his friend: 'You can come back in now, Paul.'

The mulatto, who had not ceased to fix his magnetic stare on the lover of Paquita Valdes, went off with the interpreter following him.

'Well now, here's a very romantic adventure,' thought Henri as Paul returned. 'As a result of taking part in a few intrigues in Paris, I have now become involved in one which is complicated with grave circumstances and grave perils. My God, how danger emboldens women! Hamper a woman, try to thwart her in her schemes: are you not thereby giving her the right and the courage to leap instantaneously over barriers that it would have taken her years to surmount? Come, sweet creature, take the jump. Talk of death, poor child?

354

Of poniards? Feminine fancies! They simply must give their little jest some validity. Anyway we'll think it over, Paquita. We'll think it over, darling! But, devil take me, now that I know this luscious girl, this masterpiece of nature, is mine, the escapade has lost some of its savour.'

For all these frivolous words, youth had reasserted its rights over Henri. In order to subsist to the morrow without boredom, he had recourse to extravagant pleasures: he gambled, dined and supped with friends; he drank like a fish, ate like a Teuton, and won eleven or twelve thousand francs. He left that celebrated restaurant – the Rocher de Cancale – at two in the morning, slept like a child, awoke fresh and in good complexion the next morning, and dressed for a ride in the Tuileries: he intended to see Paquita, take his exercise in order to work up an appetite and make a good dinner: all that would enable him to kill time.

At the appointed hour Henri appeared on the boulevard, spotted the carriage and gave the password to a man whom he took to be the mulatto. Whereupon the man opened the door and quickly let down the steps. Henri was so rapidly swept through Paris, and his swirl of thoughts gave him so little facility for taking note of the streets through which he was passing that he had no idea where the carriage drew to a halt. The mulatto took him into a house whose staircase led straight from the *porte-cochère*. It was a dark one, as also was the landing on which Henri was made to wait while the mulatto opened the door leading to a damp, evil-smelling, unlit apartment, each room of which, in the dim flicker provided by a candle which his guide found in the antechamber, seemed to him empty and ill-furnished, like those in a house whose occupants are away travelling. He recaptured the sensation which he had experienced when reading one of Anne Radcliffe's novels in which the hero roams through the cold, gloomy halls of some sombre and deserted habitation.

Finally the mulatto opened the door of a salon. The dilapidated state of the furniture and the faded hangings with which this room was decorated gave it the appearance of the reception-room in a brothel: the same attempt at gaudy elegance, the same clutter of tawdry ornaments, the same dust and squalor. On a sofa covered with red Utrecht velvet, at the corner of a smouldering hearth whose fire was buried in its own ashes, sat an old, drably dressed woman wearing the kind of turban which Englishwomen are apt at devising when they reach a certain age, and which would have no end of a success in China, where monstrosity is the artistic ideal. All of this: the salon, the old woman, the cold hearth, would have cast an icy spell if Paquita had not been there on a settee, in a voluptuous dressing-gown, free to dart her golden, fiery glances, free to display her arched foot, free to deploy her luminous grace of movement.

This first interview was identical with all first meetings, those arranged by two impassioned beings who have leapt across the distance separating them and who ardently desire each other even before they have come to know each other. It is impossible that there should not at first be a discordant note in such a situation, an embarrassing one until the instant comes when they find themselves in tune with each other. If desire makes the man reckless and urges him to press on towards his goal, the woman, however deeply enamoured, risking as she does her very womanliness, is frightened to find herself so swiftly at her journey's end and faced with the necessity of surrender, which for many women is tantamount to falling into an abyss with no idea of what they will find at the bottom. The woman's involuntary coldness stands in contrast to the avowed passion of the man and provokes an inevitable reaction in the most enamoured of lovers. Such adverse states of mind, which often hover nebulously round people's consciousness, induce as it were a kind of temporary malady. In the blissful journey on which two creatures embark through the beautiful regions of love, this experience is like a moor, an arid moor, which has to be crossed: by turns humid and hot with, here and there, many burning sands and intersecting swamps. But it leads to the smiling, rose-clad grove where Cupid and his retinue, dispensers of pleasure, disport themselves on carpets of fine verdure. Often a man of intelligence discovers that a foolish laugh is the only response he is capable of making to such a situation: his wits are benumbed, as it were, under the icy compression to which his desires are subjected. It is quite probable that two creatures equally good-looking, intelligent and passionate, might begin by exchanging the silliest kinds of commonplaces until a chance word, the thrill of a particular glance, a communicating spark has brought them to the welcome crossways leading them to the flower-bordered path down which they float rather than walk, yet without having the sensation of descent.

Such a state of mind is always in direct ratio to the violence of one's feelings. Two people whose love is only lukewarm have no such experience. The effect of this crisis may furthermore be compared to that produced by the blaze of the sun in a cloudless sky. At first sight nature seems to be enveloped in a veil of gauze, the blue of the firmament is so deep as to appear black, the light is so intense as to seem like darkness. Both Henri and the Spanish girl experienced an equal violence of sensation, and the law of statics by virtue of which two identical forces cancel out when they meet might also be true in the psychological sphere.

Also the embarrassment of this moment was strangely increased by the presence of the old mummy of a woman. Love is startled or cheered by all sorts of trifles; it finds a meaning in everything, and everything is of good or evil augury. The decrepit old woman was there as representing a possible conclusion to their drama, standing for the hideous fish-tail which the symbol-making genius of Greece attributed to its chimaeras and sirens, so alluring, so delusive from the waist upwards – like all passions in their beginnings. Although Henri was not a free-thinker – to call a man this is a sarcasm – but a man of extraordinarily forceful character, as great as a man having no beliefs can be, this combination of circumstances made an impression on him. For that matter the men of stoutest calibre are naturally the most impressionable, and therefore the most superstitious, if indeed we may define superstition as the prejudice arising from a first impulse, this itself no doubt being the intuition of effects arising from causes hidden from other eyes but perceptible to theirs.

The Spanish girl took advantage of this moment of stupor in order to yield herself wholly to the ecstasy of infinite admiration which seizes a woman's heart when she is truly enamoured and finds herself confronted with an idol she has longed for in vain. Her eyes expressed nothing but joy and happiness – indeed, they were sparkling with it. She was under a spell, and intoxicated beyond all fear with the prospect of a long-dreamed-of felicity. At that juncture she appeared so miraculously beautiful to Henri that all this phantasmagoria of rags and old age, of red, threadbare draperies, of armchairs upholstered with matting of green straw, the unpolished red tiles and all this infirm and sickly luxury vanished instantaneously. The salon became illuminated, and it was only through a haze that he saw the terrible harpy, rigid and mute on her red sofa, her yellow eyes betraying the servile attitude that misfortune inspires, or is caused by some vice to which one has become enslaved as to a tyrant who bestializes his victims with the flagellations of his despotism. There was a cold glitter in her eyes like that of a caged tiger who is aware of his powerlessness and finds himself obliged to choke back his lust to destroy.

'Who is this woman?' Henri asked Paquita.

Paquita gave no answer. She made a sign indicating that she knew no French and asked Henri if he spoke English. De Marsay repeated his question in English.

'She is the only woman I can trust, although she once sold me,' Paquita calmly answered. 'Dear Adolphe, she is my mother, a slave sold in Georgia for her rare beauty, not much of which is left today. She only speaks her mother tongue.'

The woman's attitude and her desire to guess, by the movements of her daughter and those of Henri, what was going on between them, suddenly became clear to the young man, and this explanation put him at his ease.

'Paquita,' he said to her. 'Shall we then never be free?'

'Never,' she said with a mournful air. 'What is more, we have few days to be together.'

She let her eyes drop, looked at his hand and with her

own right hand counted on her left-hand fingers, thus displaying the most beautiful hands Henri had ever seen.

'One, two, three . . . ' She counted up to twelve.

'Yes,' she said, 'we have twelve days.'

'And after that?'

'After that,' she said, with the absorbed air of a frail woman on her knees before the executioner's axe, and suffering death in advance because fear was stripping her of the splendid energy which nature seemed to have allotted her only in order to intensify delight and convert the grossest pleasure into unending poems. 'After,' she repeated . . . Her eyes took on a fixed stare; she seemed to be gazing at some far-off, menacing object. 'I don't know,' she said.

'The girl is mad,' thought Henri; and he himself fell into strange reflections.

It seemed to him that Paquita was preoccupied with something other than himself, like a woman under equal constraint from both passion and remorse; perhaps because she had in her heart another love which she was forgetting and remembering turn by turn. Henri's mind was instantaneously besieged with a host of contradictory thoughts. He began to look upon this girl as a mystery but, while he studied her with the expert attention of a man who was surfeited and athirst for new delights, like a potentate of Orient forever demanding that a new pleasure should be created for him – a terrible craving which takes hold of overweening souls – Henri recognized in Paquita the richest organization that Nature had ever been pleased to create for love. The calculable working of this machine – let us leave the soul out of this – would have warned off any other man than de Marsay; but he was fascinated by the rich harvest of promised pleasures and the constant variety in sensual experience which every man dreams of and which is also the goal of any woman in love. He was carried beyond himself by infinity rendered palpable and transported into the most excessive raptures created beings can experience. All that he discovered in this girl, more distinctly than ever before in his life, for she complacently let him feast his eyes on her and was happy to be admired. De Marsay's admiration became a dissimulated frenzy which however became patent in its intensity as he cast a glance at the Spanish girl: she understood it as one accustomed to being gazed on in this fashion.

'If you were not to be mine, and mine alone, I would kill you,' he cried.

Hearing these words, Paquita hid her face in her hands and naïvely exclaimed: 'Holy Virgin, into what a trap have I fallen!'

She stood up, went and threw herself upon the red sofa, plunged her head into the rags which covered her mother's breast and stayed there weeping. The old woman received her daughter without stirring and without manifesting any emotion. She possessed in the highest degree the gravity of savage tribes, the statuesque impassibility which baffles all scrutiny. Did she or did she not love her daughter? Who should say? Beneath her inscrutable face all possible sentiments might be simmering, good or bad: anything might be expected from this creature. Her glance wandered slowly from her daughter's lovely hair, which covered her like a mantilla, to Henri's face, which she was scanning with inexpressible curiosity. She seemed to be asking what sorcerer's spell had brought him there and by what caprice nature had manufactured so captivating a man.

'These women are fooling me!' Henri told himself.

Just then Paquita raised her head and threw at him one of those looks which go straight to the soul and set it on fire. She seemed so lovely to him that he swore this paragon of beauty should belong to him.

'My Paquita, be mine!'

'But you talked of killing me,' she said, in frightened, quivering, anxious tones, though she felt drawn towards him by some inexplicable force.

'Kill you? I?' he said with a smile.

Paquita gave a cry of alarm and spoke a word to the old woman, who imperiously seized Henri's hand and that of her daughter, looked long at them then released them with a sinister and significant nod.

'Be mine this evening, this instant! Come with me, don't leave me! I want you, Paquita! If you love me, come!'

Then he poured out a thousand insensate phrases with the impetuosity of a mountain torrent tumbling over rocks and repeating the same sound in a thousand different ways.

'It's the same voice,' said Paquita in a melancholy tone – de Marsay did not hear this – 'and,' she added, 'the same ardent passion.'

'Yes, yes, indeed' she replied with a passionate abandon which no words could describe. 'Yes, but not this evening. This evening, Adolphe, I have not given La Concha enough opium. She might wake up and I should be lost. Just now everybody believes I am asleep in my bedroom. In two days' time, wait at the same spot and repeat the same password to the same man. He is my foster-brother, Christemio. He adores me and would let himself be tortured to death rather than utter a word against me. Adieu,' she said, embracing Henri and twining herself around him.

The pressure of her body encircled his. She drew his head to hers, put her lips to his and gave him a kiss which so ravished their senses that de Marsay felt as if the earth were opening to engulf him and Paquita cried 'Begone!' in a voice which plainly showed how little she was mistress of herself. But she clung to him while still crying 'Begone!' and slowly guided him out to the staircase.

There, the mulatto, whose white eyes gleamed at the sight of Paquita, took the torch from the hands of his idol and escorted Henri to the street. He left the torch under the vault, opened the door, put Henri back into the carriage and with marvellous rapidity deposited him on the Boulevard des Italiens. It was as though the devil were whipping up the horses.

This scene remained like a dream for de Marsay. Yet it was the kind of dream which, when it dissolves, leaves in the soul an impression of supernatural delight that a man may try to recapture for the rest of his life. A single kiss had sufficed. No rendezvous had taken place in more decent, more chaste or perhaps in more chilly fashion, or in more horrible surroundings, or in the presence of a more hideous divinity. For Paquita's mother was haunting Henri's imagination like a thing from the underworld, a creepy creature, something cadaverous, vicious, savagely ferocious, something whose existence had not yet been divined in the fantasy of painters and poets. In truth no previous rendezvous had more exasperated his senses, opened up a vista of more daring voluptuousness or caused the spring of love to gush forth more abundantly and spread its mystic spray around a man. What he was experiencing was something sombre and mysterious, something sweet and tender, something at once restrictive and expansive; a coupling of the horrible and the heavenly, of paradise and hell, which made him virtually drunk. He was no longer himself; and yet he still had stamina enough to resist the intoxication of pleasure.

In order to render his conduct intelligible at the moment when this story reaches its climax, it is necessary to explain how his faculties had expanded at the age when, normally, young people shrink in stature as they come into contact with women or become obsessed with them. His period of growth had coincided with a conjunction of secret circumstances which invested him with an immeasurable occult power.[9] This young man held a mightier sceptre than that wielded by modern kings, almost all of whom are bridled by the law in their slightest whims. De Marsay exerted the autocratic power of an Oriental despot. But this power, so stupidly wielded in Asia by brutish men, was increased tenfold by its combination with European intelligence and *l'esprit français*, which is the keenest and sharpest of all instruments serving the intellect. Henri was able to do anything he wanted in the interest of his pleasures and vanities. The invisible effect he exerted over the social world had invested him with a real but secret majesty which he never flaunted but kept enclosed within himself. The opinion he had of himself went beyond the self-conceit of a Louis XIV. It equalled that which the proudest of Caliphs, Pharaohs or Xerxes, who believed

9. See above, Introduction, p. 9.

they were of race divine, had of themselves when they aped God by veiling themselves before their subjects on the pretext that those who looked upon them must die. So, without feeling any remorse at being both accuser and judge, de Marsay coldly condemned to death any man or woman who had seriously affronted him. Although such a sentence was often lightly pronounced, the verdict was irrevocable. Any mistake was a calamity similar to the one a thunderbolt may cause when it falls on a Parisian lady happily seated in a cab, instead of blasting the aged coachman driving her along to an assignation. And therefore the bitter and profound irony which distinguished the young man's conversation usually provoked great fear: no one felt inclined to take issue with him. Women are prodigiously fond of such men, who promote themselves to the rank of pasha and seem to go about with an escort of lions and executioners and all the paraphernalia of intimidation. This confers on them a self-assurance in action, a confidence in their own power, a pride of bearing, a leonine self-consciousness, which embody the type of strength that all women dream of. Such was de Marsay.

Happy at that moment about the prospect awaiting him, he became youthful and flexible once more and, as he went to bed, thought of nothing other than love. He dreamt of the girl with the golden eyes as all passionate young people dream: monstrous images, elusive fantasies, bathed in light and revealing invisible worlds, but always incompletely, for an intervening veil transforms the conditions of optics. The next two days he disappeared from sight without anyone being able to tell where he had gone. The power he wielded belonged to him only on certain conditions, and fortunately for him, during those two days, he was merely a private soldier in the service of the demon to whom he owed his talismanic existence. But at the appointed hour, he was at the boulevard waiting for the carriage, which was not long in coming. The mulatto approached Henri and uttered a sentence in French which he seemed to have learnt by heart. 'If you wish to come, she told me, you must allow your eyes to be bandaged.' And Christemio showed him a white silk scarf.

'Certainly not!' said Henri, revolting against this challenge to his sense of omnipotence.

He tried to climb in. The mulatto made a sign and the carriage moved off.

'Very well!' de Marsay shouted, furious at the prospect of losing the bliss he had promised himself. Moreover, he realized the impossibility of compromising with a slave whose obedience was as blind as that of the public hangman. In any case, why should his wrath fall on this passive instrument?

The mulatto gave a whistle and the carriage returned. Henri jumped in. Already a small crowd of gapers was gathering on the boulevard. Henri was a man of muscle and he decided to fool the mulatto. When the carriage started off at a swift trot he seized his wrists with the intention of overpowering his guide so as to retain the use of his faculties and find out where he was being taken. The attempt was vain. The mulatto's eyes gleamed in the darkness; he let out a choked cry of fury, struggled free, flung de Marsay away from him with iron sinews and nailed him, so to speak, to the floor of the vehicle. Then, with his free hand, he pulled out a triangular dagger and blew his whistle again. Henri was unarmed and was obliged to yield: he put his head forwards to receive the scarf. This gesture of submission pacified Christemio, who blindfolded him with such respect and care as betokened a kind of personal veneration for the man his idol loved. But before taking this precaution he had distrustfully thrust the dagger into his side-pocket and buttoned himself up to the chin.

'He might well have killed me, the black bastard!' de Marsay said to himself.

The carriage again began to rattle swiftly onwards. There was still one resource open to a young man who knew his Paris as well as Henri did. To find out where he was going, he had only to pay close attention and, gauging by the number of gutters they crossed, count the streets they passed over on the boulevards so long as the carriage continued straight ahead. In this way he could make out the side-streets they turned into, whether towards the Seine or towards the hills of Montmartre, and then guess the name or position of the street in which his guide would call the vehicle to a halt.

But the violent emotion awakened in him by his struggle, the rage which the loss of dignity had aroused in him, the vengeful thoughts to which he was yielding, the conjectures brought to his mind by the minute precautions this mysterious girl had taken in order to bring him to her, all this prevented him from applying to this purpose the blind man's attentiveness needed for such concentration of mind and such accuracy of observation. The journey lasted half an hour. When the carriage drew up it was no longer on a paved road. The mulatto and the coachman took Henri in their arms, lifted him up, placed him on a kind of stretcher and carried him through a garden – this he perceived through the scent of flowers and the fragrance peculiar to trees and verdure. Such deep silence reigned that he could discern the falling of raindrops from the drenched leaves. The two men carried him up a staircase, brought him to his feet, steered him across several rooms, and left him in a bedroom whose atmosphere was laden with perfume and whose floor was laid with thick carpets into which his feet sank. A female hand pushed him towards a divan and unknotted the scarf. Henri saw Paquita before him; but a Paquita in all the glory of her feminine voluptuousness.

That half of the boudoir in which Henri now found himself described a softly graceful curve, contrasting with the other half, which was perfectly rectangular and resplendent with a chimney-piece of white and gilded marble.[10] He had entered through a side-door hidden behind a rich *portière* with a window standing opposite. The horseshoe section was adorned with a genuine Turkish divan, which is a mattress laid on the floor, wide as a bed, a divan fifty feet in circumference, of white cashmere offset by black and poppy-red silk rosettes

10. The ensuing description tallies with the extravagantly aesthetic salon in the Rue Chaillot in the set of rooms into which Balzac moved in March 1835, while he was writing this novel. It is a moot point which came first: the real or the fictitious salon. See my biography of Balzac, pp. 74–5.

forming a lozenge pattern. The back of this huge bed rose many inches higher than the numerous cushions, the tastefulness of whose matching gave it even further richness.

This boudoir was hung with a red fabric overlaid with Indian muslin, its in-and-out folds fluted like a Corinthian column, and bound at top and bottom with bands of poppy-red material on which arabesque designs in black were worked. Under this muslin the poppy-red showed up as pink, the colour of love, repeated in the window curtains, also of Indian muslin, lined with pink taffeta and bordered with poppy-red fringes alternating with black. Six silver-gilt sconces, each of them bearing two candles, stood out from the tapestried wall at equal distances to light up the divan. The ceiling, from the centre of which hung a chandelier of dull silver-gilt, was dazzlingly white, and the cornice was gilded. The carpet was reminiscent of an Oriental shawl, reproducing as it did the designs and recalling the poetry of Persia, where the hands of slaves had worked to make it. The furniture was covered in white cashmere, set off by black and poppy-red trimmings. The clock and candelabra were of white marble and gold. There were elegant flower-stands full of all sorts of roses and white or red flowers. To sum up, every detail of decoration seemed to have been thought out with loving care. Never had wealth of adornment been more daintily disguised in order to be translated into elegance, to be expressive of taste and incite to voluptuousness. Everything there would have warmed the blood of the chilliest mortal. The iridescence of the hangings, whose colour changed as the eye looked at them from different angles, now white, now wholly pink, harmonized with the effects of light infused into the diaphanous folds of the muslin and produced an impression of mistiness. The human soul is strangely attracted to white, love has a delectation for red, and gold gives encouragement to the passions because it has the power to realize their dreams. Thus all that is vague and mysterious in man, all his unexplained affinities, found their involuntary sympathies gratified in this boudoir. There was in this perfect harmony a concerto of colour to which the soul responded with ideas which were at once voluptuous, imprecise and fluctuating.

*

It was here, in the midst of a misty atmosphere laden with exquisite perfumes, that Paquita appeared to Henri, wrapped in a white gown, bare-footed, with orange blossom in her jet-black hair.[11] She was on her knees before him, adoring him as the deity of the temple he had deigned to visit. Although de Marsay was accustomed to all the refinements of Parisian luxury, he was surprised at the sight of this shell so reminiscent of that from which Venus rose. Whether as an effect of the contrast between the dark passages from which he had emerged and the luminosity in which his soul was now steeped, or because of the swift comparison he made between this scene and that of their previous conversation together, the sensation he experienced was of such delicacy as only true poetry can give. As his gaze, in the heart of this retreat conjured up by a magic wand, fell on this masterpiece of creation, this girl whose warmly tinted complexion, whose soft skin – soft but slightly gilded by the gleams of red around her and by the strange, filmy emanations of love – sparkled as if it were reflecting the rays of light and colour, his anger, resentment and wounded vanity fell from him. Like an eagle swooping upon its prey, he took her in his arms, sat her on his knee and enjoyed the indescribable intoxication of feeling the sweet presence and soft embrace of her voluptuous body.

'Come, Paquita!' he whispered.

'You may speak out without restraint,' she said. 'This retreat was built for love. No sound can issue from it, so intense was the desire to enclose within it the accents and music of the beloved's voice. The loudest cries would be inaudible outside these walls. Murder might be committed here, but the

11. Ash-blond on p. 338. But Balzac was never pedantically consistent. He varied the tint of his women's hair according to the quality of fascination he wished to convey.

victim's plaints would be as ineffectual as if he were in the middle of the Sahara.'

'But who then is so well versed in jealousy and its dictates?'

'Never question me about that,' she replied as she undid the young man's cravat with an incredibly pretty gesture, the better no doubt to admire the graceful outline of his neck.

'Yes, there it is, the neck I love so much!' she said. 'Will you do something to please me?'

This question, asked in a tone which made it almost lascivious, drew de Marsay from the reverie into which he had been plunged by the imperious answer with which Paquita had forbidden him any further inquiry about the unknown person whose shadow hovered above them.

'What if I insisted on knowing who rules in this domain?'

Paquita looked at him trembling.

'So it is not I?' he said, rising to his feet and shaking free of the girl, who fell back on to the divan. 'I will stand alone. I will share you with no one!'

'How like! How like!' said the poor slave-girl, in the grip of terror.

'Who do you take me for? Will you answer?'

Paquita meekly rose with streaming eyes, walked over to two ebony cabinets, took a dagger from one and offered it with a submissive gesture which would have melted a tiger's fury.

'Give me such a feast of love as men give when they love,' she said, 'and then, while I sleep, kill me. I cannot answer your question. Listen. I am tethered like some wretched animal to its stake. I am amazed to have been able to throw a bridge over the gulf which divides us. Intoxicate me with love, then kill me. But no, no, no!' she implored him with clasped hands. 'Don't kill me. I am in love with life. Life is so beautiful for me! I may be a slave, but I am also a queen. I might deceive you with words, tell you that I love only you, prove it to you and take advantage of my momentary ascendancy to say to you: "Take me just as one savours the scent of a flower when one is passing through a king's garden." Then, after I had made play with a woman's cunning eloquence and unfolded the wings of pleasure, after quenching my own thirst I could have you cast into a well in which you would never be found, a well dug for the satisfaction of vengeance and immunity from the fear of justice; a well filled with quicklime which would flame up in order to consume you so that no trace of you would survive. Yet you would live on in my heart for ever mine!'

Henri looked at the girl without a tremor and his fearless gaze filled her with joy.

'But no! I will not do that. Here you have not fallen into a trap, but into the heart of a woman who adores you. I only have fallen into a well!'

'All this seems prodigiously strange to me,' de Marsay said as he gazed into her eyes. 'But you strike me as being a good-hearted girl, though not easy to fathom. By my faith, I look upon you as a flesh and blood enigma, one extremely difficult to solve.'

Paquita had no idea what the young man meant. She gazed at him lovingly through wide eyes which could never appear stupid, so vivid was the voluptuousness expressed in them.

'Come then, my love,' she said, reverting to her earlier idea. 'Will you do something to please me?'

'I'll do anything you wish, and even something you don't wish,' de Marsay replied with a laugh, having by now recovered his foppish self-composure as he made the resolve to pursue this amorous adventure to its conclusion without looking backwards or forwards. For that matter, he was perhaps counting on will-power, and his experience as a *galant homme*, to dominate this girl before long and draw all her secrets from her.

'Then ... ' she said. 'Let me dress you up as I would like to do.'

'Dress me however you like.'

In joyous mood, Paquita went to one of her two wardrobes and took from it a red velvet gown in which she robed de Marsay. Then she adorned his head with a woman's cap and wrapped a shawl around him. While indulging these follies with the naïvety of a child she went off in trills of laughter and resembled a bird with fluttering wings. But she was living only for the moment.

*

Although it is impossible to depict the indescribable transports enjoyed by these two lovely creatures, whom Heaven had created in a moment of supreme joy, it would not perhaps be superfluous to translate metaphysically the extraordinary, the almost fantastic impressions the young man received. What men of de Marsay's social station and living as he lived are most capable of recognizing is a girl's innocence. But strange to say, if the girl with the golden eyes was a virgin, she had certainly lost her innocence. The singular combination of mystery and reality, light and shade, hideousness and beauty, pleasure and peril, Eden and Hades which had already been encountered in this adventure, had its continuation in de Marsay's dalliance with this capricious, this unprecedented daughter of Eve. The most complete, the most refined, the most expert voluptuousness, every experience Henri had ever had of that poetry of the senses which goes by the name of love was excelled by the succession of delights unfolded by this girl whose dazzling eyes belied nothing of the promise that shone forth in them: a poem of Orient, radiant with the sunlight which Saadi and Hafiz[12] instilled into their impassioned stanzas. But yet neither the rhythm of Saadi, nor even that of Pindar could have expressed the mixture of ecstasy and delirium, the stupefaction which seized on the delectable girl when illusion, no longer sustained by her lover's iron will, died in her heart.

'Doomed!' she cried. 'I am doomed! Adolphe, carry me away to the ends of the earth, to an island where no one can find us. Let no traces be left of our flight, for we should be followed right down into hell! Oh God! Day is breaking. Leave me. Shall I ever see you again? Yes, I must see you tomorrow, even if such happiness had to be bought with the death of all those who watch over me. Tomorrow, then.'

There was the terror of death in the frenzy with which she

12. Persian poets of the thirteenth and fourteenth centuries.

strained him to her bosom. Then she pushed a spring which must have been connected with a bell and begged de Marsay to let himself be blindfolded again.

'But what if I refused? What if I decided to stay here?'

'You would bring me more promptly to my death,' she said. 'I am sure now that you will be the cause of my death.'

Henri complied.

To a man who has just been sated with pleasure there comes an inclination to forgetfulness, a measure of ingratitude, a desire for freedom, an urge to escape, a tinge of scorn, even perhaps of contempt, for the idol he has worshipped; in short a medley of inexplicable sentiments which reduce him to baseness and ignobility. No doubt it was the certain knowledge of this tendency, confused but genuine in hearts not illuminated by that heaven-sent light nor perfumed with that holy balm from which we draw the constancy in affection that suggested to Rousseau the adventures of My Lord Edward Bomston, related in the concluding letters of *La Nouvelle Héloïse*. Evidently Rousseau took his inspiration for this work from Richardson; but he departed from his model in a thousand particulars, and these give monumental originality to his novel. It is commended to posterity by profound ideas which it is difficult for analysis to bring out when, in our youth, we read this work with the object of finding in it a fervid description of the most physical of all our passions, whereas serious writers and philosophers never employ its images except in so far as they proceed from or point towards some epoch-making system of thought; and Lord Edward's adventures constitute one of the most delicate, most European ideas the novel contains.[13]

So then Henri found himself dominated by a medley of motives which have no place in real love. He needed, so to speak, to go through the pros and cons of comparison and to recall the magnetic pull of erotic experience before returning to a woman. True love rules especially through memory. Can a woman ever be beloved who has not graven her image

13. It is difficult to see what relevance this disquisition on Rousseau has here!

in a man's heart either by sating him with pleasure or over-whelming him with the strength of her emotions? Though Henri was unaware of it, Paquita had established a hold on him by both means. But just now, given over as he was to the lassitude, to the delicious melancholy which results from physical satisfaction, he was scarcely able to analyse the state of his heart by summoning back the savour of the most vivid delights he had ever sipped from a woman's lips. There he was, on the Boulevard Montmartre, at break of day, gazing with stupefaction at the retreating carriage. He took two cigars from his pocket, and lit one at the lantern of a worthy woman who was selling coffee and brandy to workmen, street arabs, market gardeners and others of the Parisian populace who are astir before dawn. Then he went away smoking his cigar, thrusting his hands into his trouser pockets with a jauntiness which one must confess did him little honour.

'What a fine thing a cigar is!' he exclaimed. 'It's something a man will never tire of.'

As for the girl with the golden eyes, of whom at present all the elegant young men of Paris were enamoured, he was now giving her scarcely a thought! The idea of death expressed during their raptures and the fear of it which had several times cast a shadow on the brow of this lovely creature – linked through her mother with the houris of Asia, belonging to Europe by virtue of her upbringing and to the tropics by the incident of birth – seemed to him to be typical of the frauds practised by women in the attempt to arouse the interest of men.

'She comes from Havana, from the most Spanish country there is in the New World, and so she has preferred to black-mail me with terror rather than spin me tales of suffering, or beguile me with talk of incompatibility or family obligations, as Parisian women do. Heigh-ho! By her golden eyes, I have a great wish to sleep!'

He saw a hackney cab standing at the corner outside Fras-cati's, waiting in the hope of picking up desultory gamblers. He woke the driver, had himself driven home, went to bed and slept the sleep of the unjust which, thanks to a caprice of chance which no rhymester has yet exploited as a theme, happens to be as profound as that of the innocent.[14] Perhaps this is an illustration of the proverbial axiom 'extremes meet'.

14. Cf. the English lyric: 'The rain it raineth every day
Upon the just and unjust fella;
But chiefly on the just, because
The unjust stole the just's umbrella.'

3

The call of the blood

AT about noon, de Marsay woke up, stretched himself and
felt himself in the grip of the sort of wolfish hunger which all
veteran soldiers can remember having experienced the day
after a victory. And so he was pleased to see Paul de Manerville
standing at his bed, for nothing is more agreeable than eating
in company.

'Well now,' said his friend. 'We have all been supposing
that for the last ten days you had been shut up with the girl
with the golden eyes.'

'The girl with the golden eyes? I've given up thinking of
her. I assure you I have many other fish to fry.'

'Oh, you're being discreet!'

'Why should I not?' said de Marsay with a laugh. 'My dear
fellow, discretion is the cleverest of calculations. You never
have anything to tell me, and I don't feel inclined to squander
the treasures of my strategy on you and get nothing in
return. Life is a river which serves for two-way trade. I swear
by everything I hold sacred on earth – cigars for instance –
that I am no professor of social economy adapted to the use of
simpletons. Let's go and lunch. It costs less to treat you to
a tunny omelette than to waste my grey cells on you.'

'So you count the cost with your friends?'

'Dear man,' said Henri, rarely able to resist an ironical
remark, 'since however it could happen to you (as to any
other man) to need discretion, and since I'm very fond of
you ... Yes, it's a fact! ... On my word of honour, if all
you needed were a thousand-franc note to stop you blowing
your brains out, you'd find it here, for we aren't crippled with
mortgages here, are we, Paul? Or if you had a duel on your
hands tomorrow, I would pace off the distance and load the
pistols for you to be killed in conformity with the rules.

374

Lastly if anyone other than myself took it upon him to slander you behind your back, he would have to cross swords with the hard-bitten nobleman who dwells inside my skin: that's what I call a really staunch friendship. Well, my boy, when you find yourself in need of discretion, learn this: there are two kinds, one active, one negative. Negative discretion belongs to the dolts who have recourse to silence, denial, frowning faces, the discretion which takes effect behind closed doors – sheer impotence! Active discretion proceeds by blunt assertion. If this evening at the club I were to say: "My word of honour, the girl with the golden eyes wasn't worth the expense she put me to!" everybody, once I had left, would shout out: "Did you hear that fatuous man de Marsay trying to persuade us that he has already possessed the girl with the golden eyes? He's nobody's fool: it's his way of shaking off his rivals." But a trick like that is vulgar and dangerous. Whatever gross stupidity one utters, one always finds idiots capable of believing it. The best kind of discretion is that of which clever wives take advantage when they want to fool their husbands. It consists of compromising a woman we're not keen on, or one we don't love or don't possess, in order to preserve the honour of the one we love sufficiently to respect her. The former is what one calls the *woman-screen* . . . Ah! here is Laurence. What have you got for us?'

'Ostend oysters, Monsieur le Comte.'

'Some day, Paul, you will realize how diverting it is to make fun of society by concealing from it the secret of our affections. I derive tremendous pleasure from eluding the stupid jurisdiction of the bulk of people who never know what they want or what they are made to want, who take the means for the end and alternately worship and execrate, exalt and destroy. How satisfying it is to impose emotions on them but never to receive any from them, to control but never to obey them! If there is anything to feel proud about, is it not about a power we have ourselves acquired of which we are at once the cause and effect, the principle and the result? Well, no man knows whom I love or what I want. Perhaps whom I have loved and what I have wanted will eventually be known, like the winding-up of a drama. But why let people look into my hand while the game is still going on? Weakness, gullibility! I know nothing more contemptible than strength outwitted by cunning. I am initiating myself into the ambassadorial art in a non-serious way – but is diplomacy as difficult as the art of living? I doubt it ... Are you ambitious? Do you want to get somewhere?'

'Henri, you are making fun of me. Am I not sufficiently mediocre to rise to any height?'

'Very good, Paul! Go on laughing at yourself and you'll soon be able to laugh at everybody else.'

In the course of lunch, and when he came to the cigar stage, de Marsay began to see the events of the past night in a strange light. Like many men of great intelligence, his perspicacity was not spontaneous and he could not pierce at once to the heart of things. As is the case with all natures endowed with the faculty of living predominantly in the present, the second sight he possessed needed an interval of slumber before it could identify itself with causes. Such was the case with Cardinal Richelieu, but that did not preclude in him the gift of foresight necessary for the conception of great designs. De Marsay was equipped with all the required talents, but initially he only used the weapons at his command in pursuit of his own satisfaction; not until he was sated with the pleasures to which a wealthy and influential young man devotes his first thoughts did he become one of the shrewdest politicians of his age. It is thus that a man steels his heart: he wears women down so that they may not wear him down.

At that moment then, de Marsay perceived that he had been deceived by the girl with the golden eyes, for now he could see the past night in perspective, beginning as it had done with a trickle of pleasures which in the end had swollen into a torrent of voluptuousness. By now he was able to read that page, so brilliant in its effects, and divine its hidden meaning. Paquita's purely physical innocence, the amazing quality of her joy, the few words, at first obscure but now clear, which had escaped her in the midst of that joy, everything showed him that he had posed for another person. Since no form of social corruption was a closed book to him, since he professed perfect indifference with regard to all kinds of moral deviation and believed them to be justified by the mere fact that they were capable of being satisfied, he took no umbrage at vice, being as familiar with it as one is with a friend; but he smarted at the thought of having provided it with sustenance. If his suppositions were correct he had been outraged in the tenderest part of his being. The mere suspicion put him into a fury and he let out the roar of a tiger taunted by a gazelle, the cry of a tiger uniting a wild beast's strength with the intelligence of a demon.

'Why, what's the matter?' asked Paul.

'Nothing.'

'If someone asked you whether you were on bad terms with me and you answered with so nonchalant a "Not at all!" it's a pretty sure thing that we should be fighting a duel next day.'

'I no longer fight duels,' said de Marsay.

'To me that sounds more tragic still. You go in for murder then?'

'You travesty my words. I execute.'

'My dear friend,' said Paul, 'your jokes have a very sombre colouring this evening.'

'What do you expect? Pleasure leads to ferocity. Why? That I don't know, and I'm not interested enough to seek out the cause – These cigars are excellent – Give your friend some tea – Do you know, Paul, that I live a brutish kind of life? It's high time I chose my destiny and devoted my strength to something worth living for. Life is a singular comedy. I am frightened. The inconsistencies of our social order seem ludicrous to me. The government cuts off the heads of poor devils who have killed one man and issues licences to creatures who, medically speaking, polish off a dozen young folk each winter. Morality is powerless to combat a dozen vices which are destroying society but for which there is no punishment – Another cup? – Upon my word, man is a clown dancing on the edge of a precipice. They talk about the immorality of *Les Liaisons dangereuses* or some book or other which has the name of a chambermaid for title,[1] but there exists a horrible, filthy, frightful, corrupting book, always open and never to be closed: the great book of the world; and there's yet another book, a thousand times more dangerous, one whose contents consist of everything that men whisper into each other's ears, or that women murmur behind their fans, in the evening at the ball.'

'Henri, there's certainly something extraordinary going on inside you, and it's obvious in spite of your "active" discretion.'

'True enough. But look, I have time to kill before evening comes. Let's go to the tables. Perhaps I shall be lucky enough to lose.'

De Marsay stood up, took a handful of bank-notes, stuffed them into his cigar-case, got into evening dress, and took advantage of Paul's carriage to convey him to the Salon des Étrangers, where, until dinner, he passed the time at those exciting alternations of loss and gain which are all that tensely-keyed organisms have to fall back upon when they are constrained to function in a vacuum. When evening had come, he went to the rendezvous and let himself be blindfolded without demur. Then, with the firmness of will which only exceptional men are able to bend to a single purpose, he concentrated his attention and applied his intelligence to guessing through what streets the carriage was passing. He was practically certain that he was being taken to the Rue Saint-Lazare and that the carriage halted at the little garden gate of the Hôtel San-Real. When, as on the previous occasion, he passed through this gate and was laid on a stretcher, carried, no doubt, by the mulatto and the coachman, he understood, as he heard the sand crunching under their feet, why such minute precautions were being taken. Had he been free or afoot, he might have snapped off a twig from a bush or taken note of the kind of sand sticking to his boots; whereas, being so to speak conveyed aerially into a mansion he could not hope to approach by his own initiative, his amorous adventure must perforce remain what it had been until then: a dream. But to his

1. Probably the Marquis de Sade's *Justine, or The Misfortunes of Virtue.*

despair man can never reach perfection either in good or evil deeds. All his works, intellectual or physical, are marked with the seal of destruction. There had been light rain, and the soil was damp. At night-time certain vegetal odours are much stronger than during the day, so that Henri caught the scent of mignonette the whole length of the alley along which he was being carried. This indication, he thought, would guide him during the researches he intended to make in order to rediscover the house in which Paquita's boudoir was situated. He likewise studied the detours which his bearers made in the house and thought he would be able to recall them.[2]

He found himself as on the day before on the ottoman in front of Paquita, who took off his bandage; but he saw that she was pale and changed. She had wept. On her knees like an angel at prayer, but a sad and profoundly melancholy one, the poor girl no longer resembled the curious, impatient, impetuous creature who had taken de Marsay on her wings to transport him to the seventh heaven of love. There was something so genuine in this despair veiled with voluptuousness that de Marsay, sinister as his intentions were, felt admiration rising in him for this novel paragon of nature; for a moment he forgot his main motive for keeping this rendezvous.

'What is the matter, my Paquita?'

'My love,' she replied, 'take me away this very night! Dispose of me in some place where no one can say when they see me: "That is Paquita," and where no one can reply: "There's a girl here with a golden glance and long hair." There I will give you the delights of love so long as you are willing to have them from me. Then, when you love me no more, you will leave me. I will not utter a word of complaint, and you need feel no remorse for abandoning me, because one day spent at your side, one single day during which I have gazed into your eyes, will have been worth a lifetime. But if I stay here I am lost.'

'I cannot leave Paris, little one,' Henri replied. 'I do not belong to myself alone, being bound by oath to several persons

2. All this seems to be mystery for mystery's sake (as in *La Duchesse de Langeais*). It is perfectly obvious where de Marsay has been taken.

who are to me as I am to them.[3] But I can find you a refuge in Paris where no human power can reach you.'

'No,' she said. 'You forget the power that a woman may wield.'

Never did words uttered by a human voice express more complete terror.

'But what harm could reach you if I put myself between the world and you?'

'Poison!' she cried. 'Already Doña Concha suspects you. And,' she continued with glistening tears running down her cheeks, 'it is very easy to see that I have changed from what I was. But so be it, if you abandon me to the fury of the monster who will devour me, let your blessed will be done. But come now, make it so that none of the bliss of life shall be missing in our love. For that matter, I will supplicate, weep, cry out, defend myself and perhaps succeed in escaping.'

'But who is it you will supplicate?'

'Not a word,' Paquita replied. 'If I obtain mercy, it will perhaps be thanks to my discretion.'

'Put my velvet gown on me,' said Henri coaxingly.

'No, no,' she impetuously replied. 'Remain what you are, one of the angels I had been taught to detest and whom I looked upon only as monsters, while on the contrary you are all that is loveliest under heaven,' she said as she played with Henri's hair. 'You have no idea how ignorant I am. I have been taught nothing. Since I was twelve I have been shut up and seen no one. I can neither read nor write and speak nothing but English and Spanish.'

'How then does it come about that you receive letters from London?'

'My letters? Here they are,' she said as she went to fetch some papers from a tall Japanese vase.

And on the letters she tendered to de Marsay he was surprised to see some strange figures similar to those of a rebus, traced in blood and expressing the most passionate sentiments.

'But,' he exclaimed as he puzzled out these hieroglyphs

3. The Thirteen, of course.

invented by ingenious jealousy, 'you must be under the power of some infernal genie.'

'Infernal indeed,' she repeated.

'But how did you manage to get out of your house?'

'Ah!' she said, 'that has been my ruin. I gave Doña Concha the choice between immediate death and future anger. I was possessed by the demon of curiosity; I wanted to break out of the ring of bronze drawn round between myself and creation. I wanted to see what young men were like, for the only men I knew were the marquis and Christemio. Our coachman and the valet who goes with us are too old to count.'

'But surely you have not always been shut up? Your health required . . . '

'Oh,' she replied, 'we did go out, but only at night and in the country, on the banks of the Seine far from other people.'

'Are you not proud to be loved so jealously?'

'No!' she said. 'Not now! However fully occupied, this cloistered life is darkness itself compared with life in the light of day.'

'What do you mean by the light of day?'

'You yourself, my handsome Adolphe. You, for whom I would give my life. All the passionate things that have been said to me and which I inspired, I feel them for you! At certain moments I understood nothing about existence, but now I know what it is to love. Up to now I have merely been loved without responding. I would leave everything for you. Take me away. If that is what you want, take me as a plaything, but let me be with you until you decide to break your toy!'

'You will have no regrets?'

'Not one!' she cried, letting him read in her eyes, whose golden gleam remained pure and clear.

'Am I the one she prefers?' Henri asked himself. He had an inkling of the truth about her, but was inclined to condone matters in favour of so ingenuous a love. 'I shall soon see,' he thought.

Although Paquita was in no wise accountable to him for

her past, the very memory of it was a crime in his view. So he had the regrettable strength of mind to keep his own counsel, to judge his mistress and to watch her reactions while all the time giving himself over to the most entrancing pleasures that any peri from faery regions has bestowed on her beloved. Nature seemed to have taken special care to form Paquita for love. From one night to the next her feminine genius had made the most rapid progress. Great as was this young man's prowess and his blasé attitude to pleasure, in spite of the fact that he had reached satiety on the previous occasion, he found in his golden-eyed girl the complete seraglio which a loving woman knows how to create and which a man can never refuse. Paquita responded to the craving which all truly great men feel for the infinite, that mysterious passion so dramatically expressed in *Faust*, so poetically translated in *Manfred*, which urged Don Juan to probe deep into the heart of women, hoping to find in them that infinite ideal for which so many pursuers of phantoms have searched; scientists believe they can find it in science, mystics find it in God alone. The hope of at last possessing the ideal being with whom the conflict could be constant but untiring ravished de Marsay, and for the first time in years he opened his heart. His nerves relaxed, his iciness melted in the warmth with which this ardent soul enwrapped him, his misanthropic views were dissipated and happiness coloured his existence as with the tints of Paquita's white and rose-red boudoir. Pricked by the spur of a pleasure never tasted before, he was drawn beyond the limits to which so far he had confined passion. He was unwilling to be outdone by this girl whom a somewhat artificial love had trained in advance for his emotional needs, and from then on he drew, from the vanity which urges a man to be foremost in every sphere, resources sufficient to subdue the girl; none the less, being driven over the line within which the soul is mistress of itself, he lost himself in those limbos of delight which common people so stupidly call 'imaginary space'. He became tender, kind, communicative. He stirred Paquita almost into frenzy. 'Why could we not go to Sorrento, Nice, Chiavari, and spend our whole life like this? Will you?' he asked Paquita in a voice which thrilled her.

'Need you ever say "Will you?" to me?' she exclaimed. 'Have I a will? I exist outside you only in order to be a pleasure for you. But if you want to find a retreat worthy of us, Asia is the only country where love can spread its wings.'

'You are right,' Henri replied. 'Let us go to the Indies, where spring is eternal, where the soil grows nothing but flowers, where man can unfurl all the splendour of sovereign princes without running the gauntlet of comment as in the stupid countries which try to make a reality of the chimaera of equality. Let us flee to those regions where one lives amid a population of slaves, where the sun for ever illumines a palace of unfading whiteness, where the air is pregnant with perfume, where the birds sing of love, where one dies when one can love no longer . . .'

'Where one dies together!' Paquita added. 'But don't let's wait till tomorrow. Let's go off immediately and take Christemio with us.'

'True enough, life can reach no higher climax than the bliss of love. Let's go to Asia, my child. But: such an emigration requires much money, and in order to have much money one must put one's affairs in order.'

She had no understanding of such matters.

'But there's lots of gold here! Piles of it! As high as that!' she said, lifting up her arms.

'But it's not mine.'

'What matter?' she asked. 'If we need it, let's take it.'

'It doesn't belong to you.'

'Belong! What does that mean? You took me, didn't you? Once we have taken it, it will belong to us.'

He broke into laughter.

'Dear innocent! You know nothing about things of this world!'

'Maybe not. But this is what I do know' – she drew Henri to her.

At the very moment when de Marsay was forgetting

everything and was minded to take this creature to himself for ever, in the very midst of ecstasy a dagger-stroke was dealt him which pierced his heart through and through: the first mortification it had ever received. Paquita, who had found strength enough to lift him above her as if to gaze upon him, had exclaimed:

'Oh! Mariquita!'

'Mariquita!' the young man roared out. 'Now I know all that I didn't want to believe.'

He leapt forward to the cabinet in which the long dagger was kept. Happily for her and for him it was locked. Frustration increased his fury. But he regained his self-control, pulled out his cravat and advanced towards her with an air so full of ferocious intention that Paquita, without knowing what crime she had committed, realized that he meant to kill her. Thereupon she leapt with one single bound to the far end of the room in order to avoid the fatal noose de Marsay was trying to wind round her neck. A tussle ensued: the odds were even – equal muscular suppleness, agility, vigour. To bring the scuffle to an end Paquita tossed between her lover's legs a cushion which tripped him up. She took advantage of the resultant respite to press the button of the bell for summoning her attendants. The mulatto swiftly arrived. In the twinkling of an eye Christemio pounced on de Marsay, felled him to the ground and set his foot on his chest with his heel turned towards his throat. De Marsay realized that if he continued the struggle he would be instantly crushed to death at one sign from Paquita.

'Why did you try to kill me, my love?' she asked.

De Marsay gave no answer.

'How did I displease you? Speak. Let us understand one another.'

Henri maintained the phlegmatic attitude of a strong man who knows he is beaten: a cold, mute, entirely English demeanour, a momentary resignation which revealed the consciousness of his dignity. For that matter the idea had occurred to him, in spite of his anger, that it would be imprudent to compromise himself with the law by killing the girl on an impulse and without having arranged the murder in such a way as to ensure impunity for himself.

'My beloved,' Paquita continued. 'Speak to me. Don't leave me without a loving word of farewell. I don't want my heart still to feel the terror you have just put into it. Speak then!' she shouted, stamping her foot angrily.

De Marsay's sole response was to cast a glance at her which so clearly meant: 'You shall die!' that Paquita threw herself at him.

'Very well, kill me! If my death can give you pleasure, kill me!'

She made a sign to Christemio, who lifted his foot from the young man and strode away without his face showing whether he was passing any judgement, good or bad, on Paquita.

'There's a man!' de Marsay said, pointing to the mulatto with a sombre gesture. 'The only true devotion is that which does what friendship commands without passing judgement. You have a true friend in that man.'

'If you like I will give him to you,' she replied. 'If I tell him to, he will serve you with the same devotion with which he has served me.'

She waited for a word of reply, then continued with an accent of tenderness: 'Adolphe, say one kind word to me. Daybreak is near.'

Henri made no reply. He had one regrettable characteristic: a quality, perhaps, since one is accustomed to accept as such anything which may pass for strength of will; and quite often men make a divinity of exaggeration. Henri was incapable of forgiving. The power to revise past judgements, which is certainly a sign of grace in the soul, was meaningless for him. The ruthlessness of the Northmen, with which English blood is strongly tainted, had come to him from his father. He was unshakeable both in his good and evil impulses. Paquita's exclamation was the more hateful to him because he had been hurled down from the sweetest triumph which had ever exalted his masculine vanity. Hope, love and every other emotion had risen to the highest pitch, had burst into flame in his heart and in his intelligence; then these torches, ignited to illuminate his life, had been blown out by a cold wind. Paquita, in her stupefaction and grief, had only strength enough to give the signal for departure.

'There's no need for the bandage,' she said, throwing it down. 'If he no longer loves me, if he hates me, all is over.'

She waited for a look from him, obtained none, and fell back in a faint. The mulatto flung at Henri a glance so terrifyingly menacing that, for the first time in his life, a thrill of fear passed through this young man whom everybody acknowledged to be gifted with a rare intrepidity. 'If you do not love her well, if you cause her the slightest pain, I will kill you.' Such was the drift of this lightning glance.

De Marsay was conveyed with almost servile attentiveness along a corridor which drew no direct light from the outer world, and at the end of it he emerged through a secret door into a hidden staircase which led to the garden of the San-Real mansion. The mulatto cautiously escorted him along an alley of lime trees leading to a small door opening on to a street at that time of night deserted. De Marsay took good stock of everything. The carriage was waiting. This time the mulatto conducted him no farther and, at the moment when Henri looked out through the window to take a backward glance at the gardens and the mansion, he encountered the white eyes of Christemio, and they exchanged looks of mutual challenge and defiance. It was a declaration of war as between savages, the promise of a duel which would obey no normal rules, a duel in which treachery and perfidy were fully admissible. Christemio knew that Henri had sworn Paquita's death. Henri knew that Christemio purposed to kill him before he killed Paquita. The two men understood one another marvellously well.

'This affair is becoming fascinatingly complicated,' Henri said to himself.

'Where am I to take you, sir?' the coachman asked.

De Marsay had himself driven to Paul de Manerville's house.

*

386

For over a week Henri was absent from his house without anyone knowing what he did during this time or where he was domiciled. This retirement saved him from the fury of the mulatto but brought about the destruction of the poor creature who had put all her hope in the man she loved more than any other creature ever loved on this earth. On the last day of the week, at about eleven in the evening, Henri drove in his carriage to the wicket-gate of the Hôtel San-Real garden. He had three companions.[4] The coachman was evidently a friend of his, for he sat up straight on his seat like a man who intended, as a vigilant sentinel, to listen for the slightest sound. One of the other three stood in the street outside the door. The second stood upright in the garden, leaning against the wall. The third, who held a bunch of keys in his hand, was with de Marsay.

'Henri,' his companion said to him. 'We have been betrayed.'

'By whom, my good Ferragus?'

'They are not all asleep,' the leader of the *Dévorants* replied. 'It just must be that someone in the house hasn't taken time off either to eat or to drink. Look, there's a light.'

'We have a plan of the house. Where is it shining?'

'I need no plan to know that,' Ferragus replied. 'It comes from the Marquise's bedroom.'

'Ah!' de Marsay cried. 'No doubt she's back from London today. This woman will even have robbed me of my revenge! But if she has got in before me, my good Gratien, we'll hand her over to justice.'

'But listen now! The matter is settled,' said Ferragus to Henri.

The two friends gave ear and heard some diminishing shrieks that would have softened a tiger's heart.

'It didn't occur to your marquise that sound could escape through the chimney,' said the leader of the *Dévorants*, with the laugh of a critic delighted to find a defect in an otherwise fine piece of work.

'We alone,' said Henri, 'are competent enough to foresee

4. Members of the Thirteen.

any eventuality. Wait for me. I want to go and see what is happening up above, in order to find out how they settle their little domestic quarrels. By God! I believe she is roasting her at a slow fire!'

De Marsay sprang lightly up the staircase with which he was already familiar and found his way to the boudoir. He opened the door and through him went the involuntary shudder which the sight of bloodshed inflicts even on the most callous of men. The marquise, being a woman, had calculated her vengeance with that thoroughness of perfidy which distinguishes the weaker animals. She had dissembled her wrath in order to make sure that the crime had been committed before she set about punishing it.

'Too late, my beloved!' cried the expiring Paquita, turning her pale eyes towards de Marsay.

The girl with the golden eyes lay dying, bathed in her own blood. The blaze of the candles, a delicate perfume that permeated the boudoir, a very perceptible disorder in which the eye of a man experienced in amorous matters could not but detect the mad fury common to all passion, gave evidence that the marquise had put the guilty girl to a searching interrogation. The white boudoir, in which the crimson of blood stood out so coldly, showed that a prolonged struggle had taken place. Paquita's blood-stained hands were imprinted on the cushions. There seemed to be no spot in which she had not defended herself, fought for her life, but failed to avoid the dagger blows. Whole strips of the fluted hangings had been torn down by bleeding hands which doubtless had put up a long struggle. Paquita must even have tried to scramble up the wall. There were the marks of her feet along the back of the divan, along which she had no doubt run in her flight. Her whole body, slashed by the dagger-thrusts of her executioner, showed how fiercely she had fought to save the life which Henri had made so dear to her. She was stretched out on the floor and, in her dying throes, had bitten through the muscles of Madame de San-Real's instep. The marquise was still holding her blood-stained dagger, her hair had been torn out in handfuls, she was covered with bites, several of which were still bleeding, and her tattered robe revealed her half-naked form and her lacerated breasts. She was a tragic picture.

She had the face of a fury avid for and redolent of blood. She was panting, with her mouth half-open, and her breath came too quickly for her to take the air in through her nostrils. Some animals, when roused to fury, pounce upon their enemy, bite or claw it to death and then, satisfied with their victory, appear to have forgotten their bloodthirstiness. Others circle round and round their victim, guarding it lest it should be snatched away from them and, like Homer's Achilles, drag their foe by the feet nine times round the walls of Troy. So it was with the marquise. She did not see Henri. For one thing, she was too sure of being too completely isolated to fear any witnesses; for another, she was too intoxicated with warm blood, too fighting mad, too beyond herself to have noticed even the whole of Paris had it been formed in a ring around her. A thunderbolt might have struck the house without her perceiving it. She had not even heard Paquita's dying utterance, and believed that the dead girl could still listen to her.

'Die unconfessed!' she was shrieking. 'Go straight to hell, monster of ingratitude; from henceforth belong only to the devil. For the blood you have given over to *him*, you owe me every drop of yours. Die! Die! Die a thousand deaths! I was too kind taking only an instant to kill you. Oh! If only I could have made you feel all the grief you are bequeathing to me. *I* have to go on living ... living in torment. I've only God left to love!' She gazed on the body. 'She's dead!' she told herself after a pause, with a violent revulsion of feeling. 'She's dead! Oh! The grief of it will kill me!'

The marquise was about to fling herself on the divan, so stricken with despair that her voice was choked. This movement enabled her to notice Henri de Marsay.

'Who are you?' she said, rushing upon him with raised dagger.

Henri seized her by the arm, and thus they were able to look at each other face to face. A shocking surprise chilled the blood in the veins of both of them and they stood opposite one another trembling like a pair of startled horses. In very truth, the two Menaechmi[5] could not have been more alike. In one breath they asked the same question: 'Is not Lord Dudley your father?'

Each of them gave an affirmative nod.

'She remained true to the blood,' said Henri, pointing to Paquita.

'She was as free of guilt as it is possible to be,' replied Margarita-Euphemia-Porraberil, throwing herself on Paquita's body with a cry of despair. 'Poor darling! If only I could bring you back to life! I was in the wrong. Forgive me! Paquita! You are dead, and I am still alive! I am more to be pitied than you!'

Just at this moment the revolting face of Paquita's mother came into view . . .

'You are going to tell me that you didn't sell her to me for me to kill her,' the marquise exclaimed. 'I know why you have come out of your den. I will pay for her all over again. That's enough from you.'

She went and took a bagful of gold from the ebony chest and disdainfully hurled it at the feet of the old woman. The chink of the coins was musical enough to bring a smile to the impassive face of the woman of Georgia.

'I have come at the right moment for you, sister,' said Henri. 'The law will call you to account.'

'For what?' the marquise replied. 'One person alone might have called me to account for the death of this girl: Christemio. But he is dead.'

'But what about the mother?' asked Henri, pointing to the old woman. 'Will she not always hold you to ransom?'

'She comes from a country where women are not human beings but chattels. One does what one likes with them, sells them, buys them, kills them. In fact one uses them to indulge one's whims, just as here you make use of your furniture. Moreover, she has one passion which gets the best of all the others, one which would have annihilated her mother-love if she had had any, a passion . . . '

5. Identical twins in a comedy of Plautus.

'What passion?' said Henri, abruptly interrupting his sister.

'Gambling! God keep you from it!' the marquise replied.

'But what are you going to do to get help,' asked Henri, pointing to the girl with the golden eyes, 'in order to destroy evidence relevant to this little caprice? Is the law likely to overlook it?'

'Her mother will support me,' the marquise replied, pointing to the old Georgian woman, to whom she made a sign to stay.

'We will meet again,' said Henri, thinking that his friends would be anxious and that it was high time he left.

'No, brother,' she said. 'We shall never meet again. I shall return to Spain and enter the convent of Los Dolores.'

'You are too young and beautiful for that,' said Henri, taking her in his arms and kissing her.

'Good-bye,' she said. 'Nothing can console one for having lost what constituted infinity for oneself.'

*

A week later Paul de Manerville met de Marsay in the Tuileries Gardens on the Terrasse des Feuillants.

'Well now, you rascal, what has become of our lovely *Girl with the Golden Eyes*?'

'She's dead.'

'Of what?'

'A chest ailment.'

Paris, March 1834 – April 1835